D0276706

BOUDICA AND THE LOST ROMAN

Further Titles by Mike Ripley

JUST ANOTHER ANGEL
ANGEL TOUCH
ANGEL HUNT
ANGEL IN ARMS
ANGEL CITY
ANGEL CONFIDENTIAL
FAMILY OF ANGELS
THAT ANGEL LOOK
BOOTLEGGED ANGEL
LIGHTS, CAMERA, ANGEL!
ANGEL UNDERGROUND
ANGEL ON THE INSIDE
ANGEL IN THE HOUSE

*

DOUBLE TAKE

*

(As editor, with Maxim Jakubowski)

FRESH BLOOD
FRESH BLOOD 2
FRESH BLOOD 3

*

SURVIVING A STROKE
(non-fiction)

BOUDICA AND THE LOST ROMAN

Mike Ripley

This first world edition published in Great Britain 2005 by
SEVERN HOUSE PUBLISHERS LTD of
9–15 High Street, Sutton, Surrey SM1 1DF.
This first world edition published in the USA 2006 by
SEVERN HOUSE PUBLISHERS INC of
595 Madison Avenue, New York, N.Y. 10022.

British Library Cataloguing in Publication Data

Ripley, Mike
Boudica and the lost Roman
1. Boadicea, Queen, d. 62 - Fiction
2. Great Britain - History - Roman period, 55 B.C. -449 A.D. - Fiction
3. Historical fiction
I. Title
823.9'14 [F]

ISBN-10 : 0-7278-6259-6

Except where actual historical events and characters are being described for the story line of this novel, all situations in this publication are fictitious and any resemblance to living persons is purely coincidental.

Typeset by Palimpsest Book Production Ltd.,
Polmont, Stirlingshire, Scotland.
Printed and bound in Great Britain by
MPG Books Ltd., Bodmin, Cornwall.

Author's Note

Whilst this novel is written in a modern idiom, I have tried to use only words which have a recognised Latin translation, including the obscene use of the verb *futuere* for swear words commonly thought of as good old-fashioned Anglo-Saxon.

It was also the Anglo-Saxons who named the Roman roads 'Watling Street', 'Ermine Street' and so on. We do not know what the Romans called them and I have used a simple numbering system of routes just because I wanted most of the action to take place on Route LXVI.

Any anachronisms, if funny, are deliberate. I am eternally grateful to my old *contubernalis* Colin Dexter, who patiently corrected my appalling Latin grammar and gave fascinating advice on military graffiti both past and present. *Bene facis, Magister.*

Thanks are also due to Mark Hassell of the Institute of Archaeology, University College, London, who advised on Roman military slang and corrected many naive mistakes. Any he missed are the fault of the author.

Mike Ripley, Camulodunum, MMV

Olussa

'I cannot read or write, but I am Boudica, Queen of the Iceni.'

That's what the bitch told me to write when she had my balls in one hand and a dagger in the other. So I wrote. And wrote and wrote. I scribbled for my life.

Roscius

Boudica?

That bloodthirsty barbarian whore? There's a name you don't hear any more. It must be thirty years. It *is* thirty years, come to think of it.

Know her? I didn't *know* her. But I saw her once – twice come to think of it – from a distance. Once she was coming to kill us and the other time we were coming to kill her.

Well, if you want to know what an old soldier thinks, you've come to the right place. I did my twenty-five years in the Twentieth and then some. And I'm certainly old. They gave us the title *Valeria Victrix*. The XXth Legion, I mean. After we turned over Boudica's mob.

Sure, I can tell you all about it. You'd better come in.

Are you going to write *all* this down?

BRITAIN, A.D. 60–61

I: Olussa

Why am I here? I am no spy. I have several decent trades to my name and none of them are spy.

I have some skill as a translator, having a natural gift for language and dialect, able to pick up the guttural snarl of even the crudest of the tribes in the Empire. It is a skill my father, the merchant, has made good use of especially as, being a son, I come free or at least cheaper than a local interpreter. He, of course, sees the money he spent on my education as an investment which he is now being repaid with interest. Every one of those years of learning, reading, writing, mathematics and seven styles of public speaking, was a deposit in his personal bank, another sack of grain stored away – secured in the good years in anticipation of the famines yet to come when my father would be able to make withdrawals to tide him over, or, knowing my father, the merchant, as the Fates have decreed I must, selling to the highest bidder for a tidy profit.

And in the course of working for my father as translator, bookkeeper and contract writer (three professions there, none of them spy), I have learned much of what it is to be a merchant. So, a fourth calling, the not so honourable profession of merchant, but which leads to a useful sideline as a map-maker and negotiator of trade routes (five), shipping clerk and validator of manifests to prevent smuggling (six), smuggler (seven, an automatic extension of six) and, most profitable of all, embezzler – for while my father lavished time and money on my education he wasted none on himself and he is still, at the age of almost sixty, unable to read and understand a balance sheet no matter how I present it to him, or indeed how many times I present the same one.

So, seven professions – eight, if keeping a personal history can be said to be such – but none of them spy.

Until now, when I have been made an offer; an offer neither I nor my father's business could afford to refuse. An offer from an Italian, of course.

I had been in Gallia Narbonensis for my customary two months of the year, about my father the merchant's business. Or at least that part of his business which involved the purchase and export of the fine red-gloss pottery which, in the trade, we call 'Samian' ware although in Germany, where it is increasingly popular, they insist on the term *terra sigillata* in the dog Latin they speak there. The original techniques of making Samian are, of course, Greek as is just about everything good and useful in this world (I myself am Greek) although the Gaulish industry owes much to the potters of Tuscany who migrated there thirty-odd years ago. The techniques may be Greek but the original artistic flair which spawned them has not been maintained, sad to say. The designs on most pieces are uniformly dull – hunting scene after hunting scene and damn greyhounds everywhere – and there is little to tell the work of individual potters apart other than by their name marks. Such, I suppose, are the problems of mass production but there is no denying that Samian is fashionable and commands premium prices. It is an expanding, seemingly inexhaustible market and the expression 'Get the Samian out, we've got visitors' will soon be heard in decent households across the Empire, which these days means the known world or as near as it matters.

My function in southern Gaul was to keep our regular suppliers happy, which involved much tactful deceit, flattery and downright lying (surely useful skills for a spy?) to keep our three main contract potters happy at their wheels. The three tied to the family business by a shrewd system of loans, indentures, slaves and long-term supply agreements, are Primus, Felix and Mommo, all names which are becoming well-known at the bottom of dishes and bowls and cups across six or seven provinces. None of them have any idea of how popular or well-known they are and because they hate each other as professional rivals, they are easy to play off against each other. I tell Mommo that Felix outsold him two-to-one in Belgica this year, which means Mommo immediately doubles production and cuts his wholesale price. Primus, of course, is told that Mommo and Felix are outselling him on quality and so he improves his quality wares, at no extra cost to me.

It has been said, mostly by the equestrian classes, who gossip and chatter over dinner like ringdoves on heat, that merchants with near monopolies of supply such as we have are somehow exploiting the producer, who, in this case, is an artist, a fine potter who puts thought and imagination into his work as well as clay and fire. My retort is that Olussa (and father) are respected merchants with a quality mark of their own to protect. We supply only the best at the best price, even if that means *our* best price, and people can rely on us. Surely that is worth something and gives us the right to dictate to these temperamental artisans. Anyway, if they cannot stand the heat they should get out of the kiln. This is business after all.

Which is almost exactly how the Italian introduced himself to me, saying he had 'business' to discuss. The way he said it told me immediately that he *was* a spy.

The man calling himself Marcellus – and whilst I did not believe from the start that this was his name, I was not about to argue with a spy – bearded me on the docks of Narbo Martius*. I had seen him loitering out of the corner of my eye and when he snaked his way towards me I could sense that he was some sort of government official, though obviously not a tax collector. Even in Gaul – especially in Gaul – tax collectors only appear on the docks with an armed escort.

'Olussa, son of Alexander the merchant,' he said loudly so that no one could be in doubt whom he was addressing. And his voice carried weight; the weight of an Imperial Seal.

I turned my head, knowing that to do so would be fatal, and said: 'Yes?'

And from that moment on I was a spy too.

We had lunch together. I am told that this is part of every spy's recruitment. Even the worst spies get one lunch on the

* Narbonne, on the Mediterranean coast of France.

expenses of their employer. And I was soon to discover who that employer was.

The man calling himself Marcellus ordered a Falerian wine diluted with seawater and a shellfish sausage made with celery seed, pine nuts and breadcrumbs. I ordered the same, not expecting to get a genuine Falerian (which I did) or a palatable sausage (which I did not).

'My master maintains that a little bread and some figs are enough to sustain one at the *prandium*,' said Marcellus, adding twenty oysters to his order.

And at that moment, long before the wine kicked in, I knew I was in trouble.

'You work for Seneca, don't you?' I said to him. And he nodded.

And I realised that suddenly, I did too.

It was the homily about 'a little bread and a few figs' which would do him for lunch. Everyone knew that one; it had gone the rounds the year before. Like we were supposed to feel sorry for him? We all knew that by the fourth hour of the afternoon, Seneca would be settling down to a sixteen-course banquet which would see him through until midnight give or take three or four trips to the vomitorium.

What else did we know about Seneca? He had been tutor to our Emperor Nero as a lad and now maintained some unholy position in the big wheels of government. Some would say he was in fact co-regent with Nero. Not that I would. But I did know he was rich and had been rich for a while. Long enough to have become a serious player on the stock exchange in Rome. A stock exchange which was seriously questioning its investments in one particular sector: Britannia.

The place where my father, the merchant, was based.

Thinking about it, I was surprised it had taken them this long.

'I am surprised you have not come to our attention before,' said this Marcellus creature, 'because you are ideally placed for our needs.'

There was something of a weasel about him and not just in the way he ate, though he did that with short, sharp movements of hands, teeth and gums, his eyes anywhere except on his food as if he expected me to snatch it from his grasp at any moment. He ate like a soldier on watch.

'Why should the great and noble Seneca be remotely interested in such a humble merchant as myself?'

I said it graciously I thought, with just the right tone of deference though I noted to myself how quickly, when circumstances dictated, I rushed to claim my father's profession.

The spy slurped down an oyster, then took a pinch of bread and polished the empty half shell of its juice before popping it into his mouth.

'I serve Seneca. Seneca serves Nero. Nero serves Rome,' he pronounced.

I almost broke my face at that one. Everyone knew that our mildly deranged Imperator (mildly, compared to some of them) served himself whenever and wherever he could, which usually meant when Seneca said he could.

'So now I am of interest to Rome itself,' I said, trying to sound as if this was a statement which I was deeply flattered by rather than a question which doubted the man's sanity.

'All citizens are,' said the spy, draining his wine cup and signalling for more.

'But I am not a Roman citizen,' I said, adding: 'Sadly.'

'And why not? A young man your age should have what, four or five years under canvas by now. Another fifteen and you could achieve citizenship.'

The legions recruited from seventeen years upwards and so the spy's guess at my age was accurate. And what he said was true. After twenty years' service, citizenship was indeed an option – for those who survived. But I had no stomach for the 'under canvas' life of a campaigning soldier with its petty and iron-headed rules of discipline, let alone the distinct possibility of ending up on a spit on some barbarian's camp fire. No, I looked forward to a fortieth year with all my limbs attached to my body, citizenship or not.

'I could say the same of you,' I said boldly to the spy.

'Some of us have to serve in different ways,' he answered.

'If we are slaves,' I said and his rodent eyes flashed, locking with mine.

I knew I had cut him, but whilst I did not want this man

for a friend, I could see no profit in making him an enemy, so I softened the blow.

'A trusted one, obviously, and almost certainly Seneca will make you a freedman when he dies and you can return to your native Pompeii.'

His jaw dropped at that.

'How did you know I come from Pompeii?'

'There is no trick. You ordered Falerian wine, expecting to get it, and seawater to dilute it. Only a man of Pompeii, a city famous throughout the world as a centre of wine and the export of wine, would know to ask for that here and be sure of getting it.'

I did not add that the fashion for drinking the strong, sweet, white Falerian with seawater – originally a Greek innovation – had died about the same time as the Emperor Tiberius. Only in Pompeii, a town built on the wine trade where there are bars every ten paces on every street, did they stick to the belief that Falerian was the best wine to drink, or to be seen drinking. It was a subject I knew something of as I had plans to persuade my father, the merchant, to enter the wine business. There were some interesting wines coming out of Gaul these days, red ones, which I was sure would find a good market with a little discreet promotion and the Gaulish wine growers were far less set in their ways than those of Campania around Pompeii. One day, those rich wine men (as everyone in Pompeii was rich thanks to wine) would get their come-uppance.

The spy was staring at me.

'You have a talent for this sort of work,' he said, nodding his thin head. 'Are you going to finish that sausage?'

'What sort of work?' I said, too quickly and too late.

'Information,' said the spy, spearing my sausage with his knife and landing it on his platter. 'It always pays to know the man with the information.'

I wondered if that was another of Seneca's little homilies. I had always thought of him, when I had thought of him at all, which was not often, as a man whose mutterings were taken down and transcribed into orders and philosophy by the acolytes around him, without question. Such is the reward of power. Such is the lot of the acolyte to have to listen to such rubbish and give it value.

'Surely, the noble and good Seneca is the most well-informed man in Rome and has little need of the services of such a humble trader as myself.'

I was going through the formalities of good manners which the spy knew were mere formalities but which, because I had invoked the name of his master, he had to endure as if they were sincere.

'Not so humble,' he said, chewing seafood. 'You are the son of Alexander the Greek, who trades throughout the Empire and operates several small monopolies, none of them sanctioned by Rome and several without provincial licences, but which, nonetheless, bring him an income of over 200,000 sesterces a year.'

I put my cup of wine to my mouth not to drink, but to cover my face but Marcellus was not looking at me. He was concentrating on chasing a single escaped prawn around his platter with a sponge of bread.

His information was frighteningly accurate. Not even my father knew he was worth over 200,000 sesterces a year – the salary of a provincial procurator and a sum the average foot-slogger in a legion, paid ten ases a day, would have to campaign for 219 years to earn. I realised how barbed his suggestion that I opt for the life 'under canvas' had been and vowed to take this Marcellus more seriously. Never argue with someone who knows more about you than the official tax collector.

'Obviously, any service my father can render the great and noble—'

'Your father is old, soft and knows only a tenth of what is happening in his business. You are the brains of the company. It is you we are interested in.'

'Why me?'

'Because you are in . . . a unique position . . . uniquely placed, for us.'

He stumbled over the phrase as if it was one he had learned by rote.

'How? I am a simple merchant.'

And wouldn't my father have laughed over that admission!

'Exactly,' said Marcellus, staring down at his second empty plate. 'Do they serve squid here? They should. In Rome, squid stuffed with calves' brains is all the rage.'

Typical government servant: when on expenses, stuff your face.

'Exactly? Exactly how?' I asked before he could attract the attention of a serving slave.

'You trade in Britannia, your father lives there in Londinium. More wine?'

He began to bang the table with his cup, which would have annoyed the other customers had there been any. Most of the midday diners in the Narbo docks had more sense than to sit near someone like Marcellus. They all had their own scams and rackets to hide and Marcellus reeked of officialdom. The regular clientele could smell an Imperial Seal at fifty paces. And so could the serving slaves. They slammed down wine and a dish of squid – quickly and simply fried in olive oil, unlike the Roman style which comes with a thick sweet sauce – and shot back to the kitchens, knowing that a tip was out of the question but a beating might be avoided if they were lucky.

'Yes, we trade in Britannia,' I said, wanting to get to the nub of things. The longer I spent in Marcellus' company, the more my dockside credibility would diminish and I had to work with these people. 'What is your master's interest in Britannia?'

He folded squid tentacles in a piece of flat bread and then examined the parcel when it was halfway to his mouth.

'You are a merchant there, you know the country. My master needs a merchant who knows Britannia. It really is as simple as that.'

'You want me to sell something there for you?' I struggled.

'No, we want you to take stock,' he said when he had swallowed. 'Do a taking of stock, a stock check. That is what you merchants do, isn't it? You count up your goods and assess their worth.'

'It's a little more complicated than that,' I said gently, risking a smile without patronising him. 'Anyway, a stock take of what?'

'Britannia,' he said as if I was deaf and slow.

'*What* in Britannia?' I pressed.

'All of it.'

I reached for my cup. Even the strong, pungent Falerian could not make me more confused than I already was.

* * *

It boiled down to this.

Seneca was one of the major, perhaps the biggest, private investors in Britannia and no doubt many of his upper-class friends had followed his example, thinking they were on to a good thing, the old bore being so close to Nero. But as an investment, Britannia had never really paid the dividends which had been expected of it. At the time of the old Caesar, the original one, Julius, most people were convinced that the shores of the whole island (though they weren't sure it actually *was* an island until somebody or other sailed round it) were littered with pearls, just lying there waiting to be picked up. It was naturally assumed that the native Celts were too lazy or too stupid to do so. Probably both.

When Rome finally got around to invading the place, under Claudius (though the idea had come from his predecessor, Gaius, the one they called Caligula, who really was howling mad), they didn't find many pearls. Oysters, yes, millions of them and once somebody begins to create oyster ponds and farm them properly, like Sergius Orata did at Baiae a hundred years ago, making himself a fortune in the process, then I am sure they will become a nice little money-earner. A cheap and delicious treat for the masses which will turn a handsome profit for whoever gets the distribution chain right.

But Seneca and his fat friends were not going to make a killing out of oysters. I don't really expect they believed the stories of pearls at all. They were after the mineral deposits. There was talk (there always is) of large amounts of gold just waiting to fall out of the hillsides, and also lead and silver-bearing lead, tin, copper and even coal, though that will never replace wood or charcoal. None of this materialised. Well, some of it did. There were findings of gold and silver and lead and tin and copper, but nearly all were in the uplands and most beyond the frontier which the army had established running from the south-west to the north-east.

There were other things of value there: marble, shale and jet for making jewellery and ornaments, furs and skins – and the rumour in Rome was that sealskin would be the in-fashion thing – and animals, notably hunting dogs and bears, some of which had already travelled to Rome to provide entertainment in the arena. And, of course, there was the amazing ability – amazing given the odious climate – to produce excellent harvests of wheat and barley.

But none of these offered the quick turnover and high yield on their investment which Seneca and his friends were looking for. Grants had been made to the local tribal chiefs to keep them quiet. Engineers and professional miners had been hired and sent over there. Pack animals and mule trains bought. There was even talk of building canals. All this had cost money, and money up front. Seneca had, of course, been acting on behalf of Nero and therefore Rome, as all mineral deposits in the provinces were automatically state property. And when the return on that investment started only as a trickle and then began to dry up, Seneca started to worry. If it dried completely, Nero would worry and Rome would panic.

The stock market was known to have the jitters about Britannia despite its dealings being confined to the few who had the ear of Seneca, the blessing of the Emperor and, of course, the necessary cash.

If I understood what this Marcellus was telling me and, given the amount he had drunk I think I understood better than he did, I was being asked to conduct a sort of audit. An accounting of what the island of Britannia was worth in terms of liquid, moveable and readily available assets which could be removed as suddenly as a thin topsoil is stripped off a hillside field in a high wind.

There could be only one reason why Seneca wanted this done: he had had the nod that Nero was seriously thinking of abandoning the province which continued to tie down four whole legions even after seventeen years of occupation and which was showing such poor returns. The wily old sod Seneca was making sure his investment would be covered if, and preferably before, the whole enterprise went down the sewer.

But it simply didn't make sense.

Nero, and therefore Seneca, had four legions 'in country' as they say these days. They all had quartermasters who knew pretty well down to the last rain-bedraggled sheep what the countryside was worth. The legions also had surveyors and miners who were paid to report back on any precious metals.

And then there was the Procurator, second only in influence to the Governor himself, who collected the taxes and had his own private army of enforcers. They could do you an inventory down to the last lamb chop.

What could one man alone do that they could not?

'That is a very good question,' said Marcellus stupidly. 'I was told you would ask that.'

'And what were you told to answer?' I said rudely after another infuriating pause.

He drew a long breath, racked his memory and said:

'The present machinery of accounting in Britannia is not inclusive of all the territories under Rome's influence.'

'And what does that mean?' I almost shouted.

But even as I did I had worked out the terrible answer for myself.

'You mean the frontier, don't you?' I said before Marcellus could even begin to compose a reply. 'You want me to go beyond the military frontier into the war zone – that's what it is. The new Governor has been fighting the barbarians beyond the frontier since he arrived last year. And you want me to go among them and do a stock check?'

Marcellus' bony hand moved like a snake and gripped my wrist, pinning it to the table.

'Keep your voice down,' he said in a tone which made me think he was not as drunk as he pretended. 'No one said anything about going *beyond* the military frontier. Think, man. You live there. Are there not tribes who live *inside* the frontier but who are not subject to the direct rule of Rome?'

I saw where he was going, or to be more accurate, where he had been told to go.

'You mean the so-called client kingdoms,' I said, lowering my voice. 'The tribes we have left alone as long as they accept Roman governance, or at the very least, stay neutral.'

The only good thing about the tribes of Britannia was that in the main they hated each other more than they hated Rome and so it was ridiculously easy to play one off against the other. Some, in the south-east of the island, such as the Cantii, had traded with the Romans in Gaul for generations. They quite liked the idea of joining in a unified Empire based on the mainland, seeing the benefits such a union could bring;

using the same coinage for example. One tribe in the north, the Brigantes, had actively sought an alliance with Rome simply to do down their neighbours. Then there were the downright hostiles, especially the Ordovices, who still harassed the legions from their mountain hideouts in the godforsaken west of the island, where most of the gold and copper just happened to be.

There was one tribe, however, which had been left very much to their own devices. They had not openly resisted the invasion and when there had been trouble, some ten years ago, they had been disarmed with relatively little fuss. Their territory was to the north-east of Camulodunum*, the most important British settlement when Claudius invaded (which isn't saying much as the Britons did not understand the concept that civilisation means living in a town rather than a mud hut), now the first official Roman *colonia* and something of a showpiece capital city to impress the natives.

The tribe was the Iceni and they lived, as far as I was concerned, in flat, marshy forest land and kept themselves very much to themselves. What they got up to in that misty, uninteresting eastern part of the island which bulged out into the sea, nobody knew in detail. Rumour was that if you wanted to keep your head, and not have it removed and embalmed in cedar oil, it was best not to ask.

'You mean the Iceni lands, don't you?' I said.

He smiled at me, as a teacher would at a slow pupil.

'You are one of the biggest traders with them, you know their territory.'

'My father trades with them,' I objected, 'and then only through intermediaries – wholesale, to local retailers. And I've never been north of Camulodunum in my life.'

He waved a hand dismissively; a gesture learned from one of his masters, but a lesson he had enjoyed.

'You are a good merchant,' he said magnanimously, 'and quick at languages, I hear. You have every excuse for visiting the Iceni lands, and once there, all we are really asking you to do is keep your eyes open and try not to act suspiciously.

* Colchester, Essex.

I'm told you get on well with people, which will help, and your reputation is said to be an honest one.'

I waited for him to bait the trap. It would not be subtle and it would be soon. It was.

'Surprisingly, your father has no idea you are a crook.'

I waited again. It was the most dignified thing I could do.

'Yet,' he added with a smirk.

There it was: the dagger unsheathed and at my throat.

Become a spy or my father would be – how best to put this? – brought up to date with his current (accurate) financial position. It was a disgrace. Spies became spies through loyalty to a country or a cause, or as an unavoidable contingency in war, not because minor misdemeanours could be exposed to their families. Who had ever heard of such a thing? It was unthinkable. What sort of man did he and his master think I was?

'When do I leave?' I asked.

II: Roscius

The Iceni? They're history.

I mean it; they're as dead and gone as most of the people you historians write about. But then, that's your job, isn't it?

Anyway, what I really mean is that the Iceni are gone and, actually, most of them are dead. They all would have been if the General had been given his way, but still, we did a pretty good job that autumn after the revolt. And the winter took care of many of those we missed.

It was the only way to deal with them and, between you and me, it was the only sort of language they understood. They would have done the same to us if things had gone the other way. Not that there ever was a serious chance of that happening. I mean, we had discipline and they didn't know the meaning of the word. Discipline will always win out at the end of the day. That's what we lived by in the legions and that's why we drilled so much, so we were always ready to swing into action. Discipline, you see.

Our drills were something, I can tell you. Bloodless battles, they were, and we were so well-trained that any battle we fought just became a bloody drill.

That's quite good, that. Our drills were bloodless battles and our battles bloody drills. I like that. You can use it if you want to.

What do you mean I'm getting ahead of myself?

The General.

Gaius Suetonius Paulinus; General commanding the XIV and XX Legions in the field, Consul, Governor of Britannia and the first Roman officer to cross the Atlas mountains in Mauretania.

Top man.

As soon as he was made Governor and we got to the damned island, he assessed the situation pretty damn quick and he boiled it down to two priorities.

First, we had to sort out the precious metals. The only place we had found gold was in those damned western mountains, but we knew there was copper and tin to be found to the north, deeper into the hills. Only trouble was that was where the sodding Ordovices lived, the most belligerent, bloody-minded tribe in Britain – or so we thought at the time. Compared to what the Iceni did later, of course, they were about as dangerous as a basketful of kittens, but for years they'd been buggering us about and the General decided it was time to sort them out once and for all.

So Paulinus gets a campaign underway with the XIVth Legion and quite a few of the lads from the XXth, those who weren't manning the forts along the frontier. With the auxiliaries we had it was more than enough to do the job, but in that terrain it wasn't going to be a quick campaign and by the time we'd got organised, winter was upon us, so we sat that out and started in on them in the spring.

The plan was to clear that north-west section of the mountains, and I mean clear it. Anything that breathed – on two legs or four – was killed and burned – or eaten. We didn't rush it. We took it slowly and carefully and made sure none of them doubled back behind us.

We were pushing them, you see. Pushing them right into that top corner of the region, bottling them up. Very soon they had nowhere to hide as we pushed them down from the mountains towards the sea and they began to gather on a little island just off the coast, an evil, bloody, place called the isle of Mona*.

That was the real target. Not only was there copper on Mona – we knew that – but it was also a sacred place for the Druids and the whole Druidic religion. This was Paulinus' second priority.

The Druids were behind most of the discontent and the uprisings, always had been. Their priests and their witches – oh yes, they had witches – would whip up the locals whenever they got the chance. The tribes themselves were fairly easy to pick off one at a time, or they could be played off against each other. The only thing that united them was their bloody religion. And it was a bloody religion. They collected heads, you know. Sacrificed them to their gods in sacred groves or by sacred pools. I can tell you, there were plenty of drinking places in Britain where you didn't have to dip your spoon too deep before you scooped out the skull of one of your old comrades.

It's always the same when you have a militant religion on your hands. You just can't live with it, you have to stamp it out. You know as well as I do that wherever the Empire has expanded we've usually left the local religion in place. It keeps the natives happy and usually they come round to our way of thinking. But you can't do that when the religion is the only thing everybody agrees on and when the local kings and tribal leaders take their orders from the priests rather than just looking after their own little patch.

It always leads to trouble. It did in Britain with the Druids. It did in Judaea with the Jews.

Paulinus knew this and so the plan was to hit the buggers hard where it hurt, on their sacred island of Mona, getting hold of the copper mines there while we were at it.

Take out the Druids, said the General, and the rest would realise that further resistance was useless, if only because the Druids wouldn't be there to tell them to keep resisting.

That was the plan, anyway. But, of course, we got sidetracked, didn't we?

* Anglesey, off the north coast of Wales.

Agricola?

What, Julius Agricola, the military tribune? Sure, he was there. He was on the staff with us. A bit of a Patsy, I always thought.

Patsy? It's what we used to call all the junior officers when I was in the ranks, the ones who put on airs – you know, acted like they were *patricius*, thought they were a bloody patrician with a family tree going back to Romulus.

Don't get me wrong, Agricola was all right but he was, like, just *there*. He came along for the ride. He did his bit, as you'd expect, but it was Paulinus' show right from the start.

Paulinus was the one who got a grip when everyone else was running around like headless chickens. He's the one who kept calm. He's the one who beat the bitch queen Boudica. He was the one who saved the province.

He was the one.

III: Olussa

Of course I had to cancel all my appointments with customers and dealers and wholesalers for the rest of the year (with the resultant loss of 'commission') and pay out of my own purse for a passage by sea around Hispania and the Gaulish coast as far as Gesoriacum* in Gallia Belgica, rather than follow my usual, more comfortable, route by sea, river, canal and road through Upper Germania.

Gesoriacum is a port equally as smelly as Narbo but without the beneficial climate. It is also the base of the *classis Britannica*, the British Fleet, which supplies everything imaginable to the legions in Britannia and everything else to anyone who can pay for it. I myself have done legitimate business with them, supplying some fine-quality tableware stamped CL BR, as they like to stamp on anything they touch, but their main trade (unofficial trade) is in wine. For some reason the Britons who have taken to wine, which is most of them but particularly the southern coastal tribes, are convinced that they

* Boulogne.

can buy it much cheaper in Gaul rather than through merchants in Britain. They treat it almost as if they are avoiding a tax of some sort, and it is not uncommon in the summer to see small British boats on a 'wine run' as they say, across the British Ocean, dangerously overloaded with amphorae all marked CL BR. As the temptation to tap an amphora or two on the journey home becomes too great for a lot of them, many sail straight into the white cliffs of Dubris* and their bodies are picked over by the blue-headed gulls which swarm there in great numbers.

It is said that from Gesoriacum, on a clear day, you can see the white cliffs of Dubris, but I have never encountered a clear day there, so cannot attest to this. My dealings there have been frequent, but invariably brief except when my skills as a negotiator have had to come into play to ensure that a cargo of Samian ware – or wine or spices – destined for Britannia actually gets to the ship it is supposed to be on, despite the antics of the Gaulish mule train drivers who block the harbour roads in protest at the slightest grievance.

For once, there was no protest going on in the docks and I was able to transfer to a fast galley leaving the following day with only a minimal amount of bribery and the dropping of the names of several officers of the Fleet.

I was going to have to face my father and tell him why I was home from Gaul two months early without this year's supply of pottery and that I was about to disappear for another month into Iceni territory, all expenses paid by him, whether he realised it or not.

I was beginning to learn that a spy's life was not an easy one.

My father, Alexander, son of Narcissus, the merchant, was not prone to flushing red in the face, or at least no more than any man of his age with an easy life and a liking for the wine flask. But my unexpected arrival home sent him crimson to the tips of his ears.

It was not that I had caught him with a woman. As a widower for ten years now since my mother died of a wasting fever

* Dover.

no physician could identify, my father had occasionally taken female companionship, usually a slave or a 'half-widow' of a legionary (as they are not allowed to marry legally), though I have successfully discouraged him from using the hordes of prostitutes who ply their trade in Londinium. When the need arises, he takes a woman – kindly and with suitable gifts, not by force – and is open and unashamed about it. We are Greeks, after all, and we have some style in these matters.

Unfortunately, we also have a reputation with boys, though I have never detected any inclination of that sort in my father, so it may seem odd to say that I embarrassed him by catching him with a boy.

It was not one of the prostitute boys which Londinium seems to specialise in; the ones you can rent for an afternoon. He was a boy well known to our household, because he was part of it and his name was Calpurnius. In his own way he was possibly quite famous, being, as far as we could judge, one of the first bastards to be born to an unknown Roman legionary and an equally unknown Briton woman, probably of the Cantii tribe, almost nine months to the day after Claudius' invasion force landed. That made him about sixteen years old and, despite the fact that he had never seen his father and his mother must have been waiting on the invasion beaches with her legs open, he had grown into as efficient and attentive a house slave as one could wish for. And he was not an unattractive figure of a young man, for in truth he was no longer a boy, with his short, red, curly hair and his eyebrows so fine they almost disappeared in strong sunlight. There was a pigment to the skin, light though it was, which suggested that his father could have been Italian if not Roman, which would, interestingly, have meant that his father was an officer as all the legions occupying Britannia were drawn from the provinces of the Empire, mostly the northern ones on the assumption that they could cope with the miserable climate.

However interesting Calpurnius' origins, though, and however attractive his physical features, neither of these things had anything to do with my father being embarrassed when I arrived home to find them together and engaged in an activity which I had expressly counselled against. Despite all the force of logic, several severe lectures and even threats from me, my father was doing what he had promised he would not on the eve of my departure.

He was teaching Calpurnius to read.

The number of times I had warned the old fool! An old man, far from his sharpest, alone for much of the year, confused by the complexities of business, could all too easily put his trust in an ambitious servant who had the ability to read and cook the books. Before we knew it, Calpurnius could have wormed his way to a position of power within the firm.

'I hope you are not doing what I think you are doing,' I said loudly, catching them unawares huddled over a wax tablet and having the pleasure of seeing my father's blood boil beneath his skin.

My moment of small victory was spoiled somewhat by the fact that Calpurnius himself did not turn a single curled hair. It was as if he had been expecting me and devised the whole scene purely for my benefit.

'Master Olussa,' he said with a smile, 'it is always a pleasure to welcome you home.'

'Even when you are early and unannounced,' blustered my father. 'Six weeks early by my count.'

I was tempted to retort that I was impressed my father had learned to count in my absence but I controlled myself. Letting slip such emotions in front of Calpurnius would be dangerous. Showing slaves that you care about anything – especially their presence – should be avoided.

'Yes, I have returned early and there is a reason – a business reason – which I must discuss with you.'

I waved dismissively, casually, into the air, the signal for Calpurnius to withdraw. For a moment he glanced sideways at my father but my father's eyes would not meet his and, lacking support, he scuttled out. Before he reached the door I said loudly:

'And I am sorry, father, but in my haste to return I quite forgot your request for one of the Gaulish mountain dogs. I know you so wanted a puppy to amuse you in my absence.'

'I find Calpurnius company enough,' said the red-faced old man. Then he added, rather slyly: 'Perhaps that's why I like to teach him tricks.'

'Teaching slaves to read and write is not a trick, father, it is a mistake. Rich Roman nobles may amuse themselves that way but a small family business like ours cannot afford such a luxury. Especially not with some bastard Brit. We make a reasonable living here but only because the Romans let us. You don't see them educating their British slaves and making freedmen of them, do you?'

'They will, my son, they will. They have in every other part of the Empire. That is the secret of the Roman success. They conquer a people and then offer them the benefits of the Roman way of life. When they see what the Romans can do for them they want to join in, not oppose.'

'But father, everyone knows the Britons are too stupid and too stubborn and too stuck in their Druid witchcraft to see that. They will sit around in their huts and mutter, "What have the Romans done for us, then?" for a thousand years before admitting to anything good coming out of Rome.'

'Nonsense, Olussa. One of our legions will be recruited from the natives of Britannia within the next twenty years, you mark my words. It will happen in my lifetime, you'll see.'

The prospect of the old man living that long appalled me so much I almost overlooked the fact that he had slipped into his Roman make-believe world by calling them 'our' legions.

We are, as I have written, Greeks by origin and Roman only in hope. My father has even been known to style himself after the Roman fashion as Alexander Dionysius Narcissus when his name was required on a contract; which is blissfully rare these days. Signing his name thus (and I have no idea where the Dionysius came from) is now frowned upon by the law ever since Claudius decreed that *peregrini*, which is what they call us non-Romans, should not use Roman surnames like a respectable citizen would. To satisfy his vanity he named my sister, Julia Agrippina, after the mother of the Emperor Nero, but no one minded that. She is, after all, only a girl.

Now he appears to want to claim a share of Rome's armed forces, presumably on the grounds that he pays taxes towards their upkeep. (I do not disabuse him of this theory as I have made sure that all the tax liabilities of our business are in his name.)

'Very well, father, have it your way,' I said wearily. 'There will be a legion drawn from Britannia, there will be a Consul from Britannia, there may even be an Emperor from this damned island, but there will not be a slave who can read in this house! I cannot continue to run the family business from here if there is. I have explained this many times before.'

And I knew it usually worked, for my father had a morbid fear of being left alone in his old age in what was still, after many years, a foreign country to him. To the old, loneliness is a fearsome weapon. But it was not the only weapon I had in my armoury where my father was concerned.

'A family business is a business for the family, not outsiders. Unless, of course, you are grooming Calpurnius for a partnership *by marriage* perhaps?'

My father flushed blood red again. He was too much of a snob to consider Julia Agrippina marrying anyone below equestrian rank, though where she would meet such a god in this forsaken frontier town of filthy taverns and even filthier brothels showed that my father lived more in hope than expectation.

'How could you even *think* such a thing, Olussa?' he blustered, showing that my barb had hit home.

'Others will think it,' I said smoothly.

'They will?'

A double hit, but he recovered his composure well enough.

'Julia Agrippina will join us for dinner,' he said, changing the subject. 'And you can tell us both about your trip and why you are back so early.'

I bowed politely, mostly to hide my smile of victory, and made to go to my rooms at the rear of the house, overlooking the river Tamesis. I should have known that my father would insist on the last word.

'And you can tell us why the new Procurator wishes to see you. I presume that has something to do with your untimely, however pleasing, return home.'

I covered my surprise well. It was my first lesson as a spy: there are no such things as secrets and news can travel very fast when it wants to.

Marcellus, the professional spy, had warned me that someone would contact me in Londinium with details of how and when to report my findings. I had not expected that to be the Procurator himself, nor that he would be waiting for me. But it had to have something to do with my mission for Seneca. The new Procurator would not go out of his way to pay me a courtesy call just to introduce himself. My father may have expected a visit or a summons from the new Procurator, but then my father has never really known his place in the Roman world and there was no real reason why the new Procurator should call on him. Alexander and Son were small fish in a very murky pond and I was content to keep the waters muddy.

It was possible, however, that my father had picked up some gossip which could prove useful. All I knew was the Procurator's name: Catus Decianus. He had arrived in Britannia shortly before my departure to southern Gaul and about six months after the new Governor, the noble Gaius Suetonius Paulinus, had taken office.

Not that anyone had seen much of him either. General Paulinus had arrived, gone on a rapid tour of inspection of the main garrison forts and then had disappeared off into the western hills with the legions to fight the barbarian tribes who lived there.

If my father had heard any gossip, he kept it to himself during dinner. Fortunately, my sister, Julia, is incapable of keeping gossip to herself and several of her tutors have said the only thing she hides well is her intelligence. The only problem is that Julia rarely hears gossip of any significance, spending all her time in the company of the daughters of Roman officials and merchants who were, like her, stranded in Londinium. They filled their days complaining to each other about what a crude, rough backwater the place was at the arse-end of the Empire; why they were not yet married and whether it was worth remaining a virgin. (Julia said she believed it was, judging it to be added value in a marriage settlement, which at least showed she had inherited some of the family's sense of business acumen.)

'I hear the new Procurator is unmarried,' she said casually.

'You have met the new Procurator, sister?' I asked, as casual as she.

'I certainly hope to,' said Julia, examining the platter before her as if searching for the tastiest morsel.

'He would be quite a catch,' said my father, ever the merchant. 'A Roman citizen, a salary of 200,000 sesterces a year, control over trading permits and import licences, plus the right to hand out the building franchises to develop the port.'

'A difficult catch to land,' said Julia, still looking down at her plate. 'It is said he shows little interest in women and that perhaps his tastes are more like those of my dearest brother's than—'

'Julia!' I hissed at her. Then it was for me to change the subject. 'But you forget the Procurator's one great advantage in life: the power to collect taxes.'

'Well observed, my son,' said my noble father. 'That power is indeed enough to set a man among the gods – whichever gods are in favour at the moment.'

He waved over one of the dinner slaves, a surly British girl with feet as rough and hard as crocodile skin, who silently offered him a bowl of apples. They were the latest crop from the new orchards the Romans had planted in land confiscated from the Cantii tribe south and east of Londinium. Before the invasion, the British had no conception of a ripe eating apple; the stunted and shrivelled brown fruits they called apples being good only for pickles or cooking with pork.

With apple juice running down his chin, he leaned forward.

'It cannot, I suppose, be a tax matter on which the Procurator wishes to see you, Olussa?' he said, as if the thought had just come to him and I noted that it was I alone who seemed to be responsible for tax matters.

'I am certain that it must be,' I answered, knowing full well that the question had never been far from my father's thoughts since the official summons had arrived. 'Procurators deal in taxes, that is what they do. If he had been seeking advice on the doings of merchants or the movement of ships in and out of this stinking sewer of a river port, he would surely have sent for you, father. You must be one of the senior merchants on this island by now.'

My father digested this thought along with his apple, though neither seemed to suit his stomach well.

'And if – ' I turned to my beloved sister – 'he was seeking a wife, then he also would have sent for the head of the household.'

Julia ignored me. My father simply chewed, like some moon-faced cow.

I began to pick at a plate of dates, forcing him to make the next move in our game.

'I hope you will not disparage our little outpost here in front of the new Procurator,' he said at last. 'Londinium has given this family a great opportunity to grow its business and raise our social status. The new Governor was said to have been much impressed with our town and has great plans for it.'

'So Londinium is a town now and not a fish dock?' I laughed, knowing it would wound my father's sense of civic pride. 'And how long was the new Governor here, seeing the sights, before he charged off across the frontier to find some barbarians to fight? Four days? Five?'

'General Paulinus is a soldier. He cannot seriously attend to his duties as Governor until the frontier is safe,' blustered the old man. 'And anyway, the Procurator is making his office here, moving things down from Camulodunum. That shows the way the wind is blowing. Londinium will be one of the great Roman cities.'

'You think like a Greek still, father. Londinium may have the edge on Camulodunum because the river here is bigger and can handle more ships and the more ships there are, the more money in taxes for the Procurator to collect. But once Rome realises that there is nothing worth having on this island, they will cut their losses and pull out. It's a business to them and if the business fails, they will go. What on earth would make them stay here once they stop making a profit?'

'Pah!'

Narcissus Alexander, my father and founder of the feast, spat the core of his apple across the room. It bounced off the plastered wall and came to rest by one of the crocodile feet of the dinner slave. For a moment I thought she would scoop it up and push it into her curiously small mouth. I knew my father to be generous with most forms of flesh and oysters when it came to the servants, but there were still some luxuries he thought it best they did not get the taste for. And Calpurnius, for all his youth and other failings, had trained the girl well. She looked, but did not touch and on a nod from Calpurnius –

but not before – one of the six or seven long-haired greyhounds (a breed my father had taken to) lying around the room crawled lazily over and devoured it at a gulp. The dog licked the girl's foot while he was there, found it not to his taste and slithered back to his place. Calpurnius had also trained the dogs well.

'The Romans are civilising the world,' said my father, 'and you speak as if it is just a business to them.'

'But it is, father. That is exactly what it is. Think of our own tiny empire as merchants. We make a profit on Samian ware and so we engage more potters. We dabbled in the glass trade and we made a loss, so we pulled out of glass.'

I had not chosen my example at random. It had been my father's idea to sink a considerable amount of capital (though not actually quite as much as he believed he had) into establishing a glass factory and even importing a family of glass-makers from the Rhinelands to oversee production. Not only had he grossly overestimated the domestic market for fine glass beakers and scent bottles in Britannia (there was none), but the Rhinelanders to a man – and a woman – had turned out to be drunkards and quarrelsome drunkards at that. They broke more than they ever made and we wrote the business off at a considerable loss.

'I cannot accept that, my boy. Rome is greater than a mere business, it is an idea. An idea which has become a way of life, a civilised way of life. An idea which will last a thousand years. It cannot be swayed by lowly concerns of a profit here and a loss there. You are thinking with your accounting ledgers, not with a vision of history.'

My father: so pompous and so sad, because he believed it. From the mouth of a professional orator – one of the cynic school – such a speech could have been very funny.

'Come, come, father. You have heard the rumours as well as I about the financiers and bankers in Rome who are tired of such small returns from this poxy little outpost. Britannia has never lived up to Rome's expectations and it is only a matter of time before someone counts the cost of keeping four legions here. Four legions, father, out of what? Twenty-five? More legions here than are needed in the whole of Hispania, or Africa? How does that make sense given what riches Rome extracts from them compared to the scraps of metal and brainless hunting dogs it finds here? The numbers, father, simply do not add up.'

I thrust my empty goblet into the air and waited for a slave to fill it. I had paused for breath, not dramatic effect, but there was drama and it came from my sister.

'Then you have heard the rumours about the Imperial loans?' Julia said softly.

Both my father and I stared at her. Surely she could have no idea what she was saying.

My father looked at me and I looked at him. I raised my eyebrows. My father clapped his hands.

'Leave us,' he announced and the dinner slaves began to withdraw.

'You too, Calpurnius,' I said without turning my head.

'And you, Julia,' said my father, somewhat to my (and her) surprise. 'This is politics and women have no place in politics. No place at all.'

I was never to have the opportunity to tell him how wrong he was about that.

Even without the rudest training in being a spy I was learning that the best way to discover something was to offer something in return.

'Julia is right,' I said when we were alone. 'It is about the Imperial loans.'

'So it is true?' he asked, his voice hushed.

'That depends on what it is you have heard,' I said carefully and, I thought, rather cleverly, for I had no idea what Julia had meant.

'That the grants made by the late Emperor Claudius to the local tribes are to be . . . to be . . . *recalculated* as loans. That at least is what is being said in the forum when the wholesalers meet to fix prices every morning.'

Were there no secrets at all, except from me? I began to despair, though I was impressed that my father had picked up the Roman habit of coming up with a new name for anything which might be even slightly unpalatable. Grants were now to be 'recalculated' it seemed, and not actually be grants at all. Tribes were 'resettled' rather than evicted from their land; ships of native traders or fishermen were 'impressed' into the navy, not 'stolen'.

'And what, in the collective wisdom of the wholesalers down the forum, does such a thing mean?' I said.

My father eyed me suspiciously.

'I thought you were the one summoned to see the Procurator. You should be telling me.'

'If I could, Father, if I could. But until I have actually met with Catus Decianus and received what orders he may have for me, I am unsure as to what I am allowed to say. You will appreciate, though, a man of your experience of the world, how valuable it will be for me to know what is being said in the forum before I meet the Procurator tomorrow.'

'Of course, one should always be well-informed. The key to successful business is information, information—'

'. . . and information,' I completed, having heard him say it a thousand times before. 'As you have always wisely and rightly said, father. So what is the view of the merchants if the old Imperial grants become loans overnight?'

'Well, disastrous, of course. Claudius gave the tribes massive handouts years ago to keep them docile and, naturally, they've spent it all.'

They had indeed, a small proportion of it going through the various businesses, discounting the Rhineland glass venture, of Alexander and Son.

'I shouldn't think they could come anywhere near raising the capital to repay the grants as loans,' he continued, 'let alone the interest that would be due after all these years. Most of the tribal chiefs who took the money are dead anyway.'

Several had drunk themselves to death with their grants, whilst others had died suddenly when their children had realised they had a decent inheritance.

Seneca's man Marcellus had said I was to do a stock check of what the Iceni were worth. If the rumour about the grants which were now loans was true, then Seneca was trying to get a feel of what he could recoup for Rome and at the same time gauge what effect such a 'repayment' would have on the province and his own private investments. But had the Iceni been given a grant by Claudius? If I ever knew I could not remember. If they had not, why was Seneca interested in them?

I had not mentioned the Iceni to my father, though I would have to at some point to learn what I could about them, and I decided that it would be wiser to do so after I had answered the Procurator's summons.

'I am tired from my journey, Father, and it is late. We will speak more after I have met with Catus Decianus tomorrow. Did he leave any specific instructions?'

Once again my father's eyes narrowed in suspicion.

'Only that you should report to him as soon as you crossed from Gaul. Am I to assume that you have business with the noble tax collector?'

'Yes, but not in a tax sense.'

I thought he would be relieved at that.

'So what sort of business is it?' he asked, almost demanded.

'I think the new Procurator wishes to commission me to do a study for him,' I said, choosing my words carefully. 'An economic study of sorts. An evaluation you might say. Or a *plan* – a plan of business.'

My father snorted, making the same sound he had when he spat the apple core across the room.

'So you're a spy, then?'

IV: Roscius

Druids? What do you want to know about the Druids? Bloody head-hunters, that's what the Druids were. They had a thing about heads.

They encouraged the Celts to collect heads whenever they fought amongst themselves. If they didn't have any spare heads lying about from a recent battle, then they'd execute a couple of slaves. Human sacrifice, that's what it was. That's why we had to stamp it out. A gladiator loses his head in the arena – well, that's fair enough. He's armed, like the other fellow, and it's a noble combat to the death. And the others, who make up the numbers in the bigger shows like they have in Rome, they're almost all convicted criminals or religious fanatics, so there's no loss there.

But to take a head just so they could throw it into some

stagnant pool to make a soup for their so-called gods, I ask you. Call that civilised behaviour? I think not.

There was always water involved in their rituals and they'd have sacred groves of trees around a pond or a sacred part of a river bank and the more heads they could chuck in there, the happier they were. But if there wasn't a holy pond nearby then sometimes they'd just nail your head to the nearest door or stick it on a stake and let the birds take the eyes. When they had a lean spell, like when they weren't killing each other or trying to kill us, then they'd resort to sacrificing some of the heads they'd been saving up for a rainy day, as they say over there even though it rains most days. That was another skill of the Druids, the keeping of heads. They used to embalm them in cedar oil in big jars until they needed them. I'm telling you straight. I am not making this up.

Someone once told me that they had a god called Taranis, 'the thunderer', almost the same as our Jupiter. But bugger me if Jupiter ever asked an honest man to go out and pickle heads just in case there was a shortage in the future!

I don't know where all this bloodlust and obsession with chopping heads off came from, but we couldn't allow it to go on, could we? I mean that was bad enough, though I suppose we've overlooked worse, but there was no way the Druids were going to give up the practice. They actively encouraged the tribes to do it; said it increased the magic, and that was what it was all about really.

We used to think the old Persians were dead set on magic and rituals and rites and superstition, but I tell you, they had nothing on those Celts in Britannia. I suppose it's being an island and being cut off from the rest of the world which did it. Talk about the backwoods. I've seen things in my time, dark things in the big German forests, but at least there the locals had the decency to be afraid. In Britannia, the crowds used to turn out for a ritual beheading, expecting to see some magic happen. The Druids told them the sacrifice had been accepted and their gods were happy and they swallowed it whole. Lapped it up. Couldn't get enough.

Chop off enough heads and the crops would grow, your horses would multiply, your wife would bear you sons and your enemies would lie down before you. If none of that happened, then you simply hadn't done enough heads.

Oh yes, giving head to the gods was a big thing.

But the problem – the real problem – was that the Druids who preached all this bollocks weren't stupid. They were quite clever most of them, even the women. Oh yes, they had women priests as well as witches – I'll get to them.

I don't think they believed all this human sacrifice bullshit, but they knew it impressed the hell out of the rank and file down on the farm in their filthy little round huts. Your average Celt would scratch away at a piece of mud for most of the year then go off for a bit of a ruck with some neighbouring tribe, take a few slaves, loot a few bits of jewellery, rape a few women and steal some more horses. He was happy enough as long as he got back in one piece and there was some salt fish to eat and some of their foul beer to drink through the winter. And he was happy because the Druids had told him this was what he could do. They let the locals get away with murder and they loved them for it.

It wasn't just the religion and the magic. They really did respect their priests because all the Druids came from the Celtic aristocracy. You had to be born into it, there was no way you could work your way up or buy your way in. So you had a priesthood which the locals recognised as their lords and masters because of their birth, and they could do the magic business too.

A winning combination, especially if you're a bit slow and let's face it, the Celts aren't the brightest stars out at night.

Trouble was, the Druids realised what a hold they had over the locals and of course they just couldn't resist meddling in politics. Half of them could probably have been tribal kings or queens in their own right if they hadn't had an elder brother. And don't you think they knew that? Don't you think they thought they could do the job just as well if not better?

Fact is, some of them could have. Most of them were pretty bright; some, you could say, were almost educated. Not like we'd call it, mind you. They didn't read or write things down, not like you and those scribes of yours are doing.

It was Julius Caesar who said that the Celts thought it improper to entrust their studies to writing, wasn't it? Don't look at me like that. I might be an old soldier but I've read a bit.

Even without learning, some of them Druids were sharp.

I met one once, you know. To talk to, that is, not just to kill.

I was serving with the XXth, this would be about eight years before I went back there with General Paulinus. It was frontier duty in the west, south of the hills where the gold mines were. Real bandit country that was, because the local tribe we were keeping an eye on – they were called the Silures – were probably the best the Brits ever had in terms of a fighting force. Those buggers knew what they were doing and they'd already taken on a couple of auxiliary units and given them a right seeing-to.

The commander of the XXth at the time was Manlius Valens. Yes, *that* Manlius Valens, the one who is still hanging around Rome waiting for his consulship. He's what, eighty-six or something now? They'll probably make him consul just for staying alive so long. He's already got the record for being the oldest legionary commander there ever was, as he never got promoted after being thumped by the Silures.

Anyway, my unit is camped near a small settlement and we've checked things out and there are no armed warriors for miles, just a few old women and some kids. But there is this Druid; a real ancient one, probably older than old Manlius Valens is now and he's as blind as a bat.

We didn't rate him as any sort of danger to us, though later it was policy to kill them on sight as it saved time. Truth is, he rather amused us and we took the piss out of him. He had this dog, you see, to help him see. It was a big, fat black and white bitch dog so old itself it hardly had any teeth and it drooled a lot, but it never strayed more than a yard or so from his side and when he walked, it walked by his right knee and it would lean into him to steer him round objects or stop dead if it saw somebody coming up to him.

This Druid was, I've said, bloody old and blind. He'd gone blind with age, nobody had put his eyes out or anything. He was dressed in black, like most of them are, but his robes – if you could call them that – were like sacking, not proper wool or hide. He had long white hair and a long beard in which were bits of twig and birdshite and who knows what, and by Jove, did he stink. But then most of the Brits do. Even now they're not sure what to do with hot water and a sponge.

He had tried to say something to us as we were building the camp for the night but we couldn't understand a word he was saying, so we ignored him and he just sat down on the ground, his dog next to him, and we almost forgot he was there. Then, when we were getting our mess rations for the evening, one of the lads sort of noticed he was still there and flicked a spoonful of curds from his bowl, right at the old man's face as he walked by him.

Fuck me, but the old man's hand shot up and he caught this gob of curd in mid air and whipped it into his mouth, licking the palm of his hand to make sure he'd got all of it. And I swear none of us had said a word. He couldn't have seen it coming, could he?

Naturally, some other daft footslogger does the same and he catches that as well. One-handed, sitting on the ground, without moving and the dog never moves either. Then somebody chucks a piece of bread and he catches that and eats it. By now he's got an audience and he's singing for his supper. When the lads pitch things short or too high, he just lets them go, doesn't even try for them. But when they come near, his hand shoots out and he nabs them. Both hands too, doesn't seem to make a difference to him. Never misses. And the lads love it, laughing and joking, even starting to bet on which hand he'll use.

I see what's going on and it looks pretty harmless, until the old man gets to his feet and waves the nearest trooper to come closer. One of them does – I can't remember his name, but I've a feeling he was one who copped it years later with Boudica's lot, and he stands in front of the old Druid who is jabbering away and making no sense at all.

The old man then reaches out and takes the trooper's right hand and guides it to the hilt of his sword.

Now all legionaries are taught that their *gladius* is their best friend and they should take care of it and not let anyone else touch it, so, naturally, the lads go a bit quiet at this. But the old Druid doesn't want the sword, he takes his hand away and mimes the action of a fast draw, then he takes a pace back from the trooper and holds his hands in front of him, a good two feet apart.

You won't find the quick draw in any army manual but all soldiers do it; sometimes for a bet, sometimes to exercise the sword arm and build up the muscles, and sometimes just because your life could depend on it. When you're carrying a shield into battle on your left arm, you're up tight against the man either side of you and when the order comes, you've got to get your sword out the same time as all the other guys. Otherwise you might cut off somebody's arm or – worse – be so squashed in you never can get it out of the scabbard and you've got nothing to stab with.

It's a tricky thing to get the hang of at first. You drop your hand to your hip, turn the wrist, grab the *gladius* handle, whip it out, up and then twist again. Hopefully without taking your own nose off.

Part of the quick draw game was somebody stands in front of you and you have to draw your sword before they can clap their hands. In fact if you're good, they can't clap their hands because your sword is in there between your hands, you see? Get it wrong and you could lose a finger or two.

This old Druid had heard about the game – he couldn't have seen it, could he? – and there he was challenging the lads of the XXth Legion to have a go. So they did.

I think five or six tried, maybe more, and a couple I knew were very good at the game, but none of them made it. The old man clapped his hands every time, even widening his hands after the first couple to make it easier for them.

Then I put a stop to it as tempers were starting to run by this time, ordering the lads to get back to their meal. Of course one of them had to shout out why didn't I have a go, as I was an officer (who had been a ranker) and therefore I must be good at something. Like an idiot, I did.

I squared myself up to the stinky old man and even though he couldn't understand a word, told his blind eyes that he wouldn't see this one coming. And he didn't. I drew and had my sword up as his hands slapped onto the metal and his mouth opened in surprise but he said nothing as the lads cheered.

Ever so slowly, he ran his hands down the blade until the

skin broke and a thin trickle of blood appeared where his palms had been. Then he let go and his right hand started to feel towards me, trying to locate my left hip and the scabbard.

Somebody yelled out that the old man fancied me and that broke the spell. I slapped the old Druid's hand away, wiped my blade on the grass underfoot and sheathed the sword. By the time I had done so, the old man was sat back on the ground next to his dog.

In the morning as we broke camp, a sentry reported that the old Druid and his dog had gone during the night without a sound.

We had a small unit of Thracian cavalry with us as scouts. They were from the First Ala, I remember that, a crack unit, veterans of the invasion, good trackers. I took some of them with me and we set out westwards into Silures territory and we found the old Druid, and his dog, just before midday.

We killed him on some marshy ground near the big estuary which leads to the coast.

Had to, didn't we? The old bugger had found out that officers wear their swords on the left hip, not the right like your ordinary infantryman. It was my cross draw from the left that had fooled him. You can imagine what he would have told his friends the Silures, can't you? Go for the ones with their swords on the left. Take out the officers first.

I should have seen through the cunning bastard a lot sooner and if he hadn't done a runner it might never have occurred to me.

We killed his dog as well.

Just to be sure.

V: Olussa

Despite protestations that I was unarmed, I was manhandled and searched twice as I tried to enter the Procurator's office the next morning, the second time far more roughly than was necessary (as if I would hide a dagger between the cheeks of my arse!) by a giant slave who had the arms and stench of a bear.

If this greeting was representative of the new Procurator's style of conducting business, then he would fit right into the Londinium scene.

The borough – it could not be called a town in the proper sense and did not have the status of an official *colonia* such as Camulodunum – sprawled between two small hills on the northern bank of the Tamesis, the main settlement being bisected by a grubby stream or 'brook' as the native word seemed to be, called the Wal. The official buildings, such as they were (for these were by no means grand or imposing buildings), were concentrated either in the old legionary fort to the north-west of the Wal Brook or to the south-east, overlooking the big river and the bridge. Not that the bridge was much to speak of. It had been knocked up by Aulus Plautius, the general who commanded the invasion forces seventeen years before, and had been in sore need of repair ever since. It was little used, the small settlement on the opposite bank of the Tamesis, the original camp of Aulus and his legions, being even more sordid an area of thieves and prostitutes than the rest of Londinium, and torch-bearers, bodyguards and ferrymen were reluctant to go south of the river after dark.

There had been nothing much here before Aulus Plautius' troops appeared. Even the native Britons had not bothered to settle the place, so nothing in Londinium dated from much more than fifteen years ago, when the military had decided to make it a supply base for the legions fighting in the west and south-west. Even then, it was another three years or so before civilians – mostly traders in crude and basic goods and almost totally Gaulish – began to settle and spread like a fungus in the area south of the Corn Hill, which was still used by the military as a granary.

My father, the merchant in him scenting new business, came to Britannia ten years ago after the death of my mother. We were, I suppose, the third wave of immigrants into Londinium; the Gaulish traders being the second and the prostitutes, tavern owners and professional gamblers who followed the legions being the first. And because we had capital behind us, we were able to build a house and warehouses near the Tamesis but downstream (and upwind) of the bridge and the sordid clusterings of hovels on either side of the Wal Brook which by now were threatening to expand almost as far west as the Quick, or Fleet as the locals said, River which fed the Tamesis. In ten years I had seen the streets of Londinium extend over two miles on an east-west line and if I ever complained of our living conditions in the east end of the borough, my father was quick to remind me that it was infinitely preferable to the hive of squalor, lawlessness and corruption at the west end where the streets met the Fleet.

And whilst it was not a large settlement in area – certainly not compared to decent, civilised places – it was large, and growing, in people. Perhaps fifty thousand men, women, slaves, children and sailors were crammed sweatily into the half circle of Londinium, which was in truth no more than a pimple on the edge of an otherwise impressive river bank. What had begun as a military encampment – as most proper Roman towns in the provinces do – was bulging at the sides in a chaotic maze of alleyways and shoddy, lean-to hovels. There had been no attempt at planning the place or laying out a sensible grid of streets, which showed how little the Romans thought of it. The few soldiers still around, who should have been building the basic civic amenities, were mostly confined to guard duties at the granaries on the Corn Hill or in servicing the Imperial postal system. When they were not drunk that is, as most of the seasoned officers were away with the Governor on his frontier campaign.

A few of the non-combatants had, however, been seconded to the Procurator's office for general policing duties. Unlike their comrades on hum-drum guard duty, they were corrupt, lewd and bloodthirsty as well as drunk.

It was one of these who had searched me so unnecessarily, and so *internally*, and although he had arms as hairy as a bear (and he was as rank as one) he did not actually look like a bear. I have seen many bears on my travels, even bought and sold a few, but I have never seen one with a broken nose. Moreover, his nose had been broken more than once so that his nostrils flared out from the flat of his face like a pig's snout sniffing for chestnuts.

This bear-pig wore no badge of rank apart from his shirt of green wool to which had been stitched a covering of iron mail, and a *gladius* in a scabbard on his left hip. This marked him out as someone who had the right to bear arms in a government office and the hobnail boots he wore showed he could draw supplies from the military stores. Beyond that, my powers of observation which had so impressed Marcellus the spy were failing me. In fact my entire mind was numb with fear as the giant animal man loomed over me and his breath, rippling with waves of the stagnant honey beer much favoured by the Celtic race, could only be compared to marsh gas.

'Wait here,' he said in a crude, dog Latin. 'Do not move until you are called.'

I was more than happy to wait in what appeared to be an anteroom, if only because without the bear-pig there at least the air was breathable. The walls had been recently painted with the ever popular hunting scenes bordered with streams of vine leaves. It had probably been done in honour of the new Procurator, though I noticed that little skill and even less money had gone into the design. The colours were bright but crude, with none of the deeper blue shades – blue being the most expensive colouring by far – at all. There were only two pieces of furniture in the chamber, a bench seat carved from a tree trunk (ugly, but surprisingly comfortable) and a crude and rickety three-legged table on which was precariously balanced a large Samian platter. If there had been honey cakes – or nuts, which were cheaper and more popular among the natives here – there were none now. I noted the maker's mark, Aquitanus, another potter of southern Gaul, but not one of mine. Perhaps I could persuade the new Procurator to upgrade.

It was an idea I abandoned the moment I met him.

The doors to his office were pulled open by the bear-pig with a squealing which showed the wood to be new and cheaply cut.

'Come on,' he growled, 'get a move on. You're late.'

A voice from inside the office growled even louder: 'At least a week late.'

I knew at once it was a voice I should be afraid of.

The philosophers say, or if they do not then they should, that the voice fits the man. With Catus Decianus, nothing could be further from the truth. His voice was that of the orator or the declaimer classically trained in the arts; a rich mellow tone which filled every crevice of the room he was in and which, without doubt, would reach the back seats of a theatre with ease, even the new style of amphitheatre being built these days. If his servant was a bear-pig, then Catus Decianus' voice was a world weary lion which dispensed wisdom in equal proportions to threat.

But the voice was not the man. The man was no lion; he was a weasel, a stoat, a rat. He was small and thin and quick and constantly moving as if in search of food.

I may be old fashioned, but I have always preferred my tax collectors to be fat, happy and corrupt. At least you know where you stand with people like that around you. This one had the composure of a pregnant pony during a thunderstorm.

And then I realised he was waiting for an answer.

'Most noble and generous Procurator, may I congratulate you—'

I began as I had rehearsed but got no further.

'Cut the crap, Olussa. My people in Gaul told me you should have been here a week ago.'

'The sea journey, my noble lord Procurator. These things are not exact. I was told I would be . . . that someone would make contact with me on my return. I was not told when, nor indeed that it would be someone of your honour's position. I arrived in Dubris only two days ago—'

'*Three* days ago, actually,' he said, stalking across the room in front of me. Perhaps he was a lion after all, eyeing his prey. 'On the dawn tide and you spent some considerable time with two local merchants – we have their names – negotiating the safe arrival of a shipment of pottery from southern Gaul. Hardly the actions of someone on an important mission for the Roman state, wouldn't you say? And does your father know about these negotiations in Dubris, by the way?'

My head reeled. I was no more than two paces inside his office and yet it might as well have been a court of law. I heard the doors slam behind me and from the stench I could tell that the bear-pig was still in the room, behind me; the one witness at my trial.

For a moment I considered lowering my head for the sword there and then, but had not the Procurator himself just said that I was on an important mission for Rome? What would a real spy say in these circumstances?

'I was merely laying a false trail, most noble Procurator. I am known among the merchants of this country and my early return was unexpected. It would have been *suspicious* had I returned early and not said anything to my usual contacts.'

'So what did you tell them?'

Catus had stopped pacing the room and stood immobile except for his eyes, which flashed and darted in all directions, so that I felt as if he was looking at me, over me and through me at the same time.

'I told them that I had conducted a most favourable supply deal of Samian ware and that I was hurrying back to Londinium to persuade my father that we should be expanding our distribution network before our competitors could.'

Catus considered this, tugging on the wisp of a beard hanging from his chin. I had seen better growths on the end of a centurion's fly swat.

'Very good,' he said at last. 'Perhaps the reports about you are true.'

I thought it prudent not to ask *what* reports, although I ached to do so. But a professional spy would not have had to ask. He would assume that his credentials had been thoroughly tested. He would have bowed gracefully, acknowledging that his master – his *spy*master – had in fact paid him a compliment. And so that is what I did.

When I looked up, Catus was not there. He was across the room, bending over a heavy oak chest, opening the lock with a key suspended from his neck on a leather thong.

'Who was it who briefed you?' he asked as he struggled with the lock.

'He said his name was Marcellus,' I replied, speaking to the Procurator's bending arse. 'He was Seneca's man.'

I thought it prudent to show that I had some idea of what was going on, even if in truth I had little.

'We are all Seneca's men,' said Catus, his voice booming across the room. A curious effect due to the fact that his head was almost inside the large chest now he had managed to raise the lid.

Then he raised his head, looked at me and then at the giant bear-pig guarding the door, then quickly back to me.

'Except Starbo, here. He's my man, aren't you, Starbo?'

Before the giant could reply, the Procurator's head and upper body had disappeared back into the oak trunk and for a moment I feared that he might fall in and let it engulf him entirely. But then he was suddenly walking towards me holding a leather purse and pulling the drawstrings with his teeth.

'You are a man of the world, Olussa, and are much travelled and can speak several languages and numerous dialects,' he said as he emptied something from the purse into his hand as he approached. 'This much I have heard of you. I have also heard that you are something of a sharp businessman and have been embezzling from your family firm for several years. I presume you can embezzle from yourself, if it is your family's firm? Oh, don't look so worried, I am not here to judge, although I would always advise that you embezzle from someone else's firm. I find it much more profitable. I merely raise the matter because your experience would suggest that you know what these are.'

He opened the palm of his right hand and flipped three small coins at me with all the disdain of a rich man throwing charity to the poor. One I caught out of instinct but the other two fell to the floor and I scrabbled, rather foolishly, to retrieve them.

'There was a day when a good embezzler would have caught all three!' Catus laughed and there was a grunt from behind me from the bear-pig which suggested he was also amused.

I knew I was flushing red in the cheeks but I made to examine the coins as professionally as was expected of me and not like some grubby dockside trader who checks for where the edges have been nicked by the moneylenders.

'Well?' said the Procurator, impatient for an answer.

Under his darting gaze, I examined the coins even though my hand shook. I judged them to be relatively new and in good condition. The obverse face had no likeness of a king or a god, but was embossed with a simple design of studs and quarter-moon shapes and across the middle the word ECENI. The reverse showed a prancing horse and around its head, an ear of barley. Between its legs was stamped SUBPRASTO.

'Most noble Procurator, it is an Iceni coin. It is well known that the Iceni – or Eceni as they have it here, for they have no writing skills and they have borrowed—'

'Yes, yes. Go on.'

'The Iceni are the only tribe in Britannia who stamp their name, rather than a likeness of their king on their coinage. Although on the reverse, the "Subprasto" must mean "under Prasutagus", their king.'

'What else?'

I had no idea what he wanted me to say and I screwed up my eyes at the coin for inspiration.

'The ear of barley is very common on coins of this island as it is a crop most valued for the brewing of beer. The horse symbolises the Iceni prowess in breeding fine horses, by which it is said they measure the wealth of each clan—'

'Don't talk to me about fucking horses!' snapped the Procurator.

I looked up quickly to enquire how I had caused offence, but the Procurator had moved as fast as an irritating fly trapped in a room and was over by the oak chest, which he promptly kicked to vent his temper. Then he began pacing the room, back and forth, but never in a straight line, his hands tugging, then releasing, his sparse beard.

'Everyone tells me about the Iceni horses. That's what the Iceni are famous for, that's what they breed, that's what they trade, that's what they take to bed on a winter's night for all I care,' he ranted as he paced. Did the man never stay still?

'I'm not interested in their bloody horses. What can I do with horses? What can Seneca do with a herd of knock-kneed ponies? You know there is no free-market trade in horses here. The military have a monopoly as long as there are open hostilities, which, from what I've heard of the western end of this wretched little province, will be from now until for ever. Horses go straight to the army for army use, at army prices. Who do you know in this country who deals in horses in the private sector?'

'Only butchers, your eminence,' I said nervously in case it was not the answer this madman – for surely he was – expected.

'Exactly. So don't bring me any reports mentioning horses. Is that clear?'

'Perfectly, your nobleness,' I said, though in truth I would have said anything in those circumstances. Anything which might draw the interview to a close and which would avoid getting a blade in the spine from his slave Starbo, close enough behind me that I could smell him, although in his case that could have been a substantial distance.

'Then what will you report on?'

Still Catus paced the room, but now he lengthened and slowed his stride and he had a finger in one ear as if cleaning it so that he could receive my answer more clearly.

My answer, when it came, was from a parched mouth, dry with fear.

'My understanding, your eminence, is that the great and good Seneca requires an audit of the Iceni lands and valuables in order to make certain decisions about his investments. There is a suggestion, I hear, of debts which need to be repaid. For the reasons you have stated, a private investor cannot be paid in horses. Therefore other sources of wealth must be assessed. These would normally include land, crops, precious stones, furs, pelts and—'

I held out my hand with the three silver coins, willing the hand not to shake.

'Exactly!' said the Procurator, barely pausing in his stride (and it seemed as if he was pacing out the width of the room). 'Gold. That is what we're after.'

Gold?

'But these coins are silver, your nobleness,' I said before I could stop myself. Another rule of spying I must adopt is to think before speaking.

'That is my point. The Iceni use only silver for their coinage, not gold. Such has been the case for fifty years, or so I am informed. Therefore, *where is their gold?*'

'Perhaps they have none, your eminence.'

For the first time since I had entered his office, the Procurator stopped moving and stood rigid, frozen like ice. Even his eyes did not roll as they had but transfixed me like loosed arrows.

'Oh, kill him now and let us save time, Starbo,' said Catus.

But even as I turned my head to see where the blow would come, he went on: 'No, on second thoughts, don't bother. This one is so stupid he'll fool the Iceni into thinking he's harmless. We'll never find another one as good as this.'

Starbo, the giant, odorous slave, had not moved a muscle. But he smiled at me, taking genuine amusement in my fear. And to make sure that I knew he was enjoying my discomfort, he put his hand between his legs and began to feel himself. How he knew I had pissed myself I do not know, for nothing showed through the double folds of the toga I had wrapped myself in that morning.

'Of course the Iceni have no gold of their own,' the Procurator continued speaking – and resumed walking. 'The only gold to be found in this damned country is in the west, beyond the military frontier, not in the east. We've known that for years. They have no silver of their own either, come to that. They trade for it, just as they trade for gold, which they value highly and have been known to pay silly prices for, but they do not make coins from it or use it to purchase goods. Gold goes into the Iceni territory and is never seen again. I want to know what happens to it. That's where you come in.'

What is it about the mere mention of gold which makes men forget their fear?

'How much gold do they have?' I asked. 'And how do I get them to reveal it?'

For a moment, Catus Decianus was once again almost immobile, balanced on the balls of his feet, swaying slightly as he eyed me for the first time with approval.

'You are a merchant. You offer to trade with them.'

'Trade what?'

'I have just told you what they value most.'

'Gold?'

I was speaking to the back of his head as he stalked away from me yet again, this time towards the shutters of a window which should, if I still had my bearings, open on to the river.

'Of course. Offer them something they want to win their confidence.'

'Forgive me, nobleness, but you want me to offer the Iceni gold? In exchange for what?'

The Procurator began to struggle with the latches on the shutters.

'Anything and everything, you fool!' Catus shouted, but I suspected his anger was more to do with the shutters which refused to move, rather than with me. 'Offer them gold and they'll tell you exactly what they have to barter for it. It's the only thing they really want from us. They shun everything Roman but they will take Roman gold. By all the gods, I'll pay Roman gold if you can find me a carpenter who can cut straight!'

'I am sure I can find you a competent woodworker, Procurator. It would be my pleasure. Exactly how much gold should I offer the Iceni?'

The Procurator continued to rattle the shutters although it was obvious they were not going to move.

'You take as much as you can carry safely, but it has to be enough to impress them. You tell them this will only be the first of many deals, naturally. More gold will follow. Gold will positively flow. Tell them anything you want. Then they will tell you anything you want to know. You don't know anyone who can get the heating working in this place, do you? I have no intention of spending a winter in this stinking country if there's no heating.'

'I am sure my father will know of some skilled—'

'No more than four sesterces a day, mind you,' said the Procurator, sucking his fist where he had split the skin on his knuckles rapping on the wooden shutters. 'Some of the so-called skilled workers round here are asking ten! Bastards.'

'The gold, your honour . . .' I returned to the subject at hand, '. . . which I will need for this . . . these negotiations . . . ?'

Catus turned on me and there was genuine puzzlement in his eyes.

'Well? How much can you afford?'

At that precise moment, I would have welcomed Starbo's blade. Perhaps I should have begged for it.

Not only was I being forced into becoming Seneca's spy, I was expected to finance Seneca's spying mission, the sole beneficiary of which would be Seneca!

'My lord, to be convincing – even among a barbarian tribe – the sums required would have to be . . . substantial. And liquid. I must have gold in cash or kind to show them. The Iceni are not likely to believe the promises of an unknown merchant.'

The Procurator waved a finger in the air as if I had made a good debating point, and he began to walk again, encircling me as he spoke.

'Quite right. You talk of gold but show none and the Iceni will have your head off and chucked into one of their sacred pools before you can blink. Or so I've heard. But you are a merchant, from an established firm. You must have capital.'

'Capital which is tied up in trade goods and contracts and advance payments to our suppliers . . .' I pleaded, though I expected not a glimmer of mercy or understanding. And yet . . .

'Of course, of course,' soothed the Procurator in a gentle tone which I knew, although I was hearing it for the first time, I should distrust. 'You have commitments and coinage is scarce, especially gold coin. Therefore I have made arrangements for you to draw a suitable sum from the Imperial coffers in order to finance your mission.'

I bowed low. I have found it always prudent to respect advance planning when it involves money.

'Your nobleness is wise and far-sighted,' I said as reverently as I could.

The Procurator was pacing the room again and scratching his left armpit as if he had a flea, although his movements suggested he was the flea, for the man seemed incapable of remaining still.

'I have of course drawn up a mortgage on your house and business as surety for the loan, which you will sign and seal before you leave,' he said as he scratched.

'A . . . *loan* . . . Procurator?'

'Of course. I cannot allow so much gold to wander out of the provincial treasury without some form of security, can I? If you have any problems with this, perhaps I should consult your father as to the value of your assets?'

'That will not be necessary,' I said rather sharply. 'But I had rather assumed that the great and good Seneca himself would be financing the venture as it is to his interest and fortune that we engage upon—'

'Oh, don't talk bollocks, Olussa. That bastard Seneca is into this country for forty million sesterces. Forty million! Think about it. Is he going to give a whore's fart about what you or I think?'

I should have been shocked by the Procurator's language and lack of respect for the man who, after all, had the ear of the Emperor and could control both our destinies even in this distant, dismal outpost of Rome. But I was too shocked by what he had said, not the way he had said it.

'Forty million?' I said before I could stop myself. 'I heard it was ten million.'

The Procurator held up his fingers as he bestrode the room.

'Ten million in personal investments, twenty million in government loans to the tribes – loans which he bought after the Emperor Claudius died – and something like eight and a half million in interest accrued over the years. Or so he estimates. Round it up to forty million.'

My mind raced and to my shame, it was the mind of a merchant.

'But that's an interest rate of four-in-ten.'

'Forty-two in a hundred to be precise,' said the Procurator. He was scratching at the breast of his toga with his nails. I could not see whether he actually had fleas (as does everyone in Londinium) or was trying to remove a dried soup stain.

'But that is an outrageous rate!' Again I let my mouth break free of my brain.

'Only outrageous if you are forced to agree to it,' observed Catus, pausing in mid-stride.

'The tribes will not be held to it?' I asked, lost once again.

'Oh yes. What I'm saying is that they were not forced to agree to such a rate. They simply didn't know about it. Still don't. They thought they were getting presents of money; grants, not loans, from their new Roman masters.'

'The tribes don't know? Won't they be angry?'

'Fucking furious,' smiled the Procurator. 'I would be. Which is why I wouldn't mention these loans when you are in Iceni territory if I were you.'

After a heartbeat, he added:

'In fact I wouldn't mention the question of loans to anybody. Your fellow merchants will panic if they get wind of what is going on and an over-zealous army officer might well arrest you for treason. Plus the fact that any of the tribes between here and the Iceni would kill you before you got there. Which reminds me.'

The Procurator lunged for the oak chest, his feet skidding across the tiled floor, heaving open the heavy lid and almost falling into it, scrabbling with his hands like a rodent burying food for winter. Except Catus was digging something out – a roll of papyrus tied with a red linen band from which hung an official lead seal. He checked the seal and hurled the scroll over his shoulder for me to catch.

Even before my hands closed on it, he had slammed the lid of the chest and locked it and was walking by me towards the door.

'That is my latest so-called intelligence report from one of my officials in Camulodunum, a certain Valerius Lupus. I believe he is known to you.'

Yes, he was. An old woman of an administrator who dabbled in trade as long as it involved a hefty share and no work for himself. An old drinking partner of my father who, thank the gods, would not recognise a genuine crook if he had spawned one.

'The most noble and distinguished Lupus is indeed a figure of respect in this province and known for his good judgement . . .'

Thankfully, the Procurator was not listening.

'Yes, yes, I'm sure,' he said, waving away my eulogy as the giant Starbo opened the doors for him.

In the doorway he turned and addressed me.

'You'd better read that here. Starbo will lock you in and let you out when you have finished. I don't want that document leaving this office.'

'It is confidential?' I said, stupidly.

The Procurator twisted his weasel face into a look of contempt.

'No, because I haven't read it yet, idiot. Anyway, there are too many people in your household who can read. That's always dangerous. Just remember, Olussa, that what you know – and what you will find out – could get you killed by just about everybody in this province.'

Then, as if he had remembered something important:

'But if you can find me a heating engineer in Londinium who doesn't charge over the odds and who turns up when he says he's going to, then I might just let you live.'

VI: Valerius Lupus

Camulodunum.
By Imperial Post. Strictly Private under Seal.
To await the arrival of the Procurator of all Britannia, Gn. Catus Decianus.

Most esteemed and noble Procurator, again, welcome!

I must humbly assume that my initial letter welcoming you to this island province has been received by now and so I will forgo, if you will forgive, the formalities of an official welcome and proceed to your instructions forwarded by messenger from Gesoriacum. But let me, at the risk of repeating myself, insist that you are welcome in my modest house when you visit, whenever that may be – at your lordship's convenience of course – the principal *colonia* of the province which is Camulodunum.

Your instructions require me to report on the current status of the tribal kingdoms with which I have the closest dealings.

The first of these, in proximity if not power, is the Trinovantes, who have made their home in the land around Camulodunum for many generations although Rome has not been their only conqueror in living memory.

The noble Procurator will no doubt know that at some point in history (the history of Rome, that is, for these Britons have none of their own) between the expeditions of the glorious Caesar himself over a hundred years ago, and the invasion by the God Emperor Claudius, a mere seventeen years past, the Trinovantes were subjugated by their powerful neighbours the Catuvellauni.

This, the second tribe within what may be called my remit, has its ancestral home to the west on the site of the new principia of Verulamium* which lies to the north-west of Londinium along military route LXVI (in case your eminence is unfamiliar with the geography of the province).

* To become known as St Albans.

It is said that Cassivallanus, the war chief who led the resistance to the noble Caesar's expedition, was of the Catuvellauni, whereas the Trinovantes looked much more favourably on the arrival of Caesar's legions and were not at all hostile. This obviously became a bone of contention with their neighbours, the Catuvellauni, and at some point after Caesar withdrew from this island, the Catuvellauni invaded the tribal lands of the Trinovantes.

Their king Cunobelin established his estates here at Camulodunum, but three miles or so from the site of our *colonia,* which was then known as Dun Camulos in the native tongue. It was on the death of Cunobelin that the glorious Emperor Claudius invaded and enrolled Britannia into the empire. (One of Cunobelin's sons was killed resisting the invasion force and one other, the notorious Caratacus, fled to the west and continued to foment rebellion until he was arrested by our allies the Brigantes – a mercenary tribe to the north – and taken in chains to Rome. It is said that he so impressed the Senate with his primitive courage that he was not executed, but given a pension and allowed to drink himself to death on a smallholding near Herculaneum.)

It was the wisdom of the deified Claudius who, when accepting the surrender of the tribal chiefs (or kings as they like to be called) here at Camulodunum, ordered the division of the Catuvellauni lands to restore the independence of the Trinovantes. Thus the Trinovantes owe their current independence (from Catuvellauni rule if not from Rome) to the late Emperor Claudius. It is only fitting then, that the first *colonia* to be established in this country is here in Trinovantine territory, as is the first temple to be dedicated to the God Emperor Claudius. This is indeed a rare honour for a barbarian tribe, although their current chief, who is named Tasciovanus, sends regular appeals to the prefecture here complaining about the cost of establishing the Claudian cult and the expense of the temple building work.

However, the Trinovantes can be regarded as basically a compliant tribe, unlike their truculent neighbours and one-time overlords, the Catuvellauni, who resent their loss of power and influence in the region, not to mention the Trinovantine farms they profited from for many years.

The Catuvellauni were supportive of, if not directly allied with, the Iceni in the rebellion which greeted the appointment of Publius Ostorious Scapula twelve years ago. Which brings me to the third, and strangest, of the tribes I have knowledge of and contact with.

As the Procurator will surely know, the rebellious tribes in the west, beyond the military frontier, rose up in order to catch the new Governor unawares on his arrival in Britannia. Governor Scapula was, naturally, unlikely to be confused by such a stratagem and set to the combat with a will, deeming it prudent to protect his rear in the east by ordering the disarming of those tribes who had been allowed to keep their weapons on their surrender to the God Emperor Claudius. This was a sound move as the east was left without a single legion to guard it, even the XXth Legion having left Camulodunum for action on the frontier.

When the Iceni objected and took up arms rather than laying them down, Scapula moved quickly using auxiliary troops to punish the rebellion and disarm the tribes by force. The speed with which the new Governor moved caught the tribes unaware and the conflict was short and sharp. It has been said that the trouble was fomented by hot-headed factions within the Iceni, perhaps inspired by their Druid priests, who are numerous and powerful among them. There was no evidence that the Iceni king Prasutagus was directly involved and he remains their king to this day, though only with the blessing and magnanimity of Rome.

If little was known of the Iceni before that incident twelve years ago, then even less is known now for the Iceni withdrew further into their tribal home lands which comprise a strange mixture of thickly wooded low hills, bordered to the west by marshes and swamp land and to the north and east by a desolate coast of shifting sands and pebbles swept by high winds. There are no ports along this coast and such river estuaries as there are are not used by the Iceni for trade. In fact the Iceni have little or no truck with trade by water – either sea or river – even ignoring the eating of fish, preferring meat from their herds of sheep and goats. They are seen on the coast only to gather amber, which washes up among the pebbles on the eastern shores of their land, or to race and exercise their ponies, of which they are inordinately proud.

Horses are the main currency of trade for the Iceni with the other tribes, especially fast horses for chariots, at least until the tribes were disarmed by Governor Scapula. Their land is not generally good for large-scale harvests of grain, as the quartermasters of the legions have found, though they prize their crop of barley from which they brew beer which is said to be of a fine strength. When they wish to trade, they offer wool, hides of good quality, amber turned as crude but attractive jewellery, and meat which they dry with smoke or, more commonly, they salt for they have ample supplies of sea salt. In return, they seek pots and fine ware of all descriptions (for their own pottery is both thick yet fragile), linen and the finer cloths, wine from Campania shipped through Pompeii and they have an increasing desire for the olive oil of southern Hispania, which is a major import here in Camulodunum.

Above all, though, the Iceni crave gold, for they have none of their own. Yet they do not use it in coinage and such coins as they have, which are few, are of silver and they are willing to give twenty silver pieces weight-for-weight for one gold piece where the usual market rate would be no more than five or six. Their merchants, who are not regarded highly within the tribe, visit us infrequently but are always on watch for gold as coin, bullion or dust and have a reputation for buying any gold jewellery or ornament without haggling.

It is rumoured that their Druid priests regard gold as having a magic quality above and beyond the magic which gold has always worked on men and it is perhaps to the Druids that the gold they collect goes.

It is written on the walls of the old barracks of the XXth Legion here that a local Trinovantine whore can be had for two As, which would buy you two measures of wine in any of our taverns, but a speck of gold dust could buy a hundred Iceni whores.

If I have digressed at length about the Iceni, most noble and welcome Procurator, it is because they are the least known of the tribes of Britannia – apart from the unnatural barbarians who inhabit the far north in the land, which is sometimes called Caledonia.

The Iceni are secretive, backward and barely civilised even by the rough standards of this island. They have a saying which crudely translated means that 'they keep themselves to themselves' in their thick woods and marshlands, discouraging travel by their own people and only entering into trade reluctantly.

As we have no garrison here any more, military jurisdiction for the Iceni rests with the IXth Legion based at Durobrivae* and the legate there, the noble Quintus Petillius Cerialis.

If there is any further information the Procurator requires, he has but to command this humble servant, who would be honoured to offer the Procurator such hospitality as can be mustered should he wish to visit our developing *colonia* here at Camulodunum. Have I said that a thousand welcomes are extended to him?

VII: Roscius

What did we know about the tribes in Britannia? We knew how to kill them, that was all we needed to know.

That's not fair. We didn't have to kill them all. Some of them welcomed us, especially the ones in the south. You've got to remember that the tribes on the south coast like the Cantii were a damned sight closer to Gaul than they were to tribes like the Silures, say, in the west of the island. They were the ones who saw the profit in being inside the Empire rather than out on the edge of things. Some of them couldn't wait to chuck off their furs and put the toga on.

Not like the Trinovantes, who we always thought were a bit sharp, you know, a little bit shifty, always trying to fiddle you. Oh, they welcomed us at first all right, make no mistake. We got them out from under the Catuvellauni, who had just walked in and taken them over, and they got most of their land back. But what did they do? They bitched all the time about having to pay taxes and the cost of having the army on their land, though they never missed a chance to short-change us on a grain contract or sell us rotting meat. And they certainly didn't like it when we allocated some of their farms to our veterans, but sod it, old soldiers have to live somewhere don't they?

* Water Newton, near Peterborough.

That really got to them. Probably explains why they went over to Boudica straight away.

We didn't know that much about the Iceni. Nobody did. They'd been quiet for about twelve years up to then and we left them alone. They were supposed to be disarmed, though none of us professionals ever really believed that for a minute. We'd seen it all before. A tribe agrees to give up its weapons and somebody from the Procurator's office or similar turns up to collect them a month later and gets half if he's lucky because they've had lots of time to bury the rest. They could dig them up whenever they liked. And they did.

One thing we did know about the Iceni was that they fancied themselves with the chariot and they were very proud of the horses they bred. The idea was to drive up to the enemy and get as close as you could, then the spear-thrower would jump out, shout a few insults and chuck his weapon while the driver turned the chariot and picked him up on the way back to his own lines, all in one movement without stopping. The driving was the skilled job and that was done by the war chiefs and the warriors who fancied themselves. The spear-thrower was just there to throw the spear. Anybody could do that, but handling a chariot was an art, or so they thought.

Any trooper stationed in Britannia would have read the reports of Caesar's two expeditions when his legions were faced with a chariot attack. Most of the histories, written by you people, say how confused and startled the legions were by this tactic.

Bollocks! The legions were pissing themselves laughing. No decent army has fought with chariots since the bloody Persians invaded Greece. It was just a way for the warriors driving the chariot to show off. The thing was to show how close they could get to us – get right under our noses – to impress their own mob. As long as we kept our shield-square together, they couldn't get through, in fact they bounced off us. And if they really irritated us, a couple of our best *pilum* throwers would take out one of the two horses. They carried no armour, you see, to give them the speed. That was always a laugh, watching one of their chariots trying to turn whilst dragging a dead horse.

Well, we knew the Iceni fancied the chariot for war, so we

didn't take them that seriously. Thought they were a bit backward, really. But like I said, they'd kept their noses clean for many a year and we didn't have to think about them until . . . well, until all hell broke loose.

We were more interested in those swine in the west, like the Silures, who were about the best the Brits had when it came to a fight. One of the governors of Britannia publicly condemned them for 'peculiar stubbornness'. Ostorius Scapula was it? If you say so.

Do you know what *atrocitas* means to a soldier? It's what happened to the Sugambri tribe from the Rhine under Augustus. They were stubborn and so they were eliminated – completely. Wiped off the face of the earth. After the initial slaughter, the ones who lived were transported to Gaul and the families split up, the women and children sold off as slaves. Their villages were burned, ploughed up, just wiped away, not a mud brick or a post left standing. Within ten years nobody could remember them ever being there.

We'd been told there was an *atrocitas* order out on the Silures but for various reasons it never happened.

Funnily enough, it was exactly what did happen to the Iceni, though they'd never caused us a tenth of the trouble the Silures had.

Until they went completely mad and took on the whole Empire, that is.

VIII: Olussa

'Have you been robbed?' asked my father when I finally returned home. 'You look as if you have been robbed. Did they get much?'

For my father, anyone wandering the streets of Londinium after dark was a target for the bands of young men who patronised the taverns and whorehouses, often visiting them in rotation as if on the sort of circuit athletes will run in Games in the Greek tradition. That my father saw these gangs in every shadow on every street corner was due to his age, but in a sense he was correct: I had been robbed, but robbed not by a gang of young drunks, but by an official of Rome. And not just robbed of money, which my father – the merchant – would have understood, but robbed of dignity and of liberty.

Our glorious Procurator had left me locked in his office throughout the mid-day and the entire afternoon and the early evening. Only as darkness was falling and the air was thick with the wood smoke of cooking fires, did the animal Starbo unlock the doors to release me, almost faint from thirst and hunger.

'Has the Procurator forgotten me?' I accused the giant servant.

'No,' said Starbo, shaking his head in genuine puzzlement. 'He said to remind you that you were arranging for a heating engineer to call, before we leave.'

'We?'

'I'm coming with you, part of the way at least. You didn't think he was going to trust you with Treasury gold whilst you could jump a ship to Gaul, did you? Don't worry, once you get to the tribal lands you'll be on your own.'

I stumbled out speechless and lurched into the gloom, trying to navigate my way eastwards by the glimmer of oil lamps from behind shuttered windows, but quickly admitted defeat and paid double the usual rate for two torch-bearers to guide me home. The double rate was to ensure we went directly home rather than via one of the many whorehouses on the way, for it was common practice to steer the unwary traveller to such a place where the torch-bearers were on commission. As it was, we were propositioned from the shadows four times in three languages.

'No, I have not been robbed!' I snapped at my father.

But when I saw Calpurnius, grinning like a sheep over the old man's shoulder, holding aloft a scented oil lamp, my voice moved to a roar.

'You! Get me food and drink – strong drink – and fetch it now, slave!'

As he scuttled off towards the kitchens, I remembered what the Procurator had said, almost in passing, about there being too many people in this household who could read.

It was then that I made the decision to keep the rest of this journal in a code of my own devising, an encryption which I had used many times on business journeys abroad and in the accounting of certain business ventures. From now on I shall feel free from prying eyes for no one can decipher my shorthand of code without my help. So I will write here and now that if you, Calpurnius, have been reading so far, then goodbye. The rest of this journal, for however long it may be, you can stick up your pretty little arse!

I refused to say anything of my encounter with the Procurator until I had food and wine in my stomach and then I had to waste a good hour lying to my sister, Julia, who demanded to know what sort of a man our new lord and master was. I told her that he was tall and handsome, his body bronzed and oiled like a gladiator's, that he had the deep sensuous voice of a poet and eyes the colour of the sea at Actium (she has no idea where Actium is) and that he moved with the grace of a panther.

This seemed to satisfy her, although it exhausted me. It must have tired her also as she retired to her room without prompting from my father, no doubt to weigh up the amount of currency she now had in gossip when she met with her women friends. It would, I hoped, take a few days before she discovered that her currency was counterfeit. By then, I would be gone – off into the unknown.

Which was something I had to talk to my father about once we were free of prying ears. I took him out into the garden and we sat on the low wall he had proudly built himself, which gave us a token of protection from the waters of the Tamesis – though if it ever flooded, we would need something much bigger. Out across the water we could see the lights of an Imperial Post galley floating down river and on the south bank the outlines of the fires around which the rootless mass of traders, pirates, deserters and Britons who could not afford to live in Londinium itself made their own amusement.

We sat either side of a large ceramic head of Medusa. It had been made as decoration for the end of a tile roof but my father had liked it so much he had incorporated it into the centre of his wall as a garden feature. He had spent months building his wall, claiming he had to keep himself busy while

I was away so much looking after business. And, anyway, he was doing his bit to introduce civilised building techniques to Britannia for it was a mystery to him that a country could have survived without the knowledge of mortar and cement until we (the Romans that is) arrived. I had encouraged him in his pastime, for it kept him busy and he had no idea that I had long since discovered that the Medusa's head rested on slotted joints which revealed a square void big enough to take two purses of silver *denarii* and a box of my late mother's jewellery which he had claimed had been sold two years ago to finance our disastrous entry into the glassblowing business.

'Can I trust you?' I asked, allowing my dangling heel to caress the nose (a rather big one, I thought) of the Medusa tile.

'I am your father!' he said, puffing out his chest like a pigeon on heat.

It did not answer my question but it would have to do.

'I am going to tell you what the Procurator wants of me and what it could mean, not just for us, but for the whole province. But you must swear here and now that you will discuss this with no one, and I mean no one *at all*, until I return.'

'I swear by all the gods of Rome – and of Greece, from where most of them were stolen,' pronounced my father severely, clasping his hand to his heart.

It was a good act. I had seen it many times before whenever he was cementing a deal with a non-Roman.

'Not good enough, father. Swear on my mother's ashes.'

'Very well, I do.'

'And on my sister's head.'

'I so swear,' he said after only a moment's hesitation.

He had lived in this country long enough to have been affected by Britannic superstition. All the Celtic tribes had a thing about heads, but nowhere was it stronger than in Britannia. The Druid priests out in the badlands beyond the frontier – and in the Iceni lands for all I knew – encouraged head-hunting in battle and their practice of human sacrifice, which the Romans so hated, involved casting the head of their victims into one of their sacred pools or rivers. There was nothing worse, if you were a Celt slave than to be slapped around the head by your master. Whippings, starvings, brandings, even buggery (when administered as a punishment), all were preferable to a slap about the head, which any normal parent would not think twice of doing to discipline a child.

Among the Celts, the oath 'On the head of my son' was one of the most powerful and binding between men. (Women, I suspect, have yet to find a need for the taking of oaths.) My father knew this. I had his attention.

'I have to go north, I may be gone some time,' I said with a cold gravitas.

'North? Beyond the frontier?'

'North *and east*, father, to Camulodunum and beyond, but well within the safety of the frontier.'

I considered that it would, in Britannia, be difficult to get any further behind the frontier than the Iceni lands in the east. But they were an unknown quantity and if they discovered that they suddenly owed Rome (and Seneca) a fortune, it might be no safer than the western side of the frontier.

'So it's the Iceni, is it? Well, they do need spying on.'

He said this with the wisdom of a philosopher who has never been asked a question he could not answer, which admittedly can be said of all philosophers.

'Why do you say that?'

'Because they are the one tribe who has stayed beyond the pale. They do not fight Rome, like the Silures do, nor do they ally with Rome, as the Brigantes. Nor do they trade with Rome like the Cantii, who traded for generations before the invasion. The Iceni are secretive and do not appear interested in the Romans. And Rome hates to be ignored. What is your mission, should you decide to accept it, among the Iceni?'

'In short, to find out what they are worth. I am to tempt them into trade talks, offer them things which they really want and attempt to assess their wealth,' I answered. 'And I do not have a choice in whether to accept this mission or not.'

'I see.' My father cupped his chin in his hands and looked up at the stars.

'It will not be easy,' he said at last. 'The Iceni trust no one and I suggest you adopt a similar policy from this moment on.'

'I will do as you bid, father,' I said humbly, 'though it will not come easily to me.'

He narrowed his eyes at that, but still looked to the heavens. The breeze had shifted and he shivered, partly from the cold but partly from the smell of roasting deer fat and unflushed latrines which the night air carried. From out in the night we heard a shout of anger, then a woman's scream and then a crash of splintering wood. Another fight over a whore down by the docks. From the house there followed a softer whimper. My sister, Julia, disturbed in her sleep.

'You'll have to win their confidence,' said my father, 'and that means gifts, plus you will have to offer to trade in the one thing they need and desire.'

'Which is?' I asked innocently.

'Oh, gold,' he said casually, 'everybody knows that. And don't treat them like idiots, which they are not, or savages, which they probably are but don't know it. Remember always that Celts are a vain people, all the histories say that. Or at least the Celts who have not been Romanised and shown the error of their ways. The Iceni are a backward tribe and have stayed hidden from Rome and Roman ways, so expect them to still value vanity as much as a Nubian values water. It makes them unbearable after a victory in battle and totally downcast in defeat. When Rome has a victory, she holds a triumph, declares a holiday, stages a bigger and better Games than the last one, and then gets on with life. When Rome suffers a defeat, there is an official mourning, whoever is responsible falls on their sword, and then it's back to the barrack square and build a new army better than the last one. Life, like Rome, goes on. But not for the Celts.

'A victory in battle to them is not a victory for a tribe or a state, but for an individual warrior. Often, the outcome of a battle does not matter as long as a warrior shows his bravery, usually in as dangerous and foolhardy a way as possible. And then they sing about it for generations after. But if defeated, the shame follows them to the grave. It is almost as if they give up life, preferring to wither and slowly die.'

'Perhaps they should fall on their swords,' I suggested to lighten the mood.

'It is a thought, but the Celts would see that as a coward's act, not a noble one as the Romans do. A strange people.'

'On that we are agreed, father. Now, to the matter which most—'

'Did you say you were taking gold with you?' he said suddenly.

'The Procurator is supplying me with a quantity to smooth the way,' I admitted carefully.

'How much?'

'Enough, or so I'm told.'

'You'll need an escort.'

'I already have one as far as Camulodunum. It's after that I will need help, which is . . .'

There was another soft cry from the darkened house. Julia again; dreaming.

'. . . why I need a list of men I can trust, people I can turn to for the hire of bodyguards and slaves. Good local agents that we have used in the past – your agents, your contacts. Who operates out there in the Iceni lands that you would trust with the life of your son?'

'I see,' said my father sincerely, but he was not to be distracted from his main concern. 'And what do we get out of this? We, as merchants?'

I had known it would come to this, not just quite so soon.

'Father, we get to stay alive, that is the first consideration – but only as long as we keep our mouths shut. You know what will happen in the marketplace if word gets out that I am assessing the Iceni as to the value of their worldly goods.'

'Yes, I can see that,' he said. 'The rumour is often preferable to the fact, but when the rumour becomes fact . . . There will be panic, of course.'

'I think the tribes will turn downright hostile once they realise they have to repay loans they thought were gifts,' I said.

'Very probably. I was thinking of the merchants, though. They will squeal like pigs if they wake up to find they have everything tied up in a bankrupt country.'

I felt that we were drifting from the point that I was talking about, Narcissus Alexander's one and only son and heir being stranded in the back of beyond, surrounded by bloodthirsty and suddenly impoverished barbarians. It was time to appeal to my father's better nature.

'But Alexander and Son won't wake up to that, father. We will *know* what is happening. In advance of all the other merchant houses.'

The old man caught his breath with a loud, sobbing noise. Or perhaps that had come from the house as well.

'What are you suggesting, Olussa?' he asked and there was a twinkle in his eyes which I had not seen for many a year.

'You explain my absence to your cronies in the forum by saying I am working under the Imperial seal – that always impresses them – developing new trade routes. You cannot be more specific, because it is highly secret but I have left carrying substantial amounts of Treasury gold. There will be enough rumours about that to give it credence anyway. You will say you are in the market for any tradeable commodities coming into Britannia in the next year. Fine ware, spices, wine, pots, pans, ironware, anything. You'll buy whatever they've got to sell.'

He raised a finger in protest. I raised a hand to stifle it.

'But you won't pay for anything,' I continued and the old man seemed suddenly at ease. 'You will take goods on future payment – on credit only. You will say that because I have been called back from Gaul early, which is true, to undertake this mission, our cash balance is not flowing as it might be at this time of year. Therefore, if they will extend you credit, fine. If they will not, then you say sorry, you will buy elsewhere. You create a market for the future, but it is our market. Everything you get, you ship immediately to our warehouses in Gaul. The Emperor may abandon Britannia, but he is not going to abandon Gaul. If the worst happens, we are ideally placed. If nothing happens, there will be a lot of merchants in Britannia with nothing to sell – unless they buy it back from us.'

'At a profit.'

'But of course.'

'You have learned well, young Olussa,' he said with pride.

'And you see why I need your help, Father. You will be here at the centre of things whilst I am going boldly where few clear-headed men have gone before. I need to know who I can trust out there should I need to get word back to you in case the situation changes.'

I wanted to sow at least one seed of doubt in my father's mind, for I did not want him to think I had presented him with a plan which could work without me.

'I have to tell you, Father, that the new Procurator is watching this house and will continue to do so. If you act too soon and draw attention to yourself, as if you know something which no one else does, then he will be ruthless. So will the military. They will accuse you of treason.'

'Not to mention what the Merchants' Guild will do if they think I have inside information which I have not shared.'

'Exactly. So we must tread carefully. That is why I need to know who I can trust. I want a list of your most trustworthy business partners and agents from here to Camulodunum and beyond.'

I had bargained on the first name from his lips being that of Valerius Lupus, he of the long-winded despatch and a man of some importance in the region, but I was wrong.

'Publius Oranius is your man,' he said at last. 'A former sergeant in the quartermaster's stores of the XXth Legion until he retired and married an Iceni girl. Has a farm out in the country near the Iceni lands. He and I did a lot of business when the XXth was stationed in Camulodunum. You can trust him, just mention my name.'

A corrupt quartermaster. That was a good start.

'Publius Oranius, good. Who else?' I asked, committing the name to memory.

My father thought for a while.

'Er . . . that's it.'

'What? One name? One man?'

'My dear boy,' he said smoothly, 'you did specify ones that I could trust with the life of my son . . .'

I left him sitting on his stupid wall and stomped back into the house.

From Julia's bedroom I heard a loud sob and then a quite distinct grunt.

That settled it.

Calpurnius was coming with me.

I had thought that my journey into the Iceni lands would be that of one of the *viatores* – travellers as the Romans called them, educated men who took their curiosity to new places and who made notes, just as I do as a matter of course now, albeit in secret and in code. But I was wrong. It was clear from the four days of preparation which Catus Decianus allowed me that this was going to be a nightmare journey, complicated three-fold by Starbo, mules and an evil dwarf of a second-hand mule dealer called Dumnovellaunus, or, for short (as he was), Dumno.

In fact it was not a three-fold problem, merely three aspects of the same problem: Starbo.

I had estimated that I required four *raedae* – four-wheeled carriages, which were the fastest forms of transport after single horses, and I have never professed myself a cavalryman – but Starbo insisted on six. This was an issue between us because I was expected to pay for them, something I was reluctant to do when I discovered their real purpose. They were not, as Starbo had said, for the tents and equipment of the servants and bodyguards we would need for the journey, but rather two of the carriages were earmarked to carry amphorae of concentrated fish sauce as far as Camulodunum, where it sold at a premium to the legionary veterans who had retired there. Needless to say, this was a private trading arrangement done at my expense by Starbo and without the knowledge of the Procurator. I was powerless to object and was not even offered a tenth of the value of the amphorae, which would have been customary for the transporter.

Then there was the question of the escort of twenty of Starbo's drinking pals who called themselves members of the Procurator's Special Police; at ten sesterces a day (three times what a regular soldier could expect). I did not mind the escort as such, for I knew I needed armed men around me and without doubt this was as ugly and frightening a bunch of cut-throats as you could wish for as long as they were on your side. What rankled with me was that whilst they came with their own horses, I was expected to provide a dozen mules to carry tents, food, fodder and wine (another of Starbo's sidelines) for them. And I had to buy the mules from the odious Dumno, who, if not related to Starbo, was certainly in league with him.

Dumno had somehow managed to corner the market in

mules in Londinium. The animals were ex-military and had all seen better days, their coats rippling with ticks and fleas, their legs bent and splayed and their breathing loud and laboured. Whatever Dumno had paid for them – no doubt on the quiet to a crooked quartermaster from the legions – it was probably half what he charged me.

As I opened my purse for Dumno I remarked that at these prices he should accompany us to personally nurse the animals along the way, as they would surely never make the return journey. Starbo, who was supervising the negotiations, roared with laughter at this and said it was a splendid idea: Dumno would come with us as chief muleteer and he would not listen to him say otherwise.

The look of despair which crossed Dumno's face at the prospect of leaving his Londinium nest for unknown territory where he was unlikely to make a profit, was almost worth the disgusting prospect of having him travel with us.

The poisonous little dwarf cheered up, though, when Starbo put him in charge of victualling and gave him a free hand as to where to buy supplies for our expedition. I was about to object that this would certainly mean Dumno would patronise his relatives or places where he could get a kick-back, but Starbo stared me down.

I should have known these fucking Celts would stick together and I marched back to my father's house in a filthy temper to break the good news to Calpurnius that he was coming for an educational tour of the countryside.

I saw the Procurator once more, on the night before we left. He was calm and controlled of movement to such an extent that I thought he must have taken a sleeping draught. But it was because he was officially handing over the gold I was to use on my mission and in the presence of such a sum of bullion, coin and dust, Catus Decianus showed no emotion except awe.

I had been escorted by two of Starbo's thugs to a courtyard at the rear of the Procurator's office just as darkness was falling. In the middle was a covered carriage with two knock-kneed horses harnessed to it (almost certainly hand-picked by Dumno). In the light from the wall torches the setting looked almost religious. I half-expected priests to emerge from the shadows to dispatch the horses as a sacrifice, though it would be only the most minor of gods who would have accepted such scrawny beasts.

Catus and Starbo stood by the carriage but only beckoned me to them after Starbo had told his two police auxiliaries to wait outside. The giant slave then took one of the torches from its wall bracket and held it high above his head so that the Procurator could see inside the carriage.

'Come here, Olussa,' said the Procurator, 'come and see what your arse will be guarding.'

He unthreaded a small flat key from the thong around his neck and leaned into the interior of the carriage. The key fitted a lock in the wooden panel which formed the back of the seat behind the driver. It was common enough to have a lock on such a panel, where travellers carried their personal food supplies and delicacies so they could not be pilfered by slaves whenever the horses needed resting or the traveller's bladder needed emptying. The locks are cheap and shoddily made and can be lifted quite easily with a thin-bladed dagger.

The compartment under the seat was empty, and smaller than I had expected because there was another false panel filling the space. The Procurator used the same key to open that one and lift it out completely. Behind that were bags, perhaps a dozen of different sizes, all round and fat and heavy.

'Open one, Olussa,' said the Procurator. 'Make yourself familiar with the merchandise.'

In truth, I suspected a trap of some sort but the Procurator seemed transfixed by the bags and as interested in their contents as I was. The first bag I picked up was round and firm and yet soft and yielding to the touch as I weighed it in the palm of one hand.

The Procurator nodded his head enthusiastically, urging me silently to open the drawstrings, as excited as I was, if not more so, to see inside. One of the horses farted loudly but it did not destroy the moment. Inside the bag all was a dull, beautiful yellow, the yellow of an autumn sunrise.

'Gold dust and shavings from coin stamps from the Imperial Mint in Antioch,' the Procurator said softly with awe in his voice.

Mixed with a fair proportion of iron scrapings and bronze slivers from the so-called goldsmiths of Antioch's back streets unless I was much mistaken. But it was neither polite nor prudent to mention that and, I comforted myself, a barbarian was hardly likely to notice.

The second bag – which the Procurator pressed on me, anxious for me to open it as if it were a feast-day present – contained gold *aurei*, the highest denomination coin of Rome. Yet these were no ordinary coins, for they bore the likeness of Gaius Caligula, quite the maddest of their recent rulers. And they were illegal. No coins bearing the head of Caligula had been allowed to circulate in the Empire (except those he minted in honour of the Emperor Tiberius) since his untimely, but thoroughly welcome, assassination. Most of them were supposed to have been collected in and melted down for reissue at the mints in Rome, Lyons, Nicodemia and Alexandria. It had been a profitable business for the Emperor Claudius as everyone knew that the gold content of the coins was mysteriously less when they bore Claudius' head than when Caligula smiled out at you. Nero had continued this scheme with *aurei* minted for him and had extended the policy to reducing the silver content of the *denarius* as well. Where all the 'saved' gold and silver which did not reappear in the new coins went was quite a mystery.

'Aren't these . . .?' I stuttered, holding up a Caligulan coin.

'The barbarians will never know,' said the Procurator.

Neither of us spoke again until all the bags were opened and closed and repacked in the compartment under the seat. They contained a mixture of Imperial *aurei*, some whole, many nipped, some halved, including some of the late Emperor Claudius depicting the triumphal arch he had erected in Rome to commemorate his victory over the Britons; small gold pieces issued to Celtic tribes in Gaul or in honour of Germanic chiefs to keep them quiet; coins from Thrace and Judaea; some even from Britannia minted by Cunobelin, the old king of the Catuvellauni from Camulodunum, whose death had prompted Claudius' invasion. The whole of the Empire, which means the known world, was represented as well as a bag of gold chains, small ingots or blobs of melted gold, shavings from where the coin die had missed or been deliberately punched off centre, links, pins and buckles which could have come from anywhere, the only thing certain being that the former owners were no longer alive to worry about where their valuables were now. There was more wealth there in those bags than I had ever seen in one place before. And I would be sitting on it.

As each bag swam before my eyes I tried to count, to weigh, to assess; but it was impossible to do even the crudest of calculations as to how much it was all worth.

'Four hundred and seventy-three thousand sesterces as a rough guess,' said the Procurator. 'In case you were wondering.'

I made a small gesture of deference, not to his calculation but to the bags themselves.

'That should impress the Iceni,' he said. Then, after a moment's thought, he added: 'Fuck it! That should buy them!'

He slotted the wooden false panel back into place and locked it with the key – a simple lift key, I noted. Then he replaced the panel everyone knew was there and locked that. He weighed the key in his hand.

'Starbo will carry the key,' he said, looking up at the night sky. 'Yes, Starbo will watch over the key and tonight, I will watch over Starbo. You will watch over the carriage. It will go to your house and stay there until you leave in the morning. The two men who brought you here, they will escort you and stay at your house. They will watch *you.* And before it occurs to you, I have alerted every customs official and the dockyard watch to make sure that no one boards a ship leaving on tonight's tide without a pass from me.'

I attempted to appear suitably hurt at the Procurator's implied suspicion but secretly I wondered if he knew about the Gaulish pirates who ran the small but fast slave boats from the south side of the river virtually every night when there was, as tonight, no moon. (I had not seriously considered this option as I knew I would be murdered and robbed for the clothes I stood up in let alone a carriage full of gold if I ventured south of the river after dark.)

'Your honour can have the fullest confidence in me,' I said, as it seemed the polite thing to say.

'Of that I am certainly assured, for before you leave here

you will sign and seal some documents I have had prepared as . . . surety. You may be surprised that your businesses – all of them – and your assets have been valued at . . .'

'Four hundred and seventy-three thousand sesterces,' I said without thinking.

'Exactly. That includes the house here in Londinium, the small estate you purchased in Hispania of which your father knows nothing and two vineyards near Capua which your father bought two years ago, of which you know nothing.'

Not for the first – or the last – time did Catus leave me speechless and confounded.

'Come, let us get the formalities out of the way then we can have a cup of wine to toast our enterprise and you can get a good night's sleep before your journey.'

He clasped a hand to my shoulder and it seemed to grow heavier as he said:

'By the by, that . . . valuation . . . of your assets . . . for, shall we say, insurance purposes on behalf of the Imperial Treasury . . . well, that also includes a figure for the price we would get for your father and your sister at the slave auctions. Should you not return, that is. Which I am sure will not happen. Her name is Julia, isn't it?'

My two escorts were every citizen's nightmare – slaves with swords; and worse – slaves authorised to carry weapons legally, by a Roman. Catus had recruited his police well for however wretched their condition was now (and working for the monster Starbo could hardly be a secure position) it was certainly better than anything they had before.

Their names were Rogerus and Alcides; both Celts, both illiterate and both barely comprehensible in the execrable kitchen Latin they spoke and both stank riper than the giant Starbo, as if they slept in a dog fox's latrine. The one called Rogerus was a Briton (all this I discovered later) of the Cantii tribe, taken into slavery as a boy shortly after the invasion. He had the number II branded on his forehead, though he had no idea why. I speculated that he had been sold as a lot with two or more brothers and the brand was to distinguish him on the auction block, a practice I had seen elsewhere in the Empire when a new tribe had been conquered or a new province established and for once the supply of slaves outstripped demand. Like Rogerus, Alcides had been given his name by a master, in his case somewhere in Belgic Gaul. His master had a sense of humour as Alcides was one of the family names of Hercules, yet a more unheroic figure could hardly be imagined. He was stunted of growth, only a hair taller than the awful Dumno, and thin enough that his yellowing skin stretched to show his ribs. He also had a lazy eye and was missing two fingers from his left hand. And he limped on his right foot. Whatever his uses as a slave, they must have been few. What his talents as a member of Catus' police were, I could not imagine.

I did not disclose that I could understand almost every word of the guttural Belgic dialect they spoke and when I addressed them in formal Latin, I bit my tongue as they stared blankly at me and even resorted to sign language, humiliating though it was for me, rather than reveal that I could converse in their own tongue.

With the aid of some hired torch-bearers (more expense!) we nursed the two horses and the wagon through the narrow streets to my father's house, although to be accurate it was now the house of the Procurator according to the covenant he had forced me to sign.

To my amazement – and the obvious delight of Rogerus and Alcides – the house was lit up like a Pompeiian brothel and the smell of incense mixed with roast meat greeted us as our horses hobbled into the courtyard.

My father was throwing a party was my first reaction, but on entering the house I realised it was the next best thing – a religious ceremony.

In his wisdom (a precious commodity) my father had organised a sacrifice to Mercury, the god of – what else? – commerce. The sacrifice itself being a scrawny and very smelly goat. The guests at first glance seemed to be entirely made up of his cronies from the Merchants' Guild and a dozen or so giggling girls whom I presumed were friends of Julia's. If they were not, then they were the most inept bunch of prostitutes I had ever seen and anyone hiring them for a proper ceremony would have every right to demand their money back.

The whole thing was, of course, in honour of my departure

the following day, though few of the guests (and none of the women) seemed to actually notice I was there. I moved through the crowd as if invisible, noting to myself how much wine was being drunk (a large amount – and the good stuff too!) and trying to estimate the cost of the food on offer (outrageous – the fresh fruit alone . . .) as well as how much the musicians were charging (whatever it was it was too much *and* they insisted on taking refreshment breaks at least three times an hour, but then you know what musicians are), not to mention the priests, as filthy a trio of fairground magicians as you could ever hope to meet. Where had he found them? At least they must have come cheap, for it was impossible to imagine them finding regular work in a temple anywhere, even in Londinium.

Calpurnius was, of course, in the thick of things, supposedly serving wine but in reality keeping his ears open for profitable gossip among my father's friends and his eyes and legs open for later assignations among my sister's pack of bitch dogs.

Twice he avoided my eye and when I called him by name he feigned deafness. I had to force my way across the room to catch him by the arm and be quick enough to prevent him spilling a jug of wine on my tunic.

'The two armed men who came in with me,' I hissed in his ear, 'are the Procurator's police. They are spending the night here. Make sure they have everything they need – and I do mean everything, especially plenty of wine.'

Calpurnius simply grunted and tried to pull away but I held on to his arm.

'You don't get to say goodnight to Julia until those two are asleep,' I growled. 'Is that understood?'

I felt his body relax and he looked at me and nodded, though it was a movement which would not have been detected by the people around us even if they had been sober. I released my grip and he continued to serve wine to the assembled throng, pushing one way whilst I threaded my way the other towards the rear of the house and my private rooms. Unlike the more civilised Roman habit of dining from couches, this mob had adopted the recent British practice of standing in a mass while trying to balance food and drink in one hand and gesticulating with the other, the result being chaos. (I have also noticed how those attending feasts in Londinium, whether invited or not, seem to be drawn mystically towards the kitchens.)

Apart from the occasional greeting from a fellow merchant attempting to curry favour, my progress went unnoticed, even by my father and especially by my sister, who was too busy cackling amongst her coven of friends as they eyed the hams of the serving boys, many of whom, I noticed in passing, were openly touting for business for later and all of whom could have done with a good bath.

Once I had made my escape, I hurried to my room, locking the door behind me and lighting two small lamps to work by.

I had left instructions for the house servants to gather things I would need on my expedition but I had insisted on packing them myself into two stout, iron-hasped chests. Not only did this reduce the chance of finding – when I was halfway to nowhere – that essential items had been pilfered, but I have a certain sense of order and I prefer everything to be in its place.

Into the first chest I packed a spare set of clothing to protect the outer man and jars of delicacies to look after the inner, neither of which I was prepared to share with my travelling companions. Especially not my supplies of dried figs, fish pickle and salted onions – both long and red varieties – all of which had been imported from Gaul and were scarce enough in this wilderness of a country. I had also treated myself to a jar of chives in olive oil, which the Emperor Nero consumed in vast quantity to enhance his singing voice, and, most valuable of all, a pot of chicken fat mixed with onion juice which was without doubt the best remedy for blisters, bunions and saddle sores known to man.

But it was the second chest which contained my real treasure. In that chest alone I had assembled possibly the largest collection of writing materials in civilian hands in this illiterate town. Apart from wax tablets and *styli*, which were useful for my coded note-taking, I had bought as much thinly shaved writing bark as I could find on the open market. This bark is a poor substitute for the papyrus of the Eastern Empire, but the climate of Britannia is different to that of Egypt and papyrus would not survive here. To get the best use out of the bark I had invested in three fine bronze pens and the best quality ink (something which the locals have no use for!) which I had had mixed with wormwood to deter rats and mice from eating my completed writing.

Once my valuables were securely packed and the chests relocked I lay on my bed and savoured the softness of it. I am no lover of the life under canvas and this was perhaps my last taste of civilisation for some time.

Was I fearful of the journey ahead? In truth I was not. There was no way I could avoid it that I could see and so I resolved to make the best of it, which I did when the night was at its darkest and the guests from my father's ritual had long departed.

Calpurnius had done his work well. In the stables at the rear of the house, Rogerus and Alcides lay beside each other on a pile of piss-wet straw. Two broken amphorae had been smashed against the wall, a third was still clutched by Alcides, the last of its wine trickling out as a tiny river glistening in the light of the courtyard torches. They were both snoring like elephants but still I was as quiet as I could be as I stepped around them and carefully climbed into the carriage.

One of the knock-kneed horses turned from its feed stall to stare at me as I picked the locks of the seat compartment with a long, thin blade. As I removed one of the bags – of coins, judging by the feel – the horse turned away and began to strain its hindquarters to produce a spectacularly large shit which landed a hand's width away from Alcides' head.

Neither of my noble bodyguards moved a muscle, apart from their lips which vibrated as they snored.

Nor did they stir as I relocated the panels and climbed off the creaking wagon and stepped over them and out into the night.

By touch alone, for I did not risk a lamp, I located the Medusa's head in my father's garden wall and worked the mechanism which revealed the hollow space behind. The bag of gold coins fitted easily, so easily that I considered going back for a second, but I thought it best not to tempt the Fates again.

As I made my way back across the garden, I heard one, then two, then three racking sobs from the house.

'Goodnight, Julia,' I said softly to myself. Then added: 'And Calpurnius.'

I fell asleep still puzzling over exactly how much the Procurator had thought she was worth at auction.

IX: Roscius

Camulodunum? I knew it. Not when it was a fortress, that was a bit before my time. But when it got *colonia* status and the veterans started to tart it up. Mind you, once a garrison town, always a garrison town.

I had quite a few old comrades there as most of the vets were Legio XX footsloggers who had preferred to stay in Britannia when their time was up. They had done their service, taken citizenship and fancied a bit of land and a few slaves instead of a pension back in the Rhinelands or wherever, which they probably hadn't seen for twenty years.

You've got to admit it was an attractive prospect. You could have done your twenty years and still be under forty and for the first time you could take a wife legally and own slaves. Have you any idea what that meant to a legionary? You can't have, but let me tell you that there is not much difference between a foot soldier and a pack mule, not then, not now. Every legionary carried two javelins, a shield, a sword, a saw, a basket, an axe, a pick, strap, reaphook, chain and three days' rations. We dug out a camp every night and we filled it in next morning when we moved on. If we weren't marching or fighting, we were drilling or building roads, a mile every three days. And you'll see, they'll still be using the roads we built in a thousand years' time, not like the ones they're throwing up nowadays, now they've put the contracts out to civilian tenders.

But anyway, all I'm saying is that after twenty years of that, even Britannia looks attractive if you've suddenly got a bunch of slaves to do your fetching and carrying for you. And usually the *signifer* could do you . . . the *signifer* is the standard-bearer of the legion and he always acts as the treasurer of the burial and savings club, if you didn't know. Well, he could do you a good deal in a province like Britannia because the prices were so low – both slaves and land. And a place like Camulodunum would offer you some tasty incentives to move there. They wanted to expand the place but by law, only Roman citizens could live in a *colonia* and nobody in their right minds would move there from Italy or southern Gaul or Hispania, not unless they were sick of sunshine and good wine. So where did you get Roman citizens for your settlers except from the legions? Added to which, all the lads knew how to handle themselves a bit, at least they did at first before they got fat and lazy, and that was useful when you had a tribe of surly locals like the Trinovantes in your back yard. Especially after they moved the XXth out to help fight on the frontier and the nearest garrison was the IXth.

The civilian prefects who were planning the new towns – that's what we called them, town-planners – they welcomed the vets with open arms, and the local girls welcomed them with open legs. Oh yes, the Trinny girls were dead easy that way. And life was sweet for a time. You had land, women, slaves and all the benefits of living in a provincial capital, plus you were about as far behind the frontier as you could possibly be.

Should have been safe, shouldn't you? Safe, snug and looking forward to a long, lazy retirement.

Didn't happen.

I blame the town-planners. Bunch of tossers.

They were the ones who came up with all the fancy ideas, like: let's have a theatre, let's build bigger houses with nice views and gardens with water features. They were the ones who pushed for the Temple of Claudius, which didn't half stir up the local Trinnies, as they were paying for it.

Trouble was, all these big plans involved expanding the old fortress out to the east. So what did they do? They looked at the stockade wall and the ditch and the rampart and the gate towers and they said: this lot will have to go if we're going to find room for our theatre and our temple and some nice houses with gardens instead of those draughty old barrack blocks.

And it went. They ripped down the eastern wall and the towers and then they filled in the ditch and put a road over it. Good judgement – or what? They take down their eastern defences and replace them with a road – a fucking open road. I ask you.

But it gets better, because once they'd done that, they thought: this looks nice. Why not expand on all sides, not just the east? Get a real building programme going, push the land values up a bit. Plenty of free labour around among the Trinovantes.

So they did. They didn't stop at the east wall, they took the fucking lot down; north, south and west – and they filled in all the ditches.

When Boudica turned up, not only were there no defences to stop her, there were nice new roads leading right into the town so she could just ride in.

Town planning? Suicide, I call it.

X: Valerius Lupus

Camulodunum.
By Imperial Post. SECRET, under Seal.
To the Procurator of all Britannia, Gn. Catus Decianus.

Most noble Procurator.

Now is not the time to express all the sentiments which are your due nor to repeat your open invitation to visit your *colonia* here, for there are two matters which I must report with some urgency.

Firstly, I have in previous despatches mentioned the entreaties of the chief of the Trinovantes, who is named Tasciovanus and styles himself 'king', concerning the cost of the building of the new temple to the Divine Claudius. This naturally falls upon the local Trinovantine 'nobility' yet few seem to regard it as the honour it is.

In his latest audience, this Tasciovanus has however taken it upon himself to raise further complaints in the most discourteous and belligerent of manners. Now the Trinovantes are complaining about the new appropriations of land for our settlers. Until recently, most of the land required for our colonists came from the confiscated estates of the Catuvellauni, who were themselves the conquerors of the Trinovantes. This, of course, caused little concern among the Trinovantes but with the latest quota of retiring veterans from the XXth Legion (and several of the auxiliary regiments), it has been necessary to sequester the farms of the Trinovantes themselves, including some from the Trinovantine 'royal family'. This is a policy which will continue if we are to expand as planned to an area of some thirty miles in radius, the land required in order to provide a decent standard of living for our colonists. By my calculations our present appropriations of native land measure a meagre nine miles in radius from the centre of the *colonia*.

This Tasciovanus, who seems quite incapable of recognising that we are now the masters here, is not content to complain solely about this. He has somehow got hold of a rumour that the Imperial Grants made to compliant tribes such as the Trinovantes sixteen years ago, are now to be compounded as loans and the interest and capital on them repaid. He worries this rumour as a dog would a bone and claims that it is true. His case is that the Trinovantes could not possibly pay off such a debt (even if they could remember how much it was) and contribute to the Temple of Claudius, whilst their best farmland is – quite legally – being disbursed among our new citizens.

I report this to your nobleness as a matter of urgency as I have never in all my experience known the Trinovantes to express such anger so openly. Neither is it limited to their chief. Workmen and farmhands have been failing to report for their duties and some civic building projects have been actively sabotaged. Certainly all are behind schedule. There has also been an increase in petty theft and a marked increase in rudeness and downright disobedience among the locals.

Once again I remind the noble Procurator that we have no legion here in Camulodunum any more and barely a handful of auxiliary police. Such veterans who have settled here have either sold their weapons or lost the will to train with them, concentrating their energies on their new estates and their new slaves or wives. In some cases, both. They can hardly be relied upon as a force to impose order should the Trinovantes become bolder.

Secondly, I have to report that Olussa, who is known to me as the son of Narcissus Alexander, a merchant of Londinium who is a Greek and not a citizen, has arrived in the *colonia* with the party you advised me to expect three days ago.

This Olussa carries no official ring or Imperial seal and has not divulged the nature of his mission, though I have extended every opportunity for him to do so, except that it involves an onward journey into Iceni territory for the purpose of trade. Given the sensitive nature of the situation there, as I reported in my last secret despatch, I would seek the reassurance of the Procurator that Rome's intentions towards the Iceni have not changed and that the mission of this merchant is incidental to those aims and not part of them.

I will, as I have sworn, continue to keep the Procurator informed of the health of the Iceni king, although news from the territories to the north is difficult and expensive to obtain.

On the subject of expense, I would raise for your eminence's consideration the cost of quartering and victualling of the troop of guards which attend our visitor. He seems to have little interest in their well-being and no control over them at all. On their first night in the *colonia* they have been responsible for the destruction of two taverns and the maiming of a perfectly good slave. The slave can, of course, be replaced, but assaults on property are a serious matter.

Your guidance would, as always, be welcome.

XI: Olussa

I will not detail all the horrors of our journey, except to say that they were invariably of our own making.

On my travels through the Empire trading, buying and transporting goods to make a meagre profit, I have organised shipments across every ocean, mule trains across the highest mountains and wagon trains over roads hardly worthy of the name. I have dealt with muleteers more stubborn than their animals, corrupt frontier officials, avaricious clerks, sailors (enough said!), bargemen and ferrymen determined to deceive, soldiers in open mutiny, bandits, thieves, warring tribes and tax collectors. Yet nothing in my experience could compare with the trouble caused by this motley company.

Our transport comprised two *raedae*, or covered carriages, four supply wagons and fourteen loaded mules. Quite why we needed so many was beyond me, at least to begin with, but Starbo was ill-disposed to answer questions about our provisioning – or anything else for that matter – even though I was paying for it all. There were six slaves to act as drivers and four women whose purpose was unclear until our first night's camp. Dumno, our dwarfish ostler, was accompanied by two of his sons – the ugliest boys I had ever seen in any land – and then there were my valiant bodyguards, of which it is sufficient to say that Rogerus and Alcides were by far the most admirable physical specimens, exhibiting more discipline and intelligence than the other eighteen combined.

And of course there was the sulking Calpurnius, whom I had explained away as my body slave although I had no intention of letting him anywhere near my person. For the duration of this journey and whatever it might hold, I had decided that my strength must come from within and work for me and myself alone. There could be no distractions. I, and only I, had to survive.

Route XII approaches the *colonia* from the south-west, crossing over the impressive but aimless and, ultimately, pointless defensive ditches and dykes dug by the Trinovantes – or was it the Catuvellauni? Valerius Lupus would put me right even without asking, though neither managed to keep out Claudius' conquering legions and certainly not his elephants. I knew that somewhere off to the south was what was left of the old British capital of Dun Camulos, and the remains of Claudius' temporary fort where he took the surrender of ten – or was it eleven? – tribal chiefs. It was said that the natives came and worshipped, or perhaps just stood and stared slack-jawed, at the site where the Emperor had quartered his elephants for several years after the invasion, but now the whole place is forgotten and everything revolves around our new provincial capital, Camulodunum.

And I do mean new. So new, I hardly recognised the place.

I could smell it before I saw it, but not in the way you can smell Londinium. (Sometimes, it is said, you can smell Londinium in Gaul.) These were civilised smells: woodsmoke from cooking fires, charcoal from metal workings, even, perhaps, bread baking and the smoking of meat. Animal smells too, to be sure, but healthy, prosperous smells, of cows and pigs and chickens and of straw. Clean straw. Something you rarely see in Londinium, where even soiled and spongy used straw has a second-hand value.

And yes, there was a smell of newness – of new mortar, of plaster and paint, of mud bricks drying in the weak sunlight. The smell of *clean*.

By the standards of the rest of the Empire, this was still dull, provincial, crude and rough, but for Britannia it was the height of luxury and sophistication and in comparison, Londinium was an overcrowded stench pit. It was the best this miserable island would ever achieve but after seven days on the road in the company of the demons that were supposed to be my bodyguard, I was prepared to take it to my heart.

My first reaction was surprise at how much the town had overspilled its walls and defences, for as we approached the west gate both sides of the road were edged with new houses, some of them quite substantial dwellings even if based on the traditional design of an army barracks block. The long, low houses sporting new red roof tiles had replaced the mud and reed lean-to hovels and workshops which had nested around the gate on my previous visit, giving the place a much more open, orderly look. And there were piles of cut timber, freshly baked tiles and bundles of hazel rods to hold plasterwork which suggested that the building work was far from finished.

And then, directly in front of us bestriding the road, loomed the great monumental arch in the west gate. The double arch, taller than five men standing each atop the shoulders of a stronger man (a trick perfected by itinerant tumblers from Dacia), which signified the victory of Claudius in conquering Britannia and making it clear to visitors that this was to be his City of Victory.

The only problem was the arch was there but the gate had gone. So had the stockade wall, the rampart and the defensive ditch before it.

Civilisation always has a price and in Camulodunum, the price was having to deal with Valerius Lupus.

He was a man who had been born old, believing himself destined for the patrician classes but held back only by a lack of personal fortune (or the reluctance to spend it buying influence), no military experience, and a total inability to understand politics, art or culture.

What Valerius was, and not a very good one at that, was a merchant. Not a good one – certainly far less sharp than my father and most of his cronies in Londinium – but he had been a lucky one. It was said that Valerius had come over with the Emperor Claudius and his invading elephants and that Valerius' first killing had been to corner the market in elephant dung as a fertiliser. Whatever the truth of that, old Lupus had certainly ingratiated himself with the invading army, first at the legionary fort at Dun Camulos and then from the very beginning of the fortress here at Camulodunum which was now civilianised and growing apace. It was further said that two out of every five amphorae coming into Camulodunum contained olive oil from Baetica in southern Hispania, the entire trade controlled by Valerius Lupus and, in addition, he held the officially licensed monopoly on the import of *defrutum*, the concentrated grape juice which fetched outrageously high prices among the veterans.

In the right place at the right time, Valerius had seen no reason to move on or expand his trading area; content to remain where he was in the misguided hope that his services to Rome would eventually be recognised. It never occurred to the old fool that while Rome honours and promotes the mad, the bad and the downright homicidal, the worthy but dull rarely get a look in.

Being dull was probably Valerius' most serious crime, though there were unsubstantiated rumours that he was in fact honest as well.

As was the custom when an army fortress became the basis for a civilian town, the *principia* and the neighbouring *praetorium*, or commanding officer's house, would be the prime sites for a forum and the offices of the civilian council. It was no surprise to me that Valerius Lupus had staked a claim there right in the centre of the town, constructing a new house using one corner of the old *principia* building with two storeys facing north, protected by a courtyard with thick wooden gates. His immediate neighbours were poorer, single-storey dwellings shoddily constructed on the foundations of legionary barrack blocks. Through the gaps in the houses I could see down a dusty street to where the north gate had once stood but now the street continued unhindered as a downhill track flanked by mud huts and thatched barns or warehouses, to the river.

Across that river and many miles to the north, where the roads failed to penetrate the horizon of dark forests and treacherous swamps, lay the homeland of the Iceni.

'Worthy Olussa! Your father and his family are welcome here.'

The wooden gates had opened silently on well-oiled hinges and a tall, gaunt figure clad in a white toga bent his head – a head as bald and smooth as a bowl – to look down at me.

'Are you Valerius Lupus?' growled Starbo, annoyed at being ignored.

The tall figure turned his face on one side implying that I, not he, should answer the question, but I had no idea who he was except that I knew he was not Lupus.

I shrugged my shoulders and shook my head.

'I am Horas,' said the tall man, 'servant and aide to Valerius Lupus, as I was on your last visit here, most noble Olussa.'

The impudence of the man, expecting me to remember the faces of slaves after eight years.

'Is your master expecting us?' I asked, controlling my temper.

'Of course.'

'Does he have a bath?'

The ancient Horas looked offended.

'Of course,' he said again. 'We have all modern conveniences here in the capital.'

'Do you have stables and quarters for our party?'

This from Starbo, who had shouldered his way between us, close enough to Horas to make him wrinkle his nose at the stench.

'All is arranged. The Procurator sent us warning of your arrival.' The old man continued to address me rather than Starbo. 'You will be quartered in the old cavalry barracks.'

'And what about my men?' Starbo breathed in his face, but old Horas stood his ground.

'Your men will have to share the stables with your beasts. We are a growing town here, but space is at a premium.'

'But you do have a bath for me?' I pressed him.

'I will alert the body slaves immediately,' he assured me.

'That,' I told him, 'would do nicely.'

Though it was not yet midday, Lupus' household provided a decent enough *prandium* of oysters, fish, eggs, cold mutton and beef and bread although Lupus himself pointed out that in Rome it was thought vulgar to consume a large lunch and that the choicest dishes would be reserved for dinner. Pointing this out was, of course, vulgar in itself. But once clean and fed, with Starbo and his crew out of both sight and mind, I was willing to indulge the man.

'You have travelled widely in the Empire, have you not, Olussa?' he asked as we ate.

'To almost every country and province,' I answered honestly, confident that he had not left this blighted island for sixteen years. 'From Lusitania in the west to Cappadocia in the east.'

'But never to Rome?'

He said it almost as if musing to himself, not expecting an answer.

'No, never Rome,' I said proudly. 'Italy many times but Rome has no allure for me.'

'Your father has told me you held an odd view of the world,' Lupus said haughtily.

'Odd? What is odd about a Greek wishing to remain a Greek?'

'Surely we owe our success to Rome and should serve her? The best way to serve her must be to aspire to citizenship.'

'Rome can be served in many ways,' I said, remembering that I was, after all, supposed to be a spy. 'Even by a non-Roman.'

It had the desired effect on Lupus if only for a heartbeat.

'Your mission for the Procurator, of course,' he gushed. 'Forgive an old man's memory. You must tell me what you can, for I also serve the new Procurator. But not here. Come, let me show you our new *colonia* and we can talk as we walk.'

Lupus had few immediate neighbours as the area as a whole was being cleared for redevelopment. In places, work gangs using large stone hammers were flattening old daub walls and levelling the old floor surfaces and piling rotted timbers and wattle sticks into bonfires. Two ox-drawn carts containing large grey, rough-hewn stones blocked most of the road, their drivers sat in the dirt, backs against the wheels of one cart, sharing a wineskin. When they saw Valerius Lupus approaching they stood up and began to shout for help in unloading the stones. All the other workers on the site began to look busy also.

'The town is growing,' I observed.

'One day it will be a city to rank with any in Rome's provinces,' said Lupus, glaring at the builders. 'Though we are short of craftsmen and starved of good materials.'

'You seem short of slaves, too,' I said for I had been struck by how quiet and uncrowded the streets of the *colonia* were, compared to the constant bustle and stink of Londinium.

'If anything, our programme of building is perhaps too ambitious for the resources we have. We receive precious little help from the locals. A free Trinovantine labourer – unskilled – can command six or eight sesterces a day, which I believe is more than the rate in Londinium.'

'True,' I admitted, 'but then Londinium has always been a cheap place to live.'

Lupus sighed as he watched the construction gang make heavy weather of unloading stones from the carts.

'Even when we offer them above the going rate they can hardly be bothered to turn up for work. Sometimes you will hire a crew to lay foundations in the morning but by midday they are across the town putting a roof on for someone else, or they have disappeared off to their farms to plant crops or just to sit around and complain while they drink beer until they fall over. In truth, the natives have learned much about drinking from our veteran colonists who have not set a very good example. Once the legion left, so did much of the discipline.'

Poor Lupus! A model Roman *colonia* but no model Romans!

Lupus tugged at his chin as if he had once had a beard and was now missing the good of it.

I paused to examine one of the carts more closely.

'This is poor stone,' I observed.

'It is all we have to hand hereabouts. It's a mudstone from the cliffs along the coast to the south. It is brought by barge or as ballast to our supply port some six miles downriver from where it comes up to here in small boats.'

'In Londinium we can unload from the largest ships directly into our warehouses and granaries,' I observed.

'But Londinium is not the provincial capital, Camulodunum is.'

Lupus said this with the gravitas of a soothsayer predicting that day will follow night.

'Yet you are a capital without a legion, without a city wall, without the provincial Governor and without the provincial Procurator.'

I said this to provoke Lupus for no other reason than it was pleasant to do so.

'The legion has been gone for many years,' Lupus answered, 'for we are well behind the frontier and the local tribes were disarmed twelve years ago. We have little need for walls and much need for room for expansion. Our noble Governor has been involved in fighting the barbarians in the west since his appointment. The new, and equally noble, Procurator will, I am sure, reinstate the practice of maintaining his office in Camulodunum once he has seen the facilities we can offer.'

'I am afraid I doubt that, Valerius Lupus. The new Procurator seems to be settling in quite comfortably to his new offices in Londinium.'

'You have visited him there?' Lupus asked quickly, betraying his anxiety.

'I have spent many hours there,' I said smoothly. 'I have even commented upon his furnishings – Catus has a fine taste in the better quality Samian wares – and he has even enlisted my aid in finding heating engineers for his living quarters. He seems to be settling in quite well.'

Lupus was a tall man, but now he seemed to stoop as others of his age tend to do naturally.

'The town council hopes to persuade him to relocate here when he sees the improvements we have made, and which I will show you now. Come, let us walk on. I think you will be impressed.'

'And if I am, should I tell the Procurator?'

Lupus grabbed the sleeve of my toga, all nobleness gone from him.

'Would you?'

His face was close to mine, the lines on his skin like furrows on a ploughed terrace.

'For an old and distinguished friend of my father's, of course I would.'

We walked the length of the street to where the North Gate had once stood, Lupus nodding courteously to passers-by and scowling at idle building workers in equal measure. Almost every existing building was being enlarged, re-roofed or remodelled and the crude dwellings erected when the barracks first became a civilian town were being flattened and new foundations laid for proper, rectangular Roman houses.

At the North Gate Lupus pointed down the hill to his left to a grouping of round huts and makeshift buildings nestled on the outskirts of the town, black smoke rising from six or seven small chimneys. This, he explained, was an area known as the Sheep End where smelting and blacksmithing had been practised since tribal times before the invasion. The town council had decided that all industrial workings should remain at the Sheep End rather than sully the town itself, which no doubt helped to maintain residential property prices.

There was no sign of the actual North Gate itself, the timbers almost certainly having been reused in the unseemly rush to cover the ground with houses. The defensive ditch which would have run the entire perimeter of the fort had been backfilled and stamped flat to form a crude road surface stretching for over a thousand paces. We walked westward on this road, parallel to the river down the slope to the north. I could see a ferry plying across the narrow ribbon of water immediately below us and further downstream, two ramshackle bridges cobbled together from old army pontoons.

'Are we now outside the *colonia*?' I asked Lupus, though it was clear we were: houses and building plots to our right, scrubland cleared of trees all the way down to the river on our left.

'For now, Olussa, for now,' said the old man. 'But within a few years this will be a city extending across the river. Our colonists already own the land for nine miles in every direction. We grow, we grow.'

'How many people live here?' I asked politely, interested in the potential market for fine goods.

'In the township as a whole, perhaps 15,000 people, though only those with citizenship are allowed property rights within the *colonia* itself.'

'We have at least 30,000 in Londinium,' I said, exaggerating as I knew he had.

'But Camulodunum is the provincial capital,' he said as if explaining to a slave or a particularly slow child.

'Strange that it is undefended then,' I responded as we walked. 'We still have a military presence in Londinium and we have gates.'

'It is said in polite society that the gates of Londinium are there to keep the people in, not strangers out,' Lupus said slyly.

'I have heard that also,' I conceded.

'But here, let me show you something we have but Londinium does not.'

We waited for a procession of empty ox-carts to trundle by on a new road cut down to the river. As far as I could determine, it had been the eastern defensive ditch of the fortress before those who had planned the town had filled it in. Valerius Lupus must have read my thoughts.

'The eastern side of the *colonia* is our proudest achievement, or will be. We had to reduce the stockade and fill the ditch to realise our dreams,' he said as we crossed the road where the ditch had been. 'And so it seemed logical to continue the process around the other three sides.'

Before us was a huge building site, perhaps a fifth the size of the original fortress and it was clear that this was where the main workforce of the *colonia* was concentrated. Hauliers, stonemasons, mortar-mixers and gangs of slaves rushed to and fro in a confusion of activity but it was ordered activity – ordered by the shouts of gang leaders who seemed to know what they were doing.

These gang bosses were the first armed men I had seen in Camulodunum. From their age and grizzled, if paunchy, build I guessed that they were veterans for they all wore the *gladius* short sword on their right hips. Several of them carried *puglio* daggers in leather scabbards strapped to their left forearms and at least two carried whips. They all wore the standard issue red felt cap which normally lines the legionary's helmet.

Lupus confirmed that they were mostly former engineers or shipwrights now released from the legions after their term of service. These were colonists who had shown no aptitude for farming but had preferred to return to their natural trade of bossing people about.

My host led me into the thick of the site and proudly described the order he saw emerging from the chaos as we picked our way between barrels of nails, stacks of cut and planed timber, huge buckets of lime, dumps of sand and piles of flintstones.

The whole eastern extension to the *colonia* was to be devoted to a theatre and the infamous Temple of Claudius. (When Claudius was deified, Camulodunum had been quick to declare itself the logical home of the Cult of Claudius. It was only after this that the question arose as to whether it was politically correct to worship an Emperor who was still alive. The judicial and religious authorities were still debating the matter when, fortunately, Claudius died – albeit in suspicious circumstances – and the way was clear to build a temple to him.)

Neither theatre nor temple were anywhere near complete but a good start had been made. The half-moon theatre stands were perhaps two storeys high and would, purred Lupus, come to dominate the skyline of the town as well as offering panoramic views over the river valley for those in the cheapest seats.

The temple was, I admit, impressive. The foundation trenches dug into the sandy soil and filled with stones and mortar ran for perhaps a hundred feet by forty feet to support a stone podium which in turn supported ten columns running lengthwise and eight across the width. If they ever managed to get the roof on, the whole structure would be over sixty feet high. The entrance, facing south for maximum daylight, leading to the altar was to be reached by a flight of twenty stone steps although only half of them were in place and it was possible to see into the underbelly of the temple where the foundations had created large, dark vaults under the main podium. In some temples I knew that access to these vaults was maintained by the priests should they wish to store equipment for some of the magic tricks used as special effects during ceremonies or, if their performances did not go as planned, as places to hide from disgruntled worshippers.

In the muddy ground at the foot of the incomplete stairway were two large plinths, one bearing an almost lifesize bronze (he was supposedly quite small) of the late God Emperor Claudius mounted on a charger. The other was clearly not fixed in place and bore a relatively tasteful bronze of the winged goddess of Victory.

'When the temple is complete, Victory will stand at the apex of the roof,' Lupus announced grandly, 'as a beacon to all that this was Claudius' City of Victory. It was imported at great cost.'

'It is a fine statue,' I said. 'In fact, the whole enterprise is on a scale I could not have imagined here in the wild west lands of the Empire. Who's paying for it all?'

'The local Trinovantes mainly,' Lupus said without hesitation. 'Though they grumble about the cost more each day, little realising that this is an honour for them.'

'People are strange when it comes to having honour thrust upon them,' I said but Lupus did not notice my tone.

'They will come to realise,' he continued, 'that what we are building here represents Rome and all things Roman and that their lives have now changed for the better. They will see the Roman way in all its pomp and its strength and they will come to embrace it and live as Romans. That is our mission here in the new provinces – to demonstrate in bricks and mortar that Rome is more than a great military power. It is a way of life so superior to their barbarian ways that they can only profit from it. Do you not agree?'

He may have said much more but my attention had strayed to the position of the sun and the gnawing sensation in my belly. I realised that it must be at least the fourth hour of the afternoon.

'Of course,' I said, 'of course. Is it nearly dinner time?'

It was only after a passable dinner, at which Lupus served roast ducks in a blanket of turnips and sweet wine sauce (I had eaten the same recipe but with roast crane in Lower Germania) and of course more oysters, that my host began to question me about my purpose and plans.

Or rather, my host's other guests, a selection of the great and good of Camulodunum which included several veterans with hides as grizzled and unpleasant as their table manners and some of the fattest and most flirtatious wives I had ever seen. When making these notes afterwards I could not remember a single one of their names.

Towards the end of the dinner, two of the veterans – both quite drunk by now – implored me to tell them the latest news from the Games in Rome. In particular they wished to know the fortunes of the gladiators known as Wolf, Sting and Rocky. When I told them I had no idea who Wolf, Sting and Rocky were, let alone whether they were alive or dead (and what else is there to know about a gladiator?) they did not believe me and pressed me further and again I pleaded ignorance. It was only the intervention of one of the wives, herself the worse for wine, who clutched at my thigh and told me to ignore my interrogators. It seemed that the veterans in Camulodunum gambled heavily on the outcome of fights in the arena in Rome, although news of single combat fights was a long time in reaching this far-flung outpost. They pooled their money week by week to see who was to be the latest dead and at the moment, many a pension was riding on the fortunes of Sting, Rocky and Wolf (who had probably never heard of Camulodunum or even Britannia) fighting in the sand in Rome a thousand miles away. The drunken wife even told me that her husband (whichever one he was) had a glass goblet inscribed with a gladiatorial scene and the name 'Spiculus' – Sting, his particular favourite killer. At the rate they went through gladiators in Rome, it was probably a collector's item by now.

It was an aspect of provincial life I had never considered before and I promise myself that I will, when I have time, seriously think how such a commodity – news from Rome – can be transported fresh, packaged and sold here on the frontier. After all, if I could bring the finest Samian ware from southern Gaul and Lupus could sell olive oil from southern Hispania, there was no reason why gossip from the Imperial Games should not be a regular import also.

As Lupus' guests departed, he congratulated me on the way I had handled their inquisitiveness, but in such a manner that it was clear he now expected me to tell *him* the purpose of my mission.

Instead I thanked him for the dinner and for the interesting company he had provided and asked for a slave to show me to bed.

It was only as I blew out the last lamp and settled to my first decent sleep for a week, that I thought of Calpurnius and wondered where he was.

XII: Roscius

We made our *hiberna* – our winter camp – in the Deva* fortress, which was the new base for the XXth Legion. Most of the campaigning though was done by the XIVth Legion, with the XXth lads strung out along the roads manning the forts, keeping the supplies coming, building the roads and acting as a reserve. Of course I went wherever the General went as I was on his staff by then.

Yes, so was Julius Agricola.

Why do you keep asking about him? You related to him or something?

Oh you are? Fair enough. I've no axe to grind against him. He was decent enough and he made a good career for himself afterwards, but don't go giving him any of the credit. I've already told you, it was Suetonius Paulinus who pulled our nuts out of the fire on this one. Nobody else.

Where was I?

Deva. Oh yes. Bit of a shithole in those days. Supposed to be quite a nice town now.

Anyway, there we were, which was actually north of the main base at Viroconium** where Route LXVI ended and part of the XXth's job was to build a connecting road. The XIVth's job was to exterminate the Ordovices – bunch of fucking savages – and the best way to do that was to make

* Chester.

** Wroxeter.

sure they had nothing to eat over winter. And that's what more or less happened. We all snuggled down in Deva and come the spring, the XIVth were on the march again.

There wasn't much opposition from the locals – we'd given them a pretty good hammering the year before, remember – and those with any fight left in them had moved even further westward and had struck up some sort of alliance with the pirates and the Druids on that hell hole of an island called Mona.

If it had been any other enemy, I would have said leave them there, get the fleet in to blockade the whole island and starve the buggers out. But Paulinus said no: let's go to work and finish the job.

There were two reasons we couldn't leave them sitting there on Mona. Firstly, the island had copper mines and we wanted them. It was only reasonable considering how much we'd spent conquering the damn province. Secondly, it was the Druids. I've told you about them, haven't I? About how Mona was like a sacred island to them?

Well, those were the reasons and the General set about it like a real professional.

I reckon we roped in every carpenter and shipwright living along the frontier and in the big estuary beyond Deva we built a fleet of invasion barges. While that was being done, the General had the auxiliary cavalry trained to swim in deep water alongside their horses but as most of them were from Batavi they were used to that.* Then he got the officers of the XIVth to give their lads lectures on how the Druid witches might look like devils but they could do you more harm by pissing on you than by casting a spell on you. Mind you, some of the witches *would* piss on you, given half a chance to get the angle right.

Now I'm only telling you this to show you what a good soldier Paulinus was. He knew the lads would see some pretty rough things on Mona, and he was right, and he tried to prepare them for it.

The General picked out the best archers and formed a

* The flood plains of modern Holland.

special troop whose job was to stay close up to the front line and pick off the witches. They were drilled for weeks to concentrate their arrows, even firing from the barges still at sea. Three archers to a witch was the ratio he worked to. He put the best slingers we had – and some of those lads were twice as accurate as archers over short ranges – into small units and they got the same orders: work in threes to take out a witch.

I suggested that the General put some prize money on the witches, give the boys a bit of incentive. You know, so much per head. But Paulinus wouldn't have any of that. I think he was a bit shocked by the idea.

'We're not mercenaries, Roscius my old friend,' he told me, pretending to be a real stiff-arse but he had a twinkle in his eye. 'We are Legio XIV and killing the enemies of Rome is our profession. We take pride in our work. That should be reward enough.'

He was like that, was the Old Man. That's what we called him, behind his back. Once, one night when he was doing the rounds, one of the officers asked him what his perfect victory would be. What would be the best—

No, it wasn't Agricola, it was some other Patsy.

Anyway, one of us asked him what his idea of a total victory would be, and do you know what he said? He said: One hundred thousand barbarians dead for not one drop of Roman blood.

Now that's a fucking general you want to follow. Maximum damage to the enemy, minimum cost to your own side. And he didn't just say it, he tried to do it. Train, drill, prepare, do whatever you have to, but make sure that when the shit starts to fly, it's going to fly their way not yours.

He had no time for the glory boys who went charging in without thinking. He never had any time for that prat Petillius Cerialis. Now there was a Patsy who always survived even though he left most of his men behind. The bitch Boudica took the better part of half his legion, but he made sure he got away. And that wasn't the first – or the last – time he pulled a stunt like that.

But I'll get to that.

So, the XIVth started out, marching round the coast,

sweeping up any armed resistance by the savages and when they got the word, the navy would bring the assault craft round by sea as near as they could to the straits which separated the mainland from Mona.

We didn't encounter any serious opposition, but I remember the General being really upset when one of the troops of advance scouts rode into an ambush. About ten of them made it back, saying they'd been jumped by a war party of Ordovices who had been backed up by three or four of the pirate ships operating off the island. Now these pirates were the worst sort of scum, most of them hailing from Hibernia, the big island out to the west that made Britannia look positively civilised, and we suspected they were being paid by the Druids to ferry in supplies.

Up to then, we had no real quarrel with these pirates and we'd assumed that once we started the assault on Mona, they would piss off across the sea to Hibernia and we'd never see them again. But the survivors from our scout troop all told the same story: that they'd seen a dozen or so of their comrades taken alive and packed into the pirates' ships to be ferried over to the island as sacrifices for the Druids. That really sealed their fate – the General wasn't going to let them go after that. He doubled the strength of all patrols and sent orders back to the fleet that once they'd delivered the assault craft, they should be prepared to blockade the island and make sure nothing – 'absolutely nothing' were his words – was allowed to leave by sea.

The embarkation point for the legion was on the narrowest point of the straits over to Mona. We could see the island quite clearly: the beach, the rocks, the trees – which meant that anyone on the island could see us quite clearly as well.

This didn't worry the General: he seemed to quite like the situation, even when the barbarians began gathering on the shoreline of the island, shouting and throwing stones into the water. Then the Druids came down to join them and by night they lit huge bonfires in the treeline and the screaming started.

We all knew what it was but nobody said anything and the General and all of us staff officers would walk among the men at night, joking, telling stories, anything to distract them from the screams coming over the water.

For three days we drilled and for three nights we waited and then on the fourth day the barges arrived and we were raring to go. Paulinus had the Legion assemble and climb into the barges in full view of the barbarians on the island. And by this time there was quite a crowd of them, maybe five or six thousand with their Druid priests out front, whipping them up.

And we saw the witches for the first time, there on the beach, waiting for us, giving us the evil eye and singing – if you can call it singing – their hate.

The last order the General gave before the attack was to remind the men to look scared when they got near the far shore. Told them to lay it on thick and start screaming for the gods to help them, or even their mothers if they could remember them! (That one always went down well with the lads.)

The important thing, you see, was to keep all the barbarians looking at us as we rowed towards them, which took a while because of the currents. That way they wouldn't notice the cavalry who had set off earlier further up the coast and were swimming across to Mona. They came ashore unopposed, mounted up and sneaked in behind the mob waiting for us.

Timing was crucial, because the cavalry were outnumbered ten-to-one, so if they showed themselves too soon, the Ordovices could turn round and do them, then get back down to the beach before we landed. The General had thought of that and had told the *cornicines*, the horn blowers, to develop a new signal which meant that we were about to land and the cavalry could come in anytime they liked.

How did it go? As smoothly as silk off a virgin's bottom.

We had archers in the prow of the leading barges who were there just to pick off the witches on the beach. By now they had their hair on fire and were screaming and shouting and most of them had fresh blood on their faces and their robes. They came right down to the shore and started to wade out into the sea and our archers started taking them down when we were still a hundred paces from the beach.

That made the hairy savages pull back a bit, I can tell you, but not so far they couldn't rush us when the barges landed. That was our weak spot – getting out of the boats and on to the beach so we could form up. Once a legion gets itself set in battle formation it takes more than a bunch of howling savages to dislodge them, whatever the odds. We've proved that time and time again. It's only before a legion's formed up or when it's on the march that it's vulnerable. If we didn't know that before, Boudica reminded us, for fuck's sake.

Anyway, that was where the cavalry came in, the auxiliary that Paulinus had trained up to swim across to the island. And fair play to them, because that was fucking cold water that was. They landed on the blind side of the island, formed up and, spot on signal, came charging through the trees, right up the arses of those painted savages.

The barbarians did an about-turn, all pumped-up and eager to get at the cavalry which was coming at them through *their* sacred woods. Our first units hit the beach and were formed up into wedges before they realised they'd been diverted on purpose. The first centurion ashore – nice bloke, can't remember his name – got his lads to lock shields and they went at one of the witches who was screaming and throwing handfuls of sand at them. They knocked her down with their shield bosses and just marched over her. Doubt if there was an unbroken bone in her body when they cleared it.

That got the hairies and their Druid priests all fired up and the priests were screaming to their lot to forget the cavalry and to throw our beachhead troops back into the sea. They knew that if we got a foothold it would be shortest and last day of their lives. They weren't daft, those Druid priests, but their followers were. They couldn't make up their minds whether to go for our cavalry behind them or our heavy infantry landing in front of them. They seemed to like just standing there shouting at each other. No discipline. No discipline at all.

By the time the General and us staff officers crossed, we must have had ten or eleven centuries landed and in wedge formation so all the General had to do was make his 'advance' signal – the two fingers pointing down like an upturned V sign – and we got stuck into them. It was no contest. We cut them down like wheat.

When the last units of the Legion landed, there was nobody left to kill on the beachhead, so they had to fan out and do a sweep of the island looking for targets. They complained afterwards that we hadn't left them anything worth fighting, but it was probably two or three days before we accounted for all the Ordovices there and most of the pirates and certainly we got all the Druids. Oh yes, we made sure of them.

A couple of miles inland from the beach we came across this big circle of oak trees in the forest, and there was a pond nearby too. Classic signs of a sacred Druid spot. And just to make sure we got the point, they'd nailed most of our missing scout troop to the trees – upside down – and cut off their private parts, their ears, their fingers – well, anything that stuck out. One or two of the poor bastards were even still alive, even though the General got the medical staff (and he always had them travel in the front line) to them straight away. I don't recall them saving any of them, and more than one asked for a mate to slip them the final blade. Nobody should have to do that, I don't care what you say.

XIII: Olussa

For two days now I have been mostly left to my own devices, as Lupus has been preoccupied with *colonia* business, receiving and dispatching many messages via the Imperial Post. I have made good use of this time by negotiating several new supply deals with the pottery merchants in this dismal outpost and renegotiating several existing ones made by my father. I have listed a full set of supply instructions and credit notes in the code Alexander and Son adopt for such transactions (naturally, of my devising) and will send it to my father before I depart for the unknown.

This is not an action I am looking forward to for although it is dull and provincial here, it is at least relatively safe.

This morning, as I was luxuriating in a hot scrape and cold bath under the tender hands of a household body slave, Horas announced that the Watch Commander, who is named Ulpius, wished to see me urgently.

What this Ulpius had to tell me was that Starbo and his

gang of ruffians were in the process of commandeering all pack animals and vehicles they could find, claiming they were on the Procurator's business. With only four men on the morning watch, Ulpius was unable to prevent them. As Horas shook his head slowly in dismay at such behaviour, I agreed that perhaps I should accompany them to see what was behind it all and Ulpius was immediately cheered by this. Indeed he was confident enough to ask me what should be done with the naked boy who had been sleeping with the horses for two nights.

'Calpurnius?'

'I believe that is the boy's name,' said Horas severely.

'Naked?'

'We gave him a blanket,' said Ulpius quickly.

The situation at the old barracks was little short of a circus. Starbo was in the thick of things, arguing with a group of grizzled old veterans who had armed themselves with short swords, daggers and even the odd *pilum* brought out of retirement for the occasion. All had raised their voices to the level of street-market traders and indeed it seemed that some sort of market was being held.

Through the throng of bodies and skitterish animals, I began to count a tally.

'They removed your remaining horses first,' Ulpius whispered in my ear, 'to a stables near the west gate.'

'For a quick getaway,' I murmured to myself. Then, to Ulpius: 'What do you mean *remaining*?'

'I believe there has been a question of gambling debts,' said Horas as though the words pained him.

'They have gambled away their horses?' I exclaimed. 'The Procurator's horses? *My* horses?'

'Most of the mules went first. Then the slaves, then the wagons. That was after they had run out of the money they made from the contraband fish sauce. Where have you been while all this was going on?'

Old Horas bridled even before I realised it was Calpurnius who had appeared at my side as swiftly and quietly as a rat.

'How dare you speak to your master like that?' he growled, but I waved his indignation aside for Calpurnius cut such a sorry figure; wrapped in a shit-smeared blanket tied at his slim waist with a length of hemp rope.

His hair was matted with muck, his hands and feet as black as charcoal and I thought at first his face was too but then I realised he wore the beginnings of a beard. If only Julia could see him now!

'They bet my clothes in a game of dice,' whined Calpurnius. 'And they tried to bet me! Then they tried to sell me.'

I had no chance to enquire further about Calpurnius' ordeal, for a large, weatherbeaten face, all too familiar, pressed itself close to mine. So close, I was almost overpowered by the scent of fish sauce on his breath.

'Orders,' said Starbo. 'We've had orders. We've been recalled to Londinium by the Procurator. We're requisitioning these animals as replacements.'

There was a growl of resentment from the crowd of veterans who disapproved of the idea of their property being pressed into the service of the Procurator.

'Very well,' I said, taking command of the situation. 'I am the guest of Valerius Lupus, your Magistrate. He knows that these men are on an Imperial mission for the noble Catus Decianus and will make any necessary reparations for property pressed into service for the Procurator.'

I glared at Horas until he nodded reluctantly in agreement and that seemed to satisfy the angry veterans. As they began to drift away, I realised the implication of Starbo's action.

'If you and your men are returning to Londinium, where is my escort for the remainder of my journey?' I asked the giant.

'You, my friend,' he said insolently, 'are on your own.'

XIV: Valerius Lupus

Camulodunum.
By Imperial Post.
To the Procurator of all Britannia, Gn Catus Decianus

Most Noble Decianus,

I have to report the most disturbing scenes which have surrounded your agent Olussa on his departure for the Iceni territory.

For several days, although he was an honoured guest in my house, Olussa has been conspicuous by his absence except at mealtimes. He has, it is reported to me, spent his days negotiating forward contracts and supply agreements with almost all the merchants in the *colonia*. Such, as a trader, is his right but I was led to believe he was here on official business rather than a personal mission to disrupt local monopolies and undercut established agreements.

When your orders recalling your servant Starbo arrived yesterday, word quickly spread through the *colonia* as it seems there were several matters outstanding of unpaid bills and debts, resulting from gaming, involving almost all the members of the police troop which arrived with Olussa. An ugly scene developed in the stables as tempers became heated between your police and some of our veterans who demanded payment in full before the troop departed.

Your agent Olussa proved himself incapable of restoring order and in fact seemed solely concerned with the comfort of a naked urchin who had been sleeping with the livestock. When the situation became close to violence, Olussa began to scream and wail that the whole world was against him, crying like a widow and tearing at his own clothing.

For the sake of public order, as by now fights were breaking out on the streets themselves (much to the amusement of local Trinovantine slaves), I had to intervene and negotiate a settlement between the parties.

Starbo and his men have now departed for Londinium. The slaves which accompanied them here, ten of the mules and four wagons containing a variety of trading goods have been accepted by our veterans as payment of gambling debts, for food and lodging and a small fine I have had to levy to cover various damages to property.

Olussa has, with some urging, agreed to continue his journey north. He takes the two *raedae* he arrived with but as there are no horses left ungambled, I have arranged for him to purchase – at very reasonable rates – eight oxen. He is accompanied by the muleteer and his two sons despite the fact that only four mules remain in the train, and two of Starbo's men who had lost their horses and who preferred to accompany Olussa rather than remain in the *colonia*. Olussa has also insisted that the naked urchin he claims is his body slave also accompanies them although the boy himself begged to stay in Camulodunum.

Such is the sorry state of this party, facing at least five days of travel before they reach the Iceni tribal lands, that I could not allow it to proceed without some guidance from safer hands. I have therefore, at my own expense, provided them with a guide, a trusted member of my own household who began life as an Iceni slave, and escort in the personage of our valiant Watch Commander.

They will be sorely missed and their return eagerly anticipated, unlike the other members of this expedition.

XV: Olussa

A road which is not a road, into a country which is not a country but a barbarity, in the company of a family of dwarves, two mutilated ex-slaves who would probably cut my throat at the first opportunity and two slaves – Horas and Calpurnius – who would stand by and watch them do it.

Not only has the oaf Horas been wished upon me as a translator and guide, but so has the idiot Ulpius, the so-called commander of the *colonia*'s watch. Such is the resentment among the veterans at his failure to control the unruly behaviour of Starbo's crew of thugs, that it has been deemed prudent for him to find business 'up country' as they say, until memories begin to fade.

Thus there are nine of us – a strange fellowship this – all of us spies in our own way, either for Catus, for Valerius Lupus, for Starbo, or – in Calpurnius' case – probably my father. We have a long and perilous journey ahead.

My only blessing: not one of this motley crew is talking to me.

Our departure from Camulodunum was made with indecent haste the day following Starbo's desertion. It was left to me to re-equip the expedition, again at my own expense, as most of our supplies, horses and slaves had been lost to the dedicated gamblers among the veterans of the *colonia*.

My so-called bodyguard now consists of a magnificent two: Rogerus, the Cantii slave with the numeral II branded on his forehead, and Alcides the Gaul with the lazy eye, two fingers missing from his left hand and a limp in his right foot. I can only hope that if we are ambushed by enemies, then they attack one at a time.

And I only have these two noble warriors because they have gambled away their horses and had left sufficient debts in the *colonia* that they decided it was safer to accompany me rather than stay there.

Much the same can be said for the dwarf Dumno and his sons, whose names I do not know. From the way Dumno treats them, I do not think he knows them either. Through his gambling or whoring, his string of mules has been reduced to four so he is unlikely to see a profit from this venture. I have, however, offered to pay our agreed rate for the journey on condition he handles the oxen I have been forced to buy to pull our carriages. These creatures are just as surly as the mules and while they smell sweeter, they are heavier and clumsier and could kill a man by walking over him without noticing it. I want nothing to do with them until the time comes to eat them.

Dumno's sons drive the carriages, whilst their father prefers to walk with his string of mules in the rear. The mules carry our food and cooking equipment, along with what tradeable goods I have managed to salvage from Starbo's gambling spree in the *colonia*.

My carriage, in which I travel alone, is cramped because I have to share it with our tents, bedding, torches, oil and lamps as there are no *mansiones* or *tavernae* where we are going. At least I can keep an eye on my personal luggage, my few delicacies and ointments and, most importantly, my supplies of ink and writing bark which I managed to replenish in Camulodunum quite cheaply, there being little demand for such things there.

In the second *raeda*, our personal defenders and noble warriors Rogerus and Alcides busy themselves with sharpening stones, trying to put edges on the second-hand short swords I have had to buy them.

Ulpius, thinking himself something of a soldier, has taken it upon himself to ride his horse in front of our party, scouting the way. I wonder how long it will be before he realises he will be the first to fall if we are attacked?

The road north and west from Camulodunum is little more than a track. Why should there be a road into the Iceni territory? Who would want to go there?

For several miles the trees have been cleared for timber and charcoal-burning, of which there are still many signs with thin streams of grey smoke rising to the sky across the landscape. But there are few traces of habitation apart from abandoned roundhouses and huts which I presume were once Trinovantine farms before they were confiscated by the *colonia* veterans.

Eventually, the forest closes in on both sides of us and we see even fewer signs of life: a drover herding sheep from nowhere to nowhere, an Imperial Post rider galloping south, who passes without a word. Then, but an hour or so before dusk, we find a pathetic example of a village, home to perhaps twenty surly Trinovantines who stare at us but do not speak. On the edge of the village there is a relay stable for Imperial Post horses and without asking for my permission or approval, Horas seeks out the head groom and begins to negotiate with him, though there is little to negotiate.

There is no accommodation available but we are offered the use of a pen for the animals and are graciously allowed to pitch our tents near a pool of surprisingly clean water. I resist the temptation to bathe for I must harden myself to the rigours which lie ahead among the barbarians.

Horas buys salted fish from the groom, to preserve our meagre rations, and begins to prepare a stew. Calpurnius not only helps him find wood to build a fire and set up the cooking range, but does so enthusiastically, even cheerfully. Dumno settles down the mules for the night and his sons do the same with the oxen. Rogerus and Alcides slink off into the village. They return with a flagon of beer each, though what they have bartered for it I dread to think.

All this happens without a word to me, but I do not despair.

I remain inside my carriage and use the time while they are

all busy to unlock the secret panel and examine the gold I have brought for the Iceni, using the key which Starbo had, almost as an afterthought, casually tossed to me before his departure.

The Procurator had entrusted me with nine bags, one of which was safely hidden in my father's house before we left Londinium. No matter how many times I count them, there are now only five bags in the secret compartment.

Why am I not surprised?

XVI: Roscius

The military strategy? Well, we had to make it up on the spot, didn't we?

Of course we hadn't planned for it. How can you plan for a revolt like that, coming from where it did? It was a kick up the arse, it really was. It was the arsehole of the province and we thought we'd left it quiet.

If you insist, I'll go through it slowly so that even you historians might understand. Least I can do, I suppose, seeing as how you're paying for the wine.

Yes, you are.

Yes, you better had write that down.

All right then, the order of battle – since you ask – though it won't mean much because things happened fairly quickly.

There were four legions in Britannia at the time. Got that?

There was the XXth, called Valeria after Octavian's General Valerius Messalinus. That's the Octavian who became Caesar Augustus. Oh, you knew that did you? Well, I'd forgotten you were a historian.

The XXth was my old mob. Our standard was the boar – because it was the last thing you wanted to meet on a dark night, we used to say.

Well, the XXth had built the original fortress at Camulodunum but then got moved north and then west and by the time in question was mostly occupied manning the forts along the military frontier, strung out along a line roughly south-west to north-east.

Like I've said, I was on General Suetonius' staff by then and the XXth's cavalry and our auxiliaries were attached to his expeditionary force against the Druids and the Isle of Mona.

Most of that force was the XIVth Legion Gemina, but we had Thracian archers, several regiments of Hispania cavalry as well as mixed cohorts from Batavia, Pannonia, Germania, Dalmatia, Gaul, you name it. It was a big unit, could have dealt with anything. The only trouble was it was so far away when the shit started flying.

Then there was the IXth Hispania, which was Julius Caesar's original ninth legion. They had Neptune as their standard and by the gods, they might as well have gone on a fishing trip for all the use they were.

Oh, the boys in the ranks were decent enough but they had a right prat of a legate, that Petillius Cerialis. What a tosser! – and I don't mind you writing that down one bit. Got a lot of good men killed did that shit. More than once. He always got out though. Yes, he was the one who went on to be Governor. Must have had friends in high places.

The IXth were the ones on the spot when it happened, or rather the nearest. Fat lot of good it did them. Not many of the infantry lived to tell the tale. They had to get nearly three thousand replacements from Germania after it was over to bring them up to strength.

Then there was the glorious IInd Augusta, stationed at Isca Dumnoniorum right down in the western toe of the province. They didn't exactly cover themselves with laurels, did they? Oh, they'd done all right during the invasion when Vespasian was in charge, but at the time we're talking about, most of their senior officers seemed to have gone walkabout, leaving the camp prefect in charge. Poenius Posthumous was his name. But I've told you; I'll come to that little incident.

And that was more or less it. There were bits and pieces of units guarding things like the new granaries in Londinium. For our campaigns against the Druids all our supplies were coming in that way anyway.

Then you'd have the police squads in Londinium, Camulodunum and Verulamium, which worked for the Procurator or the civil authorities and a few here and there guarding the Imperial Post or escorting the engineers building roads and bridges. There would have been about 40,000 – maybe more – of us including the auxiliaries, but we were all miles away from where the trouble started.

She was a lucky bitch in that respect. Probably explains why she got as far as she did.

There was the Governor and the XIVth Legion, with the bits of the XXth that weren't strung out on guard duty and we were – what? – two hundred and fifty miles from the capital. I mean Camulodunum of course, not Londinium like now.

The IInd – well they were in the south-west at least two hundred miles away. And the IXth, they'd be nearly a hundred miles away without a direct road and their main job was to keep an eye on the tribes to the *north*, not the east.

That was the trouble really. We were all facing the wrong way.

XVII: Olussa

For two more days we follow the track northwards. The forest thickened and then thinned over gentle hills and small valleys where the rivers and streams were easily forded by our oxen and Dumno's mules.

Riding in our van, Ulpius disturbs a wild pig. Not a ferocious wild boar, as he first thought in his panic, but a young sow, which scuttles through the legs of his horse and straight down the track towards our carriages. Before Ulpius can control his startled horse, let alone unstrap a javelin from his saddle pack, Rogerus and Alcides have jumped from their vehicle, encouraged by the witless shouting of Dumno's sons, and between them have wrestled the pig into submission in the mud. (It must have bitten Alcides for I distinctly saw him sink his teeth into its struggling hocks in revenge.)

There was naturally a delay while the pig was killed and slit open and the carcase cleaned in a perfunctory fashion in a nearby stream. I order Calpurnius to retain the liver and kidneys for me and he does so sullenly, still not speaking to me directly. They will go well with some of my private supplies of salted onions, which I had no intention of sharing with this motley crew and yet I break my own rule and invite Horas to dine with me.

He accepted my invitation with some speed. I suspect he has tired of Calpurnius' whining and constant complaints and finds the company of Rogerus and Alcides as loathsome as I do. As to Dumno and his two sons, it is probably the smell which puts him off and I can tell it gives him a secret pleasure to be regarded as an equal by me when Ulpius, who is of higher rank, is ignored.

He cooks tolerably well and tells me much. So much that I will record his experiences in shortened form as I must preserve my meagre supplies of bark and ink.

The king of the Iceni is Prasutagus. He is said to be the richest of the Iceni and has ruled the tribe for some thirty years, not by divine right of conquest or arms but by some curious system of election.

The Iceni did not oppose the invasion of Claudius and their 'surrender' was no more than a formal recognition of it. In return they were given presents or grants of money (which I now know, but they do not, to have been loans) and allowed to live their own life as a client kingdom within the province.

There were some Iceni, no doubt inspired by their Druid priests, who rebelled against this peaceful co-existence but their rebellion was swiftly crushed. Prasutagus had counselled against the rebellion and refused to send troops to aid the rebels. Because of this act he was not punished for the rebellion but had to agree to the tribe being disarmed and in the following thirteen years, little of note was heard from the Iceni.

Prasutagus had taken a much younger wife, called Boudica, who despite her youth had been unable to conceive until almost exactly nine months after Claudius' invasion. This was thought to be an omen of sorts. The child was a daughter, but healthy enough, although no subsequent offspring appeared until nine months after Governor Scapula put down the rebellious faction of the tribe. Again this was a daughter, and the superstition grew that Prasutagus could only father children when he co-operated with Rome.

Prasutagus' wealth stems in the main from horses, as is evident from the horse design on most of his coinage; and sea salt which they collect from the coast to the north. What meat they have can thus be cured and a surplus of barley and wheat each year sees them comfortably through the winters. They are self-sufficient and rely on their neighbours for nothing.

'Except gold, it is said,' I prompted him.

'Because they have none of their own and they prize it above all else,' replied Horas.

'But what do they use it for if they are not interested in trade? They do not use it in their coinage.'

'They like to be buried with it,' said Horas with a shrug of his shoulders.

We have arrived at the farmstead of Publius Oranius. It has a substantial house; by no means a villa but a good solid house, the building of which is a major achievement in the depths of this wilderness. But then Publius Oranius is a former quartermaster of the XXth Legion and was no doubt able to enlist the help of the legion's tilemakers, carpenters and blacksmiths as well as obtaining a good discount on his building materials. However it was financed, the roof is tiled and the walls of sound plaster and I shall not spend the night under damp canvas.

Oranius himself is a stout man, not tall but broad of frame though he seems fit and active for his years. He greets us as if he was expecting us, presenting us with wine and local delicacies – thin strips of smoked boar and scraps of lettuce leaves which have been pickled in honey and vinegar – as soon as we dismount from our vehicles. Ulpius performs the introductions in the formal manner and proves surprisingly good at it.

Oranius growls a greeting to each of us and bids us welcome to his humble home 'out here in the wild lands' as he puts it. I am delighted to see that he transfixes his gaze on the numeral II branded on Rogerus' forehead until Rogerus squirms and bows his head, shuffling his feet in the dirt, although Oranius has made no comment or accusation. He obviously knows what the branding signifies and I must remember to ask him, perhaps over dinner.

We are attended by twenty or more slaves and grooms. Oranius is doing well for himself as he says there are another ten at work in the fields and he even has to hire six labourers to dig or unblock his boundary ditches after the winter and then again to help with the harvest.

I ask if they are Iceni and he says loudly, 'No, they're Roman senators down on their luck,' and we all have to laugh along with him out of politeness.

A small, dark-haired, slim-hipped woman walks unsmiling behind him. This, when he remembers that she is there, is his wife Borrach, which he says means 'Glad Courage' in the Iceni tongue but is also their name for the herb borage. She is the best wife he has had so far, he says with a nudge and a wink to us as if we were back in the barracks, old soldiers together. Borrach does not respond but constantly dips into a leather pouch hanging from her girdle to remove a few seeds or herb stalks which she slips into her mouth to chew delicately. There is a faint musty smell about her which I cannot place.

'Rest awhile and then we shall dine tonight from the egg to the apple,' announces Oranius, adding: 'That is what they say in Rome, isn't it?'

It is indeed when a twenty-course banquet is planned with time allowed for visits to the vomitorium. I doubted that Oranius' hospitality ran so large, but I smiled politely.

In truth the dinner was better than I had expected, but almost anything could have been served such was the simple pleasure of being able to eat seated on crude but comfortable couches in a room lit by a hundred small lamps (no doubt army issue) with servants to wait upon us.

Oranius had asked Ulpius and Horas to join us and I could not protest as I was his guest. His wife was with us but she did not eat so much as peck at a few dishes and though she had changed her robe, she still wore the pouch of seeds around her waist and would regularly dip her fingers into it and then into her mouth when she thought no one was observing her.

We were served oysters, both fresh from one of Oranius' barrels and smoked, which was how he preserved them when supplies faltered, then a white fish cooked in vinegar with cummin spice, turnips – both the mashed root and the boiled leaves, parsnips cooked in honey and the previous summer's raspberries and blackberries preserved in mead in sealed jars. And there was wine, imported from Rhodes no less, of which Oranius was almost insufferably proud though it had not travelled.

While the servants were still present I was content to eat and relax and engage in what smalltalk arose, though most of it concerned Camulodunum.

'How goes the building work in the *colonia*?' asked our host.

'It goes apace, Publius Oranius,' said Ulpius. 'There are more houses every day, new shops every week and the temple to the Divine Claudius is half finished.'

I was surprised at this assessment as the building work I had seen was sporadic at best and the temple was surely no more than a fifth complete.

'Are the Trinnies not giving you any trouble then? Because that's not what I hear.'

'There have been grumblings,' said Horas. 'And some of the work is not as far advanced as we would wish.'

'Slaves are deserting you, so I'm told. Can't get labour without paying for it and at a pretty high rate I believe.'

'That is the situation in Londinium,' I said, feeling I should contribute to the discussion. 'Even the Procurator has trouble finding a reliable heating engineer who does not charge the earth.'

'Well, that's Londinium for you,' said Oranius, slapping his chest with one hand and spilling wine from the cup held in the other. Why do soldiers think they have to shout to make a point? 'A nest of whorehouses, a refuge for pirates and a bolt-hole for deserters, where only smugglers and gamblers make a profit.'

'And merchants,' Horas pointed out slyly.

'Pah! The honest ones make a profit, as all merchants do, but the dishonest ones in Londinium have the honest ones outnumbered by ten-to-one!' He finally caught my eye. 'Saving, of course, the noble – and honest – Narcissus Alexander. How is your father, young Olussa?'

'He is well and sends his greetings to his old friend. In fact he has sent with me a few goods – the latest and most fashionable things a merchant can offer – as presents for your household.'

'Presents, eh? You're sure they're not just free samples to tempt us into buying more than we need or can afford?'

'My father would always be willing to satisfy any order you may place and, of course, extend credit to his old friend . . .'

Oranius laughed aloud and slapped his own meaty thigh this time.

'By Jove, that sounds just like your father. Is he still cutting sharp deals like he used to?'

I had doubts that my father could cut his way out of a cobweb with a sword, but then they were supposed to be old friends.

'He claims never to have been sharp enough to get round you, Publius Oranius.'

This provoked much more laughter than it deserved.

'In fact, he would like you to consider a potentially profitable partnership with the firm of Alexander and Son,' I added. Having wounded him with good humour, I now went for his purse.

'Oh he does, does he? How could a small farmer here in the wilds help the business of Alexander and Son, which surely stretches across the Empire by now?'

'Our business hardly covers the Empire,' I demurred graciously. 'For example, we have no agent further north than Camulodunum; something we are seeking to rectify if we can find a trustworthy partner, with minimal capital but good holdings of land, carts and oxen or mules.'

'That sounds like you, Oranius,' slurred Ulpius, who had showed early in the meal that he had no head for drink.

Oranius pretended to think it through, tugging his beard and screwing up his eyes.

'Let me see. I might have a small amount of capital to invest. I certainly have good holdings of land and I could have buildings for storage and warehousing easily enough. I have no mules and only a few oxen, but I have access to horses aplenty. Yes, it could be me. But one vital ingredient is missing from the stew.'

'And what might that be?' I asked, thinking this was merely the opening gambit in a bid for an equal partnership, which did not worry me as this was one business venture which was never going to get off the ground.

'Customers, my young merchant, customers. You may have

noticed, I have few neighbours. There is simply no one here in the outlands to buy the expensive, though no doubt high-quality, goods which Alexander and Son could supply. I am trying my best to produce a son or three or four but I am not getting any younger.' He put a hand to his mouth to cover his speech: 'Though my wives are!'

If she heard or understood, the woman Borrach showed no sign.

'My father was thinking of establishing a trading relationship with the Iceni,' I said. 'He feels there is a market there which is sadly unexploited.'

'Hah!' shouted Oranius loudly. 'What do you think the Iceni would want from you?'

'Spices, olive oil, wine, dried figs and the best-quality pottery in the Empire.'

'Think again, Olussa. If this was your father's idea then he should know better. The Iceni want none of those, except maybe the wine which they will take and wait until it is sour and then use it for pickling vegetables. Everything you offer smells of Rome to them. The only thing they want from us – and everybody knows it well enough – is gold. If you have brought enough gold with you, the Iceni will give you all the horses and all the sea salt and all the wool you'll ever want. A fistful of gold will also buy you enough Iceni women to service the whole XXth Legion twice a night!'

Ulpius spluttered into his wine again and held out his cup for a refill. I was not happy with the way the conversation was turning in this company, for although Ulpius would remember none of it, Horas was not missing a word. And neither were Oranius' wife and slaves.

'I have heard that the Iceni are a proud and noble tribe and surely will want to better themselves with the benefits the Empire can provide. The Empire is, after all, a single economic trade unit and it makes no sense to stay outside its boundaries.'

'That's not the way the Iceni see it. They are not interested in what's going on in Rome or what any other part of the Empire has to offer. As long as Rome leaves them alone, they go on pretending that Rome doesn't exist and . . .'

He paused as a thought struck him.

'. . . Rome. That reminds me, have you heard the news from Rome?'

'What news?' I asked, puzzled.

'*Any* news. About the Games.'

'I do not understand.'

His complexion began to glow from red to purple.

'The gladiators, man, in the Games. Who survives, who triumphs? Rocky, Wolf, Sting and Prudes – the careful one. They are the ones in the veterans of the XXth's syndicate. You must know the latest results. There's a lot of money riding on those four.'

I realised why I had been so keenly questioned in Camulodunum. The veterans had a 'death pool' running on their nominated gladiators, those backing the survivor scooping the winnings.

'The only thing I can tell you is that Prudes is not spoken of any more,' I said, based on the fact that no one had mentioned his name to me in the *colonia*. Gladiators are quickly forgotten when they are dead.

'Damn!' muttered Oranius.

'Prudes was not careful enough!' giggled Ulpius.

I thought this quite a good joke too, but not in front of Oranius.

'So your mission is to establish trade links with the Iceni, then?' he said, recovering his temper.

'Exactly so, and with your help if Fate allows.'

'Exactly so, but exactly *how*?'

'Perhaps you could introduce me to the elders of the tribe, for whom I will certainly provide presents. I have no wish to enter their lands as a common peddler moving from village to village.'

'Hah!' he scoffed, holding his cup for more wine. 'You'd never find half their villages. More than six huts in one place is their idea of a town – and they don't like towns. And anyway, you'd be wasting your time trying to talk to the elders right now, they won't want to know.'

'And why not?'

'Because they will be too busy making arrangements for the funeral,' said Oranius as if addressing a slow-witted Gaul.

'Funeral?'

On the couch beside me, Horas sat bolt upright and planted his boots with a thump on the packed clay floor.

'The king,' he said softly.

'That's right, old Prasutagus, the king. He snuffed it about a week ago. They'll all be so busy with the funeral you won't get sense out of any of them.'

XVIII: Valerius Lupus

Camulodunum. By Imperial Post. Under seal.
To the Procurator of all Britannia: Gn Catus Decianus
Most Secret

Most Noble Procurator,

I have received the news you have been waiting for these past months from one of our settlers to the north, though when it came it came without warning.

The Iceni king Prasutagus died on or before the Ides of the month. By custom, the succession will not be decided until after the funeral but if it follows the wishes expressed in the king's will, the legal conditions will be in place and our plan can be executed as soon as the Governor returns from front-line duty with the required troops.

I crave your indulgence when asking if I can be informed of when this is likely to be so that I may arrange suitable supplies and provisions for the legions. As agreed, I will do this using my personal lines of credit, to avoid arousing suspicion, but I humbly remind the Procurator that I will require a post-dated requisition form for the expense involved.

I would also remind the Procurator that the expedition of the merchant Olussa is on course to enter the Iceni territory any day now, unless some mishap has befallen them.

Among that company I have placed two of my most trusted subordinates who have instructions to report immediately any unusual developments. They have, of course, no idea of the importance of the events which are now about to unfold.

XIX: Olussa

The dinner party broke up in some confusion.

Clearly there was more Oranius wanted to say on the subject but not in front of his slaves. Horas, having listened keenly to him, suddenly professed exhaustion and begged permission to retire to the room he had been given. (A room only slightly smaller than mine, I had noted earlier.) And Ulpius had begun to turn a distinct shade of green in the face.

When conversation faltered, I suggested that perhaps we should inspect the lodgings of my animals, to ensure their comfort; and also my assorted bag of servants, to ensure they were up to no mischief. Oranius agreed with alacrity and suggested we take torches and step outside. He even provided me with a brown woollen cloak (army issue no doubt) which smelled only slightly of wet dog.

I assumed that the house slaves slept in the kitchens as was the custom, but the land slaves and his hired-in farm labourers preferred the thatched round huts of the native tribes. Beyond a capacious barn and an extensive network of animal pens and drainage ditches, I could make out four of these huts from the glow of fires inside them.

'I've given your people the end hut,' Oranius said, pointing with his torch, 'and told my people not to mix with them. Nothing personal, it's just I don't allow drinking or gambling and certainly not what that swarthy one gets up to. The one who's been branded.'

He tapped his own forehead and then held out two fingers towards me.

'You mean Rogerus?'

'That's his name?' he smiled.

'You know the meaning of that brand? For I do not. And he is not my property, I have somehow inherited him from the Procurator.'

'Who was probably glad to see the back of him. Yes I know

what that II means. It's what the boys in the IInd Legion used to do.'

'He was a legionary?'

'I doubt that. The boys in the IInd didn't do it to themselves, they did it to anyone they caught in the act.'

'In the act of what?'

'Buggery.'

I had no idea the legions were so strict.

'Now that we are far enough from prying ears, shall we do some honest talking young Olussa?'

Crouched in a damp field decorated with sheep droppings under a cloudy night sky was not my idea of an ideal location for a conference, but then spies cannot be choosers. 'My father says you are a man I can trust,' I began.

'Aye, that's true. In this neck of the woods I'm the *only* man you can trust.'

My father had said that too.

'I believe you have a long history of business dealings together.'

'You could say that, though you'd better not say it too loudly to a tax inspector. But you've not come up here to tempt me into a business partnership, have you?'

Perhaps when I have been longer a spy I will be able to tell who is not as stupid as they first appear.

'No, you are right. My mission here is from the Procurator, Catus Decianus, and the story of trading with the Iceni is merely,' I sought the right word, ' – a cloaking story, to cover my real purpose.'

'You're not going in there to tell them about the loans, are you? Fuck me, that would take a braver man than I am.'

I assured Oranius that I had received no instructions to tell the Iceni anything about Imperial loans, but as everyone I had met since leaving Londinium seemed to know the loans were about to be called in, there was a good chance the Iceni did also. I was merely there to assess how much and how quickly they could repay them. Discreetly, of course.

Oranius sank into the damp heather to sit cross-legged, wrapping his cloak tightly around him and pushing his torch into the soft, sandy earth until it stood upright. When he had settled his ample buttocks, he shook his head slowly from side to side.

'Go home, Olussa,' he said eventually. 'Go home. There is nothing here for you. There is no trade, no profit, and I suggest that spying is not the best career path to a long and comfortable old age. Go home and live off your father's money.'

'Would that it were so simple, old friend of my family. I am here on the orders of the Procurator, his most insistent orders. I cannot go back to Londinium, he has a knife at my throat.'

'Boudica will hold one somewhere a damn sight more interesting than your throat if you disrespect the Iceni when they're in mourning.'

'Who is this Boudica?' I asked and Oranius looked at me as he would look upon a prisoner being led to the gibbet.

'I can see your career as a spy is destined to be a short one. What amazes me is how you have survived so long.'

'But my mission has not yet truly started,' I protested.

'And your point is – what? Is there anything you want me to tell your father when I take him your ashes?'

From across the fields torchlight flashed across the entrance to one of the roundhouses, then there came a scream followed by the sound of pottery breaking.

'That's your lot, fighting among themselves,' Oranius observed. 'Do you trust any of them?'

'Not a one,' I replied

'Then perhaps there is some hope for you. Distance yourself from them, better still, sell them or give them to the Iceni as a gift.'

'They are not mine to give, except Calpurnius.'

'The boy with the cheeky smile?'

I was glad of the night to hide my blushes.

'Be careful, Olussa. The Druids do not approve of Greek practices, at least not with boys. You really have no idea what you are getting in to, have you?'

'All I have to do is win their trust, keep my eyes open, make notes and report back to the Procurator in London. I pose them no threat and I bring them gifts, that is the plan.'

'That is a plan?' he snorted. 'You'll only win their trust if you bring them sacks full of gold, that's the only sort of trust they understand.' Frightened as I was, I was not going to fall into his trap of admitting what I was transporting in the secret compartment of my carriage. 'And you should worry about *keeping* your eyes if they catch you snooping around, not to mention your hands if they catch you writing notes. They're very strange about people who read and write, you know, as they don't believe in it themselves. And I wouldn't worry too much about reporting to the Procurator in Londinium. If I know that greedy little weasel – and I do – then he's already on his way here.'

'Here? Catus is coming here?'

'I'd bet the farm on it. He won't be able to resist. You, my son, and your mission, have been overtaken by events. You're history.'

XX: Valerius Lupus

Camulodunum. By urgent Imperial Post.

Most Noble Procurator, Gn. Catus Decianus,

I have received your instructions with some trepidation, and I must respectfully suggest that this is not the wisest of times to press our business with the Iceni.

If the Governor continues to campaign beyond the military frontier, it would be prudent to appeal to the Prefect of the Legio IX Hispana for troops which could, I am assured by the veterans here, reach the *colonia* within six days. I crave that the most noble Procurator at least considers this course of action rather than relying solely on his police auxiliaries.

There is no possibility of any additional troops from the *colonia* itself. Despite a population consisting in the main of veterans of the legions, few have maintained the fitness or discipline required by the army. Few actually bother to maintain their weapons and the civil police here number no more than 100, none with active service experience.

Their regular tasks and duties are already proving a burden as the local Trinovantes become increasingly sullen and unruly. Public works here in the *colonia* are in danger of coming to a complete halt, such is the level of absenteeism by local labourers and craftsmen. The number of slaves reported as runaways increases daily and there is growing evidence of actual sabotage to some projects, particularly the temple to the Divine Claudius, which is now months behind schedule. Druidic symbols are painted on new walls, which then collapse overnight. Newly thatched roofs catch fire. An entire morning's production of tiles was scrapped when goats trampled over the drying racks, leaving hoof prints (an omen of bad luck) in nine out of ten tiles. Other portents of doom are seen in every cloud or passing flock of seagulls. If crows are seen in any number, there is panic in the streets.

The Night Watch does what it can and several groups of veterans have taken to patrolling the streets at dusk – although they soon retire to the taverns. But the increasing number of summary executions does little to deter this disobedience. As I write there are three gibbets on the west road down to the Sheep End factories, but it has to be said that three crucifixions a night hardly makes an impression on the problem.

I beg the Procurator to note me well when I say we could face serious civil disobedience from these Trinovantes, who become bolder each day. It would be prudent not to offend the Iceni as well while our military resources are so stretched.

If your Honour insists, I will of course make the arrangements for the reception and quartering of your police, naturally at a discounted rate.

XXI: Olussa

'You must tell me everything you know about this woman!' I commanded, startling old Horas so much that he clutched his chest and sucked at the air like a landed fish.

In truth, he had startled me as much as I had shocked him when I had burst into his room unannounced – but when are visitors to a slave's quarters ever announced?

It was what he was doing which shocked me, for there he was, reclining on his bed as if it was the most natural thing in the world, writing furiously with a thin metal stylus on small squares of bark smeared with wax. Guiltily he scooped these cards, used in the Imperial Post, into the sleeves of his robe and stood before me, eyes downcast, showing that he at least remembered his position.

'I know nothing about her, except that it is curious that she eats little but nettle seeds when Oranius claims he is trying to produce a son.'

'Have you been drinking that stagnant Celtic beer?' I accused. 'You are making no sense.'

'But I have not set eyes on the woman Borrach until today,' he squirmed.

'I'm not talking about Borrach,' I snapped, then reconsidered. 'What do you mean? What you said about the nettles?'

'The pouch she wears at her waist and eats from. They are nettle seeds, or perhaps the ripe seeds of hemp. The Iceni women believe they prevent the female from getting with child.'

'An interesting plant, the nettle,' I mused while I considered this. I had heard that the first legions in Britannia had used bunches of nettles as flails on their own bare legs, stinging them to warm themselves against the cold. Very soon, though, they had copied the idea of wearing trousers which, as the cavalry auxiliaries had discovered, were far more suited to the climate.

'And you think Oranius knows nothing of this?'

Horas shrugged his shoulders, holding on to the sleeve of his robe so the bark posting cards did not fall out.

'It is not my place to tell him,' he said quietly.

'Nor mine. We will speak no more of it, but now you will tell me all you know of this Boudica woman, and how important her standing among the Iceni.'

'If the king Prasutagus is dead, her standing could be of the highest, for they have no son. Therefore it is most likely that the Iceni will elect her Queen, unless she has sons-in-law to make a claim. It all depends on what Prasutagus put in his will.'

'His will? I didn't know the Celtic tribes made wills. I didn't know the Iceni king could read and write.'

'They don't – and he couldn't. And therein lies the problem.'

XXII: Roscius

It wasn't just politics. For Nero, Seneca and the fat cats in Rome, and that shit of a Procurator, it was mostly about money.

Prasutagus, Boudica's late husband, had not been a complete fool. He must have known that client kingdoms within the Empire only lasted as long as the client king did. Once the king died, the kingdom was subsumed into the province. A client kingdom was only for life, not for ever. But he made the big mistake of thinking that if Rome could do business with *him*, he could do business with Rome. So when a few years pass and he realises he's not going to produce a son he can put forward as a suitable successor, he tries to protect his two daughters by making a Roman will.

He leaves, on his death, half the kingdom to Nero – good move that, keep in with the boss – and the other half to be shared between his two daughters, both of them young, both non-political – hardly a threat to Rome, which has, legally, got the lion's share of Prasutagus' wealth anyway, so he thinks they'll be left in peace. Trouble is, nobody tells him Roman law doesn't recognise the girls' claim, so if it went to an Imperial court, Rome would get the lot eventually.

But times were hard and people were greedy. Think of poor old Seneca, he was probably down to his last fifty million sesterces and getting desperate. The powers that be, in the Senate and in the counting houses, just couldn't wait. They wanted it now.

So that bloody Procurator decides to go in and take everything he could get his hands on, no doubt creaming a little something off the top for himself.

He wasn't expecting trouble, why should he? That's why he only took a couple of troops of his special police, a bunch of thugs with plenty of experience on the *wrong* side of the law; most had taken a branding and all of them had felt the lash.

After all, the Iceni were supposed to be disarmed and they had no king to rally round. The widow Boudica was no natural leader and certainly no general – didn't know the first thing about organising an army and had never seen a battle, let alone been in one.

There was no reason for her to be made their War Queen, she would probably have been happy wearing widow's weeds and ashes or whatever it is they do, for the rest of her life. After all, she wasn't even mentioned in the king's will. Nobody expected her to step up like that and take command – there was no reason for her to.

Not until the Procurator gave her a reason to get mad – and the rest of the tribe with her. A damned good reason, come to think of it.

XXIII: Olussa

For a night and a day I have milked Horas like a she-goat, but instead of milk I have been straining information – the lifeblood of the spy. I forget which of the great historians, probably one of the Greek ones, said that a man asked in the correct manner would reveal everything. It is undoubtedly true and the trick to dealing with Horas was to treat him as an equal. I have learned a valuable lesson in spying, as well as much about the Iceni and their widow queen, Boudica, which means 'victory' in their tongue. Both will be important from now on as we are entering enemy territory, although as a 'non-Roman' I sometimes feel I am always in enemy territory.

I have discovered that my secret cache of gold has diminished yet again. Now there are only three bags left, one of them the sweepings from the floor of an Imperial mint. Naturally, because he was the one man my father said I could trust, I suspect Oranius.

As we follow his directions west and then north along a well-worn pathway almost as wide as a Roman road, I use a bone needle and thread and a square of leather to fashion a sheath for the thin-bladed knife I carry in my luggage. This I strap to my left forearm and it is invisible under the sleeve of my tunic. The knife is razor sharp on both edges and with a quick tug on the hilt, it will easily cut its way out of the sheath. Rogerus calls out like a fishwife, commenting on my feminine skills with a needle but I ignore him. If the Iceni are not choosy, I will make them a present of him at the first opportunity.

But from what Horas has told me, the Iceni can be choosy, especially the women, when it comes to the finer things. He has urged me not to dismiss them as barbarians, and whilst their own hand-made pottery is rough and crude in the extreme, some of their metalworking shows high skill and not a small amount of artistic taste. Bronze hand mirrors are highly prized by the tribeswomen, just as highly decorated harness and bridle rings, as well as brooches, are symbols of high status among the men. Both sexes aspire to that ultimate display of wealth: the gold torc – strands of solid gold twisted together until thick as a man's wrist, worn around the neck. They have skill in fabrics also, not just wool, which they dye many colours, but also other materials such as leather and the bark from trees which they cut into strips and then cure as if it was the hide of an animal, producing belts and straps and shoes both soft and strong as with the finest leather. They use box wood and elder to make flutes, pipes and trumpets which produce music as finely pitched as anything heard in Nero's palace, though quite how Horas would know that beggars belief. And, he boasted that the Iceni had considerable expertise in the use of plants in medicine. Most notable was their use of the roots of the marshmallow, crushed and boiled in wine to make a poultice for wounds. Even more impressive than this, if it is to be believed, is their use of woad. Fermented woad leaves are widely known for their use in dyeing cloth blue, and their use by certain Celtic tribes as war paint is also famous. What I had not known was that the properties of woad act to heal wounds, reduce swelling and congeal blood, so in effect, an Iceni warrior who paints himself blue before a battle is preparing himself for the wounds to come. He thus, claimed Horas, feels invincible from the outset and perhaps this explains the reputation for fearlessness of the Iceni.

I questioned him closer on this and he admitted that as the Iceni had been peaceful for so many years, tales of their warriors' fearlessness were just that – tales, recounted as history by their Druids, whom Horas described as 'the keepers of memory'.

'And they are powerful, these Druids?'

Horas was intelligent enough to know that I was not talking about magic powers, and answered that most fine metal-working – and brewing – within the tribal territory was done under the control of the Druids almost as a state monopoly, whilst weaving, pottery and the salting of food (vital and profitable industries in any civilised economy) were done at a household level by the women of the tribe.

I took heart from this as what goods I carried in my ramshackle caravan were the things that most appealed to women and what talents I lacked as a spy were more than balanced by my skills as a salesman of fine table wares and delicacies. I was good at selling to women. And this Boudica – was she not a woman? From what Horas had told me, she sounded to be a woman I could do business with.

He described her as having a kindly, round face, framed by long strands of red hair hanging almost like curtains down to her waist. She was renowned as a cook within the Iceni lands and never happier than when teaching the young women of the tribe how to prepare the simplest of dishes, which she did slowly and with care so that even the most stupid of them could understand. Even if a wench had never stirred a pot in her life, following Boudica's instructions exactly would result in complete satisfaction. Her other love was her children, over whom she was fiercely protective, as unsophisticated mothers often are, willing to defend them instinctively, like a she-wolf or a newly delivered she-bear. The elder daughter, named Prisca, had been recently married to a man called Adminius whilst the younger, called Erda, was, not before time at the age of thirteen, betrothed to one of the young bucks of the tribe.

There was one other aspect of Boudica's character or reputation which is worthy of note. She has some skill in driving the Celtic chariot, if that indeed can be said to be a worthy asset for a woman. These chariots are light, their frames made of wickerwork and their floors suspended by hemp ropes and straps, so that to the occupants it must feel as if they are standing on springy marsh grass and they have to concentrate hard on keeping their balance, though the system is said to absorb the shocks of driving over rough ground much better than the more solid-frame racing chariots of Rome. They favour only two horses – the small shaggy ponies they breed and which are depicted on their coins – to pull them and the driving of them is a respected skill, much practised.

'If Oranius' directions are correct, we should be within the precincts of the Iceni's western camp by tomorrow night,' I observed.

'Then your honour may wish to dress more suitably for formal presentation to Queen Boudica.'

'If indeed she is a queen,' I said.

'It is best to be prepared for any eventuality,' he said, and I agreed with that.

But nothing could have prepared me for that first meeting with the Iceni and their queen.

It was the morning of the third day after leaving Oranius' personal outpost of the Empire and we had made an early start, our company oddly silent and uncomplaining. The early morning mist had risen from the bracken, which grew taller than a man in places, lining the trackway as it snaked across the heathland avoiding patches of dark brown marsh. So lush was the bracken it appeared as impenetrable as the thickest German forest and the only view I had was down the track in front of me; a view limited to the rear end of Ulpius' horse.

Suddenly I was presented with sight of Ulpius' own rear end as he leaned forward over the neck of his nag to peer at the ground beneath him. I had not expected the commander of a *colonia* Town Watch to have any skills in scouting or tracking, in fact I was mildly surprised that he had stayed on his horse for so long.

Twisting in his saddle, he shouted back: 'A cart has passed this way recently.'

From where I sat next to my driver (one or other of Dumno's sons) even I could make out the lines of wheel marks and the gouges of hooves in the damp, sandy earth.

'The road is not reserved for us,' I proclaimed loudly. 'We use it only so that it may bring us closer to our friends the Iceni.'

I just hoped that if anyone was hiding in the bracken, they were friendly, and they understood Latin.

'What's going on?' asked Calpurnius, who had left the second carriage and appeared walking at the side of our oxen.

'Our fearless bodyguard has made the discovery that there is other traffic on this road.' I was tempted to add that this was hardly any of his business, but now he was talking to me again, that would have been churlish.

'Those two back there – ' he jerked a thumb back towards Rogerus and Alcides – 'have been smelling natives since daybreak, or so they say.'

'Smelling them? Over their own stench?'

Calpurnius shrugged his bony shoulders and climbed, unbidden, on to the driving seat and then on to the roof, placing a hand on my forearm to help haul himself upright. Standing there, he shielded his eyes against the sun and gazed into the distance, over the bracken. The fine blond hairs on his thighs beneath the hem of his short tunic were level with my eyes.

'It was a chariot, with two ponies, not a cart,' he said.

'His eyes are young and sharp,' commented Horas from inside the carriage.

I did not add that they were also of the deepest blue, merely pointed out that this was a profound deduction to make from a few lines in the mud.

'I can see it,' said Calpurnius, 'up ahead, no more than a hundred paces away. They appear to be waiting for us; or rather he does. There's only one of them.'

'One man alone?' someone asked.

'Yes, but he's a big one.'

I gave orders that we should approach on foot: myself, Ulpius, Horas and Calpurnius. Dumno and his sons were to stay and guard the animals and carriages. Rogerus and Alcides were to guard Dumno and his sons. The arrangement seemed to suit all concerned.

We set off with a surprisingly sprightly step, following the trackway as it curved around a thicket of bracken and we glimpsed our first sight of the Iceni.

'We must demand an immediate audience with the Queen,' Horas whispered in my ear.

'We must plead for an audience,' I corrected him, 'at which we can pay our respects to the grieving widow.'

Neither plea nor demand was necessary for we were to meet the Queen of the Iceni there and then. Just as soon as she had finished pissing like a carthorse in the bracken, which was, thankfully, shoulder high.

XXIV: Roscius

How would I know what she looked like? I told you, I only saw her twice. The first time we were well over a mile away and believe me, that was as close as we wanted to get to that rabble. The last time was on the battlefield and we saw her driving off into the distance. Neither were what you might call social occasions – what does it matter anyway?

We knew it was her because of the chariot. She was driving and she had the two daughters in with her – that's how you knew it was Boudica – and she was always out in front when there was trouble, like she didn't worry about getting killed at all. There were those who said she was looking for it, but then there were those who said she had red hair because she washed it in Roman blood. People will say anything when something like Boudica happens and you historians usually believe it.

Say what you like about her – you will anyway. Say she was ten feet tall and built like a barracks latrine. Say she could fight six men at once whilst weaving a blanket and cooking a stew at the same time. Say that she slaughtered civilians by the thousand, because that's true, cutting the dicks off the men and throwing them to the hens, but treating the women even worse, especially those she thought had been to bed with a Roman. Those poor tarts had the breast sliced right off and then sewn into their mouths: to stop them suckling the enemy, see? Say that she breathed fire and farted sulphur. Say that she kept snakes in her hair and put swords on the wheels of her chariot – oh yes, I've even heard that one.

Say what you will. It's your history, you write it.

Truth is, I never got near enough to the bitch to look her in the face and I thank my ancestors for that. And by the time we'd finished with the Iceni, I doubt there was anyone left alive who could have told you what she looked like.

XXV: Olussa

'Come forward, strangers!' the warrior shouted to us.

'He is saying: "Advance, friends",' whispered Horas to me.

Just in time I stopped myself from revealing the fact that I could understand the big man's dialect, which was similar to the language of the more backward Belgic tribes I had traded with. They also used the same word for strangers as they did for friends; something which has always made me uneasy.

The man speaking dwarfed the two ponies whose bridles he was holding. He was the largest man I have ever seen – far larger than the thuggish Starbo – his shoulders and meaty arms straining under a bearskin cloak fastened on his chest with a large, circular bronze pin. He wore leather trousers and from his belt hung a leather scabbard containing a sword twice the length of a legionary *gladius*.

'He doesn't look disarmed to me,' I hissed at Horas.

'The carrying of arms is permissible for self-protection on a journey, under the edict of the great Caesar Julius,' he hissed back.

'I know that, but who told them? Announce us.'

He stared at me.

'As what?' said the old fool.

I stared at Horas but I had no time to summon up my anger, for the giant warrior, who was stroking the head of one of the ponies, almost oblivious to our approach, said, as if to his horses:

'They'll have come to see the new Queen, won't they, my lovely boys?'

I remembered to turn to Horas and not betray (yet) the fact that I understood him.

'He says—'

But before Horas could translate, Calpurnius hushed him with the command he had no right to give: 'Be quiet! Listen.'

We listened, all of us, to the sound of rushing water and instinctively we looked towards the two horses in their harnesses, but they were not the source of the stream, which ceased almost as soon as it had begun, to be followed by a loud rustling – the noise of bracken being trampled.

And then out of the bracken, near the giant warrior and the chariot, stepped a short woman smoothing down the folds of her skirts. She had a blank, round, moon of a face and long red hair which she wore in two plaited lengths draped over her ample bosom. When she spoke it was to the giant warrior, calling him by a name which sounds like Tarex.

'I feel much better for that. Come, Tarex, have you not welcomed our visitors?'

I did not comment at the time, of course, but I have since remembered that in some parts of the Empire whilst the native word for 'friend' might be the same as for 'stranger', very often the word for 'visitor' is the same as that for 'enemy.'

Thus were we formally presented to the new-elected (as we have since discovered) Queen of the Iceni; no fuss, no pomp. The renting of a prostitute in Londinium required more diplomatic ritual and ceremony, even south of the river.

Horas bowed to her and Ulpius slapped his right arm across his chest and then threw her a passable military salute, which drew a snort from the giant holding the horses and a flicker of a smile from the woman we were all staring at.

She spoke with the same lilting accent as her bodyguard, though softly and slowly, as though talking to a nervous child, and although she addressed Horas, her eyes were on each of us in turn. I think I did well to disguise the fact that I understood almost every word without having to wait for Horas' rather pedantic translation.

'I recognise you, old man. You were a house slave to a cousin of my husband many years ago,' she said, although this came out as 'a loyal and trusted servant' rather than slave in the Horas version. 'You were sold to the Trinovantes, I believe. You seem to have done well for yourself.'

The loyal dog of a servant bristled with pride that he had been recognised and I was not dismayed that he seemed to be the centre of attention, for it gave me a chance to cast a closer eye over this native queen. I was aware that as I did so, her bodyguard was casting a giant eye over us.

'I have a position of some trust,' said Horas, as near as I could understand. He was far from fluent in the dialect, which, after all, he had probably not spoken for some years.

'A trusted guide, to bring guests to the funeral,' said the woman quite calmly and with a certain dignity, then she smiled at Calpurnius (who did not understand a word) and added: 'Though he looks as if he could do with a decent meal right now.'

We were at a loss, for the situation was like nothing I had encountered before. In the middle of a heathland, miles from civilisation, we had stumbled – or had we? – across a woman who had no fear of us and had emptied her bowels virtually in front of us, who had one bodyguard whilst we were nine (although, like the gamblers in Camulodunum, I would have bet on the giant bodyguard to survive the dead pool rather than the nine of our shoddy fellowship), and yet there was no doubt that these were her woods, this was her heathland, we were on her trackway and we were her guests.

Perhaps that was what being a queen was all about. Instinctively we shuffled ourselves into a line so that we could be identified to her by Horas. I was naturally first (a much travelled merchant!), then Ulpius (representing the noble magistrates of Camulodunum) and finally Calpurnius (a noble youth in my employ!). I had to bite my tongue at Horas' descriptions and particularly that of me as a mere merchant, though it was the one thing he said which lit a distinct fire in the native woman's eyes.

She spoke rapidly to Horas who then said: 'Perhaps now would be a good time to call up the carriages and baggage. It is customary among these peoples to present a gift or two of goodwill.'

I agreed instantly and made a show of clapping my hands and instructing Calpurnius to run back along the track to lead on the others, if they were still there and sober.

I had not only seen it in her eyes, but I had understood what she had said to Horas after he had mentioned that I was a merchant. She had hissed, 'Does he have any free samples?'

I did not think I would have any trouble with this woman.

We reached the western Iceni settlement by mid-afternoon. It was hardly worth calling a village but it contained more people than we had seen since leaving the *colonia*.

I counted eight large round houses, all inhabited and with their roofs recently thatched and repaired, thin drizzles of smoke wafting skywards. As was the custom of nearly all the primitive tribes I had encountered, their doorways faced south-east. One structure was no more than a thatched canopy on four poles above a deep square pit cut into the sandy soil. A gentle fire smoked in the bottom of the pit to slowly cure the dozens of gutted eels suspended on twine from the thatch.

Native tribesmen, and particularly their women, reek of the smoke of their round houses, so much so that I have heard veterans speak of being able to smell a barbarian ambush before it was sprung. The smoke does, however, do much to discourage the lice which are rife in thatch, something I should perhaps point out to Dumno, his sons, Rogerus and Alcides.

I note this fact simply because I soon realised there was a different smell about Boudica who carried no trace of domestic smoke, but the strong sharp scent of pine. Perhaps it is some mark of status and I must remember to ask Horas about it.

Although she is short and plump, with an expressionless face and says little, Boudica certainly commands respect within her tribe. She neither wears nor carries any badge of office, although the giant warrior Tarex is never far from her shoulder. Her own forearms match his for muscles which can easily control the ponies pulling her chariot and balancing on its suspended wickerwork floor has given her a rolling gait when she walks. I have seen sailors walk the same way and it is not entirely due to drink.

We are given the use of a pen for our animals, which Dumno objects to, not wishing to be parted from his remaining mules. The Iceni – mostly women and children – take little interest in the mules or us, but they do eye the oxen with what appears to be envy. Under directions from the bodyguard Tarex, who continues to openly wear a sword even though he can no longer be said to be on a journey, we make our camp on the northern edge of the village. There is a trickle of a stream nearby but the water has a brownish tinge and tastes of iron and ash. Our animals, now penned with the Iceni ponies and a few milking sheep, have water from a dug channel which looks clean and clear. Rogerus and Alcides ask me for some samples of pottery so that they might trade for beer, which, they argue, will be safer than the water. Reluctantly I agree and supply them with some inferior cooking pots we were unable to offload on the Londinium market.

When examining our baggage out on the road, Boudica has already made it clear that she is impressed with the finer Samian ware and particularly a *mortaria* for grinding and mixing, such things being unknown in Iceni territory, indeed in all Britannia, which may explain much about their food.

And yet the smell of foodstuff cooking, sweetmeats and savouries, permeates the camp. They are preparing a feast but it is not in our honour.

XXVI: Olussa

To Valerius Lupus, Magistrate, Camulodunum
By the hand of Ulpius Frontius

Most noble Magistrate,

I write to report progress on our journey to the tribal lands beyond the outlying settlements where we have been greeted with all due dignity and hospitality, far more than our true station warrants as the Iceni have assumed we are an official delegation from the *colonia* to the funeral of their king, Prasutagus.

I have not disabused them of this notion and many of the presents and trade goods I have dispensed among them have been in your name. We can discuss terms of reimbursement on my return.

Such gifts have brought us close to the hearts of the Iceni and their new queen, Boudica, who met us on the road and escorted us herself to the western settlement which contains the royal family's hunting lodge and private temple. For the past three days the Queen has had to meet and greet visitors who are to attend the funeral. These have included another queen – Cartimandua, of the northern Brigantes, who has travelled far and fast with a large retinue of slaves and bodyguards to be here.

Other notables, at least among the natives, are a chieftain calling himself Tasciovanus, of the Trinovantes, who is known to Horas. He has made his feelings concerning all things Roman very clear but there are rules of hospitality and respect for the dead even among the savages, so for the moment, he behaves himself.

The so-called king of the Catuvellauni tribe is here too, one Verica, who has, from his appearance, demeanour and speech, adapted to life in the new town of Verulamium, which Horas tells me is built around the native's own settlement of Verlamion. This Verica is approachable and diplomatic in every way Tasciovanus is not and that the Trinovantine dislike him is plain for all to see. Horas maintains it is a tribal feud which dates back to before the arrival of the divine Claudius. In those days, the Catuvellauni saw Rome as a mortal enemy, whilst the Trinovantes saw her as a liberator. Now the positions seem reversed, with the Trinovantes spreading rumour and ill-will while the Catuvellauni have taken to the toga.

Yet we do not feel threatened. The Iceni seem to accept us and are openly curious in the way babies and dumb animals are.

Queen Cartimandua is also well known as an ally of Rome and has boasted within our presence that she has met the Governor, General Paulinus.

The king's funeral is to take place tomorrow and it is not before time, for the king's body, which lies in the temple here, is becoming ripe despite the constant burning of juniper wood and beeswax mixed with lavender.

We are unlikely to be allowed to witness the burial itself for the location of Prasutagus' grave is reserved for followers of the old religion and we are told that our presence would be an affront to the god of the woodlands which they call Faunus. I suspect that offending their gods is of little concern compared to knowledge of the location of the grave and its considerable grave goods, which will include much gold. In this, the Iceni have reason to mistrust the motives of some of our fellowship, who have already been caught attempting to barter my personal stock of preserves and spices for picks and shovels.

I trust you will inform my father by the earliest despatch to Londinium that I am well and have established excellent relations with the natives which promise much future trade. From what I have calculated so far, they can supply salt and small furs in quantities equal to the current trade for the whole province and abundant supplies of wool. They have horses in abundance, which surely must interest the Army quartermasters, as will the wheat and barley they grow in excess of their needs. In trade they are eager for fine-quality pottery, for their own is sandy and gritty in texture and decorated, if at all, with a monotonous circular device. All the women and especially the Queen herself have expressed a preference for the wares Alexander and Son can offer in fair trade.

Command my father that I see many opportunities here in the outlands beyond the *colonia.* There is much business to be done here and I remain his son, his agent, his partner, in good health.

Olussa

XXVII: Olussa

I have sent a despatch to Lupus at Camulodunum in order to keep Horas quiet. Since he witnessed the arrival of this Tasciovanus, accompanied by what looks like a war party of 'Trinnies' as Rogerus calls them, the old slave has been agitated beyond reason and anxious to inform his master of the fact that they are here and openly carrying weapons, though I am unsure as to whether the general edict to disarm applied to them as it did the Iceni.

They are without doubt a fearsome bunch, but they have brought gifts for the funeral as well as a cartload of amphorae of the finest Greek wine which, in all likelihood, has gone missing from a merchant's store in Camulodunum. Within the

Iceni encampment, which is growing daily, they behave themselves for the most part though they talk loudly in our presence about the tyranny of Roman taxes and Roman masters and Roman religion. The three things appear to be linked, their Roman masters insisting on higher taxes to pay for the new temple to the divine Claudius. They mutter darkly that 'things will change' and that there have been 'omens' and that they 'are ready'. I am sure they would regard a dog sniffing its own backside as an omen if the mood took them, but I promised Horas I would write to Lupus to keep him informed of the situation.

At least it keeps him quiet and it has the distinct advantage of getting rid of Ulpius, who has done nothing but skulk around the camp since we arrived. He is convinced we will be murdered in our beds and Alcides does not help matters by pointing out that the Iceni would prefer us to be standing when they behead us. Ulpius jumped at the chance to take my letter back to the *colonia* and I fear his poor horse is in danger of being ridden into the ground.

Boudica's personal guard, the giant Tarex, escorted him through the woods to the trackway we arrived on, which the Iceni refer to as The Pathway. All the tribes know this and use it for trade and, no doubt in less civilised times, for war. The Catuvellauni delegation under the chief Verica have followed it for several days from their tribal home around the second city of Verulamium, so this Pathway must stretch for well over a hundred miles to the south and west, where it is said to cut Route LXVI, the road the legions built from Londinium to the north-west frontier. Knowledge of such a trade route may well be of use in the future.

My ability to write and the Iceni's inability to read is a source of wonderment and amusement in the village. Almost all the children have attempted to copy my actions when writing with a stylus on wax, which I do not mind, though I am reluctant to let them see me making good copies on bark in ink, which I do in the privacy of my tent each night. Boudica has even brought her daughters to meet me and have me show them their names in script. The girls – princesses I suppose we must call them – are plain but not offensively so and fairly clean. The elder, Prisca – which is a name I have seen written many times in southern Gaul (usually on the walls of tavern latrines) – is, I would say, seventeen and married to a gentle, fair-haired boy called Adminius, who asks many questions about Roman law and customs. For his sake I pretend I am interested and answer honestly to the best of my ability (perhaps not all of it) and he is in awe of me. And why not? I have travelled the world – he has not left the forest. The younger brat is different entirely. This one is tall and thin and pale and has no manners, questioning everything I say but in the manner of an Imperial torturer, not a pupil. She does not wish to learn, merely to argue. Erda is thirteen and betrothed to a warrior, Togobin, twice her age. Boudica tells me (and by now she realises I can understand her, so we have no need for an official Horas translation) that Togobin's first wife died from blows to the head administered by her husband and this is just the sort of man to take control of the spirited Erda. I am unsure whether this is a joke I have misunderstood or a joke at all.

I have made a present to the queen of a flawed and slightly lopsided glass bowl which I picked up cheaply on credit in Camulodunum. Despite the bowl being flawed from the outset, an engraver with enthusiasm but not skill has taken some trouble to depict a pair of gladiators in combat and there is a crudely engraved legend running around the rim: *Moneo ut quis quem vicerit occidat*. When young Erda stabs in frustration at the engraving, for clearly she can think of no word for 'writing', I translate as best I can into the native tongue: *Give no quarter to the fallen no matter who he be.* Erda is unimpressed by the sentiment and shrugs her thin shoulders, saying to her mother, 'What's all that about, then?'

'It's a good rule of life,' Boudica tells her, avoiding my eye. 'Remember it well.' She looks at Erda's betrothed, Togobin, who has the hang-dog expression of a warrior returning from a battle on the losing side, and says: 'And you too.'

Togobin looks at his second-wife-to-be and sighs, already wearied by the future.

On another occasion, Boudica visits my tent after dark. She has her bodyguard Tarex with her (and by now I know that he does more to her body than just guard it) and he can only just squeeze through the flaps of the tent. When he is seated on the ground, the leather side walls bulge outwards. I am working by lamplight making good copies of my notes and I would have cleared away all my ink and writing equipment had I only heard them approach, but these Iceni can be quiet when they want to be, no matter what their size.

She makes herself comfortable, sitting cross-legged on the earth and moves her hand and wrist like a squirming snake. It is her way of signifying writing.

'*Scriptum*,' I tell her, pointing to the words and she repeats it until she is comfortable saying it. I have taught the Queen of the Iceni a new word.

'What is the point of this writing?' she asks, genuinely curious.

'It is so we can record the history of what has happened to us.'

'And so you will show these . . . pieces of writing . . . to others, so they may learn?'

'Yes. The writing can be made into a book and it can be read by people anywhere in the world.'

'In Rome?' She reaches out to touch the edge of a piece of bark as if it is magical, which to her it must be.

'Yes, even in Rome.'

I do not tell her that such is the general ignorance in Rome that even the highest classes prefer to be read to rather than do it themselves. Thus most of Rome's histories are written as if for the theatre: to be performed, not studied. Real life is rarely as dramatic as history.

'In our tribe, the Druids are the guardians of the stories; the stories of our past. They speak to us of events long ago. It is a skill which is taught from generation to generation and much valued.'

'I would be interested to hear these storytellers,' I say, but purely out of politeness.

'Oh you will,' growls Tarex, but then I realise he was not growling at me but has raised his eyes to the night sky and is allowing the shadow of a smile to play around his square, but by no means unhandsome jaw. 'Get the Druids talking and nothing will shut them up.'

The Queen takes up her braided hair and using it as a whip, strikes Tarex across the face. His smile becomes a lecherous grin and he nods his head towards the tent flaps and Boudica begins to get to her feet.

'I will arrange for stories to be told and we will leave you to your . . . writing.'

She stumbles over the new word but her smile turns her face into a friendly summer's moon, and then she is gone almost as silently as she arrived, with Tarex on her heels.

As if he had been waiting for them to leave, Horas bursts in on me and demands to know what the Queen wanted. I prevent him from entering – for I do not want him perusing these notes – and ease him outside into the night where we conduct our conversation in whispers.

'We talked of reading and of writing and how the Druids are the keepers of their history, but by recalling the legends of the past from memory, not from scripture.'

Whether Horas was satisfied with this answer or not I do not know. He puts one hand on my chest and raises a finger to his lips, demanding silence.

Over the night air comes the sound of male grunts and female howls in equal number. There is one thing not even the Iceni can do quietly, but where the sound of the love-making is coming from I cannot determine, other than that it is somewhere close by in the waist-high heather.

'That explains the scent of pine,' whispers Horas.

'It does?' I ask for I have no idea what he is talking about.

'On *her*. The smell of pine resin. The Iceni women rub it into their . . . their . . . wombs afterwards, to prevent babies.'

I think of Oranius' wife and her constant chewing of nettle seeds and now this revelation. What is it about the Iceni that made them so cautious about breeding? Does the whole tribe have a death wish of some sort?

Today was the funeral of King Prasutagus and though we were not expected to attend, we were expected to contribute.

I was awakened just before dawn by a terrified, near naked Calpurnius, who seemed to be trying to get into bed with me.

'Do not let them take me! Use the gold and save us all! Wake up, wake up!'

I was in too undignified a position to remonstrate with him with any authority but eventually I wrestled him off me, put a foot in his stomach and pushed, so that he went sprawling against the tent skins.

As I stood, pulling a blanket around me against the morning chill, Calpurnius flung himself to the ground and grovelled at my feet. His thin frame was wracked with huge sobs as he clawed at the sandy dirt. He was wearing only threadbare underwear – some of father's cast-offs I suspected, knowing how he had always spoilt the boy – which suggested he too had been disturbed from his, or somebody else's, bed.

'What have you done, now?' I asked him sternly, but stroking the nape of his neck to calm him down. He began to kiss my hands.

'They've come for us, the men in black.'

'Don't be a blockhead,' I soothed, but through the tent flaps I could see the flicker of torchlight against the slowly brightening sky.

'Roman! Are you awake, or taking your beauty sleep?' came a voice and it was a voice of authority, one used to commanding an audience if not an army.

I flung a cloak around my shoulders and stepped out into the morning to face Calpurnius' spectre.

'I am no Roman, but I am awake,' I answered loudly in the Iceni tongue.

The two men awaiting me were indeed dressed in black robes, as were the dozen or so figures at a distance, forming a rough circle around our little encampment. Some held torches, but none had weapons I could see. At least three of the black figures were female. Calpurnius' men in black were Druids and the women in black were their witches.

'If not Roman, what are you?' asked the taller of the two figures confronting me and for a moment I was shocked for the priest spoke in Latin. True, it was kitchen Latin at its roughest and bluntest, but Latin nonetheless, signifying something far more dangerous than swords and spears: learning.

'I am a Greek, from a country superior to Rome in every way except power and influence,' I replied in Greek.

My inquisitor maintained his dignity and kept a straight face though it was clear to me he had not understood a word. A man with less than two languages should not cross wits with one who commands six or seven.

Eventually the tall, thin Druid nodded his head and slipped back into his native tongue.

'I am told you are Olussa, sent from Rome if not of Rome.'

I acknowledged the point, replying in the Iceni dialect.

'The Romans call me *peregrinus*. I am of the world of Rome but not a citizen,' I said, though now I was the one struggling to translate. 'A Roman who is not a Roman.'

'A Lost Roman?' he said in all seriousness.

'In your tongue, that is perhaps the best way to say it,' I admitted.

'I am Aneurin,' he continued sternly, 'High Priest of the Iceni, nephew to Queen Boudica and cousin of King Prasutagus.'

At least that is what I think he said. In less than a week I have learned that these backwoods folk are vague on actual family relationships, though they value clans and kinsfolk highly.

I acknowledged him with a short bow. He is not a noble fellow, this Aneurin. Tall and wiry with a head of black curls and a short black beard which is crisp enough to have been cut by the priciest Spanish barber.

I was wrong about him being unarmed. As the dawn broke around us, I could see something glistening at his belt in the watery light. He carried a curved dagger; curved like the blade of a scythe or a small hand sickle. I learn later that this is used by the Druids for pruning their sacred plant mistletoe – a weed which attaches itself to healthy trees and lives off them. It is a very impractical weapon for combat and no match for the blade I have strapped to my arm, but it has other qualities and it glints because it is made of gold.

'We have come to perform the sacred ceremonies which will take King Prasutagus into the Other World,' he said, full of solemnity and reverence. 'You must entrust us with your parting gift for the burial grove is sacred and forbidden to all but his tribe.'

To make sure I got the point, his shorter, older, companion held out a hand towards me, like a crow proffering a claw.

I gestured them to wait and plunged back into the tent,

tripping over Calpurnius, who was still sobbing quietly in a heap on the ground.

'What do they want?' he asked me, his voice trembling.

'Your head if you don't behave,' I snapped and, kicking him away, I began to scrabble at my luggage. I had removed it from our carriage as soon as we arrived so I could keep an eye on my three remaining bags of the Procurator's gold.

I correct myself. My *one* remaining bag of the Procurator's gold and, such is my luck, it was the bag of shavings, ingot scraps and sweepings from the floor of the Imperial mint at Antioch. I was speechless with rage. My personal possessions have been violated, not once, but many times along this journey.

I kicked Calpurnius again for relief and took the solitary bag outside to where the circle of crows has drawn tighter, like a noose. As far as I could tell, my trusted advisor Horas, not to mention my so-called bodyguards Rogerus and Alcides, slept on.

Aneurin the Druid and his smaller shadow had not moved. The small one's talons still outstretched. I prepared to make my speech but my mouth was dry.

'I am a stranger in a strange land,' I said, 'and I came to trade with the living, not to honour the dead. But the dead must be honoured, especially when high born and of rank and so, unprepared though I am, and poor merchant that I am, I offer these few scraps of gold, which is poor tribute I know, but all that I have.'

Despite the eloquence of this sentiment, which would have been much more impressive declaimed in Greek or even Latin at a pinch, the smaller black crow snatched the bag from my hand like a forum thief and pulled at the draw strings.

'Excellent!' he said when he looked inside and for a moment I thought I had misunderstood, but no, he was genuinely delighted.

'The perfect gift for the king's journey!'

I was still confused but the tall and serious Aneurin explained and his voice had a strange lilting quality almost as if everything he said was a confidence he was sharing.

'This is Esico, goldsmith and coinmaker to the king. He follows the old beliefs that no king should go to the Other

World without gold which can be fashioned for him by the smiths and coinmakers who await him. It is a belief these workers in metal hold dear and this is truly a noble gift for the king to take with him.'

It is they who now bowed to me.

'We will return by nightfall for the feast,' said Aneurin and he and the Druids faded away into the village and the breaking dawn.

It is said that it is better to have luck than good intentions and I feel I have proved that axiom.

I came here as a spy, was greeted as a mere merchant, and now am an honoured guest at a royal funeral feast.

I looked across into the animal pen and noticed that two of our oxen are missing. I suspect we will be eating beef tonight.

XXVIII: Valerius Lupus

By Imperial Post. Most urgent and strictly private.
To Narcissus Alexander, Merchant, Londinium.

Dearest and oldest of friends,

I bring you news of your son, who is alive and well and instructs me to tell you such and to say that his business plans are continuing with good fortune. I know not what Olussa's plans are, either his business venture or whatever mission he may have undertaken for a higher authority, but I bring you his words, along with my own, for I do fear for his safety.

He has travelled far from the security of the *colonia* into Iceni territory and has sent a dispatch with one of my most trusted officers. This officer informs me that Olussa has been bewitched by the Iceni queen Boudica and takes an unmanly interest in her and the tribe's way of life, seemingly oblivious to the dangers that both surround him and that approach him. My officer, who was at his side barely ten days ago, claims he is more interested in the cooking skills and pottery requirements of the women of the Iceni than he is concerned for his own safety. Perhaps I should have warned him more strongly when he was in Camulodunum, but he is beyond my counsel now.

The news may have reached Londinium – I know not – but the king of the Iceni, the rich and always compliant Prasutagus, has died. For his funeral, the tribes are gathering from far and wide, including some of our local troublemakers from the Trinovantes, whose sole purpose is to stir up dissent and resentment against Imperial rule.

Into this cauldron now enters the Procurator who, as you will know, left Londinium with a force of special police and is presently quartered (at my expense) here in the *colonia*. His intention is to enforce the conditions of King Prasutagus' will, or rather to enforce the logical conclusions of that will under Imperial Law.

That he has the law on his side is not in doubt, but I fear that with civil unrest growing to alarming levels among the Trinovantes here, and the Governor still far to the west on campaign, this is not the wisest of times to unsettle the Iceni, after so many years of peace. Yet he is determined on an expedition into the tribal lands, where your son innocently waits.

I intend to write to Petillius Cerialis, the Legate of the IXth Legion, who commands the closest troops to our situation. In the meantime, dear friend, I wish you to take the enclosed bills of credit and promissory notes all drawn on members of the Merchants' Guild of Londinium, and go to the forum and get for them in goods or cash what you can. I would expect you to secure such goods or monies until I can send you further instructions or collect them in person. This would be, of course, minus your usual handling fee.

Your friend from the past and always of the future,
Valerius Lupus.

XXIX: Roscius

Legio IXth Hispana? Yes, I knew those boys. A funny bunch, mostly from Pannonia on the Danube. We used to say the IXth was always trying to be something it wasn't – the XXth! Get it? Please yourselves.

At the time in question, the IXth was based at Durobrivae so they could cover the north-eastern arc of the military frontier, in a temporary fortress that probably isn't there now. Their legate was Quintus Petillius Cerialis Caesius Rufus, a right Patsy, but he really was well-connected. He survived more battles when his men didn't than any officer has a right to, however high born. That was his trick. He survived, his poor bloody infantry didn't.

He went on to become Governor of Britannia, you know, well, yes, of course you do, you're historians, aren't you?

Not that there is much in the official histories about what happened to the IXth or even where it happened. It must have been three or four months afterwards before a funeral detachment went looking for them and they didn't find much. A few bits of bodies hanging in the trees were recognisable as men but not as people, the rest were just lumps of meat and bone or whatever the animals of the forest had left. All the armour and weapons had gone of course, mind you, that was to be expected, but it was said they never found a head – not one.

There's a thought for you: those fucking Druids carting off two – three? – thousand heads. They would have needed a few carts, I can tell you that. And what for? What do you do with that many heads?

I mean, I can understand it if, say, you were besieging a town. A dozen or so heads chucked over the walls by catapult – that's a good trick. Puts the shits up the defenders, that's for sure. I've done that in my time, but this was just butchery for the sake of it.

It was bloodlust gone mad. Mind you, it scared the bowels out of Petillius. He galloped back to his fortress, strengthened the walls and stayed there for the rest of the year just about. General Paulinus had to order him out when it was all over; threatened to go in and drag him out if he didn't come willing.

Not exactly a noble war record for old Petillius, though he wasn't the only officer you could say that about.

Agricola? No, he behaved himself; just followed orders. Tell the truth I never thought Agricola had the imagination to be scared by what we were up against. Just as well. You need soldiers like that on every campaign.

I know you're his son-in-law, so I know that he'll come

out of it smelling sweetly, whatever I say. He's paying you to write this, isn't he?

The only thing I want is some credit to go to the foot-sloggers for once. They are the ones who did for that barbarian bitch after others had stirred her up.

Those men Catus took into the Iceni lands – the Procurator's Special Police they called them – scum of the sewers they were. Don't you dare refer to them as soldiers. Lions in the arena would have turned their noses up at most of them. Deserters, pirates, bandits, escaped slaves, you name it. They were in it for anything they could get. No discipline and no balls either when the chips were down.

Actually, quite a lot of them really didn't have any balls when Boudica had finished with them.

That slime deserved all they got for what they started.

But it was only to be expected, sending the wild bunch in there. It was always going to end in tears.

Our job was to make sure they were Boudica's, not Rome's.

XXX: Olussa

The funeral has taken place with due reverence but the funeral feast was one of the wildest orgies of food and drink I have ever attended, and that includes a wine-pressing festival in Pompeii and *Saturnalia* in Syracuse one year.

The beer has been flowing all day – wheat beer, rye beer, and strong beer thickened with oats. With the funeral feast has come wine, a much-travelled if unspectacular vintage which is decanted out of amphorae marked with the official CB stamp of the *Classis Britannicus*, and, strongest of all, they serve mead fermented from honey, after which it is impossible to taste food properly, but by now few are in a state to eat.

The Iceni are naturally showing off to the representatives of the other tribes as well as providing Prasutagus with a good send off to the Other World. I cannot assess how impressed they are by the feasting, for the Trinovantes and the Catuvellauni contingents, who are both used to Roman standards and the civic amenities of towns, will have tasted better and more exotic things. The Brigantes from the north are solely interested in quantity, not quality, in both food and beer, but mainly beer, and they are suspicious of food they do not recognise, which means they mostly eat my oxen and they treat the appetiser with suspicion, which is their loss for the Iceni have brought fresh crabs from the coast which they serve simply boiled with a vegetable they call samphire, a smaller and coarser relative of asparagus.

The funeral was, as they always are, an occasion not for the dead, but for the living; for the living to show off their wealth, their position and the fact that they are still alive.

There is one two-storey building in the village, approached by an avenue of planted saplings and protected by a triple ditch, though the ditches are for keeping animals in rather than intruders out. This building, which dominates all the other round houses, is where they stored the dead king. Only the Druids and Boudica and her family were allowed in there until now, when the king is carried out for his last journey. The pall-bearers are clearly of the warrior caste and are dressed in their most colourful clothes and finest furs. From their cloaks, and indeed from their beards and hair, hang dozens of small gold bells which tinkle as they move. It is perhaps the only time anyone will be able to hear an Iceni warrior approaching.

Tarex the bodyguard – and former champion of the king I learn – leads them and I recognise Boudica's son-in-law, Adminius, and son-in-law-to-be Togobin among those shouldering the hefty planks on which the shrouded body is balanced.

With due reverence the corpse is placed on the back of a cart drawn by two washed and groomed ponies, their bridles and bits glistening with gold decoration and the cart itself bedecked with yellow heather, holly and ivy strands twisted into ropes.

Our view of what happens is restricted by six of Aneurin's Druid acolytes, who form a line which clearly tells us thus far but no further, as the king is prepared for his last journey.

One by one, every member of the Iceni and the representatives of the visiting tribes, approaches the cart and places an offering. For some it is a handful of grain, for others a simple hand-made beaker, several present bronze-backed mirrors. For Esico, the goldsmith, it is the familiar purse of gold shavings swept from the floor of the Antioch mint, to which he adds a fired crucible and a pair of metal tongs. I doubt whether any other gift will have come so far to be buried in this damp outpost on an island at the edge of the world.

Boudica and her family finally approach in procession from the two-storey pavilion. The crowd, by now several hundred in number, though I have no idea where they have all come from, is open in its appreciation of the ritual gifts which will accompany their king to his grave. They mutter approval and gasp aloud and there is no wailing or tearing of clothes, as there would be at a Roman funeral, but in truth there is much to impress them.

The queen and her two daughters are dressed in highly patterned woollen dresses which have been dyed with every colour in a rainbow's arc. They too have small bells sewn on to the material as well as gold and silver braiding in the famous Celtic double circle pattern. They wear heavy necklaces of shells hanging low on their bosoms, but no one pays them much attention for all eyes are fixed on the torcs of twisted gold, thicker than a man's arm, at their throats. From the way the younger girl walks, it is an effort to hold her head up such is the weight of wealth around her neck and I cannot help thinking that this would make a fine dowry indeed – all three of them would buy a consulship. And then I notice there is a fourth, grander and heavier than the others, which Boudica is carrying in her hands in front of her body, turning this way and that as she walks to allow the crowd a glimpse, drawing many a grunt of admiration.

Behind me, in the little enclave into which we have been herded by the priests, I hear Rogerus gasp, but in greed not admiration.

Boudica reaches the funeral cart and places the torc she is carrying on the shrouded chest of her late husband. The cart has been lined with herbs and wild garlic from the woods and several of the Druids have started small incense fires, so the smell of the king is just tolerable. She then removes the torc from her throat and lays that next to the first, larger, one. Her daughters follow suit.

The final touches are from Tarex and the pallbearers who

place in the cart two spears, a large oval shield with a painted boss and, wrapped in linen, though it is first shown to the crowd, a long sword in a leather scabbard decorated with bronze clasps.

It is Aneurin who leads the ponies and cart away, although another horse is brought through the village – a fine mare with some breeding – and its bridle tied to the rear of the cart. The horse sniffs the air and its nostrils flare at the scent of death.

It is the normally mute Dumno who whispers: 'What a fine animal. Too good to waste like this.'

I realise that they intend to slaughter the beast and bury it with the king.

'Give them one of your mangy mules instead!' Alcides suggests and I curse them to be quiet and show some respect for the dead, or at least until the living are out of earshot.

The crowd forms into a column to follow the funeral cart as it disappears along one of the tracks to the north, into the high bracken and the darker forest beyond. Yet before it has gone from sight, a dozen or more women and young boys begin to urge us back to our campsite and to tempt us they have plates of food and jugs of beer. It is hardly the fourth hour of the morning, the sun still well short of its midday height, and the drinking has already begun.

The funeral feast proper did not begin until about the tenth hour, by which time the women and boys left in the village had placed torches on every vantage point and used carts with no wheels and planks laid between tree stumps as tables, covering every surface with prepared dishes. When the wind had changed in the afternoon we were able to smell the fire pit at the other end of the village where one of our oxen had duly sacrificed himself in the name of Prasutagus. We were encouraged not to stray from the area of our tents and food, beer and wine were brought to us in a constant stream. It was clear from the gestures of the women that we were expected to sit and wait for the real funeral guests to return from whatever they were doing in the forest. Although no guards were put on us, I had no doubt that the younger boys had instructions to run for help should we attempt to follow the procession.

Having finished his third flagon of beer, Rogerus rose unsteadily to his feet.

'They don't trust us, do they? These barbarian bastards don't trust us enough to let us see where they are burying all that gold. To hell with them!'

I have no doubt he would have fallen over without the vicious clip around the ear he received from the odious Alcides who hissed: 'Shut your fucking mouth, you blockhead! I don't trust you, why should they?'

The heroic dwarf then planted a boot firmly into Rogerus' stomach, before pulling him up by an arm and leading him to the tent they shared muttering that it was time 'to sleep it off' before the serious drinking began that night.

I did not see Boudica return until the feasting was well underway and night had fallen. By then our little party had built its own fire and we were joined by the goldsmith Esico and the betrothed Togobin, possibly seeking sanctuary from his future wife, as well as a pair of Trinovantes, probably there to keep an eye on us, and six or seven Druid priests who were keeping watch over the Trinovantes.

Any questions about the funeral itself were discouraged by the Druids who preferred to call loudly for more beer and then distracted us with interminable stories of Iceni history. Had the food not been so good, the night not dry and the beer and wine never-ending, we would have been bored to death, but there was no escape now that they realised I understood their language and, as Horas pointed out, since they have no written history, these stories were important to them and it was only polite to listen.

So listen we did – for hours – to the story of a prince and his three brothers out hunting when they meet an old hag who demands that they make love to her. Only one does and so he, of course, turns out to be the true king, whereupon the old hag turns into a beautiful princess (if you hadn't guessed) and takes her suitor to a house with a ridge pole of white gold (at least I think that was what the storyteller said) and in this house she conjures down the smoke hole the ghost of the late king, his father. We all snorted and grunted our approval of this story, though I doubt even the Iceni knew what it was supposed to mean. And then there was the mildly interesting tale of the Celtic god who showed men the secret of brewing beer, when a flooded grain pit was burnt out (as is the annual custom to clear any rotting grain) and how the combination of water and then fire on the barley corns had produced a sweet malt from which beer could be made. And I liked the legend of the blacksmith who posed the riddle to his king that he could pull a sword out of a stone, meaning that he knew the secret of smelting iron from the ore-bearing rock. That one, I felt had promise as a test in a philosophy class, but I did not understand at all the tale of the warrior who went bear hunting, demanding of the gods that they give him 'the biggest fucking spear there is'. Despite the size of his weapons, this warrior was always being defeated by the cunning bears of the forest, and punished in a truly bestial way. The natives laughed almost until seizures took them at this and Horas whispered to me that it was not a part of their spoken history, but a joke of some sort. I racked my brains for a joke I had once heard and began to tell them of the Roman who sets out to walk into Gaul and of the Gaul who sets out to walk to Rome, and how they pass each other without acknowledging each other on the Alps, but I forgot what happens next and this turned out to be funnier than the joke could ever have been for wine was called for this time and I received many hearty thumps on the back.

In a moment of clear-headedness whilst I was relieving my bladder into a boundary ditch, I discovered Calpurnius was of like mind and for a while we played 'crossing the streams' – something we had not done for many years.

'You are popular with the natives,' he told me. 'A real diplomat. Old Horas is quite jealous of you.'

'I bring gifts, I eat their food without complaint and I listen to their stories,' I said, although the words seem to be slow in emerging from my mouth. 'What more is there to being a diplomat?'

'We shall see,' he said and then was gone.

His warning, if that is what it was, comes back to me with the next morning's dawn as I am booted awake, though neither body nor mind responds well, and I feel a hand grab my ankle and I am hauled across the ground. All I can think of is that an exotic bird must have somehow died in my mouth, and some time ago at that, probably whilst I was crossing a desert, for I am in desperate need of a draught of water.

My wish is granted surprisingly soon as I am lifted into the air by the grip on my leg and my head is lowered into the iron-coloured brackish stream which trickles across our campsite.

Despite what the Romans say I do not hold that a death can be dignified, at least not mine, and not by drowning in a few fingers of water, so I struggled and kicked as wildly as I could and my reward was to be dumped on my back in the stream which had obviously been used by several creatures for the emptying of their bowels, and not all of them had been animals.

'Are we awake, Roman?' boomed a voice like thunder in my ear.

I felt sick and promptly vomited into the stream. The air shook with noise which I gradually realised was laughter. It seemed the whole Iceni nation was gathered to witness my humiliation at the hands – or hand – of the giant Tarex, for it was he who had dragged me from my sleep. Calpurnius and Horas were in the crowd too, but neither were enjoying my discomfort which I mistakenly presumed was out of loyalty to me.

'You'd better count your people,' Tarex shouted at me, bending so that his grizzled face could be near enough to mine for me to smell his stale-beer breath.

I began to splutter that I did not understand and then I caught the flickering of Calpurnius' eyes to something over towards the north end of the village. Tarex hauled me to my feet so that I could see better, but so shocked and weak was I that I had to lean against his chest to remain upright.

'See?' the giant breathed in my face. 'You lost a fine pair during the night. A pair of night owls out hunting on forbidden land.'

Coming through the heather and into the village, the crowd parting in silence to make way, was small, deformed Alcides flanked by two pairs of Iceni men still in their funeral best dress but carrying short hunting bows, with arrows notched. Alcides had blood flowing down his face from a wound on his scalp yet it did not deter him, though the bowmen gave him little choice, from his task of dragging an inert figure along the ground after him. All I could see were the soles of two boots in Alcides' hand. I knew the body he was dragging was that of Rogerus and was, in truth, unsurprised to find on closer inspection that there were three feathered shafts protruding from the chest. He was no longer burdened with the 'II' brand on his forehead, for his corpse no longer had a head.

Alcides sank to his knees and let go of his burden.

From the crowd the gaunt figure of Aneurin stepped forward.

'Do you know what these wretches have done?' he asked me.

'I can guess,' I replied.

And then Alcides began to babble, blowing and snorting the blood away from his mouth.

'You know what we're here for and it's not to swap recipes with these people. You should make up your mind which side you're on before they get here.'

I levered myself away from Tarex and planted my feet apart which gave me some semblance of authority

'What is the penalty for . . .?' I could not think how to say 'desecration' so that they would understand, and Horas, from the crowd, had to supply the word.

When Aneurin said 'Death', it needed no translation.

I nodded once and drew my finger across my throat; even as I did so I felt Tarex move behind me and heard him unsheathing his sword.

'Make it quick!' I shouted, and Tarex did so. There was a murmur of approval at my pronouncement from the Iceni and then a collective intake of breath as Tarex's blade flashed and the head of Alcides flew from his shoulders, over a fence and into the animal pen.

The Druid Aneurin nodded to me as if to say I had made the right decision. I already knew I had; I wanted Alcides dead before any of them realised what he was talking about.

During the next night, Dumno and his two sons left the village taking their remaining mules with them. The Iceni men are impressed with this feat. So confident are they that no one could approach the village without them knowing, they had not considered the possibility of someone leaving it so quietly. Where they have gone or why I do not know, although Calpurnius says Dumno was upset by the fact that Alcides' head had landed among his mules and it was some time before he could get them to stop playing with it.

On the whole, yesterday was a quiet day. A very public execution before breakfast dampens the spirits, although the Brigantes, preparing to leave for home, thought the spectacle was laid on as a parting gift. Queen Cartimandua, wrapped in furs and mounted on a pony sturdy enough to carry both her and the weight of her jewellery, paused in her procession to congratulate Tarex on his swift and clean stroke. She even said that that was what she called entertainment.

Tasciovanus, the surly chieftain of the Trinovantes, rode his horse as close to Alcides' body as possible without trampling it, then he pointedly looked over to where Horas and I stood and levelled a finger in our direction as if to say that we were next. Horas took this almost as if one of the Druid witches had cursed him and disappeared inside his tent faster than a scalded cat and he took much persuading to come out again until he was sure the Trinovantes had left the village. I think only the prospect of meeting them on the road back to the *colonia* prevented him from leaving as well.

I made Calpurnius build up a fire and heat clean water in the largest pots he could find, so that he could wash me all over as well as my clothes, removing the stains I had received from my own erupting stomach, from the stream I had been near drowned in and several sprays of blood, which I took to be from Alcides.

It was a poor substitute for a visit to a proper bath-house (one of the few truly great marks of Roman civilisation) but it proved just as public. Calpurnius had found a large deep dish in which I could stand while he poured hot water over my shoulders and rubbed oil into my back. There was little the boy did not know of the art of oiling and I was grateful that my loincloth protected my decency and disguised my lust. It was as he was scraping the dirty oil from my back and using my long-bladed knife to do so, that we were approached by Boudica with a retinue which included her daughters in tow. The elder, Prisca, for once did not have her husband with her, but still made a show of averting her eyes from my toilet. Erda had no such modesty, giggling wide eyed as Calpurnius massaged my body as if it was the most unnatural thing in the world.

I acknowledged the Queen's presence but she raised a hand as if in apology, not wishing to interrupt us. She watched Calpurnius carefully, especially when he wiped off the oily blade on his own tunic.

'So you do have one slave that you can trust,' she said, confident that the boy could not understand, though I was sure he was picking up the dialect almost as quickly as I was.

Many a noble I knew would have agreed with her and much mutual moaning about how difficult it was to find good slaves these days would have followed. But before I could explain that I am not a slave-owner of any importance (for Calpurnius, in law, belongs to my father) Boudica summoned from the crowd around her two young warrior types. The Celts as a rule do not go in for body armour, but warriors are easily distinguished by thick leather sleeveless coats which they wear open to reveal their manly chests, often painted or tattooed. These two, both healthy, fair-haired specimens, looked the part, complete with red and blue chequered trousers tied at the knee with leather gaiters, long drooping moustaches and long broadswords in decorated scabbards hanging from their belts.

'I cannot replace your slaves,' said the Queen, 'but I can provide these two guards. Their names are – '

But their Celtic names defeated even me. 'I thank the Queen of the Iceni,' I said formally from my shallow bath. 'I shall call them Nero and Claudius.'

Behind me Calpurnius snorted in derision.

'Haven't you always wanted to give Nero one up the arse? Well, now you can,' he hissed with malicious glee.

XXXI: Olussa

They say there is a special part of Hell reserved especially for criminals. It is true, I have spent two days there.

I write what I write now while it is still fresh on the eye

and sour on the memory, though there is no one to read it and perhaps never will be but I have witnessed terrible things and must be a witness for history, even if only my history. So I write what I saw and what was said.

Catus Decianus, noble Procurator of Britannia, appointment of the Roman Senate and second only in rank to the Governor of the province, rode into the village yesterday morning, two hours after dawn. He had with him some thirty men who gave the appearance of auxiliary light cavalry, lightly armoured and carrying long spears, round shields and short swords. And though he wore an armoured visor on his helmet to hide his face, there was no hiding the bulk of that thug, thief and most likely assassin, Starbo.

My one cheerful thought was that Starbo would meet his match in the even larger Tarex but as the Iceni gathered to meet their visitors, the Iceni warrior was nowhere to be seen.

I had ordered Claudius and Nero to stay close to our diminished encampment and now I took young Nero by the shoulders and demanded to know where the late king's champion was.

'Gone to his farm,' said the boy, 'to supervise his slaves and the planting of his crops. It is two days walk to the north from here.'

'Then you had better run. But go slowly and quietly until you are out of sight. Bring Tarex. Tell him his queen needs him.'

The boy was too confused to question me and disappeared behind our tents and not before time for I was halted in my tracks by the sound of my name.

'Olussa the merchant! A man who owes me money!'

He kneed his horse forwards and reined it in until its nostril breath was close enough to warm my face.

'Well, Olussa, I trust you have enjoyed your little holiday among the savages.'

'Procurator, I have much to report but my official report will need tabulating before I can—'

'Just tell me where my gold is.'

'What little I had left on my arrival here has been put to good use. For the rest, it might be prudent to enquire amongst your own men.'

'Prudent! Don't you dare tell me to be prudent, you vulgar little foreigner.'

And with that the Procurator of all Britannia planted the sole of his boot in my face and all was darkness.

I awoke in my tent, lying on the ground with a rolled up sheepskin for a pillow. Claudius, my personal Iceni warrior, was kneeling over me, wiping my face with a damp cloth. My fingers met his and I could trace the individual impressions of the hobnails left by Catus' boot. Of Horas and Calpurnius there was no sign.

Claudius put his finger to his lips and then pointed to the tent flap. Lying on my belly I then witnessed what befell the Iceni in all its shame.

Catus had ridden straight into the village with only a third of his force, to test his reception among the Iceni. Amongst his riders was the muleteer Dumno, uncomfortably perched on a horse for once, who must have run into the Procurator on the trail.

As usual, Fortune favoured the evil, for there were not more than ten adult men among the Iceni, all of them stooped and toothless and I had only seen Claudius and Nero carrying arms. When the thug Starbo realised this, he blew sharply on a wooden whistle and from north and south there appeared more men, similarly armed and dressed in a mixture of military cast-offs. In total Catus commanded more than a hundred of these mounted pirates and the Iceni village, and Queen, were at his mercy.

The Iceni, curious to see their visitors (ironically, their word for enemies) gathered in the centre of the village and instinctively formed themselves into a circle around Boudica and her daughters. There was no sign of Prisca's husband Adminius, nor of young Erda's betrothed. Like the other warriors, Togobin had land and slaves to see to elsewhere.

Without dismounting, his horse actually pushing against the massed villagers, Catus announced that he had come to claim for Rome that which was Rome's, which in fact was everything and that all lands and goods owned by the royal family were from this moment forfeit.

The Iceni showed little sign of understanding Catus' address, though his intentions seeped through in his curt manner and obvious disdain. The villagers began to wail and shout their objections, which only caused Starbo and several other riders to start laying about them with dog whips.

Then I heard a familiar voice above the tumult. It was Horas, declaiming like an actor and translating what Catus had just ordered. He added that to resist the law of Rome would be futile. Ever the loyal civil servant, Horas had offered his services before Catus had got off his horse and I noticed that his horse was now being held at the bridle by none other than Calpurnius. How soon one is alone.

But I was forgotten in the heat of the moment.

Catus gave orders and his men charged through the village, securing the perimeter. A squad of them fell upon one of our carriages – fortunately not the one in which I had stored my copied notes – and dragged it with some effort, for these were not the fittest of soldiers, to the path leading to Boudica's two-storey residence.

Catus' instructions did not really need translation – he was ordering the carriage to be filled with whatever was not tied down. Other men were already into the animal pens, throwing rope halters over horses and milk cows and tying the hind legs of sheep and pigs together. The few ducks and hens which roamed free in and about the round houses fared less well. Most had the necks wrung or their throats slit on the spot.

All this the Iceni took in stoic silence. It was behaviour they were probably familiar with from raids by other barbarian tribes in the past, raids which Roman Law was supposed to have brought to an end, and the confiscation of their livestock was only the beginning.

The killing started when Catus' men rushed towards Boudica's lodge. The first to enter let out a scream such that it halted for a brief moment the melee between the mounted troops and the villagers and all eyes turned towards it.

We saw the lead soldier staggering backwards out of the lodge, a long pig-sticking spear protruding from both his chest and back. The man screamed something none of us understood. It may have been a call to one of the gods, it may have been the name of his mother, for it is said that is very common when men of violence die by violence. His companions, three or four of them nearby, made no move to help him. They simply checked their run into the lodge and waited. Which was the clever thing to do as it is true what they say about the fearless Celts – they cannot resist getting in among their enemies.

It was Adminius who had speared that first man and now he came tearing out of the lodge wielding a long sword, determined to take on the whole of Catus' force. He engaged the nearest one and with a slashing blow removed his opponent's sword arm and caught a second across the face, removing most of his lower jaw. He used his shoulder, for he had no shield, to bowl a third over and then he paused long enough to swipe at the man's hamstrings as he lay prone.

Beside me, young Claudius screamed in anger and began to draw his sword, but I grabbed his wrist and ordered him to wait, for neither he nor Adminius had seen what I had.

In the central confusion where horses now bucked and men shouted and women and children ran without direction, a single figure stood out of the crowd in my eyes. Amidst the dust and noise there was Calpurnius holding on to the bridle of Catus' horse with one hand and pointing, arm outstretched, towards the Princess Prisca.

Ever the helpful servant, Calpurnius handed Catus' men the advantage which they seized with speed and violence. Prisca was cut out of the crowd like a troublesome animal, forced to her knees and a sword held at her throat. Seeing this, the child bride Erda flung herself on to the back of one of her sister's attackers, screeching like the Druid witches are supposed to do in battle, but with little effect as her opponent was able to throw her over his shoulders with ease.

Most spectacular was the Queen herself. Hemmed in by riders, Boudica chose to attack the nearest horse rather than horseman. Scooping up a large pebble from the ground, she swung her fist in a boxer's blow on the jaw of the nearest horse. Stunned or surprised or both, the horse staggered sideways by which time Boudica had it by the bridle and was pulling downwards. The horse buckled and collapsed, its rider tumbling at her feet. With a speed my eyes could not believe she stamped a foot across the rider's windpipe then relieved him of his sword and returned it to him through his stomach. She managed to withdraw the bloody blade just before she was felled by a rain of spear butts.

With their Queen beaten to the ground and her daughter about to have her throat slit, resistance drained from the villagers, though this was not to save them. Adminius stopped his lethal charge from the lodge and threw down his sword. He too was attacked and beaten with shields and the flats of swords, which was too much for the young Claudius to bear. With a cry, he wriggled by me and out of the tent, drawing his sword and shouting at the enemy as he rushed to his comrade's aid. An arrow in the chest felled him before he had gone ten paces. One of the mounted men galloped over to him and speared him like a fish to make certain.

I withdrew behind my tent flap until I was sure that the rider had gone, for by now I realised I was unlikely to be spared.

In the centre of the village, the Iceni were being cut down without mercy and the first round house was beginning to burn.

Catus and Starbo, with the faithful Calpurnius holding their horses for them, had to whip their frenzied men to order. Boudica, still unconscious, was bound upright to a tethering stake, her face crushed into the wood. Adminius was hog-tied hand and foot as was his wife Prisca, at her feet, while the young Erda was bound to one of the wheels of the carriage they were loading with a poor haul of loot.

Finding nothing of value except a few silver coins, the animals and much of the pottery I had brought in trade (most of which was broken or chipped thanks to the rough handling), Catus' rage knew fresh boundaries. Was this the wealth of Prasutagus? I heard him shout along with 'Where is the gold?'

For a while, calm returned like an ocean after a storm.

Catus began to organise his men into small search teams and some were, grudgingly, set to work putting out the fires that had caught two of the round huts. He was not totally mad, then, for he had realised that the smoke from a burning house could well act as a trumpet call for the Iceni scattered out in the woods and fields. When the searchers discovered two large pots containing the heads of Rogerus and Alcides, marinading in cedar oil, Catus had to cool the blood lust of his men – if only temporarily – by dispensing as much wine and beer as could be found in the village, which despite the recent feastings was a considerable amount, and by raiding the huts for mattresses and furs to sit on, making themselves comfortable as if at ease in a well-planted garden.

As the search teams went more methodically about their business I decided to move my position. Using the blade strapped to my arm I cut my way out of the side of the tent and managed to crawl unseen into the heather, which was tall enough to offer concealment as long as I lay prone. Although I could not hear anything except the loudest shouted orders, I could see everything.

I saw Adminius being questioned, his feet held in a cooking fire, his chest pierced twenty or thirty times with just the point of a dagger and then sea salt rubbed into the cuts. I saw, as he did, his wife stripped naked and beaten about the face until she fell unconscious to the ground only to be revived with the whip, plied with great enthusiasm by that boar Starbo.

Boudica, tied to the post, had her clothes cut off her to the waist and two of the Police took it in turns to lash her with triple-thonged leather whips of the type used on slaves but never animals. And when her two assailants were staggering with exhaustion, two more took their place, first turning her so that her back was to the hitching post and her naked breasts could take the full force of the new onslaught.

It was not then that Boudica cried out, even though her body was a mass of raw meat.

It was not until mid-afternoon, after Catus and his men had cooked and eaten a meal in front of her, that the Procurator, after consulting with Starbo and some of his gruesome lieutenants, gave instructions for the Princess Prisca to be staked out with rope and tent pegs on a bearskin. Even before the last rope was tied, a squad of men were lining up, jostling for position, loosening their armour and their trousers.

Adminius, now barely alive and lying tightly bound in the dirt, was forced to watch everything. After the first man had brutally, though swiftly, taken Prisca and ceded his place to a second, with a third waiting at his shoulder, Adminius' head sank in shame.

Six of them had had their way with his wife before she had to be doused with a bucket of water and then young Erda was likewise spreadeagled next to her sister.

It was only now that Boudica shouted so loudly she could be heard above the cracking of the whips and the animal laughter of her enemies.

'Harder! Strike harder!' she cried at her bemused tormentors, who, not understanding her, did just that.

As the assaults on them continued throughout the afternoon, mother and both daughters had to be regularly revived from their ordeals with dousings of water, and many of the Police, having slaked their thirst as well as their lust, were collapsing where they stood. Some took their pick of the other Iceni women, dragging them off into the nearest hut but only emerging alone.

Throughout all this, Catus sat sprawled on a sheepskin, drinking and eating what looked to be the last of my store of preserved delicacies. Calpurnius was never far from his ear and it could have been his suggestion which made the Procurator order that the two girls be turned over and pegged down so that they could be taken from the rear.

Two lines of willing rapists quickly formed as the almost inert bodies of the princesses were manhandled into position. It was then that Horas, who had been well-concealed from me for most of the day, stepped into view in front of the reclining Procurator.

I thought, with a feeling of shame, that the old fool was showing more courage than I had but he was not intervening on behalf of the princesses. He was merely offering to translate what the bound and tortured Adminius was trying to say – that he was willing to show them the way to the grave of King Prasutagus.

It was dusk when Catus led most of his men out of the village, following poor Adminius, a rope round his neck like a leash. His men spent the last hour of daylight sobering up, making torches, but not lighting them, and muffling the feet of their horse with whatever cloth they could find.

This silent, ghost-like column moved slowly northwards through the heather and into the darkness. I counted eighty-six mounted men disappearing into the gloom. There could not be more than twenty left as a guard on the meagre plunder they had amassed so far and I could see, as torches began to flare in the village, that many were sprawled senseless on the ground.

I began to crawl on my belly towards the nearest hut only to discover that it had been used by Catus' men and there were three Iceni women lying with their throats slit and their female parts mutilated. One of them had served me boiled crabs and samphire at the funeral feast.

I had no wish to stay in their company, or that of the rats which were already squeezing through holes they had made in the walls, but I used the shelter to spy out the situation.

In the flickering light of torches that had been stuck in the ground around them, I could see Boudica, bloodied and uncovered, her body straining at the ropes which bound her but which kept her limp body upright. For her daughters, prostrate before her like some cruel sacrifice, there was no respite.

Six or seven very drunk soldiers were drawing lots as to who would pleasure themselves first in the rumps of the girls. Calpurnius was among them and, as always, had the luck of the gods with him. He took his place at the start of the line.

I also caught sight of Horas, seated on the ground, holding a torch, his back turned on the drama about to be enacted.

It was then that I decided to kill them both.

I am not a brave man; I am a spy and spies are not expected to be brave. Neither are they expected to make a confession, for this is what this history now becomes.

I did not kill them, that is my confession, my failure. In my mind I killed them, but in my mind I also wished to be able to cut the throats of Erda and Prisca and put them out of their misery. But that too proved beyond me.

I managed to hide myself in the dark under the carriage they were using for their loot and I waited until the men lusted no more and the two girls had no strength left to scream.

I must have fallen asleep as it was full dark and only one or two torches were struggling to stay alight when I was jabbed awake by something prodding my ribs. A filthy, dung and straw-coated hand was slapped across my mouth.

'Come quickly if you want to live,' hissed a voice speaking the Iceni tongue, but all I could see was a shapeless bundle of rags. It was easy enough to follow the smell, however, and

I did so on my hands and knees like an animal, away from the carriage and into the nearest thatched hut, one of the ripest I had encountered. Several kinds of animal had over-wintered there and the place had not been cleaned out. My guide lit a small beeswax candle with a flint and tinder. It gave off just enough light for me to see that she was an old woman, but not enough to be seen outside.

'The Queen told me to hide you here,' she said.

'The Queen is alive?' In the gloom I thought I could see the outline of Boudica still tied to the hitching post but I could not be sure.

'She breathes but cannot run, so has chosen to stay near her daughters. She watched you as you hid and tells you not to try and rescue her. There are too many of them and the others are returning. She has caught their scent on the wind.'

And with that the old hag found my hand with hers, placed the candle there and disappeared.

But she – and Boudica – were right about the approaching horsemen – four of them, carrying torches raced into the village shouting for their comrades to wake up and hitch a pair of horses to the carriage I had been hiding under.

They had, it transpired, discovered so much loot at Prasutagus' grave that the carriage was needed to transport it as the idiot muleteer's sons had got lost in the woods somewhere along with their (formerly my) mules. Catus and his heavily burdened men were already on their way back.

The carriage creaked away into the dark with its escort and what men were left soon began to stir as dawn broke. I counted twenty-two, not including Horas, of whom there was no sign. Some kicked at a cooking fire until it spluttered into life, some discovered untapped wine jugs and several flagons of beer. Four, unbelievably, made ready to have their unnatural way with young Erda's bitten and bruised body, and were hotly debating whether it was preferable to wake her first.

Of the Iceni there was no sign to be seen. Those left alive had drifted off into the forest during the night.

Two of the men dragged a sheep by its hind legs from the pens and made a bloody spectacle of slaughtering and skinning it, then spitting the carcase over a cooking fire. A fight then broke out as to who was to collect more firewood.

The argument was not resolved and the sheep not a quarter cooked before Catus and his convoy appeared through the heather heading for the village at a fast trot, so fast that it did not appear to intend stopping. It did not.

In the vanguard, Catus slowed his horse just enough so that his shouted orders could be understood.

'You lot can finish up here. Round up the animals and bring them to the house of Publius Oranius. We will wait for you there to share out our profits.' This raised a desultory cheer, and some confused questions about why they could not all travel together, but these went unanswered as Catus raised an arm in command and instructed: 'Torch the village!'

Fortunately most of the men were too unsteady from their exertions to react promptly; for the most part they just stood and watched as Catus led his troop off to the south, my former carriage, now heavily laden but moving at a fair clip, driven by none other than Calpurnius. Bringing up the rear, hanging on to his horse's neck for dear life, was Horas, who must have been hiding in the animal pens.

The stragglers, realising that the Procurator had abandoned them, began to argue among themselves, milling around the pens at the west end of the village desperately trying to find a mount to enable them to catch up with their comrades.

Several were mounted, although far from in control of their horses, when Tarex appeared, with the first rays of dawn, from the east.

There was no fanfare, he was just there – in the middle of the village, between the horsemen and where Boudica and her daughters were still on display. He was naked to the waist, his torso coated in blue woad dye and he carried an enormous spear with the girth of a stout sapling and more than twice his height, topped with an iron barb.

With his left fist, he beat his chest and shouted one terrible word as if three.

'Boo-de-ka!'

Drunk and probably only half awake, one of the Special Police urged his horse towards the giant, determined to ride him down. I saw the charge. Or rather, both charges, for as soon as the horseman set off with a battle cry of his own, so too Tarex charged, hefting the spear to his shoulder and running towards the oncoming horseman.

I am no student of military history but I have read of the heroes of old and this was a sight to rank with the noblest of exploits.

As man and horseman closed on each other, there seemed to be only one outcome, then suddenly Tarex dropped to one knee and jammed the butt of his spear into the earth, holding the shaft at an angle so that the iron barb was ideally placed for the horse's breastbone. As horse and rider hit the spear point, Tarex rose up and pulled. My Greek heritage has given me an admiration (if no aptitude) for mathematics and I could appreciate the way the force of the horse and the lever provided by the spear combined. Both horse and rider went flying over Tarex's head, rider parting company with beast at the top of the arc and both hitting the ground behind the Iceni warrior. I was impressed. The other Police were terrified, unsure whether to fight or run, given that to follow Catus would have meant passing Tarex, who was busy wringing the neck of the unseated horseman to the accompaniment of the dying squeals of his horse.

Deciding that what had happened to their comrade could not happen to them all and there was safety in numbers, the Police charged Tarex as one, bringing with them as many animals from the pen as their whips could make break into a trot. Tarex reluctantly dropped his lifeless victim to the ground and ran to the fallen and skewered horse. With a foot on the horse's neck he pulled his long spear free of its chest. One swift blow to the neck finished the horse and Tarex went into a crouch behind its lifeless body.

The charging ponies and cows (plus my remaining oxen) avoided the dead horse just as Tarex knew they would, swerving and causing confusion among the horsemen who were loath to come near him. He had no such scruples and the giant spear, swung like a club, gave him a huge reach, as at least three dismounted horsemen discovered. But unhorsing his enemies was not his main aim. Even in the confusion of battle, Tarex had realised that the headlong rush of horsemen and beasts would eventually run across the pegged out bodies of Erda and Prisca.

I could say that it was now my time to be a hero, as I burst from my hiding place to rescue the princesses, albeit late in the day. And run I did, but only to find half a dozen Iceni women already standing over them – though where they had come from I do not know – tugging at their ropes. At least I was able to lend them a knife.

As the women struggled to drag the lifeless bodies to safety, one of the horsemen who had avoided Tarex bore down on me, sword ready to slash and cut. I had no weapon, nowhere to run, and the sudden, utterly convincing belief that I would die here unnoticed by anyone of consequence and thus saving my father the cost of a tombstone and an equally expensive florid inscription.

A witch saved me. A black-robed Druid witch who appeared as if from the earth itself and flung herself under the legs of the oncoming horse, bringing it tumbling down on top of her. Like panthers, the old women who had been freeing the royal princesses dropped their bruised and battered charges and launched themselves on the hapless and now unseated horseman.

So there I was, the noble rescuer rescued, by a dead witch and half a dozen old crones, who proceeded to rip the soldier's face from his skull with their fingers.

Hearing his screams, two of his comrades rode to his aid, letting out screams of their own soon enough as a dozen arrows pierced each of their horses, bringing them down, as Aneurin the Druid emerged from the heather with a line of Iceni bowmen. And then I must have fainted clean away.

Seventeen of Catus' assassins were captured alive by the Iceni, and kept alive for three days while the Queen recovered.

In that time I was nursed as if a hero, with almost every whim catered for, or offered, by the women of the tribe. I was given a clean hut and Tarex himself brought my supplies of writing materials which had evaded Catus' raiders. I was fed on clean, weak beer, mutton broth and oat porridge and given daily reports on the health of the Queen and her daughters.

On that third day, Boudica walked through the village and I was helped from my sick bed, though I was hardly sick, to greet her. In fact she said nothing to me, merely nodded to acknowledge my presence. Her movements were stiff, almost wooden, like a doll, but the fact that she lived spoke much about the skills of the Druids and the Iceni women. No mention was made of her daughters.

A great crowd of Iceni had gathered – perhaps a thousand of them, more than had been present at the king's funeral – and it was clear that something of importance was about to happen.

From out of the west, Tarex drove Boudica's chariot into the village, the chariot I had not seen since that first day when we met out on the road. Drawing up in the middle of the village, Tarex dismounted and made a show of presenting the reins to Boudica. She climbed unsteadily into the chariot and called out for the Druid Aneurin.

In his black robes, Aneurin stepped forward holding a sheathed sword – the sword I had last seen going to Prasutagus' grave. With the help of several other Druids, he jammed the hilt of the sword into the hub of the chariot's right side wheel and lashed it there with rope, only then removing the scabbard to allow the shiny, polished blade to glisten and dazzle in the sunlight.

Boudica pulled the horses to her left, though the effort seemed great, and ordered that the prisoners be released, shouting 'Let's be having you' in a deep-throated roar.

Those who had been abandoned by the Procurator then paid for their crimes. Unable to escape to the side through the massed lines of the Iceni, the prisoners were forced to run in front of Boudica's wheels as she swerved and turned to make sure that the whirling sword did its work. If they avoided that turning blade, hissing at their legs, they fell beneath the hooves of her ponies. It was butchery not slaughter, for only a few of the lucky ones died straight away, as she pursued them out of the village. The last of them were cut down at the knees in a water meadow near a stream about a mile away and allowed to bleed to death in peace as Boudica turned her chariot back to the village with one arm raised in salute, her spinning blade dulled with blood. Aneurin then unleashed his priests to follow in her wake, taking the heads from the limbless and gutted prisoners, many of whom welcomed death rather than their crippling injuries.

That night the Druids disappeared into the woods with their gruesome trophies and when they returned, there was much singing and drinking around the banked-up camp fires.

I was almost the honoured guest though there were many who kept their distance. I summoned up the courage to ask Aneurin what had happened to Adminius, who had not returned from the forest. The Romans, I was told, had nailed him upside down to a tree and cut the veins in his neck so he could watch himself bleed to death. It was just as well, he added casually, for had they found him alive, the Druids would have been obliged to kill him themselves, for treachery and desecration, no matter who his mother-in-law was.

Four days after the slaughter of the prisoners, Boudica presented her daughters to the village – to a village which had quietly doubled in size every morning as the Iceni deserted their farmlands, seeped out of the forest and rallied to their Queen. The three women rode in Boudica's chariot, slowly tracing the boundary of the village so that the newcomers camped on the outskirts could get a good look. Princess Erda's face was cruelly disfigured, her nose broken and almost flattened against her face, one eye still closed with bruises and she had few teeth left. The scars on Prisca ran deeper. Her face was unmarked and a slight limp seemed to be her only wound, until that is, you looked *into* her face. Where there had once been a precocious, not to say stubborn girl, there was now nothing, just a death mask. She no longer talked nor, whispered the old women, did she blink her eyelids.

There was an other-worldly silence as Boudica addressed the massed tribe. Speaking so that many had to strain to hear her, she said that the insult and indignity forced upon the tribe by Rome would be revenged but as the outrage had been against the family of Prasutagus, it was the family that must seek revenge whatever else happened and that her intention was to follow the Roman Catus to wherever he chose to hide and deliver on him the vengeance of an Iceni Queen, widow and mother.

This was greeted with a growling cheer which rolled like distant thunder through the village as her words floated over the crowd.

She told them to make ready, to round up horses and animals, turn their carts back into chariots and get the elders of the tribe to remember where they had buried their weapons all those years ago as part of the *Lex Julia* disarmament laws. Every blacksmith and metalworker in the tribe would be kept busy shaping and sharpening weapons. Every woman should gather provisions for a long march, every man out in the fields must abandon them, for until Catus was found, the Iceni were no longer farmers. They would, instead, live off the Romans, taking what they needed as they found it, for dead men have no need of possessions.

It was somewhere around the last week of spring or the first week of summer when Boudica set fire to her own lodge, took the reins of her chariot with her daughters at her side, and led the entire tribe out of the village to war.

XXXII: Valerius Lupus

From Valerius Lupus, Magistrate, Colonia of Camulodunum
By urgent dispatch to the most noble Legate Quintus Petillius Cerialis, Headquarters Legio IX at Durobrivae.

Legate,

I beseech you to consider our request for aid in these most troubled times.

The actions of the Procurator of all Britannia, the noble Catus Decianus, have enraged the Iceni peoples to such an extent that there is now open rebellion sweeping the farms and homesteads to the north of the *colonia.*

No news has been received from the outlying settlements for two weeks now and the Imperial Post riders are refusing to go more than five miles due north. The ones that did have not returned.

I am sure I need not impress upon the noble Legate what this has done to property and land prices in the area. I urge him most sincerely to send us a considerable show of force to protect the *colonia*, to put these barbarians in their place and to restore order and law.

Legate, make haste.

Valerius Lupus.

XXXIII: Roscius

Where was I when I heard?

We'd still be on Mona when the first report came through. It was a message from Cerialis saying that the *colonia* at Camulodunum had asked the IXth for help and he was off for a stroll in the woods with his cavalry and the best part of a brigade, maybe two or three thousand *grex* – that's squaddies to someone like you, the poor bloody infantry. I was there when it was read to General Paulinus and I saw him raise his eyes to the sky as if to say: 'What's that blockhead up to now?'

I remember thinking that Cerialis didn't ask for permission to move his legion, he just told us he was going, but then that was only to be expected from the likes of him, but I don't think the General was too worried at the time. Two thousand trained legionaries were thought to be more than enough to handle some barbarian war party on the rampage.

The Iceni had already managed to do a considerable amount of damage. Afterwards, sometime that winter, I took a squad out into Iceni country to find what had happened to an old XXth Legion vet, the former quartermaster who took his pension in land and a few slaves and even married an Iceni girl, man called Publius Oranius.

His farm had been one of the first to be hit and it had been flattened and I do mean flattened. Some of the animals hadn't even been stolen, they'd just been killed and left to rot. The water was poisoned, all his possessions smashed to pieces. But they'd saved the best for him and his child bride. Know what they did? They stuffed them into a half-full barrel of oysters – he always had a passion for oysters did Oranius – both of them together, head first, just stuffed them in so they drowned. Then they nailed the lid on and buried the fucking thing in the ground.

What a way to go, eh?

You expect the settlers out in the country to be the first to get it in the neck, they always are. And where there's a mixed marriage like that, it always gets nasty. But nobody really thought the mad bitch would start attacking and burning the towns.

That's when it got serious.

XXXIV: Olussa

It was not a campaign march, it was more a migration interrupted by murder.

Boudica's army grew by the hour as the tribe came out of the woods and marshes to join the snaking mass. Warriors and charioteers in the vanguard and then women, children, carts, cattle, sheep and spare horses in any order in the body of the column. Entire families would spring from the bracken complete with as much food as they could carry and a weapon of some sort, ranging from a bent and rusted sword to a stout club with its head blackened in a fire to harden it.

Black-robed Druids would scour the outlying wilderness in groups of three or four riders, always returning with another family or two and however hesitant the newcomers were at first, they became enthusiastic camp followers once they caught sight of so many warriors in their blue war paint, with Druid witches casting spells over them to make them invincible, and just the sheer numbers of so many Iceni gathered together with a purpose, along with Boudica, proud and cruel, leading the exodus. And, of course, the killing helped. That was very popular.

That rough and ready character Publius Oranius and his Iceni wife – her name will come to me – were among the first to feel Boudica's revenge, bound together as if making love and then half-drowned upside down in a barrel of oysters before being buried alive.

It was after the third or fourth Imperial Post rider had been disembowelled along the track that I began to notice, when a break in the forest allowed for it, columns of smoke rising from twenty or thirty sites on both sides of our line of march. Aneurin and his Druids were kept busy organising these raids and returning with the heads of their victims, often tied by their hair to a hemp rope and slung over their horses' necks. Every stream we crossed and at every pond we saw, a head would be offered up in sacrifice to their god Taranis. When a head was thrown into whichever patch of water was handy, they would wait and watch the ripples spreading outwards. This, it seems, is an omen which can be read if you have the skill. Only the Druids have the skill of course, just as the Roman priests are the only ones able to read the hidden meanings in a pigeon's entrails.

Boudica and her daughters would attend all these ceremonies, though I doubt whether the blank-faced Erda understood what was happening. Perhaps she did, for as a sacrifice was about to be made, Boudica would ask the officiating Druid 'Where is Catus?' and every time their gods seemed to answer 'He has passed this way', which would be the signal for the Iceni host to resume its march.

When we fell upon one of the staging posts which held reserve horses for the Imperial Post riders, it was the Princess Erda who put her unblinking face next to that of a cowering and drooling stable hand and asked, 'Where is Catus?' She did not wait for a reply but sliced off the man's genitals there and then with a downward stroke of a hand sickle, but at least she had recovered her power of speech.

No one other than perhaps her mother, though, was ever to hear her speak anything except the words 'Where is Catus?' and it was taken up as 'Erda's war cry' by some of the young bucks of the tribe as the bloodshed continued.

Aneurin has told me that tomorrow I will be with the Queen when she meets with a party of Trinovantes at a ford in the river marking the ancient boundary between their two tribes.

Is this an honour? A mark of trust? Or am I to be a sacrifice to the gods they share?

Boudica is to be accompanied by her inner circle of advisors who are the chiefs of the various Iceni clans or extended families. Tarex is a clan chief and well-established in his role as the Queen's General, yet Aneurin too is a clan chief, as are many of the senior Druids, which gives the priests the double influence of politics and religion. A dangerous mix at the best of times, as Rome has often found out.

'But what can I do?' I pleaded. 'I am no soldier.'

'It is not clear what you are, Olussa the Lost Roman,' he said dangerously, 'but think on this. You are still alive and from here north to the coast, there is not another invader who is.'

'I am a merchant, not an invader,' I protested.

'And because of that, you may live a little longer but you will help Boudica, not just because I think you can, but because she wants you to.'

'She does?' I said, surprised, for the Queen had not spoken to me or even noticed me since the killing started.

Aneurin nodded his head. 'Yes, but she has her own reasons of which I know nothing. No doubt she will tell you in time. Priests will collect you at dawn and bring you to the meeting.'

'You are asking me to become a spy?' I said boldly.

'I am asking if you want to live,' he answered and then he was gone into the night.

I have since thought long and hard if the Celts have a word for 'traitor' but I cannot bring it to mind.

I am not a traitor, I am a spy with different masters.

At the war council on the riverbank (I cannot be precise to the location except that by general agreement, Camulodunum is to the south) the Trinovantes' delegation, led by Tasciovanus, proposed that before anything else, I was to be beheaded and sacrificed to the river.

Aneurin had sent three black-robed priests to wake me and provide a breakfast, as we walked, of a piece of salted fish and a flask of strong, sweet honey mead. At the council, these priests surrounded me and for once I was glad of their presence. At Tasciovanus' suggestion, they closed ranks until their bodies formed a living shield around me. If it had not been for the smell coming off their robes, it was almost comfortable, for the morning was chill and the sun had not yet burned off the early mist.

Boudica handed the reins of her horses to her daughter Prisca and stepped down from her wicker chariot, holding the hand of the frail and damaged Erda. The Queen carried no weapon, though Erda seemed to be collecting them, wearing a hand sickle and two short stabbing knives through a cord around the waist of her dress – a dress stained brown with blood. Yet Boudica needed no weapons or symbols to exert her authority. In the sharpest and roughest of terms she dismissed Tasciovanus' suggestion, saying that if the Trinovantes wanted a sacrifice they should try taking prisoners of their own.

The discomfort of the Trinovantes and the smug expressions of the Iceni told me that the Trinovantes were not yet in open rebellion even though all carried arms openly and wore stripes of blue warpaint across their cheeks and brows.

It was Aneurin who opened proceedings with a long and rambling speech detailing the history of the two tribes which mostly seemed to concern ancient trading agreements, notable instances of inter-marriage and the formal exchange of prisoners and slaves after raids on each other's territories in the days before the Roman invasion. In fact, I suspect he was referring to the days before the great Caesar's expedition, but the incidents were of so little consequence they made for a poor oration and when the formalities were complete, the tribes – about thirty on each side – sat down in a rough circle in the damp grass on the Iceni bank of the river. Once the Iceni Druids had produced a dozen flagons of beer for circulation among all present except me, the talking began and went on until almost midday.

The Trinovantes' case, as put by their clan chiefs, was one of pure hatred and the bitterest animosity aimed mostly at the legionary veterans who had been settled upon them. Each clan chief listed an inventory of farms, animals and slaves which had been appropriated by the veterans, but even more venom was reserved for the temple being built to the divine Claudius, which was seen as the symbol of seventeen years of Roman misrule. What clearly hurt these chiefs – nobles, I suppose – was that they had all been 'elected' to serve as priests in the Temple of Claudius; not only forced to honour a strange religion, but expected to cover the cost of building the temple itself – 'forced to pour out our fortunes like water' as one of them said.

The Iceni clan chiefs responded by detailing the insults and injuries laid upon their royal family, claiming that Iceni honour was worth more than the strain on Trinovantine purses, but Boudica herself put an end to that discussion, preferring to ask about the defences of Camulodunum.

It was Tasciovanus himself who spoke on the defences of the *colonia*, which he described, quite eloquently, as 'carelessly guarded as if the whole world was at peace'. He described what I had seen with my own eyes – what Valerius Lupus had shown me until I was bored to exhaustion – that the deep ditches and steep ramparts built for the original fortress no longer existed. It was in effect, an open city ripe for invasion.

Neither was there any force to meet an attacker outside the *colonia*, resumed Tasciovanus, for the Town Watch were few in number, the veterans themselves were old and fat thanks to a life of luxury at the Trinovantes' expense, and the only relief force to arrive from Londinium had been two hundred auxiliary troops who were poorly armed, if they had a weapon at all.

In the *colonia* itself there was much panic with many omens of doom for the inhabitants, who were fleeing every day, some by river to the sea and many into the woods and coastal marshes to the south.

It was Aneurin who asked how many people were left in Camulodunum and here the Trinovantes displayed only a basic grasp of mathematics. Eventually, after much conferring and muttering, they estimated that no more than three thousand civilians remained in the town, the majority of them women and children, many of them the wives and slaves of the colonists rich enough to have bought passage to the coast. This population was defended by no more than three hundred armed men, although the town magistrates had ordered all the workshops and foundries in the industrial area they called the Sheep End to work day and night forging and sharpening weapons.

This news provoked much heated, and thirsty, discussion and after more beer had arrived, along with some roasted pigeons, I saw Boudica conferring with her chief Druid, both of them looking in my direction.

Aneurin got to his feet and signalled that I be brought forward with my escort to stand in front of the Trinovantes, who, if they were not eating or drinking, snarled and snapped like dogs at my heels.

'Can it be true, what they say about the defences of this great town?' Aneurin asked me in a loud clear voice.

'You will take the word of a Roman above mine?' roared Tasciovanus, making to rise but wisely not attempting to draw his sword for the giant Tarex was quickly at his side.

'This man claims not to be a Roman,' said Aneurin, 'and has suffered as an enemy of Rome. Hear him.'

All eyes were upon me as I answered, including those of the Queen and, more worryingly, those of young Erda.

'I cannot speak as to how many citizens remain in Camulodunum, nor how many soldiers they have to defend them, but I can tell you that with a combination of arrogance and greed, those who govern in the *colonia* have taken no steps to protect themselves. In fact they have abandoned what defences were left by the legions. It is as Tasciovanus says. He speaks the truth.'

This brought a murmur of approval from the Trinovantes.

'And where is the Roman army?' Aneurin addressed the council like an advocate, but he looked to me for an answer.

'It is with the Governor, General Paulinus, many miles to the north and west,' I said confidently.

That seemed to satisfy them for which I was grateful for I had no desire to try and explain to these tribes that there was a whole province out there beyond their tribal homelands. Nor did I want to get into debate about how fast a legion could travel on a Roman road, something else they would have no concept of. Nor did I feel it prudent, under Aneurin's beady eye, to mention that the Governor's mission in the north-west was the extermination of the Druids there.

'How long will it take this General and his army to come to the aid of the colony?' Aneurin fixed me with a stare. All the war council did, even young Erda, although she held her head on one side like a dog expecting a bone.

'Too long,' I said.

It seemed to be the answer they wanted.

That afternoon the Iceni crossed the river at fords marked for them by the Trinovantes. By the time the last carts and animals had crossed, a camp had been established some three miles away in a part of the forest where many trees had been felled for charcoal production.

Cooking fires were lit with no attempt to conceal them and patrols of horsemen carrying torches rode out into the night. An old crone brought me hot food and beer. She gave the impression of having adopted me, although I suspect she was constantly at my side on the orders of the Queen, and even offered, through sign language (for even I could not understand her thick accent) to patch and sew my one good pair of woollen trousers. I was thus standing in my underpants, with a cloak around my shoulders when Aneurin, flanked by a pair of black-robed Druids almost invisible against the night, announced that the Queen wished to see me.

My Iceni stepmother cackled her toothless laugh and made a great show of sewing faster, muttering something I could not understand, but Aneurin did and he snapped at her to be quiet and when one of his priests took but one step towards her, the blood drained from her face and she put her eyes down and her fingers made the bone needle fly.

Thinking that he had need to explain, Aneurin said: 'Tonight the Queen will lie with Tarex, for she will need his strength in the battle to come. This hag dared to suggest you might be the Queen's choice for tonight.'

Fortunately, the Queen had other – military – matters on her mind when we reached her encampment. She was holding court by the light of a small bonfire, her clan chiefs and the most blessed and honoured Tarex sitting cross-legged on the earth around her. Tasciovanus and several of his war chiefs were present, as was young Erda, who was seldom far from her mother's side these days.

Boudica did not acknowledge my presence, but continued to talk to her chiefs and her allies.

'Our patrols report no Romans outside the walls of Camulodunum. Even better – there are no walls to Camulodunum. There are no defences worth speaking of.'

This speech received a chorus of grunting and slapping of chests which the Queen allowed to run its course. Then she said:

'Tomorrow we will attack with all force. Chariots and

horsemen will form a spear point along the road until we reach the outskirts of the town, then we divide. Iceni to the west, Trinovantes to the east, and encircle. We meet in the centre with fire and sword, sword and fire.'

It was a noble speech, nobly said and I knew that even as I was scratching it into a wax tablet, the Druids would be repeating it to themselves, making memory serve as history for these were days when history was being made, and for once they might have something worth remembering.

One of the Trinovantes, an older chief with a long mane of white hair, saw me at my writing and scrambled to his feet, extending a scrawny finger.

'Look, we have a spy among us!' he shouted in an accent which grated on the ear. 'He is writing down our words.'

I did not start or flinch, for so completely had I accepted my role as a spy that my only thought was that the old blockhead was telling no more than the truth.

Before things could turn ugly, Boudica herself strode out of the firelight towards me, declaiming over her shoulder:

'So he is, but who can he tell? Do the Romans not know we are coming? Tomorrow they will!'

This produced a cheer all round, but Boudica did not pause in her purposeful stride until she was face-to-face in front of me, so close I could smell the pine sap on her. And then I knew that I should be very afraid, for in one hand she held a dagger which had appeared as if from the night air. Her other hand lunged forward and grabbed my private parts through my newly darned trousers. Needless to say, this brought another cheer from her chiefs.

'I cannot read or write,' she announced, 'but I am Boudica, Queen of the Iceni and from today I shall decide what is to be written. You, merchant, trader, spy, whatever you are, you will write for me.'

I nodded enthusiastically as the pressure of her grip forced me on to my toes.

And then the pain was gone and so was she, turning to accept the thigh-slapping and hooting of her chiefs. But where she had stood a moment ago, there stood young Erda, idly fingering the hand sickle on her belt. The princess said nothing, merely looked into my eyes and then she too turned away and resumed her place at her mother's side and I knew I had known real fear and when I sank, trembling, to the earth, I could feel dampness in my crotch.

I thought I would be dismissed along with the chiefs, to allow Boudica and Tarex to do whatever they had to, but Aneurin signalled me to wait until the company had melted into the trees. Only then did Boudica leave Erda with Tarex and approach to speak with her Chief Druid and her historian/spy.

'Tomorrow,' she said in a serious and low voice, 'we will take back Dun Camulos, the ancient home of our war god. You will stay close to my priests and you will seek out the . . .'

She faltered, almost embarrassed and looked to Aneurin for help.

'*Medicamentarius*,' he said hesitantly and Boudica nodded, making no attempt to pronounce the word.

'An apothecary? I saw at least three in the *colonia*. They do a good trade in poultices and herbal drinks.' I told her as if it was the most natural topic for discussion under the sun.

'You will,' said the Queen, 'obtain poison for me. The strongest and surest poison there is. Priests will accompany you and you will say nothing of this to anyone.'

'Or we will test the poison on you,' said Aneurin in an unnecessary threat considering those I had already suffered that night.

'I ask a favour in return for this service,' I said boldly.

'You do not bargain with Boudica!' snapped Aneurin but the Queen raised a hand to silence him and she nodded permission for me to continue.

'My supplies of writing materials are almost exhausted and if I am to write the glorious history of Boudica, Queen of the Iceni, who defied Rome, then I will need more . . .' I held up the wax tablet and stylus I always carried, not knowing if she would understand what I meant by ink, papyrus, parchment or writing bark, for the Iceni had no need of words for them.

'Keep the priests close tomorrow, they will help you collect whatever you need,' said Boudica, 'but gather your booty quickly. Anything that burns *will* burn.'

* * *

The Iceni horde approached the capital of Britannia from the north. To the inhabitants of the *colonia*, it must have seemed as if a flood wave of dark water was seeping out the forest, running as if through a funnel, towards the small wooden bridge crossing the muddy river. The last time I had seen this prospect, dozens of small boats plied their trade between the bridge and the large, ocean-going ships moored downstream towards the coast. Now there was no sign of a sail, no sound of an oar and no sight of man nor beast. The bridge was undefended and intact, the road up the hill to the north gate of the *colonia* completely empty.

I had been placed in a chariot with two Druid priests. It was not one of the light, wickerwork chariots such as Boudica drove, but a heavier, wooden contraption probably cut down from a two-axle cart or wagon and thankfully much slower, so that by the time I reached the bridge, Boudica and one hundred and fifty war chariots plus over a thousand horsemen, many of them Trinovantes, were already knocking on the north gate of the town.

Or would have been, had there been a gate. The chariots simply rolled on in, a third of the cavalry swinging to the right around the side of the hill, to attack the west gate and the Sheep End smithies and workshops.

From the throng of foot soldiers crossing the bridge, perhaps five thousand strong including the armed and painted women, a low growl grew into a shout:

'Boo-dee-ka! Boo-de-ka!'

And then the host was across the bridge and spreading out to advance up the hill and already the first fires were taking hold.

It was a battle – if it could be said to be a battle at all – fought in a fog of smoke and hot ash. On that first day, the only inhabitants of the *colonia* I saw were dead ones lying in the streets and gutters where they had been speared or clubbed. Many still had their heads.

The Druids in the chariot had been instructed by Aneurin to get me about the Queen's business and they were not going to allow me to forget my duties even if they did not know what they were, which, of course, was to my advantage.

Coughing from the smoke from burning thatch, I tried to get my bearings in the midst of a sea of moving human flesh, for by now, the Iceni women and children were pushing into the town and I saw Trinovantine warriors coming to join the throng from the direction of the west gate, all of them shouting their war chants and many carrying the heads of their victims impaled on their spears. One of the heads, I was sure, belonged to Ulpius, formerly of the Town Watch and my one-time bodyguard.

I chose a direction at random and pointed so that my Druid guards understood where I was going. One of them indicated that he was to go with me and he showed me the haft of a long sword to make sure I knew I had no say in the matter, but at least the second stayed with our chariot.

I was grateful for my Druid escort for his black robes guaranteed us a passage through the crowd, though our progress was slow. There was a chance that I would be mistaken for a colonist, especially by the Trinovantes who had never seen me before, although my own torn and dirty clothing, an Iceni woollen cloak and clasp-pin, coupled with a week's worth of beard and several weeks without a proper bath helped me to blend in with the rabble.

I tapped my Druid on the shoulder and pointed through the smoke to a house I recognised. With little respect for his kinsmen he forced a path through them for me until we reached the gates of the house of Valerius Lupus.

We were not the first intruders. Already, smoke and flecks of hot ash were billowing from the upper-storey windows and the gates and doors had been forced open, but for the moment, the vengeful natives had passed on their way. They would be coming back to loot the house, for loot there was in abundance, from exquisite bronze deities to the finest decorated vases, silk drapes, cushions and goose-down mattresses, and some fine oak furniture such as the large couch in the entrance hall. It had not been in the hallway when I had stayed with Lupus, but then neither had Horas the faithful servant been skewered to it by a spear.

'Olussa . . .'

So he was alive, but only just. My Druid moved to draw his sword as soon as he heard the old man croak my name but I held up a hand to stay his. I had to lean over Horas' face to hear him over the din of destruction outside. He had no strength left as he had exhausted himself trying to pull himself along the shaft of the spear sticking out of his chest. They must have held him against the couch and run it through him for the point to embed itself in the wood so deeply. There could not be much blood left in him, but he had made it to within three or four inches of the end of the red and slick haft.

'Horas the loyal servant,' I addressed him, 'you are about to die, and your world with you.'

'It is your world too, Olussa,' he said faintly.

'Not any more, old man, it has abandoned me. I am, as the Iceni call me, a Lost Roman.'

'Help me now and I will tell you where the gold is.'

I was staggered. He was trying to buy his life.

'I did not come here for gold,' I said in Latin, hoping that my Druid guard could not understand.

'Yes you did,' the old man coughed and blood came out with his words, 'your sort always do.'

'You are wrong, slave,' I was angry now. 'You know nothing.'

'A man like you wants gold, always,' he sighed.

'I came here for parchment and bark and writing materials, not the gold you stole from me on our way to the Iceni lands. I care nothing for it now.'

'We . . . hid . . . it . . . under the barn at Publius Oranius' farm. Calpurnius and I were to collect it on our return but the Procurator would not halt, wishing to get back to civilisation as soon as possible.'

'So Calpurnius lives?'

'He rode with the Procurator to Londinium.'

'He would. I fear he will never see that gold now.'

'It could be yours,' gasped the old, dying, man. 'And Lupus has gold and silver coins hidden in the garden. I could show you . . .'

I felt something, perhaps it was pity, for him.

'But Horas,' I said, my face close to his, 'there is nowhere left to spend it. Give me Lupus' pens and inks and I can buy my life. Nothing can buy yours.'

As I straightened up I nodded to my Druid shadow but turned my face away as he drew his sword. I heard two thudding strokes before Horas' head bounced on the floor and rolled away across the still cool tiles.

In the office of Valerius Lupus I found all the writing materials I needed. My Druid ripped down a drape and made a crude sack in which to carry them and whilst he was occupied, I found and read a copy of a letter from Lupus to the Legate of the IXth Legion at Duriobrivae, appealing for help.

My Druid and I did not linger and fortunately, one of the apothecary shops I had remembered was almost intact. The owner had stayed to defend his property from his doorway, defying the intruders. They had nailed him to the door for his trouble.

Inside the shop was dark and cool and I turned my Druid into a lamp-bearer once I had located a pair of circular oil lamps (imported from Gaul, and a profitable item for me in another life). By their flickering light I examined the apothecary's stock, recognising only a few of the hundreds of items in jars and boxes on his shelves. And there were many I was glad I did not recognise knowing what charlatans most apothecaries were.

In a neat row of pottery flasks (good Samian ware I noted, a special order, wondering who his supplier had been), I could feel with my fingertips that three at the end had lettering embedded into them before firing. The letters were *Ven.*, which I took to mean *venenum*, or poison.

Given the quantities in which apothecaries usually sold such mixtures, there seemed to be enough in one flask to kill a rich man's herd of cows.

I took all three flasks, just to be sure.

Boudica's headquarters, if they could be called such, were in what would have been the precincts of the Temple of the Divine Claudius, the centrepiece of the Empire's latest cult. The foreground of the temple was a heaving mass of warriors hooting and dancing in victory, with many, especially the Trinovantes, involved in toppling the bronze equestrian statue of Claudius from its plinth by the incomplete steps.

On the opposing plinth, the winged goddess of Victory, which the Romans had based on the Greek deity Nike, had ropes straining to drag her down, though the statue seemed to have been damaged already. The ropes were held by Iceni women but the goddess proved reluctant to jump off her pedestal.

'Oh just do it!' a voice bellowed – that of the Queen herself, who was seated with her daughters on a piece of marble destined never to be used now. The Iceni charioteers had ranked their chariots in a semi-circle facing the temple and released their horses from the shafts, so that they could be fed and watered. Apart from the attempted desecration of the temple's statues, the fighting seemed to be over.

As I approached the Queen, Aneurin – his face blackened with soot – intercepted me.

'You have found what you were told to find?'

'Yes, though as to its content and effectiveness I cannot swear,' I said showing him the three flasks I clutched under my cloak.

'Give them to me,' he ordered, which I was pleased to do.

'And I have found more,' I said, to hold his attention. 'I must speak with the Queen.'

'Go. But be careful of Erda. She is enjoying this too much.'

Boudica was drinking wine from a flagon, Erda was kneeling behind her, playing with the braids in her mother's hair. Her other daughter, Prisca was sternly putting an edge on a Roman *gladius* with a whetstone. From the amount of blood – not hers – on her face and in her hair, I suspected it had been well used that day.

The giant Tarex stepped in front of me to block my route to the Queen. He was also smeared in the blood of others, as if he had washed in the stuff.

'What do you want, little lost Roman?' his voice rumbled like thunder.

'I have news for the Queen. The colonists have sent word to the legions for help.'

'They wait in vain,' said Boudica rising to her feet and moving the colossus aside with the lightest of touches on his bare shoulder.

'I do not understand,' I said truthfully.

'Those who still live are in there. They have sealed themselves under ground . . . I do not know the word.'

'In the vaults?'

'There must be nearly two thousand of them. They have little if any water, no light and if they have weapons they are in no position to use them. It is foolishness.'

'They are waiting for their army. It is based to the north, but it will come,' I warned.

'They are on their way,' said Boudica. 'They crossed into Trinovantes land this morning, but they have still far to march.'

I was astounded by the speed and accuracy of her spies.

'A Roman legion can march fast,' I warned.

'But it cannot fly over the forest, it must march through it. They will not be here for two days and we will not wait for them here. We will go and meet them. Do not worry, Olussa the not-Roman. Our gods are with us. Come, there is something else you must explain to me.'

I followed her, with Tarex following me and a troop of Iceni bowmen following him, to a narrow street, no more than an alley, off what had been marked out as the temple precincts. It was an alley of poor housing, crudely converted military barrack blocks which Valerius Lupus had probably earmarked for demolition in his grand plans for the *colonia.* Boudica picked her way across broken furniture, rubble and more than one body, until she stopped and pointed to an unimpressive piece of mud wall.

'Is there anything the Romans do not write on?' she asked me, pointing to some lines of scribble in the pink daub.

'It is of no importance, Queen, merely the scratchings of idle soldiers.'

Even above and beyond the smell of burning, it was obvious to all our noses that this was an old army latrine block which had been none-too-carefully filled in. Only the back wall remained standing and it was covered in crude lettering.

'If even the lowest Roman soldier has the skill and time to write, I want to know what it says,' Boudica repeated.

I scanned the writings, my eyes watering in the smoky air, to see if any could be translated easily. From what I knew of the Queen, I doubted she would be shocked by anything here.

'It is common to what you would find in any Roman fort,'

I said, still reading, for it was obvious that the wall was, ironically, one of the few original military defences left standing by the new town's planners.

'Somebody called Laurentius, who had served his time with the legions in Cambria, had a good shit here.'

There was a general belly laugh all round at that one, but I had interpreted it truthfully.

'And here,' I read down the wall, 'a comment by somebody called I. Silva. No, a comment *about* them. *I. Silva Podex perfectus es*, which means "Silva, you are a complete arsehole." And these others, they are what you might expect from crude and rough soldiers.'

'And that one?' asked Boudica, pointing a stubby finger at the one inscription carved with some care.

'*Res rarissima virgo inter Trinovantes,**' I read. 'It means that it is a rare thing indeed to find a virgin among the local women, the Trinovantes.'

This got the biggest laugh of all but Boudica merely nodded, content.

'So I had heard,' she said.

From somewhere behind us came a roar from a thousand throats as the statue of Claudius crashed down on to his temple steps.

By nightfall Boudica's army had gathered carts of straw, storage jars of oil and enough timber to build a bonfire twenty feet high on the beams which formed the roof of the temple vault. On a signal from Tarex, warriors pitched torches on to the mound and the wood caught fire immediately.

Very soon after we were able to hear the screams of the women and children trapped beneath.

Boudica and her daughters mounted her chariot, intent on spending the night in a camp outside the town.

'Spread the fire,' she said to Tarex, 'Burn everything. I want only ash by morning. Ash as far as the horizon.'

Tarex saluted her and began to gather his clan chiefs about him. In that moment, just as Boudica pulled on the reins to control her horses, who were disconcerted by the flames

* In modern parlance, given the geography: 'Essex girls are easy.'

leaping skywards above the temple, not to mention the wild singing of several Druid witches who were dancing so close their hair was catching fire – just then, the young Erda tugged at her mother's sleeve and I heard her voice quite distinctly.

'Where is Catus?'

XXXV: Roscius

Cerialis and the IXth, well, they walked right into it, didn't they? The one time when a legion is vulnerable, when it's on the march through woodland. That's why all military roads have the trees at the sides cut back the length of a bowshot so the bastards can't surprise us and we have time to get the shields off our backs. They say the sword is the soldier's best friend, but it's really his shield. A legionary calls it his 'biscuit' – after the bread of the same shape – and just like a man needs bread to survive, a soldier needs his biscuit.

From what I heard afterwards from the survivors – all of them cavalry men, please note – the infantry was marching in a thin file along a narrow path following a river valley somewhere north-west of the *colonia*. Of course they didn't know then that the *colonia* looked like the rakings from a blacksmith's furnace and they weren't near enough to smell the burning bodies.

The Celts must have been lying in ambush all night, keeping quiet, having got rid of their ponies. One moment the legion was marching along the bank of a river, the next moment, ten thousand painted savages were coming out of the trees at them getting in up close and personal very fast so that most of the lads didn't even have time to draw swords let alone get their shields and javelins off their backs. A lot of them were tumbled straight into the river and they sank like stones because of their armour and all the stuff they were carrying. Those that managed to float, well, they were finished off by the Celts jumping in after them, with knives in their teeth.

Cerialis was with the vanguard cavalry and there was another unit of cavalry acting as a rearguard. At least he made an attempt at a fight – he might have been an idiot, but he was no coward – though he must have known right from the start that they'd been caught cold. He leads the vanguard at a gallop through the trees, back along the line of the column, but now the Iceni and the Trinnies are right in amongst our boys and anyway, you can't operate cavalry in woods like that. By the time he links up with the rearguard, having taken quite a few hits himself, it's almost all over. In the time it takes a hungry man to eat a good dinner, one of them told me, over two thousand troopers had been cut down and were in the process of being chopped up.

Anyway, that was Boudica's one and only victory over Rome and she probably wasn't even there herself. I don't count Camulodunum because there was hardly any defence put up at all, and even less in Londinium and Verulamium. Those weren't battles, they were slaughter.

But after that victory, her fate was sealed. Whatever the political situation, and we heard all the rumours about how much it cost to keep four legions in Britannia and how the economics of it all didn't add up and how Nero and Seneca wanted their money back, which meant that given a fair wind and a nod and a wink from a Vestal Virgin, Rome would clear out of that bloody island for good.

Couldn't happen now, though could it? We couldn't allow a Roman army to be defeated by a woman, could we?

XXXVI: Olussa

The victorious Iceni have returned to camp with a thousand heads or more, some still encased in their army helmets and red caps; some with the eyes poked out, just for fun.

Yesterday, an hour before midday, Tarex and Tasciovanus led the Iceni and Trinovantes into the forest to the north-west of the ruin that was Camulodunum. By nightfall, their scouts had located the overnight camp of the IXth Legion and, hobbling their horses well away from the track and downwind and leaving their chariots hidden, they took up positions on foot in the bracken and underbrush, only an arm's length away from where the unsuspecting legionaries would march the next day. There they stayed all night, silent and motionless, a battle line nearly half-a-mile long and four men deep, invisible from the trackway, which ran alongside a gently curving river. In the morning they allowed the cavalry vanguard to pass unharmed and waited until the legion's infantrymen were strung out opposite their own lines. Then they attacked from the side, sweeping many of the enemy straight into the river, overwhelming and dismembering the rest.

Some fifty pack mules carrying the legion's tents and cooking gear were captured and loaded with the weapons of the dead while several chariots were pressed into service as wagons to carry the trophy heads, piled in them like a harvest of turnips. With Celtic bravado, all Roman armour stripped from the corpses was thrown carelessly into the nearby river.

All this we heard, for the first time, from Druid messengers who had ridden on ahead to the *colonia* as soon as the battle had finished but while the butchery was just getting underway.

Yet those of us away from the battle had not been devoid of entertainment that day.

The fires over the Temple of Claudius had died down to leave blackened and still glowing timbers over the top of the vaults. The great game from the Trinovantes, who seemed far keener than the Iceni in this, was to walk along two beams, thrusting downwards with a spear to hopefully skewer a victim, or at the very least bringing mortar and masonry crashing down on their heads. Not all had died in the smoke of this makeshift oven and their cries and screams only encouraged the Trinovantes to more acts of cruelty. One warrior developed a great game, standing astride two smouldering beams and pouring a goatskin of wine in a thin stream through a hole he had made, on to the people below. As the goatskin emptied, he fumbled with his trousers and began to replace one stream of water with another to howls of encouragement from the onlookers, who began to throw stones and bricks on to the timbers to bring them crashing in on the heads of the survivors.

And then, at around the third hour after noon, or the tenth hour of the day as they would call it in Rome, the crowd fell silent as an ominous crack, like the snapping of a giant's leg, came from the bowels of the temple. One of the main cross beams had finally been consumed by the fire and the splitting of it began the collapse of the vault's roof. To us spectators above, it looked like a whirlpool was opening up, but a whirl of mortar and wood and ash, not water.

The screams from inside these fiery catacombs were drowned out by the cheers of the crowd outside and the instant the roof began to cave in, the first warriors were standing at the edge stabbing their spears downwards as if fishing in a stream.

In truth, the tribesmen could not kill fast enough and survivors actually began to emerge on to the temple precinct, having escaped from their tomb by climbing the mounting pile of their dead comrades. Those survivors managed to claim a few moments of daylight before they were swallowed by the crowd and torn apart, mostly – as is always the way – by the women.

Boudica and Prisca had front-row seats for this bloody spectacle, watching calmly from a pile of bear skins laid out on the rubble. The younger Erda was somewhere in the thick of things, wielding one of the curved knives she had acquired. Even above the screams of the victims, many of them as black as Nubians with soot and smoke as they were pulled out of one torment and into another, it was possible to hear Erda's shrill voice as she screamed, 'Where is Catus?' into the faces of those pitiful wretches.

Cautiously, I made my way through the crowd to where Boudica was seated, carefully identifying myself and showing that I was unarmed to the pack of black-robed Druids who provided a protective circle around her.

'My Queen,' I said, though it felt odd as she was not my Queen, but I could think of no other form of diplomatic address which she would either understand or expect. 'My Queen, one of them may know.'

'Know what, my Lost Roman merchant?'

'Where Catus the Procurator is,' I said, though I knew already he would be back in his office in Londinium packing his bags with as much Iceni gold as he could carry.

For a heartbeat, Boudica said nothing, then she sprang to

her feet and barked a command which I understood as 'Erda! Don't you now do that!' and she motioned her Druid guard to clear a space in the crowd, which they did by swinging thick lengths of knotted rope in front of them, although carefully avoiding the blood-soaked Princess Erda.

I fear I made a rod for my own back that afternoon, for Boudica insisted that I stay near the hole in the Temple vaults from which the few remaining colonists were dragged one by one. I witnessed them all put to death, without pity and without exception, after being asked 'Where is Catus?' by the mad (for surely she was by now) Erda, or in Latin by me if they could not understand the tribal dialect or Erda was busying herself with her knives.

At one point, the single womanly cry of 'Mercy!' came from underground and a baby was thrown into the air, out of the pyre. It was caught by a Druid who in one movement, took it by a leg and smashed its brains out on the ground, with no more effort than he would use if stunning a freshly caught fish.

And then one of the blackened, barely human, figures dragged from one hell into another had an answer to the question.

'Londinium,' gasped Valerius Lupus, his voice a hoarse croak.

I had not recognised him, his clothes and skin covered in grime and soot and shit and blood, his hair matted with sweat and filth, his tongue swollen with thirst.

The Iceni pulled him from the vaults across a pile of broken bricks and the Druids held back the press of Trinovantine women who had also realised who he was.

'So the Procurator has fled south?' I said to him in Greek, which I knew he understood and in which he answered me.

'To Londinium. Olussa – is that you? Have you come to save us?'

I had to kneel beside him and lower my head to his to catch his words and there were murmurings from the crowd who could not understand what we were saying.

'No, Valerius, I cannot save you. You could have saved me, but you let me blunder into the tribal lands knowing that this storm was coming. And now it is too late. I cannot save you. I do not think they will even let me bury you.'

'Your father—' he croaked.

'My father never liked you, and certainly never trusted you. It is the same with me. I could forgive your greed and your treachery, and the ideas you had above your station, but it was your power to wield boredom like a sword – that alone means you are not worth saving.'

I stood up and turned away, showing the crowd that we had finished our business, although Valerius had the last words: 'Your father . . . knows . . .', but they were no more than the wanderings of a lost mind.

'This man was an official of the town and he says Catus is in Londinium, to the south. He has no reason to lie – not now,' I announced, disappointing some who had thought I might plead for him.

'This man is known to the Trinovantes,' said Boudica, 'whom he has mistreated and abused cruelly, taking their property and their slaves without payment. Shall I give him to them?'

I do not think Boudica expected an answer and I gave none.

It was decided that as Valerius Lupus was said to have introduced crucifixion to the Trinovantes, it was only just that they should practise it on him. There was no shortage of volunteers to go into the forest and cut fresh timber.

XXXVII: Roscius

The Governor didn't hang about.

All the staff officers were summoned to the General's quarters where he provided bread and wine and cold meats and had about a hundred lamps lit so that we could see the big map of Britannia he'd had drawn on a calfskin. Yes, Agricola was there, taking down the orders and feeding them to the despatch riders.

General Paulinus used a dagger to stab the map and there were some holes in it by the time he had finished, I can tell you!

'Petillius Cerialis and the IXth have been defeated by the Iceni,' he told us, 'and we must assume Camulodunum to be lost. It is likely that the Trinovantes have joined in this uprising and perhaps other tribes will ally with them. Our main problem is guessing where Boudica will strike next.'

'Verulamium, surely. It is the second city,' someone said.

'But Londinium has granaries and warehouses,' countered the General, 'and if she takes Londinium, she could cut the road to the ports of Rutupiae* and Dubris, which means no reinforcements or resupply.'

We knew it would also mean no escape from this bloody island, though none of us said that out loud.

He began to stab at the map with the point of his dagger.

'The XIVth is here, on Mona. I want orders sent tonight that it breaks camp immediately and comes to Deva. I want riders out to all forts to the north and south, telling the XXth to join them here. Strip the forts and outposts of three out of four legionaries and all the auxiliaries. Once they are assembled, I want the entire force to march south down Route LXVI.'

I told you Paulinus was the man, didn't I? Even then, when he didn't know where the enemy was, or how strong they were, he was planning an attacking victory, not a heroic defence.

'Now, we must send word to the IInd Legion down here in Isca,' said Paulinus, using his dagger on the map again, this time near the bottom corner. 'Who is in command there?'

'The acting commander is Peonius Posthumous, sir,' said Agricola. Now that was Agricola, I do remember that, because he always knew the whereabouts of staff officers. 'The legate and the deputy commander are both in Rome, attending a family wedding.'

We all saw the General's eyebrows go up at that.

'Get orders to him with all speed. Tell him to mobilise and march north to . . .' He looked at the map and stabbed yet another hole in it, this time near the centre. '. . . Venonis**. I want them, the whole IInd Legion and their auxiliaries, to rendezvous with the XIVth and XXth there in nine days' time. No, make that eight days, just to push them. Tell them minimum supply trains and no artillery and they can live off the land where they can, under my seal.'

* Richborough

** Near Nuneaton.

If we didn't think things were serious before, we did then, because the General, who was also the Governor, remember, was giving his blessing to wholesale confiscation of private property not only from Brits – which nobody really minded – but also any Roman citizens with farms or granaries who got in the way. That usually led to legal disputes and reparations cases which went on for years.

The General put Julius Agricola in charge of the rendezvous at Venonis – I thought you'd like that. Given the circumstances, it was quite a responsibility for someone on their first posting as military tribune, but Agricola was well thought of, mainly because his father was supposed to be an expert on wine and vine-growing, even written a book about it, though I've never read it. Anyway, he wouldn't have that much to do if everything went to plan. The XIVth Legion with odds and sods from the XXth would be coming down the road, the IInd coming up from the south. All they had to do was meet up and keep on going, next stop Verulamium and then Londinium. It wasn't Agricola's fault it went shit-faced on us, he did his bit, and it was a good plan of campaign.

What made it a great plan – and Suetonius Paulinus has never got the proper credit for it – was what he ordered next.

'I want half an *ala* of cavalry and my personal bodyguard,' he said, and that of course included me, 'ready to ride fast and hard at daybreak.'

Now half an *ala* – a cavalry wing – is eight troops, about 250 men. That's not enough to fight a battle with, hardly enough to do a major scouting job, and you don't go scouting with a General in tow.

'If we use the roads and she doesn't, we could be in Londinium before that mad bitch Boudica!'

'The General's presence alone will make Londinium impregnable!' gushed one spotty young officer trying to lick a few boots on his way to the top. The General was having none of that.

'Stupid boy,' he said under his breath. 'We are not going to defend it, we're going to make sure she captures it!'

XXXVIII: Olussa

It has taken them two days to decide on the order of march to Londinium. Not the order of battle, simply who should lead this triumph down the road, as if there was an audience lining the way, waiting to throw flowers in our path.

At first it seemed as if the Iceni would have the honour of leading the march south. After all, there were many more Iceni warriors than there were Trinovantes and they had done the bulk of the fighting in the ambush of the IXth Legion. The Trinovantes argued that they had been responsible for slaughtering more civilians in Camulodunum and that by leading the army on the road to Londinium, they would attract the local population, who were, of course, Trinovantes, thus swelling our strength. Warrior chiefs such as Tarex maintained that Roman insults and the outrage committed by Catus Decianus on the Iceni, gave them the right to be seen leading the fight against Rome and the only question to be decided was which Iceni clan took precedence.

Tasciovanus made the point that there were Roman military forts along the road and the Trinovantes knew the lie of the land better – it once having been their land. The Iceni responded, rather undiplomatically, that a tribe who had lost its land to an invader it had originally welcomed, had few battle honours to display.

And so it went on for two days, with supplies of fodder for the animals running out and even the hardiest of warriors complaining about a diet of Imperial Army mule stew. Then the Druids came up with the strategy that Tarex's clan would lead the Iceni forces, acting as Boudica's personal bodyguard. The Trinovantes, or at least their cavalry under Tasciovanus and his noble kinsmen, would scout ahead of the army, seeking out recruits to the rebellion, Romans and supplies, though not necessarily in that order and eventually, the army began to move, uncoiling and stretching like a fat worm down the road.

I have one *raeda* to worry about and I must be my own *raedarius*. Everything I have in the world is carried within it; the second carriage and all my oxen have disappeared but I have inherited two Iceni ponies, gifts from the Queen brought to me by a pair of curly-haired twins aged no more than ten or eleven years. The twins, who are cheerful enough, are guarded by their mother, an Iceni warrior woman with a dagger in her belt, a legionary javelin in her fist and an oval shield slung across her back. She speaks with an accent even I have trouble understanding, but eventually I begin to follow what she is trying to say to me. She is of the Eastern Iceni as far as I can judge, and has few relatives or clansmen left among the native army. If I have understood her, she has lost a husband, two brothers and two brothers-in-law in the ambush of the IXth Legion, leaving her with children, female relatives and ponies to feed.

I foresee what is coming and accept with good grace. I agree to take the twin boys, whom I call Romulus and Remus, as well as the ponies. One pair can look after the other, for I am not good with animals or young boys. Both ponies attempt to bite me as I stroke them, to accustom them to my smell, and to show my generous nature I offer both boys a share of my last jar of salted red onions, which they taste briefly before spitting on to the road. I would rather they had also tried to bite me.

I search the carriage for something to give the mother – a pot or plate or perhaps a brooch – but my supplies are exhausted. What has not been given away has been lost or stolen. I have the clothes I stand up in (and they are so rank they could almost stand alone) and my writing materials, though they are worth nothing in the world I now find myself in.

I do not expect my fortunes to improve greatly in Londinium. In fact I am certain that the Procurator has already taken steps to liquidate the business of Alexander and Son, sequester my father's property and sell my sister into slavery. And somehow I will still end up owing him 473,000 sesterces.

Unless, that is, the Princess Erda finds him first.

XXXIX: Roscius

We beat her to it, though only the gods knew how.

It took six days of hard riding for us to get to Londinium down Route LXVI and the General didn't lose a single man. Plenty of horses, though. We raided every Imperial Post stable on the way, sending on our fastest riders to warn them we were coming, then we'd charge in like it was an enemy camp, take every fresh horse standing and all the feed we could carry and then we would be off, leaving the ostlers with dust in their mouths and a corral of lame, broken-winded nags, good only for the knackers' yards.

We didn't see a single hostile. They probably saw us but we were moving so fast that they couldn't organise an ambush. Maybe there just weren't any hostiles. We didn't see much sign, though afterwards all the reports back to Rome spoke of the 'British' rebellion as if all the bloody tribes had sided with Boudica, just to make it sound more dramatic. Anyone who served there – even Agricola – could have told you that the British tribes hated each other more than us.

Boudica had the Iceni, naturally, and she had just about all of them; it was almost a migration for the tribe, like the Helvetii tried under old Julius, they left virtually nobody back in the tribal lands while they went on the warpath. Half their season's crops never got planted and the other half never got harvested. They were doomed from the start.

The Trinovantes joined in, of course they did, and they probably had good reasons given the way they'd been treated by the veterans of the XXth, and I am a vet of the XXth so I can say that. Agricola was as well, come to think of it. There were plenty of Trinnies, though, who buggered off into the woods at the first sign of trouble and stayed there until it was all over. Some of the poor bastards looked for shelter in Londinium thinking we were coming to save them, and they got the worst of it when the fellow tribesmen arrived, I can tell you.

But right from the off, the most belligerent of the Trinnies were really in it to settle some old scores with the Catuvellauni at Verulamium. Once they'd done that, most of them pissed off and left the Iceni to face the music.

Yes, I know, I'm getting ahead of myself.

So, on the fifth day on the road, we fetched up in Verulamium, covered in saddle sores and dust, as black as Africans, and yet the civic authorities and the townsfolk turned out for us like they were giving us a triumph, showering us with rose water from the roofs and the women rushing out to wipe down our horses with their cloaks, giggling and getting all excited like they were collecting gladiator sweat.

Thank the gods there was a sensible military man to clear a path for us and provide feed and water for the horses and onion and chicken fat poultices for us to ease our saddle sores, because I can tell you, five days hard riding in those rigid square saddles, can rub your delicates red raw.* Sometimes through two pairs of necessaries.

Necessaries? It's what we called underpants and a good cavalryman never went anywhere without a spare pair.

The chap who greeted us in Verulamium was a cavalryman, an officer in an auxiliary unit of Thracians – good riders and good archers. He was called Rufus Sita and he was a good bloke, one of us. He knew that what we needed was a poultice, a jug of decent wine and news of where the enemy was and he gave us all three.

The General was mightily impressed with him and included him in the officers' call. Rufus Sita had been sending out scouts to the east as soon as word had come through about the ambush of the IXth Legion. He estimated that Boudica was still on Route XII, burning and drinking everything in her path, her army covering between six and eight miles a day as if they were going for a stroll in the market. Sita put them somewhere south of Caesaromagus**, approaching the Old Ford on the

* At this time, Roman cavalry did not have stirrups and the rider sat in a bone-framed box saddle, controlling the horse with the knees.

** Chelmsford, Essex.

outskirts of Londinium and their strength at perhaps fifty to sixty thousand, though he couldn't swear to that.

'How soon could she be in Londinium?' the General asked him, adding: 'Be honest. Tell me as a soldier, do not try and impress a Governor.'

Sita did not hesitate and he told Paulinus straight, where many an officer, especially from the auxiliaries, would have offered to soap and sponge the General's arse.

'Her army is strung out over many miles. She seems to have no idea of how to use the roads properly and when night comes they camp where they are, so they waste much time bringing supplies up from the rear. But if none oppose them, they will be setting fires in the forum in Londinium in four days' time. They have already sent a message to the populace – slave chains and neck irons.'

'Chains?' said the General, his thoughts interrupted.

'From the fort at Caesaromagus, where there was a slave market. They loaded up three horses with them and spurred them down the road ahead of their army. The beasts virtually bit their genitals off so maddened by the way they were spurred. Some of my scouts put them out of their misery, but not before the locals had seen them. Now there is panic about an uprising of slaves in the town.'

'For which there would be cause, if that is what the message of the Iceni means,' said the General.

'What else could it mean?' asked one of the other officers – you can say it was Agricola if you like, though he wasn't there.

'I think it means the Iceni do not need neck irons and slave chains because they have no intention of taking any prisoners. They want blood, not slaves. They want victims for their rituals. You remember what we saw on Mona, Roscius?'

'Too right, General. Every pond and grove of oak was stuffed with the heads of sacrificed prisoners.'

'There are about 17,000 civilian heads left in Londinium,' said Rufus Sita.

'And Londinium sits on a large river, bigger than anything the Iceni know in their homelands. They will not be able to resist making a substantial sacrifice,' replied the General looking him straight in the eyes.

'Which should delay them for quite a while,' said Sita.

'Exactly,' said the General, recognising a kindred spirit. 'Rufus Sita, I appoint you military commander of Verulamium. You have one task and absolute authority to carry it out. Assemble every man with military training in the town, arm them and have them ready to move north in two days' time. Do this without encouraging the civilian population here to join you.'

'You can rely on my Thracians, General, as long as I can assure them of a place in the battle you are planning,' said Sita even though most of the regular staff officers were still trying to work out what Paulinus had in mind.

'I can promise you that, Rufus Sita, but I cannot tell you when it will be.'

'Londinium and Verulamium should delay her for a week, ten days if we are lucky,' said Sita to a chorus of muffled gasps from the staffers, most of whom had only just caught on to the fact that we were about to abandon the second city of the island as well as Londinium to the enemy. It was quite a gamble.

The General always said he liked to pick lucky commanders and Rufus Sita must have been lucky. I never saw him again, but his Thracians did everything that was expected of them and more, and Sita lived to retire and claim citizenship and a pension. Got himself a place near Glevum* I heard, which is where he's buried.

At dawn the next day we were on the move again. None of us had got much sleep, it was summer, remember, and the nights were short, but Rufus Sita had organised fresh remounts, each with a small flask of wine and loaf of bread lashed to the saddle. Only a cavalryman would think of that.

The General's orders were quite specific. We would get into town about the eighth hour that day, find quarters for the night and then round up every spare mount and every spare military man we could find, burn the bridges to the south bank of the Tamesis, torch all the granaries, and get back on the road by noon tomorrow. All without scaring the populus.

* Gloucester.

That last order was easy; we didn't have to worry about scaring the good citizens of Londinium, they were well scared already.

The clever ones – or at least the richer ones – were long gone, mostly by boat. The rest were divided into two camps – those who were stupid enough to think they could stack all their possessions on a cart and use the roads to get to safety without the protection of a military escort, and those who were extra stupid and thought they would stay put because the Governor would protect them.

We met the first column of refugees, heading north, about five miles from Londinium. They actually cheered us, maybe thinking that the legions couldn't be far behind us although our boys wouldn't have made the rendezvous at Venonis yet.

The nearer we got to the town, the thicker became the fleeing crowd.

'At least they're keeping some sort of order,' said the General over his shoulder, 'not running and trampling the children.'

'There'll be plenty of time for that,' I replied.

We halted in the cemetery outside the north-west gate of the old stockade. The gate had been left open in order to allow civilians out and our passage was temporarily blocked until the duty centurion, recognising the General's standard, turned out the Guard to clear the crowds with their shields. Thus we entered Londinium riding in a column of fours, General Paulinus at our head, following Route LXVI to the heart of the settlement and the government buildings down by the river. As we rode the General pointed out the Imperial granaries in the distance to our left and, as arranged, two troops peeled off from our column, their mission being to prepare fire or flood to ruin the contents of them and to recruit their guards to our ranks. Another troop headed on towards the bridges spanning the Tamesis to prepare them for destruction, although the weight of fleeing civilians seemed likely to do the job for us.

The remaining five troops and we of the General's bodyguard dismounted in the market place near the new residence of the Procurator. I didn't get a proper chance to stretch my legs before I was following Paulinus up the steps to the palace of Catus Decianus – a man the General was anxious to see.

But Paulinus was to be disappointed, for the palace was empty – not even guarded – and had been empty for several days. Amazingly the place had not been looted and there were plenty of fine bronzes, wall-hangings and imported pottery and glassware going begging.

The General had brought along two personal body slaves, who walked bow-legged following the ride south, and he sent them to the kitchens to see if there was any food there, which there was in abundance. Not even the Procurator's unguarded larder had tempted the local criminal element.

Paulinus ordered the kitchen fires to be lit and bread baked to go with whatever cold cuts could accompany the excellent wines found in the Procurator's cellars. He also asked for every lamp in the palace to be filled with oil and made ready for dusk in the main reception rooms, which would be his command centre rather than the Governor's residence further to the east.

From the Procurator's Palace, we sent out a stream of runners and throughout the afternoon they returned with news, with appeals from civic leaders, with excuses, with bribes, with requests for audiences. I posted sentries at all the entrances to the palace and took up position myself on the steps outside, fending off the growing crowd which gathered to petition the General in person.

One delegation comprised half a dozen prostitutes from the docks led by a fierce, redheaded Celt with an accent thick enough to cut with a knife. She demanded to see the General because she was sure he would want to see her. I told her to get back to the fish docks in no uncertain terms and threatened to put my fist between her eyes.

'You Palace Police always liked it rough!' she shouted in my face. 'Half our business has gone now the Procurator's shut up shop! You could at least compensate us, you bastards.'

I grabbed a handful of her greasy hair and pulled her down on to her knees and told her she should tell me what she knew of the noble Procurator's whereabouts before she found herself counting her teeth on the steps beneath her.

'They say he took a ship. He'll be in Gaul by now. Went two, three days ago,' she said between gasps of pain, for I was twisting my grip and her hair was coming out like straw from a pillow.

'And what of his bodyguard, his slaves, his secretaries and clerks?'

'He left alone with only what he could carry, they say. As for the rest, I do not know except for his Chief of Police, an animal called Starbo. An animal who has a bite worse than his bark, believe me, and a stench on him that repels dung flies.'

'Where do I find this arsehole?'

'He's working his way down the street of taverns by the docks. Been there for a couple of days now. He's drunk so much, we are of no use to him, which is a pity for just this once he has plenty of cash on him. Gold coins – loads of them.'

I let go of her hair but instead of trying to stand, she remained on her knees, reaching forward for my thighs.

'That was worth something, wasn't it?'

'It's worth some good advice,' I told her, pulling her up on to her feet and holding her close enough so that the rest of the crowd couldn't hear, but far enough away that I didn't have to smell her breath. I didn't know what she'd had in her mouth that day, but I could guess. 'Take your girlfriends and go south of the river. Go now while the bridges still stand and keep going. Trust me, that's valuable advice.'

'It's not as good as money, though, is it? What do we do for money on the south bank of the river?'

'The same you do on the north, you old whore. You know where your fortune lies, you're sitting on it. Now fuck off and prosper!'

Our patrols found this Starbo character in the third tavern they tried. Finding him wasn't difficult, they just followed the trail of broken furniture and smashed pottery. He was a big fucker and tried to take them all on, but the cavalry in those days were tough boys, not quite as hard as the legionaries but tough enough. Two of them held him down while a third cut the hamstrings on his left leg. They were used to dealing with horses, you see, so even a big shithead like him didn't worry them.

Lying there in front of the General on the stone palace floor, he didn't look so big. He was still drunk enough not to realise he would never walk straight again, or worry about the shame of emptying his bladder right there in front of us all. I didn't think there was much hope of getting anything out of him, and I was right. Every question the General asked brought a blubbering answer which made no sense. Then a junior officer from the patrol that had brought him in asked permission to speak and suggested we tried our questions on the big animal's slave. Apparently, this Starbo had a naked boy with him on his tavern crawling, a boy with a rope around his neck and, like a dog, had been tied to the leg of every table he had slumped over.

'Will the dog turn on his master?' mused Paulinus and ordered the boy brought in, though not before he had been sluiced with water and given some trousers and a tunic.

Even though he was still filthy, his skin as brown as a Spaniard's though from dirt not sun, and he stank like a latrine in high summer, it was still possible to see why men such as Starbo would lust after him. His eyes were as blue as the sea at Philippi – not that I've ever been to Philippi, but that's what the Greek writers always used to say, isn't it?

Paulinus used his vine stick – his swagger stick, we called it when we were on parade – under Starbo's chin to raise his face towards the boy and then he said:

'Is this man your owner?'

The boy's eyes flashed.

'He is my jailer!' the boy spat, in educated Latin. 'My master is Narcissus Alexander the merchant, but I have not been allowed to go to him since my return. This pig has kept me prisoner.'

'Returned from where?' asked the General softly.

The boy hesitated before he answered: 'From Camulodunum.'

'You know that the *colonia* is no more?' The boy nodded, his eyes to the floor and the General went on gently. 'I would be very grateful and generous to anyone who could tell of the events which led up to the loss of that city.'

'I know of some things,' said the boy, almost childlike.

'Excellent,' said Paulinus. 'Let me hear your story over some food and wine, while this piece of shit on the floor sobers up.'

The General stepped over to the boy to put an arm around his shoulders, but he made sure he trod on the wounded man's leg as he did so. The former Chief of Police moaned loudly, made a gulping sound as if he was about to vomit, and fainted.

The boy's story, once he got going, was a cracking one, just like the history we were taught when young, of the heroes and kings of ancient times. Naturally, we didn't believe a word of it, but the lad knew how to entertain, I'll give him that. He held the floor for a good two hours while we brought in chairs and sat and listened. He never once lost his thread, even with messengers coming in and whispering in my ear or the General's every few minutes.

He had, or so he said, been an unwilling traveller in the land of the Iceni on an expedition led by somebody called Olussa, the son of his owner, who pretended to be an honest merchant but was long suspected in the household of being an embezzler and although he claimed he was in Iceni territory to establish trade links, it was well-known that he was a spy in the pay of the Procurator, Catus Decianus.

The General asked what this Olussa had learned about the Iceni and how he sent his information back to the Procurator, but the boy could not answer. The General then said that this Olussa must have been a pretty poor spy and the boy, who said his name was Calpurnius, agreed that indeed he was, spending most of his time talking to the women of the tribe, exchanging recipes!

I remember we all had a good laugh at that and then the General pointed out that the war chief of the Iceni seemed to be a woman and perhaps Calpurnius could prove to be a better spy and tell us something about Queen Boudica.

'She's as tall as any man,' he said, 'and has a voice like a man, deep and rough. And she has thick red hair so long that it hangs over her arse. Although she is not long a widow she shags anything that moves, sometimes taking two lovers at once.'

'There seem to have been few secrets in the land of the Iceni,' the General said dryly, then asked: 'How was the noble Procurator received on his visit?'

To hear the boy tell it, Catus Decianus had been the perfect

Roman ambassador – gracious, understanding and generous to a fault, there to negotiate the terms of the late King Prasutagus' will. It was nobody's fault that the mad red-haired bitch encouraged her people to argue with the Procurator, and disobey him, in fact openly attack him until he was forced to flee back to Camulodunum and then Londinium.

'And then elsewhere . . .' the General muttered under his breath, then he slammed his wine cup on the table so that we all sat up and took notice and he said: 'Roscius, get a blade and cut off this little bastard's ears. Then the end of his nose, then his eyelids. Cut something off every time he tells me another lie and feed the bits to the dogs. Leave his tongue, so that he can still earn a living.'

I had hardly got to my feet let alone drawn my sword, before this Calpurnius was on his knees and talking for all he was worth. It was then we got the true story, which we all know now as it came out in the Senatorial inquiry. The kid couldn't talk fast enough, telling us how Catus and his men had gone into the tribal lands, lifting every piece of loot they could carry, even to desecrating the old king's grave and a couple of Druid shrines for good measure. And when Boudica had objected, they'd flogged her in public – instead of just fucking killing her like a soldier would have. They had also had their way with her daughters and again, the stupid fuckers had left them alive. The dead tend not to be able to lead reprisal raids, it's a well known fact. Survivors make better heroes, or heroines in this case and Catus had provided the Iceni with three of them.

'And what did the noble Catus do next?' the General asked politely.

'He commandeered the Imperial Post Galley and sailed on the first tide for Gaul.'

'He travelled alone?' the General pressed.

'Without even a body slave,' said the boy as if disappointed.

'Where did he leave the loot?'

Now that was why Paulinus was a General. He was the first to realise that Catus may have bullied his way on board the Post Galley, but there was no way he could have smuggled his Iceni plunder on with him. The captains of Post Galleys had strict operating instructions about the weight they carried and were, in the main, incorruptible. But what the boy said next I think surprised even him.

'There are three wagons full of Iceni plunder, including much gold, in the stables at the rear of this palace. The gates are not even locked.'

The General shook his head in wonderment. 'I had not realised that even the thieves were of such poor quality here in Londinium. This will never be a great city until it has a decent criminal class. Put sentries out, Roscius. Take the boy to show you.'

Before I could take him by the scruff of the neck, this Calpurnius prostrated himself on the floor before Paulinus.

'My Lord, you must return me to my master,' he pleaded.

Paulinus looked at him over the rim of his wine cup and said:

'I am Governor of this province, Commander of the British Fleet and General of four legions. There is nothing I *must* do. Keep this young pup out of sight, I don't want him gossiping to anyone.'

And so we hogtied the little imp and left him face down in a pile of straw in the stables he took us to. There were no animals there, only the three wagons he had promised. I posted two junior centurions as guards and they looked a bit surly at first as they, like us staff officers, were *immunes* – exempt from fatigues and guard duties. But their eyes popped like eggs when they saw what was in the wagons – the gold jewellery and coins, the bronze mirrors, the silver bowls and spoons, even a couple of sickles made out of gold, I swear – all piled up in no particular order. And of course the gold torcs, those big thick twists of spun gold which the Celts wore around their necks. You never hear a story about Boudica without a gold torc getting a mention, but I can tell you I've seen them, held them in my hand. I've even seen one on her, the bloodthirsty bitch herself!

I know, I know, stick to the history. Where was I?

Oh yes. Well I could see what those young officers were thinking and I just asked them how much extra weight they thought their horses could carry back up the road to where our legions would be waiting, which might be a hundred miles of hard riding with some very bad-tempered Iceni on their tails all the way. I left them thinking about that and went to report to the General.

Paulinus heard me out and then ordered the recall for senior officers to be sounded by the trumpeters. That not only brought in our men but the crowd outside the palace tripled in size within the space of a few minutes.

The General wasn't worried about that, in fact he said we should start to make as much noise as we could. The enemy knew where we were so there was no point in hiding and there were probably spies already planted in the crowd, so it was best to look busy.

He heard the reports from the units we had sent out into the town and then gave his orders. We would burn the bridges across the river, but not the granaries, which raised a few eyebrows, I can tell you. The east gate out on to Route XII, the old road to the capital Camulodunum, was to be sealed and barricaded and defended by any auxiliaries from the Londinium garrison, members of the Town Watch and the *vigiles*, the night shift police, who couldn't find a horse. Those that had a mount would come with us. The civilian population would be encouraged to evacuate the town immediately and head for Verulamium but carts and wagons were not to be allowed on the road. All transport in civilian hands must be left in Londinium. It was to be our present to Boudica: no organised defence, granaries stuffed with grain for the taking and plenty of wagons to carry it, along with whatever plunder could be found in the dock and warehouse district. We would even leave the Iceni treasure looted by the noble Procurator unguarded and inviting.

'That should slow them down,' said the General.

It was almost dark when Paulinus addressed the crowd from the palace steps by the light of a hundred torches.

He told them he would not turn their city into a battlefield but there would be a defence of the eastern gate which should deter the rebels long enough, as they were an undisciplined rabble and had no experience of besieging a place as big as Londinium. The very size of the town, compared to the mud huts the rebels lived in, would be enough to deter them. The gates were stout and the defence would be led by the Procurator, Catus Decianus himself.

Now this bit came as a shock to most of us on the General's staff, but he pressed on without pause, telling the crowd that the Procurator was recovering from a fever and had sworn to take personal command of the Town Watch on the next day. (By which time, we would be out of there, we realised.) His deputy would be the auxiliary policeman Starbo, who was known to all. And at this point, a pair of burly troopers brought Starbo forth from the Palace. He wore a long cloak pinned up tightly at the throat. He reeked of vomit and piss and was kept steady on his feet by the two troopers who had firm grips on his elbows. It was dark, and they kept him out of direct torchlight, so nobody noticed.

The General ended by saying that those who wanted to leave the city should take the bridges to the south bank before dawn or travel on foot to Verulamium, but no transports were allowed as he had to keep the road clear for he was riding to meet his legions – three full legions who, at that very moment, were racing to defeat the rebellious little British shits.

That last bit actually got a cheer from the good citizens of Londinium who didn't realise they had had the wool cap pulled firmly down over their eyes.

The General gave them a wave, then turned on his heel and marched back into the palace. He was unbuckling his armour and calling for his body slaves while we were closing the doors, but not before one of the *ala*'s standard-bearers had grabbed my arm, saying there was something the General might want to know.

We had put scouts out down the riverbank as soon as we had arrived and they had reported back that there was nothing left in the port of Londinium that could float except for a converted bireme anchored on one of the mud islands in mid-stream. For a while a crowd had gathered on the north bank and shouted curses and obscenities at it, then offered bribes for safe passage and one or two had even tried to swim to it though they were prevented from climbing aboard by the crew wielding their oars. More than one head had been staved in and a couple of bodies were floating upriver as the tide came in.

As I was telling the General this, he said: 'Don't let a few murders worry you, Roscius old friend, there will be plenty more soon enough.'

'It's not that, sir,' I said, feeling guilty at keeping him from his bed, 'it's just that there's a man outside, a merchant, who claims to be the boat's owner and he says he has information for you.'

'It sounds as if he has the only safe passage out of here, never mind any information. Better let him in before the crowd get wind and rip him to pieces.'

The standard-bearer pushed his way into the mob and pulled out a white-bearded old man clutching a hide bag to his chest. He wore a toga which had been white once but now was stained with dust and sweat and good-quality sandals of brushed pigskin, the sort the merchants call 'quiet little dogs'.

'My name is Narcissus Alexander,' he said, breathing heavily.

'And the Governor is my Lord General C. Suetonius Paulinus,' I told him, 'and you are coming between him and his supper, and soldiers don't like that. So make it important, and make it swift.'

The old fart almost kissed my hands in gratitude as I showed him inside and he stood quivering in front of the General's supper table. His slaves had found some cold cuts of roasted duck preserved in fat and even some fruit, and prepared him some hot wine with nutmeg and aniseed – he used to drink that all year round before retiring for the night.

The old man repeated his name and bowed, adding that he was a leading figure in the merchants' guild in Londinium.

'The last one left, I should think,' observed Paulinus. 'And now, I am told, you command the only vessel left in the merchant fleet of this port.'

'I have a ship, my Lord, with captain and crew and eighty-eight oarsmen and marines all paid for. I place it entirely at the disposal of the Governor. I am told the ship is fast and given tide and wind, could easily make the coast of Gaul in the hours of daylight.'

'Then why,' said Paulinus, 'is not Narcissus Alexander, his wife and children and all his considerable personal fortune, already in Gaul?'

'Because of this,' said the merchant and he produced a letter from the bag he was clutching and handed it over so the General could read it aloud.

XL: Valerius Lupus

By Imperial Post. Most urgent and secret.
To Narcissus Alexander, Merchant, Londinium.

Dearest and oldest et cetera,

I write you this last time with the gravest of news. The *colonia* here is under attack from savages whose muster is as thick as the forest. It is doubtful that help will arrive in time, if, indeed, any help is on the way. I am consigning this letter to the last Imperial Post rider to leave. I fear you will not hear from me again, my old partner and friend.

I have more news, which for you will bring the utmost sadness. In amongst the panic and the fear that grips our city, the rumour is widespread that a Roman rides with the enemy, aiding Trinovantes and Iceni alike and acting as a *consiliarius* to the barbarian queen Boudica herself. The stories about this mysterious adviser to the enemy of Rome grow more outlandish each day. In the slave market there is talk that he directs their campaign and the tribal war chiefs pay him homage; that he has adopted the Druidic religion and participates in human sacrifices and drinks blood; even that he is the lover of Boudica.

This so-called Roman can be no other than your son, Olussa and there is nothing I can say to explain or predict his actions, but I did warn you in my last letter that I feared for his safety. Now I have to inform you of his treachery and know how much this must hurt your heart, you who have always been a loyal servant of Rome, as have I.

I trust that you have called in the bills of credit and promissory notes which I sent to you. As I have neither wife nor children, I make you my sole heir and as such I expect you to make arrangements for a suitable tombstone for me here in Camulodunum.

Goodbye friend,
Valerius Lupus.

XLI: Roscius

Paulinus finished reading and went back to eating his supper. The only thing he said was: 'What has this to do with me?'

The old man reached into his hide sack again and hefted a bag which he placed delicately on the table in front of the Governor. The place was so silent we could hear the chink of coins as they settled.

I remembered the last time someone had tried to bribe Paulinus, and how we made him pick his teeth out of a camp fire, so most of us in the bodyguard were already measuring this Olussa character for his coffin. But the old man talked himself out of trouble. Maybe he was an honourable merchant. You do occasionally meet them.

'I would ask only that my Lord Governor does not believe these allegations against my son. My old friend Valerius Lupus must have been deranged when he wrote that letter, but if they are indeed the last words of a man facing death, they must be respected. I'm sure he must be mistaken, but if my son is allied with these rebels against Rome, I ask only for a fair trial for him.'

Paulinus stared him down and said: 'I dispense Roman law, I do not sell it.'

'Forgive me, my Lord,' the old man quivered, his legs shaking, 'those coins are for any of your men who will search the battlefield for his body if it comes to that, and for a decent funeral, that is all.'

'You said you had a ship,' said the General.

'It is yours to command, I would ask only safe passage for my daughter Julia, who is already on board.'

'And for yourself, I presume?' the General asked him, and the old man surprised us all yet again.

'No, my Lord. I have decided to remain here in Londinium. I think it is important that Roman values and Roman life are not seen to fold their tents and run at the first sign of trouble.'

'Are you saying that is what the army has done?' said the General with a real edge to his voice.

'The gold I bring for my son's burial surely shows that I believe the army will do its job. I only say that Rome is more than just its army; Rome brings trade, law, learning, civilisation. I have always believed this. I will to the end, and though it might be my end, it will not be the end of Rome.'

The old man said all that looking Paulinus in the eyes.

'A noble speech,' said the General. 'Rome should be proud of such citizens. But it is likely to cost you dear. I cannot protect your houses or your property, and I am taking your ship and sending it to Gaul. Have you any other family who would sail with it?'

'My daughter Julia is on board and apart from my son, I have no other children. There was a slave – a trusted house slave – whom I had thought to make a freeman. The last I heard, he was serving with the Procurator's police, but I have been unable to find him,' answered the merchant with real sadness.

None of us said a word – well, we wouldn't unless the General did, and he was playing it straight, his face as blank as a ceremonial cavalry helmet mask.

'Your daughter will be taken to safety,' was all the General said.

As he was escorted out by the standard-bearer, the merchant turned back to look at Paulinus, just once, and he said:

'My son and I, we never achieved citizenship, and though we have always served Rome, we are, at the end, non-Romans.'

That was all he said, and there were tears in his eyes as he did.

The General's next lot of orders were for me, and me alone, which is why you won't find them mentioned in the official reports.

'If I don't come through this, Roscius, my old comrade,' he told me, 'then I want to make sure our beloved Procurator does not either. I suspect you will find him at the Imperial Treasury in Gesoriacum. Take this merchant's ship to Gaul and give my best wishes to Catus Decianus. My *very* best wishes – you understand?'

I touched the hilt of the dagger at my belt and told him I

understood very well what he was asking me to do, but I wasn't going to leave him on the eve of a serious battle.

He said: 'The legions will take care of the rebels; I have to stay with the legions. I will sleep easier and be a better general in the knowledge that our greedy shithead of a Procurator is no more. Now do as I say. Take the merchant's boat on the night tide and the merchant's gold for your expenses.'

I hefted the bag of coins which Narcissus Alexander had left on the table.

'If these are gold, there's a fortune in here. I might be tempted not to come back,' I said.

He smiled at that. 'Use what you need for bribes – you might need them to get near to him. If you can't drink your way through the rest, then give it to the merchant's daughter. You'll make sure she travels safely, won't you? Of course you will, you've never failed me. Take care, old friend.'

And with that, we embraced as old comrades and then I stepped back and gave him my best salute: back straight, heels together, fist to the heart and then arm outstretched.

Before we parted I asked him why he had not told the merchant that his missing house slave was at that moment tied up on the floor of the stables at the back of the palace.

'That boy is a wastrel,' he answered, 'and I would not trust him further than I could throw him. How he has survived this long is a mystery and I suspect the Iceni will have plans for him if they find him. The old merchant has suffered enough. Let him know his daughter will be safe and that he has done Rome a great service by providing you with a ship. He will die happier that way.'

The merchant was as good as his word. He signalled his ship from the steps of the Palace wharf using a small lamp and square of red glass and the boat answered with a torch waved twice through an arc. Then we heard a slap on the water as they launched the coracle to pick us up. The river was flat calm and the night was moonless, I remember that. And the coracle had to make two trips because the General had insisted I took a couple of the lads along with me, to watch my back. They were good messmates that I'd known for years before we served in the Governor's bodyguard. There was Sextilius

Germanus, who copped it a few years later in Judea, and T. Flavius Niger, who stayed on in Britannia when he retired and started farming oysters, would you believe, not far from Camulodunum, and he made a fortune once things calmed down.

The bireme's captain was pleased to see us for it meant he could get under way. He was feeling a bit exposed, being the only ship in the river and his oarsmen and marines were getting nervous, so they were glad to have something to do and I slipped the captain a fistful of *aurei* to keep up morale.

The ship had been converted for speed: the tower in the stern, where they usually mount the artillery and the bowmen, had been removed and replaced with a square tent. The captain told us that was where the merchant's daughter was and he hoped she would stay there as she'd already offered herself to two of his oarsmen, which could only lead to trouble among the other eighty-six.

The oars set a steady pace and we glided through the night towards the dawn and the sea. Londinium was dark and ominously quiet.

The next time I saw it, it was a pile of glowing embers.

XLII: Olussa

Londinium burned and I have seen horrors and cruelties such as I had never thought I could dream.

Tonight the vanguard of the army camps in the streets and squares of the city. Warriors collapse where they stand, exhausted, though not from battle. Many are too drunk to stand, some stagger under the weight of booty. All are tired from the killing. Not the fighting, but the killing. Old men and women do not put up much of a fight.

The so-called defenders managed to launch one volley of javelins before their nerves broke at the sight of the concentrated infantry attack by the tribes. The plan agreed by the war chiefs had been to pile wood and bracken cut from the forest against the gates and set it alight. It proved unnecessary, for the defenders fled their posts, allowing the British to climb over the stockade walls and open the gates from the inside.

The Druids sent word along the length of the army for Boudica to come forward. She did so driving a war chariot herself, with both her daughters beside her as spear-carriers. All three women were naked to the waist, their breasts decorated with blue circles of woad paint, and all wore cloaks fastened at the throat by large bronze pins forged into the shape of a curled snake.

A huge cheer went up from the army as she drove through the open gateway, but she gave no new orders and made no speeches. The warriors followed her chariot and the slaughter began.

Only the Druids seemed to lag behind, collecting up the wood gathered against the stockade walls, wielding axes to sharpen branches and saplings into long pointed stakes.

The attack on the gate started around noon, or the sixth hour of the day; by the end of the seventh hour, the air was thick with smoke and the war cries of the army were drowned by the screams of their victims.

The lucky ones were the ones who were killed in the first rush. Among them, much to the dismay of the Iceni royal family, was the giant Starbo, Catus' right-hand man, found face down in a street drain with a spear through his liver.

The discovery was greeted by a howl of anger from the Iceni warriors and a howl of despair from the Princess Erda when the body was dragged before the queen's chariot. Boudica herself remained impassive as her daughter walked over, spat on and stabbed the body of the dead giant, all the time screaming, 'Where is Catus?'

A flock of Iceni women carrying knives and sickles gathered around Boudica's chariot and when they saw that Erda's fury had run its course, they set upon the body like flies upon carrion.

They stripped the body of all its clothes, including the trousers which Starbo had soiled extensively in death or its anticipation, and then they stripped it of its skin, cutting lengths two inches wide from throat to groin and then down the legs. So many and so expert were the willing butchers that within minutes Starbo's body was a pattern of raw meat, although the head they left intact. Then the bloodied women called out to the Druids for one of the stakes they had fashioned at the gate and between them they spitted and skewered the rest of Starbo.

By nightfall the town was well alight and the victims of the British were numbered in their thousands. Most were the old and lame and many were children pulled roughly from cellars and hiding places. But the true savagery of the tribes was reserved for the women.

To Boudica, the women of Londinium had suckled and nursed Rome and had therefore to suffer the most. Where there was a wooden frame on a building, or a door or porch, a woman was crucified. When they ran out of space, two stout stakes planted in an X in the ground would do. In almost all cases, the women had one or both breasts cut off and the teat sewn to their mouth with coarse twine and a bone needle.

I took no pleasure in the bloodlust of the Iceni women, who would be too busy mutilating and sewing to cook a dinner for the army, so I made my way through the streets towards the river in search of food.

The taverns near the docks had been thoroughly wrecked but in one of them I found a pot of fish stew on a hearth. Cold and already scummy with the ash and soot that was falling like the first snow of winter, it was palatable and I ate it with the stirring ladle whilst walking around the tavern, stepping over splintered furniture and broken jugs. The toe of my boot found one flagon intact; its contents were vinegar, but they helped to dilute the taste of salted fish.

The street of taverns was ghostly in its emptiness, as the British had charged through the area to get to the river. Along the bank and the quays of the docks, thousands of them had gathered to stare in amazement at the Tamesis, for most had never seen a river so wide, the greasy black water reflected in a supernatural yellow light.

The bridge to the south bank had been burned by the Romans just before dawn and was now a blackened and glowing skeleton, and not the source of the light. That, I realised, came from a hundred or more large torches planted in the mud of the riverbank. And then I saw that the torches were humans, impaled from buttocks to throat on a stake, covered in pitch or oil and ignited.

In the hour before dawn, some of Tarex's clansmen found me sitting in the mud of the riverbank, watching headless corpses float down river on the turning tide. They told me I must report to the Queen and I allowed them to lead me back into the city centre, towards the Procurator's Palace.

On the way, I checked the face of every body we passed: bodies in ditches, bodies in open sewers, bodies nailed to timber-work, bodies impaled on stakes, heads on spears and strung from the belts of Iceni warriors. None of them was my father.

Boudica, her daughters and a troop of Druids were holding court on the steps of the Procurator's Palace. To either side of them large bonfires were fuelled by timbers, furniture, drapes and cushions from the Palace itself. The steps are ankle-deep in smashed glass and pottery and blood.

No Iceni or Trinovantes warrior has frightened me as much as the Princess Erda did that night. Boudica and Prisca had been splashed with blood, but Erda had bathed in it. From her face to her waist and all down her arms, she was covered and her hair was matted and plastered to her skull. She reminded me of a hunting dog which had plunged its snout into the innards of its kill.

All three women remained bare-breasted, though Boudica and Prisca held their cloaks close around their bodies for warmth.

Where before the cloaks were held in place by bronze pins at the throat, now they displayed magnificent golden torques of such size and weight they could only be the ones I glimpsed at Prasutagus' funeral.

I tore my eyes from the gold around her neck and looked around the square. In the crowd of armed men and blood-spattered women were three wagons, one of them mine, over-flowing with large jars, bronze mirrors, weapons, furs and bottles, everything covered with a sheen of gold and silver coins. The Iceni had recovered the treasure stolen from them by Catus, and were adding the contents of the Procurator's treasury to the load.

'We have taken back our goods, but not our honour,' Boudica announced proudly.

'They are paying for that in blood,' said Prisca.

They spoke as if I was not there and Boudica placed a gentle hand on the shoulder of young Erda, who was not speaking but making a low keening noise, staring into the flames of one of the bonfires.

'But there is not enough, my brave girls, not nearly enough,' said the Queen and then she turned to me, her face as calm and bland as if she was in her kitchen. 'Some of Togobin's clansmen have found something of yours, Olussa the lost Roman. Over there, in the house of Catus.'

At the top of the steps, the double doors to the Procurator's Palace lay torn from their hinges and smoke billowed out over them.

I climbed the Palace steps with a heavy tread as if in a fog, not hearing the chants of the victorious army saluting Boudica, the screams of its victims floating on the smoky air or the constant crash of falling masonry. I had to step over many bodies and from one of them, a young house slave I guessed though it was difficult to tell without the head, I ripped the sleeve from his tunic and wrapped it around my face against the smoke.

Togobin was in charge of the destruction of the Palace, a task he warmed to with great enthusiasm.

'The great Lost Roman!' he greeted me, for the name had gained great popularity among the Iceni.

'The Queen has sent me,' I told him.

He rested his hands on the hilt of his long sword, the point gently prising loose a polished floor tile.

'Are you here to scratch your stories?'

'I am here because the Queen says you have found property of mine, though I cannot think what it could be.'

Togobin raised his sword and then pointed over his shoulder.

'Through there,' was all he said.

I followed his directions towards one of the ante rooms, peering through the thickening smoke. Togobin's men ignored me, too busy carrying caskets of official documents outside to fuel the fires and amphorae of wine from the kitchens to fuel the crowd.

I heard something moving in the room, something which sounded to be crashing into the furniture and then, a figure staggered towards me, its arms stretched out as if to feel a way through the smoke. I knew before I saw his face that it was Calpurnius. But he could not see me.

They had burned his eyes out.

Togobin, who had appeared suddenly by my side, told me that the Iceni had thought I might wish to talk with Calpurnius, as he was after all my slave, before they impaled him on a stake and planted him at the roadside.

I thanked him and them for their consideration but I had nothing to say to the wretch, whose ravaged face turned towards me at the sound of my voice, albeit muffled by the cloth mask I was wearing. Yet he was my property now, for surely my father must be dead as he would not have abandoned him. And ownership involves responsibility.

He was moaning as I put my hand on that smooth chest, smooth like the skin of a baby, and pushed him gently back against the wall. I massaged the area above his heart and the gentle circular movement seemed to calm him, as stroking would calm an animal. He made no attempt to remove my hand and when he began to whimper, I hushed him as a nurse would hush a child. If he recognised the sound of my voice, he made no acknowledgment.

I traced the shape of his ribs with the fingers of my left hand while I removed the thin blade from my sleeve with my right.

It was an easy matter to put the point of the blade between my splayed fingers and then lean on the hilt of the dagger. Calpurnius' body bucked and shied against me and his warm blood spurted through my fingers.

If he said anything with his last breath, I did not hear it.

He died as he had never lived: quiet, obedient, and in my arms.

XLIII: Roscius

By dawn the oarsmen had got us almost to the wide mouth of the Tamesis, where the water was salty and the wind was fresh enough for the crew to unfurl the big square sail.

Behind us, in the distance we could see a plume of smoke rising high into the sky.

Sextilius Germanus and Flavius Niger were both keen to know why we were crossing to Gaul without calling in at either Rutupiae or Dubris, the main military ports. I told them to mind their own business, because I was on the General's business. Then I gave them five gold coins apiece and told them not to flash them around in front of the crew.

Funnily enough, the crew gave us absolutely no trouble. I thought at first it was down to their delight in getting off the island, but after a few hours it became clear that the other passenger, the merchant's daughter, was entertaining the younger, fitter oarsmen in her tent in the stern, sometimes two at a time.

I only caught a glimpse of her and she was quite a beauty, but then any woman on a boat with nearly a hundred sailors or marines would look good. But this one was a soldier's dream. She didn't charge, she didn't want to talk and she didn't get tired.

By the time we saw the coast of Gaul that afternoon, it was a good thing the wind was with us because half the oarsmen were exhausted.

The harbour at Gesoriacum was crowded with ships of all sizes from Londinium and the Londinium Merchants' Guild were operating from tables on the dockside like common fish-wives. Still, it meant we could get rid of the girl easy enough. Once she had made herself decent and we had hired servants to carry her luggage, she disembarked like a right royal princess and was greeted by a dozen shouts of welcome from the Londinium contingent. They all wanted to know where her father was, of course, and whether the warehouses they had left behind were still standing. I was as honest as I could be with them, saying that when I had last seen the girl's father – Julia, that was her name, the tart – he was in conference with the Governor discussing the defence of the town.

It gave them a bit of hope and one of them readily agreed to let Julia stay at his villa on the outskirts of Gesoriacum and if she's still there, she's probably gone through most of the British Fleet by now.

We took the captain of the bireme for a fish dinner and

some decent wine at a tavern on the quay and I asked him how soon the ship could return to Britannia. He almost choked on his mussels in white wine and chive sauce and wanted to know why the fuck we wanted to go back there. We told him because that was where our General was, but I'm not sure he believed us. He took a lot more notice of the gold I slid across the table at him and said that the wind showed no sign of changing direction, so if we wanted to get anywhere, we would have to rely on the oarsmen to get us well out into the channel before we could use the sail. That would mean keeping the crew together and that would take more gold. I hinted that there would be more when we landed, adding that once we were safely ashore, the ship was his to do with as he pleased. The merchant's daughter had no need of it any more and would not object (granted, I had no intention of asking her permission). That sealed the deal. The captain used some of his advance gold to buy several amphorae of cheap but strong wine and have them sent to the ship. He then negotiated with the tavern owner to have some girls from the brothel down the street delivered with the wine. The tavern owner agreed enthusiastically as he was no doubt on a healthy discount from the brothel. The captain estimated that the tide would be right for us to slip the harbour around the eighth watch of the night – the last hour before dawn. I said that would be fine as I was sure we could complete our business that evening.

We had no trouble finding the Procurator, we just asked the first patrol of the Town Watch we came across. We were in uniform, we were regulars from the legions and we outranked them, so they told us that Catus Decianus had indeed taken up residence in the private quarters attached to the Imperial Treasury office. They were usually reserved for travelling tax inspectors, so nobody had thought much about it, though his arrival from Britannia had been sudden and unannounced.

We found the place well before dusk, just to scout it out, and counted four sentries guarding the entire Treasury complex, only one of them on the door to the residential quarters.

When it was dark we just marched straight up to him like a squad of the Praetorian Guard and asked if the Procurator of all Britannia was in residence. The sentry was some poor auxiliary footslogger from Dalmatia or somewhere, who had trouble understanding Latin, but he didn't misunderstand our tone, so he said yes, Catus was at home, but he was not to be disturbed. Except by messengers from the Governor of Britannia who had the authority to flog anyone who delayed them, I pointed out.

Once inside, I sent Flavius towards the kitchens to dismiss the house slaves and told Sextilius to watch my back as we took a pair of lamps from a small altar near the door and made our way upstairs as quietly as we could.

There was light coming from only one room on the upper floor.

I used hand signals, like we do on night patrol, to tell Sextilius to guard the corridor and stepped into the room alone. That way there would be no witnesses.

'Who the fuck are you?' was how the Procurator greeted me, though I suppose my arrival was a bit of a surprise.

'I bring the best wishes – the very best wishes – of General Suetonius Paulinus, the Governor of Britannia,' I said and as I spoke I could see in his little rat face that he recognised me. He had seen me often enough, standing at the Governor's shoulder.

'You have come to take me back to Londinium?' he asked, which is something only a guilty man would ask.

'I doubt if there is a Londinium to take you back to,' I answered him. 'Though I am sure Boudica would welcome you with open arms. It is her city now.'

He had been sitting at a table piled high with scrolls of papyri and wax tablets, most of which seemed to be covered with columns of figures, but there were also plates, jugs and beakers, bowls of fruit and nuts and half-eaten loaves cluttering the surface. I had to follow his gaze to see that at the end of the table, under the mess, was a sword in its scabbard.

He made a lunge for it but I got there first. The scabbard was on a fine leather belt, really excellent workmanship, but the *gladius* itself was of the old, curved, Mainz-style blade maybe twenty years old. The army had long since moved over to the straight *gladius*, what they call the Pompeii design, so this was a bit of a throwback and probably only intended for ceremonial use. It wasn't even very sharp.

You should have seen old Catus's face when I handed it back to him. He knew what was coming.

'The Governor expects me to kill myself?' he asked me, as if it was negotiable.

'Your rapacity has goaded the province into war. Britannia is a disaster area thanks to you,' I told him. 'For that, the Governor expects your life. He does not necessarily expect you to take it yourself.'

That was when the panic took him and he began to rush around the room, scattering papers and turning over chairs. He shouted for help, but when it was Sextilius who appeared in the doorway with his sword drawn, his screaming died away.

He clutched his ornamental sword, still sheathed, to his chest as I walked over to him and stood almost toe-to-toe in front of him, so close I could smell the sour sweat on him. He gripped the hilt of his *gladius* with his right hand. I did the same. He did not look like a man who had practised the sword quick draw every day for fifteen years.

'You wouldn't dare,' he said in my face.

I gutted him where he stood before he had drawn his sword an inch and I managed to wipe my blade clean of blood on his toga and put it back in its scabbard before his body fell backwards and hit the floor.

He was not quite dead; blood bubbled from his mouth for another fifteen minutes or so; long enough for Sextilius and I to eat the bowl of chestnuts and some pickled dates we found on the table.

XLIV: Olussa

The corpse of Londinium has been picked clean and now the army marches north, its pace slower than ever, as if it is bloated on blood. Catus Decianus may have escaped the wrath of the tribes, but nothing else has.

Heavy with plunder and grain, the army has impressed almost a thousand carts and every living animal larger than a dog but even using a major Roman road, progress is painfully slow.

Our destination is the second city of Verulamium, home of the Catuvellauni, the detested neighbours of the Trinovantes, who now lead us, urging a faster pace, so anxious are they to confront their old enemies.

The grand strategy of the rebels is to destroy Verulamium (the Trinnies demand nothing less) and then use the ancient Pathway to take the Iceni home in time for a late summer harvest. Yet the Iceni are strangely unexcited by the prospect, almost listless. It is as if their thirst for loot and slaughter has been quenched even though they have failed to take their revenge on Catus, the true instigator of this war. The Procurator has escaped to the safety of Gaul and whilst that pig Starbo and his men now sleep with the fishes of the Tamesis, this brings little cheer to the royal family and in particular the Princess Erda.

The old crones who cook and cackle around the fires every night now talk openly about the madness of the girl. There is a rumour that she has a cart full of the heads of Londinium citizens and when the army camps, she plays with them as a child would play with dolls or puppets. This is said to be the reason Boudica's retinue travels at the rear of our long column, as Erda's wagon-load of heads is attracting flies by day and rats by night.

Verulamium was obliterated this morning while most of the Iceni were still at breakfast.

Boudica will almost certainly be blamed by history, but the attack was by Tasciovanus and his Trinovantes and the slaughter of the townsfolk was mercifully swift. The bulk of the Iceni were camped some five miles from the city when the smoke began to rise and for the whole day they did nothing but sit idly by the side of the road. As dusk fell, the rumour rippled down the length of the army: Tasciovanus and his troops are not coming back. They have taken their revenge for the slights of the past and as much plunder as they can carry and have ridden due east back into Trinovantine territory.

Will Boudica order a pursuit and punish this desertion? When I suggest this to the women who are serving the evening stew (lamb, I think), they stare at me as if I have lost my wits and I realise that this army has absolutely no concept of discipline.

Next morning, Druids rode the length of the camp, which stretched for more than two miles, with a spare pony in tow. The pony was for me, as I was summoned to a war council in the rear.

Boudica, her daughters and clan chiefs were camped in the walled gardens of a half-built villa. The original owner had taken care to plant flower beds to service a series of beehives in the sunniest spot. The Iceni had trampled over the garden, but appreciated the honeycombs, though the scent from the flower beds and the kitchen herbs planted alongside disguised other smells coming from the south wall where a two-wheel cart rests, its axle pole pointing to the sky.

The cart contained human heads stacked as if they were turnips fresh from the field.

'Sit with me, my Lost Roman,' was how Boudica greeted me and I took my place on the ground as the council convened in the shade of the half-completed villa.

It quickly became clear that the clans were divided on what the army should do next. Some were convinced that the war was over and all that was left to do was go home to their farms. Others, including Aneurin the Druid, believed that the legions had yet to give battle and argued that a battle here on Catuvellauni land was preferable to one in the Iceni homeland.

With some difficulty I managed to hide my feelings and still my tongue. These savages have no concept of what they have done, treating their war as they would a series of raids on a neighbouring tribe. If they did but know it, they had opened a hole in the western frontier of the entire Roman Empire. Rome could not allow that to happen; the Empire would surely strike back.

Eventually, the moment I was dreading came when Boudica turned her round, homely face to me and asked me if I thought there would be a battle.

I pointed to the north, along the line of the road to Verulamium and beyond.

'The Roman Governor of Britannia and his army are out there somewhere,' I told them. 'And he will seek vengeance for his lost cities. He can do no other.'

One of the older chiefs, a small, wizened creature, his beard matted with honey muttered, 'What is this Britannia?' to one of his compatriots.

'Then let us go find this Roman!' boomed the giant Tarex. 'We have food, we have weapons, we no longer have to worry about those thieving Trinovantes. Let us have a good battle and go home to our farms. Who knows? Perhaps the Druids will have some new stories to sing this winter!'

It was a fine speech which produced much deep-throated cheering and Boudica clapped her hands and called for supplies of beer in which to drink a toast to their war gods. But, as is the way with these people, it never stops at just one toast.

Orders were given to send the swiftest riders down the road in advance of the army to scout for signs of the enemy and the chiefs began to disperse to join their clans in the order of march.

Unnoticed by the war council until now, the Princess Erda had drifted into the villa's garden and was humming to herself as she carefully removed heads, one at a time, from that gruesome cart.

Holding each head carefully with both hands, she looked into the face as if trying to read it somehow, then she placed them on the ground in a pattern – a pattern in her mind only – as though laying out the pieces of a board game.

I was transfixed by her actions and tried to see in those dead faces, what she saw; to guess what answers she was seeking.

From one of the heads she used as a gaming piece, I learned something that Erda did not. I learned that my father had not escaped from Londinium after all.

XLV: Roscius

It took four days and all my remaining gold coins to get that fucking ship back to Britannia. First it was waiting for the wind to change, then it was waiting for the tide, then it was waiting for the oarsmen to decide how much extra pay they wanted, once they saw the smouldering ruin that was Londinium.

The wind and the tide I could do nothing about but the oarsmen I could bribe. They soon came round to my way of thinking, especially when I explained that I wanted the ship to stick to the middle of the river, well out of spear or arrow range, and go several miles upriver beyond Londinium until we even thought about going ashore. And even then, the ship's crew had no need to get out of the boat themselves. All they had to do was put me, Sextilius and Flavius ashore and then they could sail to the ends of the earth for all I cared as it would be their ship.

We were rowed past Londinium at dusk, the sail down but with the tide. There was nobody watching the river; in fact there seemed to be nobody in Londinium at all, not that there was much of Londinium left.

They had burned it to the ground. Hardly one brick left on top of another. All the warehouses were gone and all the riverside statues toppled. It was impossible to pick out any features. I could not recognise a single building or wall. What was left of the town still glowed red and the smoke seemed to make the dusk fall quicker. Not a living thing moved except for the dogs which raced in a pack along the river bank like a cavalry troop in training.

As my eyes became accustomed to the twilight, I could make out that the dogs were running in and out of hundreds of stakes planted in the muddy bank. On each stake were some remains of a man, or woman, or child; but only the bits that remained after the sword, fire and the dogs had taken their share.

The oarsmen needed no further bribes that night, so anxious were they to put Londinium behind us, and by dawn we were at the point in the river where the main stream loops south, then north, then south and then north again.

By midday we were approaching the town of Pontes*, which lies on the main military road from Londinium to the southwest and Isca, where the IInd Legion was based.

Of course we didn't know if Boudica's mob was heading there as well, we only knew she hadn't got there yet because the place wasn't on fire.

* Staines.

Pontes wasn't much of a settlement, but it did have a big Imperial Post station, which if nothing else meant horses.

Sextilius, Flavius and I disembarked at a wooden jetty, so at least we kept our feet dry, and straight away a small squad of auxiliaries came quick marching out of the town towards us. The ship's crew decided not to hang around and pushed off again as soon as they saw them, but to us it was a relief to see there was some discipline left in the province, even though the junior centurion in charge of the squad tried to arrest us!

We soon put him straight, though, pointing out that if we were deserters, we would hardly be likely to be requisitioning horses to take us *towards* the fighting. And we pointed out that if he delayed or harmed us in any way, the Governor himself would personally deliver the first fifty strokes of the lash.

I'm not sure that lad actually believed we were members of the General's bodyguard, but he knew regular army when he saw it and muttered something about us being 'more hard cases'.

When we got into Pontes we saw what he meant by that, for camped near the stables were two troops – about sixty men – of legionary cavalry. I went straight over to them as soon as I saw their standard with the badges of Capricorn and Pegasus. I grabbed their standard-bearer by the throat and gave him a damned good shaking, demanding to know just what the fuck cavalry from the IInd Legion were doing here, when they should be at the rendezvous with Agricola at Venonis, miles to the north.

To give him his due, he demanded to know just who the fuck I was, even though his wind-pipe must have been suffering, so I told him I was a staff officer for the Governor who knew exactly what orders had been sent to the IInd Legion, two weeks ago, telling them to get their arses moving.

Well, of course, it turned out they hadn't moved at all. Not an inch.

The standard-bearer, once he got his breath back, told me that the acting legate, Poenius Posthumus, had decided that his legion was better employed guarding the south-west in case the tribes down there joined in the rebellion.

I put it to the standard-bearer that perhaps this Poenius Posthumus was a cowardly little shit who had let down Rome, the Governor and the IInd Legion in that order. My new friend said that I could say that, but he couldn't possibly comment, but what he could say for sure was that these two troops of the legion's cavalry had accidentally extended their scouting mission – by about 150 miles! – and that was too far to go back to the fortress at Isca, so they might as well find the Governor and ask him if they might possibly be of use to him, as they did not feel they were much needed by their commander. Though they didn't know precisely where the Governor was – and could I possibly help?

Well, of course I could, as I had a rough idea of where Paulinus would be and when I told our new friends that we had been in Gaul and had chosen to come back to fight, that got me elected leader straight away and within the hour we had horses, packhorses, clean clothes and a good meal inside us and we were ready to depart. Someone even came up with the name Roscius' Auxiliary – and we set off to ride to the rescue!

In total, sixty-seven of us rode north from Pontes, but as we couldn't use the main road, we had to travel parallel to it and so the going was slow but we had a stroke of luck early on. Ten miles outside of Pontes we ran across a family of Catuvellauni, refugees from the Verulamium area, who had been on the run for several days. They told us that they feared the worst for the town. They had farmed on the outskirts and as soon as their neighbours got hit by a murderous mob of Trinovantes, they upped stakes and ran for the woods. Just in time, they reckoned, as the next thing up the road from Londinium was an army of Iceni as thick on the ground as an ant colony – 200,000 of them they said, though we took that with a brick of salt.

These locals said they were blood kin of Verica, one of their chiefs or something, and no friends of the barbarians who followed the bloody queen Boudica and her mad daughters. They offered to show us the forest paths, even though we had no gold left to give them. They did it for nothing. Once we got near Verulamium – the smoke rising from the ruins was a good guide for us – we put scouts out on our right flank and on the third or fourth day, they reported movement on Route LXVI to the north of the town. Flavius and I went to have a look for ourselves, hobbling our horses and covering the last mile on foot until we were on the treeline of a hill and we could see the road below us.

That was the first time I saw her, like I told you, and she was coming to kill us – the legions I mean. How mad was that?

Her army was spread along the road out of Verulamium like a snake that had just eaten. I had to look twice to make sure it was moving at all. By the gods, they were slow and sloppy. Not a single outrider on the flanks and her infantry was mixed in with cavalry which in turn was mixed with baggage wagons, women and children. Boudica herself rode with the war chariots in the rear. In the rear – I ask you! There they were, the pride of the Iceni, a hundred war chariots and tactically in the worst position possible. Mind you, she wasn't expecting to be attacked and, to be fair, nobody was going to attack her on the move. If I knew Paulinus, and I did, then he would stick to the training manual and he would pick a nice flat piece of ground where he could manoeuvre and he would invite them to come on to him.

Anyway, I saw her down there, on the road. It must have been her, for even at that distance, the sunlight clearly reflected off something sizeable and gold around her neck. And there was all that long red hair flowing down her back. It must have been her. And she was driving the horses herself, with two other females in the chariot with her. Must have been her.

You could see the Druids too, with their black robes. A whole bunch of them rode near Boudica like a bodyguard, but others rode up and down the line of march using whips and clubs in an attempt to keep the column moving.

Even as we watched, various parts of the marching column would stop and they would crack open some flagons of wine or they would wander off the road to graze their animals.

Flavius and I watched them all afternoon as they passed by our position, unaware and unconcerned that they were being spied on.

We estimated their strength at about 25,000 armed men and boys, with another 10,000 women and children dragging along with them.

Flavius summed it up perfectly.

'When this lot meet the legions, they're dead meat, aren't they?'

I couldn't have put it better myself.

That night we camped well to the west of the road and come the dawn, we were on the move again, parallel to the rebels but now ahead of them. We risked another look at the road from the hills overlooking Durocobrivis*, a nothing place with two houses and some huts, all of which had been abandoned. But it was the place where the army road running roughly north-south crossed the old Celtic Pathway running south-west to north-east, ending up in Iceni territory.

I could hear the General's voice in my head. He knew about the Pathway – army surveyors had checked it out soon after the invasion with a view to turning it into a proper road in the future. I reckoned that Paulinus was trying to lure them up to this crossroads. If they turned right and headed home, the legion could follow and catch them in the rear. If they didn't run for home and carried on up the road, Paulinus would pick the ground and set out the legion in battle order, inviting the barbarians to attack him. They would not be able to resist and the outcome was inevitable.

I was tempted to stay in our vantage point and watch the crossroads, but around noon there was movement down on the road. Two riders, each holding the bridle of a spare horse, galloped towards the oncoming Iceni army as if they had something to report.

There was nothing in the direction they were coming from except a *mansio* and an Imperial Post stable at a place known as Magiovinium**, not nearly enough to scare anyone. The riders must have seen something else.

We rode about another five miles, then we ran into a patrol

* Dunstable.

** Dropshort.

of auxiliary cavalry from the XIVth Legion and I can tell you, I was glad to see them, though they were a bit touchy to say the least as we surprised them coming out of the woods like that.

The *prefectus* in charge ordered me to stop and give the password for the day. I told him to go fuck himself. How was I supposed to know the password?

It turned out to be 'Mercury sanctus' answered by 'Jupiter sanctus', though I just told the prefect to find General Paulinus bloody quick and tell him that his 'deliverer of best wishes had just returned from Gaul'.

By nightfall I was sitting in the General's tent eating a roast chicken and drinking some of Paulinus' private stock of wine. The tent was in the middle of a thousand other tents behind a properly organised ditch and rampart defence. We were surrounded by the smells of hundreds of cooking fires and the sounds of weapons being sharpened, horses calmed and trumpet calls rehearsed. As far as I could estimate, we were only outnumbered by three or four to one. All seemed right with the world.

Paulinus looked relaxed, all things considered.

'Did you find the noble Procurator?' he asked me. But only after calling for food and wine and making sure that Flavius and Sextilius were seen to.

'Easily,' I told him.

'How did he receive my best wishes?' he said.

'Quickly,' I answered, 'but they left a lasting impression.'

The General nodded at that and refilled my wine cup himself from one of his personal silver jugs.

'Later,' he said, 'I may wish you to convey my best wishes elsewhere.'

'To Poenius Posthumus, perhaps?' I ventured.

He was surprised to find that I knew about the disgraceful behaviour of the acting-commander of the IInd Legion who had refused to march to the rendezvous at Venonis, so I told him about the two troops of cavalry I had met at Pontes and ridden north with, saying they were all good lads eager to join in the fight.

'Send them back to Isca,' Paulinus said. 'Spread the word among the men that an advance guard of cavalry from the

IInd Augusta has arrived but that I have sent them back to their headquarters because there are simply not enough barbarians to go around. There will be little enough glory for the XIVth in beating this rabble; we do not wish to share it with the IInd.'

I had to smile at the General's plan and I told him I could get the camp's gossips spreading the word within the hour. There was nothing a soldier liked more on the eve of a battle than a good rumour especially if it was a slander against another regiment.

I asked the General if he was confident we could win. Any other staff officer would have been flogged for such a question.

'As long as the men believe we can, we will. We have discipline, they do not. We have armour and artillery, they do not. I have already selected the field of battle, they have no say in the matter. We do not have our wives and children and mothers with us, they do. They are fighting far from home. When we fight, we *are* at home.'

I told him he should say that in an address to the troops in the morning, but the General argued that he did not want the men to think this battle was anything out of the ordinary. There was no need for stirring speeches, this was just another day's work for the legions.

'Leave the stirring speeches to the historians,' he said. 'They write them so much better than soldiers do.'

I'll tell you something, though, no historian could match the General for sheer cunning. He gave me one last order before I got some sleep. I had to find the senior quartermaster who commanded the camp cooks and requisition all the bay leaves in the supply wagons.

Now that was a genius stroke. Boudica and her mob never stood a chance.

XLVI: Olussa

I write this by the one lamp I am allowed in my enclosed carriage, the smoke stinging my eyes. We must not show light, we only eat cold food. We avoid roads and paths; we flinch at shadows in the forest. How our fortunes have changed.

Scouts brought us the news that we had found the legions, or perhaps they had found us, and on that night we heard their trumpet calls for the first time. The Iceni camp remained sober and actually posted sentries. All through the night, clan chiefs and Druids rode the length of the camp counting men, weapons and horses, with each clan negotiating for a place in the front of the attack, in order to impress their kinfolk. The warriors were already stripped to the waist, though the night was cool, and all the women were busy cooking or brewing up batches of woad paint. I was twice asked to contribute my piss to this cause, which I did gladly in exchange for a bowl of hot soup made with lamb and a bitter herb I did not recognise. No one could sleep much that night, especially the Druids, who held interminable rituals and ceremonies in the darkness of the forest, betrayed only by pin pricks of orange torchlight through the leaves.

The battle was not to come with the next dawn, though, for it would take all of that day for the Iceni to position themselves in battle order. Not that there was much order in the army's movements, with cavalry and chariots mixed in with foot soldiers, women and children. Nor was there any direction from Boudica herself. She and her daughters stayed in the rear, and none seemed to think the worse of her for this.

As men and horsemen moved up, I allowed my wagon to fall behind in the column of the army until I was travelling with the baggage train as was Boudica herself. The wagons and carts, at least a thousand of them, now carried not only the Iceni's supplies and plunder, but all the women and children judged too weak, too young or too old to join in the fighting. A grandmother clutching two babies in a sheepskin sling had adopted my carriage and made herself my new travelling companion.

At midday the road cut across a more ancient track which ran away to the north-east following the ridges of the undulating landscape. This was The Pathway as the Iceni called it, running all the way to the Iceni lands and then the sea.

And then the army drifted off the road to the right on to

sparsely wooded rolling uplands and the baggage train followed at a crawling pace until the infantry were almost out of sight.

About two hours before dusk the army halted on the top of a ridge and the wagons were allowed to catch up. Only then did Boudica show herself, alone in her chariot, driving fast to the brow of the ridge where she was met by her war chiefs, who formed a protective circle around her with their horses.

A rider eventually broke away from this circle and rode down the baggage column. It was Esico, the coinmaker, his chest and arms painted blue, a thin gold twisted band around his neck. A long sword lay across his saddle and a large iron hammer was slung over his back on a strap of leather.

'You! The Lost Roman!' he hailed me. 'The Queen wishes to speak to you.'

The grandmother at my side dug her elbow into my ribs.

'You had better run, Roman,' she cackled.

Indeed, I had to run in the tracks of Esico's horse, to the caterwauling of the women in the baggage train, but there were no jeers or mockery from the army on the brow of the ridge. For they were looking to their front, not at a lone lost Roman stumbling up the hill behind them. They were fixed silently on a host of Romans who were anything but lost, camped in the distance towards the dipping afternoon sun.

Iceni horses, their flanks decorated with blue hand-prints of woad paint, nudged and pushed me towards the circle of chieftains who attended the Queen. From this part of the ridge we could see over the heads of the army to where the ground sloped into a gentle valley, no more than a defile, clear of trees, although both sides of the defile were thickly wooded. At the end of this depression in the earth but before the ground rose again into undulating hills, lay the Roman camp, tiny in the distance but still a seething mass of movement, of colour, of reflecting metal and rising breaths of dust.

I found myself against the wheel of Boudica's chariot, the Queen's moon-shaped face staring down into mine. Strands of her long red hair brushed against my knuckles as I gripped the chariot's wicker frame.

'Olussa, my historian,' she greeted me. It was a word I had taught her and I was surprised she had remembered. 'Tell me what you see.'

I shaded my eyes with one hand and looked to the west. What I saw was the end of the Iceni, but I could not say that.

'It is a legion, my Queen, in its marching camp.'

'How many men?'

'Five or six thousand, plus auxiliaries and cavalry, perhaps eight thousand in all, perhaps more.'

I was doubtful how much of this she understood for few of the Iceni seemed to be able to count accurately.

'We are more,' she said, gazing into the distance and then she asked: 'Will they fight?'

'Not today,' I told her. 'Tomorrow, in the morning, they will come out of their camp looking for battle.'

'And we will be waiting for them.'

Then Boudica, lowering her head towards mine so that none around could hear, said: 'There is nothing else we can do, is there?'

To which I answered: 'No.'

The army camped where they stood, down from the ridge top on the gentle slope leading to the valley floor. They were encouraged to light as many fires as they could to confuse the Roman lookouts and to sing and talk and drink and offer prayers to their gods, while the women in the baggage train passed out baskets of cold meat and rock-hard bread.

I was disturbed at some time in the darkness of the night by Aneurin the Druid accompanied by the Princess Prisca and several torch-bearers.

Prisca, fully armed and carrying a round leather shield, spoke not a word to me, leaving Aneurin to ask her questions for her.

'We have sent scouts to the very edge of the Roman camp,' he said. 'They report that the Romans have many more men than horses and no chariots. We wish to know how they will fight.'

'I am no soldier,' I told them.

'Do the Romans not write the history of their battles?' the Druid asked, though I suspected he already knew the answer.

'I have read of the battles of the past, it is true,' I admitted, 'but that is the only knowledge I have.'

'How will they fight tomorrow?' Aneurin repeated seriously.

'They do not use chariots and their cavalry is for scouting and skirmishing only. Their main weapon is the heavy infantry, which they will place in the centre of their line.'

'They wear coats of iron and move slowly,' said the Druid. 'We have defeated them once already.'

'You have defeated part of a legion on the march. This is a full legion which will be in battle order, working to a battle plan.'

A disciplined battle was a concept unknown to the Iceni, and to most Celts.

'So how do we attack them?' he said.

'You do not have to. They will attack you.'

In the morning the Iceni army moved down into the defile, the baggage train following them and then spreading out in a line across the valley so that the women and children could watch the battle.

The legion had broken camp in the night and had advanced across the valley floor. Dawn had shown them formed in two lines of cohorts; infantry in the centre and cavalry on the wings.

When the legion was half a mile from the Iceni, they halted their march and we could see riders speeding along their lines.

Boudica sent a Druid priest to find my carriage. Her scouts closest to the legion had reported that the riders in the Roman ranks were distributing bunches of green leaves which the front line were tying to the points of their javelins, and what did it mean?

I knew of the tradition where a legion after a battle would decorate their weapons with bay leaves as a symbol of victory.

This legion was so sure of the outcome of the battle, they were celebrating already.

I told Boudica's rider that they were doing it for luck, that was all.

XLVII: Roscius

The rumour about not needing the IInd Legion and issuing the bay leaves as victory garlands before the battle even started put the men in an excellent mood.

No one had any doubts that we would win as we lined up across the width of that defile. The General had chosen the place well. It was a flat-bottomed valley, just wide enough for us to roll forward over the Brits, the wooded sides meant they couldn't outflank us in any strength and there were so many of them bunched up together that they couldn't use their cavalry effectively and their chariots not at all.

We broke camp before dawn and my first duty was to accompany Suetonius Paulinus to the official sacrifices conducted by the legion's *haruspices*. I asked him, on the quiet, what would happen if these priests and soothsayers came up with unfavourable omens for the day ahead. He just smiled and said that the omens would be what he had told the priests they would be.

Paulinus made no big speeches to the troops, he just said what he always said before a big battle – *Me signante emittite canes infernos** – but nobody will remember that with pride except those of us who were there. Then he would make an upturned V shape with his fingers and pushed them forward like a wedge. That was our real signal to start moving.

Even above the racket the Brits were making, there was a real comfort in the steady, solid thumping noise our boys made as they started to march down that defile.

The Brits, who were still about half-a-mile away, faltered for a minute. I mean, it just hadn't occurred to them that we would attack *them* as they outnumbered us at least threefold. But then they came on because there was nowhere much for them to go. You see, they had all these wagons and carts with them, a bloody huge baggage train of maybe a thousand vehicles, and they had

* 'At my signal, unleash the dogs of hell.'

arranged them in a semicircle halfway down the slope at the far end of the defile. When we got a bit nearer, we saw this wasn't a defensive fall-back line, but the wagons had been arranged like that to provide a place for the women and children to sit and watch the battle. The Brits had created a tier of seating just like in a theatre; and had brought their families to watch the show!

As soon as Paulinus saw this, he sent messages by rider to the cavalry on both flanks and gave orders to bring up our own horse-drawn carts – we had about a dozen – on which were mounted the *carroballistae.* Those artillery crews were a breed apart. They loved their lethal contraptions – called them their 'scorpions' because of their sting – and they trained hard so that a good crew could put an iron bolt through an armoured breastplate at two hundred paces. And remember, the Brits didn't wear armour.

I reckon there must have been thirty-five thousand of them in the field and that includes plenty of women armed with clubs and sharpened sticks. In total we had around ten thousand men. Those sort of odds don't frighten a legion, but you can inflate the numbers if you like to make it sound better. You probably will, anyway.

It began, as it usually does, at a walking pace until the two armies were a hundred paces apart. We were still in formation but they were already falling all over themselves. In the crush they couldn't use their chariots and their horsemen, all mixed in with the infantry, were next to useless.

We had to get them closer, to within javelin range. On Paulinus' signals, the cavalry skirmished forward, just to get the Brits stirred up. And then the artillery started up, firing bolts deep into their ranks, sometimes going through the front man and even the one behind him. That shook them up but still they refused to charge us.

Then the General gave the order for the auxiliaries to advance on the wings along with the cavalry, so that more pressure could be put on *their* flanks, and their centre would start being squeezed. What with that pressure and the artillery keeping up a steady stream of bolts, and every horse that was hit crushing three or four warriors on its way down, that mob couldn't stand it for long and they charged us and then it was all over bar the slaughter.

As the Brits closed on our front line, yelling their heads off, we let them have two volleys at killing range. The Legion put about four thousand javelins in the air in the time in takes a man to swallow a mouthful of wine. So tightly were they packed, you just couldn't miss, and suddenly there was a forest of spear shafts in front of our army, each one stuck in a fallen enemy, and the whole field went quiet.

At that moment, the front line cohorts drew their swords and, I tell you, just the sound of that happening was enough to make a normal man loosen his bowels. I dare say some of the Iceni would have run away if they could have, but by then they were pretty much trapped.

Paulinus now sent the cavalry up the sides of the valley and they worked their way through the trees, outflanking the barbarians and coming down the slopes behind them to attack their baggage train. The orders he had given the cavalry were quite specific: avoid the main throng of the Iceni army completely and concentrate on those carts, specifically the animals pulling them. They were the real target and our horsemen used their spears and arrows to good effect, cutting down animals in their harnesses in a good half of the vehicles before the Iceni army realised what was happening in their rear and sent their own cavalry to chase off ours. By then the damage was done. The semicircle of wagons which had provided an amphitheatre for the Iceni women and children was now an immoveable obstacle, which prevented their army from escaping.

And it soon became clear that the Iceni needed an escape route.

Paulinus made his famous inverted 'V' signal with his fingers and our army started to move at walking pace, shoulder to shoulder, shields up and the blades of their short swords flicking in and out of the line like the teeth of a saw. We always used to say that a legionary's best weapon was his shield boss, which really did some damage when smashed into the face of an enemy. If that is true, then his *gladius* was his third-best. You know what comes second best? His boots. A pair of stout leather boots with hobnails inflicts more damage than you can imagine, unless you have ever been there in the middle of a cohort moving forward over an enemy. Because that's what we did, we walked over them, crunching bones and crushing the breath out of those who weren't dead yet.

Our second line came up and threw their javelins over the heads of our front line, cutting another swathe across the Iceni. Our lads didn't have to aim, they simply couldn't miss. Pretty soon every trooper was standing on the body of a dead Iceni rather than on grass.

The auxiliaries, cavalry and light infantry, squeezed them on the flanks while the centre just kept going, pressing them back up the defile and on to their own wagons, which were not going anywhere. That baggage train was the wall we eventually pinned them to. I have no idea how many of them were crushed to death by their own people, but our lads accounted for plenty, I can tell you.

The Legion held its formation right to the end. Normally there is a temptation to break ranks and charge, which usually makes the enemy turn and run, but these stupid Brits had nowhere to run to. They had given themselves so little room that they couldn't even swing those long swords of theirs and their big oval shields were nicely painted, but fucking useless at stopping *carroballistae* bolts.

With their backs to their own wagons, the Brits just stood there until they got chopped down. It was about then, as the General and the command staff moved up, that we saw her.

Beyond the killing area around the baggage train, on the very rim of the far ridge, was a chariot with a lone figure controlling the horses. We couldn't see a face at that distance of course, just a shape dressed in blueish cloth with a cloak, and then there was a flash of gold in the morning sunlight and we knew it was her. As she wheeled her horses around, long tresses of red hair flew out behind her and then she and the chariot disappeared over the ridge.

'Let her go,' said Paulinus. 'There's a lot of killing still to do before lunchtime.'

The Legion exhausted itself before it ran out of victims. About a thousand Brits, trapped against their own wagons and squashed by their dead kinfolk, managed to wriggle and crawl away between the wheels. Our cavalry gave chase to ride them down, but it had been a long hot day and horses and men needed water and rest. The men also needed a wash, the legs of every one of our lads were red from the knees down with Iceni blood.

When the trumpeters sounded the Stand Down. Paulinus sent in the regimental priests – whose prophecies had been proved absolutely right – to do the body count. The Legion had lost 400 men killed and just over a thousand wounded, including amputations. The auxiliaries, a couple of thousand dead and the same wounded but no one ever counts them. The regimental standard-bearers, who also looked after the men's savings and funeral fund, did a double check of the dead and we started collecting up weapons and stripping their armour – that was a standing order, not one piece of metal was left for a potential enemy to pick up – and preparing the funeral pyres.

We cleared out the Iceni wagons of all the valuables they had stolen while they were on the warpath. We found souvenirs from Camulodunum which could not have meant anything to the Iceni – ornamental roof tiles, for example, embossed with the wild boar emblem of the XXth Legion. What use could that have been to the Brits in the mud huts? And we also turned up a bag of gold coins, *aurei* with the head of Caligula on them, wherever they had come from.

We kept everything worth keeping and butchered the animals which had died in their harnesses – there was plenty of beef to eat that night – then we made four huge pyres out of the vehicles and started to stack up the dead Brits. That took the rest of the day and we didn't light the pyres until after dark, after making sure that the wind would take the smell away from our camp.

Our tally was just over twenty thousand Iceni dead. There were no wounded – we made sure of that – and we took no prisoners. The General had told us that there was to be no future for the Iceni. He was right.

XLVIII: Olussa

The battle is now a blur of memory, a dream of screams and blood and the sound of metal cutting flesh. I have seen the legions in action and I have survived, but few others have.

The ponies hitched to my carriage were among the few Iceni haulage animals to survive the attack of the Roman light cavalry, thanks to the old crone who was my travelling companion and, briefly, my bodyguard. I saw it all from under the *raedae*, from behind the front wheel, as one lone rider came towards us, his spear raised and aimed at the ponies who were squirming and chomping at their bits in terror. With a scream, the old Iceni woman flung herself from the driving seat of the carriage on to the neck of the cavalryman's horse. His horse stumbled and went down, crushing the old crone and throwing its rider forward. He hit the ground face first, so close to where I was hiding that I heard his neck snap.

Neither the Roman, his horse, nor the old Iceni woman moved again and I remained under my carriage until the legs of another horse stomped into my view.

'Where are you, Lost Roman?'

It was Tarex, who had led the Iceni charge to see off the Roman cavalry. He looked down at me from his horse and said: 'Withdraw from here and join Boudica and her daughters. She has ordered it and will not leave without you. You must get her away.'

'Is the battle lost?' I asked as I scuttled crab-like from under my carriage.

'The battle was lost the day the first Roman saw this land,' he answered grimly. 'Come, hurry. Boudica must not be taken, alive or dead. We have to get her home.'

My ponies, smelling blood, were as anxious as I to leave that field of death and reacted to the lightest of touches on the reins. It was only when the carriage was a mile away from the fighting that I remembered the old crone's two grandchildren were still on board.

With great gentleness for a giant, Tarex took the babies in his arms and placed them on the ground in the heather and the gorse. Then he scraped up a fistful of dirt and sprinkled it evenly across both bundles of rags.

I do not know what the gesture meant, nor why Boudica was fleeing the battle while her loyal subjects were being exterminated. There is much about these people I do not understand.

We fled north until first the forest, and then the night, hid us.

Boudica rode alone in one chariot, her two daughters in another. There are three other wagons besides mine, all driven by women of the tribe. Boudica's escort is less than a hundred riders, either Druids or kinsmen of Tarex. Many of them are wounded – one has lost his right arm below the elbow – and many have no weapons. Aneurin is among them, grey-faced and silent, but there is no sign of Esico the coinmaker and Tarex confirms that Togobin, betrothed of the Princess Erda, has fallen bravely charging the legion's centre. Whole clans of the Iceni have been wiped out as have hundreds if not thousands of Iceni women of child-bearing age.

These are things I should add to my history of Boudica, Tarex tells me, and by the light of my single lamp in my cramped and curtained carriage, I write and write and write.

XLIX: Roscius

Where was the battle? Well, I've told you as far as I can remember. The Legion did mark the nearest milestone when they marched back on to Route LXVI, but I can't remember which one it was. Why would anyone want to know something like that?

Some of us, of course, had work to do and I had to find myself some clean underwear and fresh horses for the long ride west.

I took Sextilius Germanus with me and we followed Route III back to Pontes, where we had landed from Gaul only about a week before, and stayed on the road to Calleva*, where we turned south-west and rode over the hills towards the coast.

There was more traffic here, for this was one of the main mining areas of the province – mining for salt and shale as well as quarrying stone. Here and there were units of the IInd Legion and when they saw our insignia their eyes dropped in shame, but to be fair, they offered us first-rate hospitality in their barracks in Durnovaria** where they showed us the massive aqueduct they were building up the valley and also the huge hill fort where the Durotriges had defied Claudius' legions during the invasion. Vespasian had commanded the siege there, yes, *that* Vespasian, who went on to become Emperor.

From there it was really quite a pleasant journey along the cliff pathways looking down on to those long pebble beaches and then we veered inland and the hills got steeper but the grass was lush and green until we came to the fortress of Isca.

Imperial Post riders and regular cavalry patrols had noted our presence two days out so our arrival came as no surprise and when the big gates creaked open one of the duty officers was there to greet us and ask me what we needed.

'To be shown to the acting commander, Poenius Posthumus,' I told him, 'for I bring the very best wishes of the Governor, General Suetonius Paulinus.'

L: Olussa

Twenty days since the battle and our numbers have dwindled even further. We are well into Iceni territory but no longer does the tribe flock to protect Boudica's honour. Her few remaining soldiers disappear into the trees to find their way home and when we stop at an isolated farm, seeking food and fodder, we are met with surly silence. Neither does Aneurin and his handful of Druid priests command the respect they once did. Perhaps the Iceni have lost faith in their soothsayers and sorcerers, who never foresaw such a defeat. Only Tarex

* Silchester.

** Dorchester.

and the few of his clan who ride with him, are still obeyed without question.

These Celts are a peculiar race, as many have said in the past. In victory they show only pride and boastfulness, never counting the cost and never, ever, showing mercy to the vanquished. But in defeat, they are abject. They hang their heads, cannot look each other in the eye and they neglect themselves, their children, their animals and their crops. They are like bewildered dogs, spurned by a master for sins they do not realise they have committed. It is as if their gods have deserted them, but none can say that the Celtic blood gods have not been paid their due in sacrifice this summer.

The fields and hedgerows of the Iceni lands are lush and heavy with the best harvest any of them can remember, though there are now not enough men to cut and gather the grain and not enough women and children to strip the hedges of their berries and preserve them for the winter. I had not thought until now how many of the tribe's children have been lost this summer. Those who survived the fighting around the baggage train and fled into the forest, will now be slaves of the Catuvellauni or, if they have wandered further east, of the Trinovantes, their former allies.

There is no talk of missing friends or kin becoming slaves of the Romans. Seeing the legions in action left no doubt that the Empire was striking back as hard as it could and the legions were taking no prisoners.

I have suspected it for some time, but it is here in the tribal territory where cows go unmilked, eggs go uncollected and ripe crops remain unharvested, that I am convinced.

The Iceni will be exterminated.

And I think Boudica has known this from the start.

LI: Roscius

We were shown directly to Poenius Posthumus, who was still acting commander even though the IInd Legion's legate was supposedly hurrying back from wherever he'd been drinking or fornicating.

Posthumus even offered us wine, which of course Sextilius and I accepted – it would have been rude not to – and asked after the General's health.

'He is well,' I said, 'and happy with the completeness of his victory.'

'The battle went well?' Poenius enquired formally. He was wearing a sword but no armour, which meant he had been expecting us.

'The Iceni were completely destroyed for the loss of only four hundred from the legions.'

'A great victory indeed,' Poenius agreed, sadness in his voice.

'It was a sight to see,' I said and he nodded in agreement, then he drew his sword.

'On the table there are letters and rings for my wife in Bononia*, if you would be so kind. There is money also, for the Imperial Post.'

'I will see to it,' I said.

He sank to his knees there in the middle of his office, and reversed the sword until he was holding the hilt with both hands and the point was at his stomach.

'I may need help,' he said.

'I will see to that also,' I told him in farewell.

Sextilius and I had been away on our mission for about two weeks.

The army had rested up, sharpened its swords and been issued with fresh supplies of javelins and boots, which the General had only got from the army quartermasters in Gaul so quickly by threatening to flog ten of them for every day's delay.

It took another week to put a supply train together as most of the food and fodder had to come up from the supply bases on the coast – what grain the Iceni had not stolen, they had spoiled – and by then the Legion was itching to be on the move again. Face it, there was nothing for them to do in Londinium except get posted on to some boring civic duty like road repairs or cleaning up the mess the Iceni had made of most of the public buildings.

* Bologna in Italy.

So when the order came, all the boys were up for it, although Paulinus had no intention of taking his whole force. A fair chunk of the legion stayed behind in Londinium to get the rebuilding under way, and a couple of cohorts were sent due north to Durobrivae to relieve Petillius Cerialis and the survivors of the IXth.

For the rest of the Boudican campaign, we used mostly the auxiliaries – the cavalry and the light infantry, keeping the Legion in reserve. Paulinus was not expecting to fight a pitched battle; this was going to be a hunting party and he wanted it over and done with before winter.

So we were still well away from the first frost when we marched out of Londinium and up the big north road, but the leaves were turning brown even if they had not started to drop yet.

It took us three days to reach the old tribal track they called The Pathway and we followed that right into Iceni territory. Along the way we found plenty of examples of small bands, maybe families, of Iceni who had been caught fleeing the battle and had been killed for their loot, or their weapons, or their horses. Not by us, mind you, but by the other tribes. Catching them asleep in the middle of the night and slitting their throats seemed to be the favourite way, though we came across several hangings and more than one really messy crucifixion.

We picked up about fifty Catuvellauni who offered to act as scouts and trackers for us and when we thought we were more or less in Iceni territory, we started to slash and burn. All the livestock we couldn't eat or use ourselves were killed, piled up and left to rot. Similarly, any grain we couldn't carry was burnt, whether in granaries or still in the field. Storage pits we used as latrines.

All the Iceni we found – and I mean all – we killed and dismembered, leaving them and their limbs piled up at the doorways of their huts. We were working our way from west to east, driving the tribe before us. Eventually they would end up in the sea, which was fine by us.

Advancing across a broad front, we swept up every village we found and we didn't miss many. Our Catuvellauni scouts would ride on our flanks and double-back in the evening in a sweep to catch every last woodsman's hut and hunter's hide.

And I'd say we found them all – every piece of shelter that might keep an Iceni family warm and dry and snug in winter – and we burned the bloody lot.

We also found dozens of Druid temples tucked away in among the trees. They weren't temples like we know. They were made of wood, not stone, and they often had living oak trees as part of the structure. And they were always near water, though what you'd find if you put a fishing net in some of those ponds on streams doesn't bear thinking about.

We found their temples and we burned them. We found their sacred groves which were perfect circles of oak trees. We chopped them down. If we found Druids alive, we would crucify them to any bit of wood that was handy. Some of the lads would carve *FTR** into the cross beam – 'Happy Days Are Here Again' – just to show who was back in charge.

We found large stocks of sea salt. They had obviously had a thriving business there, though they probably didn't know it. When we took some of the Iceni alive, we would burn their barley fields and then make them plough salt into the ashes just to make sure that if there were any who didn't starve to death over the winter, they wouldn't be growing any more crops next year.

And we found all the food they had stored away for winter, even some buried barrels of beer brewed from malted barley and oats. I reckon there wasn't a piece of salted fish or a bucket of flour or a pot of honey we didn't find that autumn.

But Boudica? No, we never found her.

LII: Olussa

The Princess Prisca cries continuously. It is a small tearful sobbing sound that she makes rather than the professional widow's tormented howling, but it is persistent and we are as accustomed to it now as we are to the wind in the trees or the creaking of the wheels of our small caravan. The Princess Erda, on the other hand, makes no sound at all and has taken

* *Felix Temporum Repartio.*

to wandering off into the forest without direction or purpose or warning. At night, Boudica ties her ankles together as she would hobble a horse and although Erda carries several knives and a sickle at her belt, she remains tied every morning.

We wander without purpose, or no purpose that is clear to me. Boudica seems determined to seek out every surviving member of her tribe and present them with a piece of her rapidly diminishing supply of plunder. Those that were left behind are the old and the lame. If they accept anything, it is a pot or a plate or a skillet. They will not take gold or silver coin, nor jewellery, nor any bronze figurine of Roman design. They know what will happen to them if the legions come and find them.

But it is no longer 'if' the legions come, they are here, in Iceni territory, their presence betrayed by the smoke pyres from burning fields and round houses to the west. For days we have fled east with the smoke rising at our backs, but soon there will be nowhere to go. The lands of the Iceni end at the sea and the Iceni have no ships.

It is left to Aneurin the Druid, to make a decision.

He and Tarex spent a day riding side by side talking quietly and earnestly. That night Tarex quietly led his horse away from the camp before mounting and riding into the night.

At dawn, as our small camp, well-hidden among the trees, began to stir, Aneurin woke the three Druids who remain with us and they risked a small fire, selecting only the driest wood they could find, to boil a pot of water to which they added ground oats and a piece of honeycomb one of them unwrapped from a cloth heavily stained with what looked like blood.

Aneurin himself served this porridge breakfast to Boudica and her daughters while his fellow priests scurried into the woods to forage for berries. One of them has a bow and a few arrows and each day goes out in the hope of seeing a deer or wild pig; each day he comes back empty handed.

As we await Tarex's return, I use the daylight to transcribe the few notes I have taken since the battle, as working at night with only one small lamp is affecting my eyesight. Boudica saw me writing (making spare use of the last of my ink) and sent her daughters to the nearby stream, telling them to wash themselves all over. Then she moved to sit with me. She no longer smells of pine resin, but of dirt and sweat and fear.

'My faithful Lost Roman Olussa,' Boudica asked, 'how is your work on my history?'

'It awaits an ending,' I told her.

'You will have one soon,' she said, 'though perhaps not the one you expected.'

I told her that I did not know what to expect of the Iceni, and never had. As a people, I told her, they were *aenigma* – an enigma, though the Queen had trouble with the word and I tried to explain.

'Others have said we had magic,' she said, misunderstanding.

I tried with all my skill to explain that the Iceni are an enigma because they are – were – the one tribe which neither welcomed nor opposed the Romans. They were outsiders in an Empire which welcomed and rewarded insiders, and did not tolerate outsiders. They had not fought against the invading Emperor Claudius, yet when insulted, they had mobilised the entire tribe, marched hundreds of miles from their lands, destroyed a Roman army and three cities. Had they defied Claudius with such strength, Britannia might never have become an imperial province.

'I did not know this Claudius,' said Boudica, 'but I know he did not insult us in the way the Roman Catus did. He would not have treated my husband the king in such a way. He would not have had me flogged and my daughters would not have been forced to lie under his men.'

I said nothing but my thoughts were that the Queen was wrong.

'What is done cannot be undone,' I said.

'But it has been revenged,' she answered with a smugness that chilled my blood. 'Have the Iceni not made the Romans tremble?'

'At a price,' I said, looking around me, 'at a terrible price.'

'Which is why your history is important, my Lost Roman. We will have no story-tellers left. Yours will be the only story of the Iceni. You have it safe?'

I showed Boudica the inside of my battered carriage and the piles of wax tablets, papyri and sheets of writing bark, things which she valued highly but understood not at all. She ran her fingers over a hinged double wax tablet as if it was the most precious jewel she had ever seen.

'They will see this and know our story?' she whispered.

'Anyone who can read will know the story of the Iceni and of their Queen Boudica and her fight against Roman tyranny.'

Her eyes turned on me and they were like knives, and there was iron in her voice: 'Her fight to regain her honour,' she corrected me.

'Of course, my Queen, of course,' I said quickly.

All I have seen; all I have suffered; all I have sacrificed for them; and no matter how long I live, I will never understand these bloody savages.

Tarex has returned and he and Aneurin spend an hour talking with Boudica, their voices low, their heads close together. The three Druids still with us begin to break camp, scattering the ashes of our small fire and using branches from the trees to sweep the ground clear of any signs of our presence.

Not before an hour has passed does Aneurin walk over to my carriage to address me. Tarex has seen the enemy to the south and west of us. By moving through the forest on an old hunting track we can pass to the north of them and we will spend the night in the hut of an Iceni charcoal burner, a man so isolated that he had no idea the Iceni had even gone to war.

When I ask the Druid what will happen after that, he does not answer me.

The charcoal burner's hut is small and stinks of dog, but it is warm and dry which is important, for the first of the autumn rains has fallen. The ground will be softer now and our tracks easier to see so it is decided to abandon our carriages and carts.

We roast and eat a wild pig which the charcoal burner's dogs have brought down that very day. The hut, the ground and even the trees all smell of ash and damp soot, so there is no point in not having a cooking fire and hot meat. I even manage to reserve the pig's kidney for myself.

The charcoal burner has a pair of beeswax candles, which I use to write by, though he regards this as some evil magic ritual and is only reassured when Boudica herself speaks for me.

In the morning we will pack everything on to the horses

and leave the wagons for the charcoal burner to destroy. In return for this service, he is given a bag of silver coins which also covers the price of a pair of shovels and a mattock, though he looks anything but pleased to have become the proud owner of his own fleet of transport. He is also offered some gold coins, but refuses them, saying mysteriously that the Queen's need is greater. Boudica's chariot, I note, is not included in the transaction, though I do not know what this might mean either.

The Queen sleeps on a mangy bearskin, her arms around her daughters, one on each side of her, and she says no more this night.

I write in haste for we have just heard the faint blast of a Roman trumpet.

As Boudica said, this is an ending.

We leave the charcoal burner's hut at dawn. Boudica, Prisca and Erda riding in the Queen's chariot, with Tarex and Aneurin leading the way. The three Druids and I ride to the rear, each of us holding the reins to a pack horse, mine being loaded down with all my writing materials wrapped in the Queen's tent canvas.

We reach our destination at the sixth hour of the morning, a sheltered grove deep in the forest, where both sunlight and rain only penetrate with difficulty, away from any trod path or track.

The Druids clear the thick bramble undergrowth with hand scythes and sickles, but almost as if they are combing it back to the edge of the grove rather than cutting it, until a square of dark brown sandy earth is revealed some twenty paces by twenty.

We dig for three hours, taking turns with the shovels and the mattock. The earth is soft from years of dead leaves and with Tarex doing the work of four men, we can stand waist-deep in the hole.

The square hole is a grave but none call it that. As we dig, Boudica and her daughters walk in the forest and return with a harvest of berries, walnuts and mushrooms, also some blue flowers whose long green stems taste of onion and garlic. Prisca, who is not crying today, produces some cold cuts of roast pig cooked by the charcoal burner and all the food we are to share is placed on Tarex's round shield and served by the two princesses.

When the grave is judged to be of a sufficient depth, the Druids bow before Boudica, who stands with an arm around the shoulders of her daughters, and then begins to drift into the surrounding trees, dismissed by Aneurin. I do not know whether to follow or not and it is Boudica herself who resolves my doubts.

'You must stay, Olussa the Lost Roman. Stay for the end of the story.'

From the folds of her cloak, Boudica took a small bag containing a flask of drink and two of the smaller pottery flasks of poison I had obtained for her in Camulodunum.

She sat down at the base of an old oak and pulled her daughters to the ground, one either side of her. Princess Prisca began to sob again but her younger sister Erda accepted the poison her mother offered without question or surprise. Erda drank first and then Boudica lifted her chin so she could kiss her on the lips. By the time Boudica broke the embrace, Erda was dead in her arms.

The Queen had to help Prisca, raising the flask to her lips for her and whispering soft noises of comfort, offering her daughter a draught of honey mead from the larger flask to wash the poison down.

It was not necessary. The poison took effect quickly. Prisca let out a short, sharp cry and her back arched in spasm. Her feet drummed against the earth and she died.

No words were spoken, no orders given.

Tarex helped her lay her daughters in the grave on the damp earth, their tunics and skirts straightened, their cloaks covering them to the neck, a space left between the two bodies.

Aneurin unstrapped a large leather pack from one of the horses and unrolled the hide on the ground and for a moment it was as if I could no longer breathe. There in the leaves and the dirt lay the treasure of the Iceni: six large gold torques, necklaces of pearls and of jet, bags of coins – some of them the very bags I had left Londinium with, gold and silver bowls and dishes and looted silver spoons.

The treasure was placed at the feet of the princesses, except for two torques, which Boudica placed around their necks, choosing a third to wear herself.

Tarex unloaded another pack, removing a long sword in a scabbard on a leather belt, which he offered to Boudica. She held back the folds of her cloak so that he could tie the sword belt around her waist, his fingers hovering gently for a moment over her belly.

In return Boudica unplugged the flask of mead she still held and offered it to him. They shared the contents, staring into each other's eyes, but not speaking. When the flask was empty, Boudica raised a hand and touched the giant warrior gently on the cheek.

'One more service,' she said quietly.

Tarex bowed and turned back to his pack from which he withdrew a long-handled iron hammer of the sort a blacksmith would use, turning its leather strap around his wrist. Swiftly he cut the traces holding the two ponies to Boudica's chariot and led the larger of the two by the mouth bit to the side of the grave.

He swung the hammer once and brought the iron head down between the horse's eyes. As it buckled at the knees, he put his shoulder to its flank and pushed it over and into the open grave, jumping in after it. Exchanging the hammer for a knife, he slit its throat, the blood gushing over his arms before soaking into the earth.

Aneurin the Druid also stepped into the grave to place sprigs of mistletoe, which even had a few white berries though it was not yet winter, on the bellies of the two princesses. I can only guess that this was a necessary ritual for their journey to the Other World as they called it.

I called out to Boudica that I too had a gift.

I gave her the only thing of value I had left: a metal stylus and an unused *diptych*, a double wax writing tablet, both plundered from the house of Valerius Lupus.

She looked at the blank wax squares and asked me what it could mean and so I wrote on one of the faces *Bdicca * Prsca * Erd* in the shortened writing that I use for my notes.

I told her those were the names of the Queen of the Iceni and her daughters, which now would always be remembered.

'In the Other World, if not this one,' was how she replied and I thought perhaps I had committed some sacrilege against their gods. If the Iceni did not need to read or write in this life, why should they in the next? But Boudica showed no sign of anger.

'You will finish the story and then my Lord Tarex will take care of you,' she said to me and those were the last words she spoke in this life.

Boudica held the wax tablet to her breasts as she lay down in the grave between her two daughters. Then she broke the seal on the remaining flask of poison and drained it, lying back on the cold earth to stare at the sky until her eyes closed and she breathed no more.

Her general, champion and lover, Tarex, gently covered the heads and chests of the three females with his cloak, then he placed his round shield and a knife at Boudica's feet. With the iron hammer, he smashed the wheels from her chariot and laid them flat in the grave. With his sword he slashed the wicker sides and floor and covered the bodies with them, finally pulling the axle pole until it lay along one side of the grave.

Her priest and counsellor, Aneurin, produced a sickle made of gold from his own packhorse and swung it against the trunk of the nearest tree. When the blade was buckled, he cast the sickle into the grave near the head of the dead horse, which was still leaking blood.

It took the three of us until dusk to fill in the grave and cover the site with brambles and leaves. Then with Tarex leading the way, we rode through the darkening forest until we came to a small, slow river and we camped on its banks. I have memorised as many natural features as I can in order to find my way back there.

I write by the light of one lamp, shrouded by my tent canvas strung from two saplings, to finish this history of the Iceni at war.

Where we will go tomorrow I do not know, but Tarex has said he will keep his oath to Boudica to take care of me.

LIII: Roscius

Strangest thing.

We were about halfway across Iceni territory, destroying everything in our path. By the time of the first snow that year there wasn't a fucking thing for any survivors to eat, not that there were many survivors. Paulinus was working to a plan of reducing the population down to a manageable level – say about a tenth of what it had been. Those that were allowed to live had to do so in a special settlement where everything was run on Roman lines. Normally, the policy of Romanisation was a matter of the carrot then the stick, leading the stupid natives like the mules they were. But this place up in the Iceni lands, Venta* I think they called it, was run like a slave camp, except that slaves have a value, the Iceni didn't.

Then the strangest thing happened.

Our scouts found this charcoal-burner miles from anywhere in the forest, just one man living with his dogs, smelling of soot and his hands black as a Nubian's. They would normally have killed him and burned his place without a thought, except they find an Iceni war chariot, two carts and a four-wheel Roman style carriage on his land. So they do the sensible thing, they kill his dogs, who are making a hell of a racket, and they send word to the General who just happens to be no more than an hour away.

By the time we get there, the scouts have had time to search the place properly and buried in this old boy's hut they find a bag containing over fifty silver *denarii*, though it was doubtful the old woodsman could count up to five let alone fifty. Then, even stranger, in one of the wagons, we find empty bottles of ink, some used quills, a wax note tablet, some offcuts of writing bark and bits of vellum. Now there is no way this old forest monkey is able to read or write, so where did he get them? In no time at all our scouts have got the

* Caistor near Norwich.

poor old sod stretched out over one of his own charcoal fires and are giving him a slow roasting.

Paulinus himself examined the wax tablet, then tossed it on the fire and asked the old man himself, through one of the Catuvellauni we used as a translator, where the wagons came from. The old man did his best to spit in the General's face, but he had no spit left. Paulinus gave one of his hand signals and the archers in the bodyguard opened up from close range. The charcoal burner's body looked like a pin cushion and we left it smouldering on the fire.

Paulinus organised us into roving patrols in every direction with instructions to ride for two hours whatever the terrain then turn right, ride for one hour more and then return. That gave us the best chance of finding tracks in the daylight that was left, or flushing our quarry into the path of another patrol. Not that I was exactly clear what our quarry was. You've got to remember, there wasn't a big hunt on for Boudica, there wasn't even a price on her head. The army's line was that if she just disappeared, nobody would remember her by the time spring came.

The troop I rode with were skirmishers; mostly Spaniards, a mixture of archers and slingers and the ideal combination for a fast ride through woodland. They were good trackers too and they thought nothing of climbing the tallest tree to get the lie of the land.

They found fresh sign of horses, on the banks of a small river and we followed their tracks for three miles or more until one of our flanking scouts made a sighting of six horses and three riders moving slowly up ahead, about to emerge from the forest and cross a wide water meadow, which would give them no cover at all.

I moved my men up quietly and we attacked them at an angle from the side, charging across the meadow at them and the archers and the slingers were in range almost immediately.

The lead rider was a huge man, a real warrior, naked to the waist and with that blue woad paint all over his chest. His companion was head-to-toe in black robes which picked him out as a Druid. There was a third rider, lagging behind them, hunched over the neck of his horse, a cloak pulled up over his head.

Strangest thing.

The Druid took one look at us rolling out of the trees and he started shouting, but not at us. He was yelling at the big warrior at his side. One of our archers told me afterwards that he had shouted, 'Now! Do it now!' but at the time, I just couldn't believe my eyes.

That big painted bugger raised his arm and he brought this bloody great hammer down on the Druid's head. Just like that, and of course his skull cracked like an egg.

But before the dead Druid had fallen off his horse, this savage had turned his horse until he was facing us and now he was shouting and his voice boomed out across the meadow. I didn't need a translator to tell me what he was saying. It was a challenge. He was telling us to fill our hands with a weapon, for he was coming to kill us sons-of-bitches.

You had to admire him, I suppose. He took the reins of his horse between his teeth, transferred the hammer to his left hand and drew a bloody great sword with his right and came at us, waving both and determined to take some of us with him.

We didn't let him, of course. Our archers peppered his horse and our slingers got at least ten hits on him, any one of which would have knocked a normal man out of the saddle. Both he and his horse were down and dead before they got close enough to touch us.

I dismounted to get a closer look at this giant and bugger me, but he wasn't quite dead even then, so I put my foot on his chest while I drove my sword through his throat. One of our Brit scouts said he thought it could be one of the Iceni's war chiefs, but he couldn't think of his name. As far as we were concerned it was one Iceni less, that was all we were worried about, then one of the lads said I had better take a look at the other two.

There was not much to see of the Druid unless you were a doctor interested in head wounds, but the third rider turned out to be still alive.

His horse had gone down under him, with arrows in its belly and a slinger's bullet between the eyes, but the rider had been thrown clear, bundled in his cloak.

I thought at first that the slingers had got him as well, for he wasn't moving much until I turned him over with my boot.

He was whimpering like a whipped dog as I pulled the cloak off him and it was obvious to see why. I don't know what crime that poor sod had committed, but it must have been something terrible.

The Iceni had pulled out his tongue so he couldn't tell us. They had also cut off both his hands so he couldn't have written us a message – not that it was likely he could read or write – to tell us why he was a prisoner of the Iceni.

But you know what was the saddest thing of all? They had left him his knife, a really nice long thin blade, a fine piece of work. He had carried it in a scabbard strapped to his arm and it was still there. How long had he wanted to put himself out of his misery, but couldn't because he didn't have any hands to use it?

Cruel, I call it.

When he saw me, or rather the uniform, he began to go into convulsions, trying to speak, holding the stumps of his arms out to me as if pleading with me. I knew what he wanted and I gave it to him quick, through the heart so he didn't feel a thing. It was the least I could do.

When we went through their pack horses, we found a load of pages of writing, a complete mixture of vellum, papyri and bark sheets and some wax tablets. So perhaps I had misjudged him, and he could read and write, whoever he was. But when we looked at the pages, they made no sense at all and half of it seemed to be in some sort of code. We searched the rest of their goods but found nothing of value except the giant warrior's weapons, which we confiscated. Standing orders were to make sure not a scrap of food was left in the Iceni territory, so we gathered some dry wood and we burned the dead horses and the three bodies together. We used the papyri and the vellum sheets to get the fire going.

I've often thought of that prisoner since. They must have had a good reason for cutting his tongue out and the hands? Well, that was probably one of their superstitions. They would have been terrified of anyone who could read and write. So why didn't they put his eyes out? Maybe they were happy for him to see things, but they didn't want him telling anyone about them.

Well, it was all a long time ago and it does not really matter now, does it? Boudica would have been forgotten already if fellows like you had not come round asking questions. Only a few old boys like me can still remember and we'll all be dead soon and you can write what you like. You will anyway.

That prisoner, by the way, the one without the hands, I took his knife for a souvenir and I think I've still got it somewhere.

Would you like to see it?

Oh well, please yourself.

Finis